After distinguished naval service during the Second World War, Alexander Fullerton learnt Russian at Cambridge, on a Joint Services course, then worked in Germany with Red Army units. He predicted the lowering of the Iron Curtain, a forecast that was rejected by the SIS, whose Russian desk was at that time manned by Kim Philby. After passing the interpretership exam (CS) he was at once returned to sea in submarines. He resigned and was released in 1949, and worked in South Africa as an insurance clerk, in a Swedish shipping agency and as a publisher's representative. His first novel was published in 1953. In 1959 he returned to Britain to pursue a publishing career, but abandoned it in 1967 to write full-time. He is now the author of over thirty novels.

SPECIAL DECEPTION

Alexander Fullerton

SPHERE BOOKS LIMITED

SPHERE BOOKS LTD

Published by the Penguin Group
27 Wrights Lane, London w8 5tz, England
Viking Penguin Inc., 40 West 23rd Street, New York, New York 10010, USA
Penguin Books Australia Ltd, Ringwood, Victoria, Australia
Penguin Books Canada Ltd, 2801 John Street, Markham, Ontario, Canada l3r 1b4
Penguin Books (NZ) Ltd, 182–190 Wairau Road, Auckland 10, New Zealand

Penguin Books Ltd, Registered Offices: Harmondsworth, Middlesex, England

First published by Macmillan London Ltd 1988
Published by Sphere Books 1989

Printed and bound in Great Britain by
Richard Clay Ltd, Bungay, Suffolk

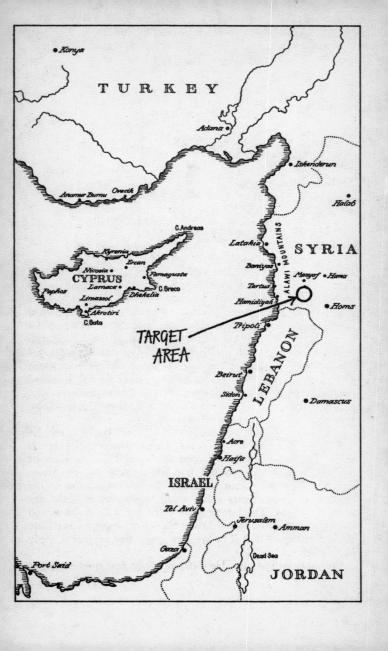

1

Charlie poured himself two thick fingers of Black Label and added a little water. It hadn't been a bad day, for a Monday. He'd taken a firm order for a near-new Rolls – it was to have less than ten thousand on the clock and be either pale-blue or silver, but there'd be no quibbling over price – and sold a C-registered Porsche 928 S Automatic for £35,000. The Saudi princeling who'd ordered the Rolls wanted it by the weekend – some tart to impress, obviously – and Charlie had spent about an hour on the blower chasing up possibles; this had taken up the slack in the warm, Indian-summer autumn day, and he'd missed his usual skinful at the pub in Bruton Place, which in its way was also a source of satisfaction.

Might kick the habit altogether if one really tried, he thought. He knew he wouldn't. Didn't want to, except it would be nice to believe it when one said, 'I can do without it, give it up tomorrow if I had to.' Saying this to Anne: not actually to her, not recently, but addressing her in his imagination, sometimes aloud when he was alone in the flat as he was now. The last time he'd tried to talk to her she'd hung up as soon as she'd heard his voice, and another time she'd threatened that if he went on pestering her she'd apply for a court order.

Probably would, too. He'd drunk about half the Scotch, he

7

noticed. He put the glass down. If you hung on to it you sipped at it without thinking. But it was astonishing how tough a woman could be, once she felt she had cause. Even Anne: sweet, lovely, ultra-gentle Anne.

Once she felt really hurt, that was the thing. Once you'd drawn blood, hit the nerve.

But – *for ever?*

Staring at his buckskin shoes. From Trickers in Jermyn Street. Long legs out straight, pale grey against blue carpet. Props of up-and-coming spiv, adulterer and piss-artist. Strange to recall that so short a time ago the same shanks had been encased not in lightweight flannel but in camouflage-pattern, tattered DPMs – rain-soaked, filthy . . .

Happy days, though he'd barely known it at the time. Hadn't paused to think about it. He sighed, quoted mentally *Fools, for I also had my hour* . . . Like that other bloody donkey. His glass was empty . . . He reminded himself, *But you blew it.* Everything that had ever really mattered, for – *nothing* . . . He was staring into the bottom of the glass, thinking about this without the least understanding of his own actions – which of course made them impossible to explain, let alone excuse, although he'd tried a few times – and also thinking about getting up for a refill, when the door-answering device buzzed. He pushed himself out of the chair, crossed the room and put the glass down beside the bottles on his way out into the hall.

This would be Paula, he guessed. It was a bit early for her, but he wasn't expecting anyone else.

'Yup?'

'Captain Swale?'

Male voice. Charlie told it, 'Never heard of him.'

'*Charlie* Swale?'

'Who wants *him*, for God's sake?'

'My name's Knox. You don't know me, but – well, it's sort of official, in a way, I can't explain over this—'

'Inland Revenue, or Customs and Excise?'

'Neither.' A pause. 'I'm not trying to sell a car, either. May I come up?'

Charlie pressed the button to release the catch on the street door. 'Second floor, turn left.'

Selling some damn thing, he guessed. Insurance, time-share . . . But he'd said 'official'. He paced to the window, stood gazing down at greenery and through the gaps in it at the slow swirl of evening traffic. His own reflection misty in the window-pane: darkish, dark eyes, the planes and angles of his face still well defined although there was padding on the bones which hadn't been there a year ago. Mostly in the mind's eye, this; the window glass showed only a ghostly outline, and the fatcat look was in his imagination because he was uncomfortably aware of it – of having been both a soldier and an athlete and of having converted now into *Homo Westendus Repulsivus*.

Success, some people called it.

Doorbell.

He was slightly on the alert as he twisted the knob and opened the door from the side, not from directly behind it. Old precautionary habit lingering, despite awareness that having been out of the swim for a while now it wasn't likely that any of the entrenched enemies of the realm would still consider him a worthwhile target. But you couldn't be entirely sure: and they liked their targets soft . . .

Knox wasn't swarthy, but at first sight you wouldn't have taken him for Anglo-Saxon either. If he'd walked into the showroom, Charlie would have had him down for an Arab. Except for the light-blue eyes: and until he spoke – Scottish overlay on standard English. Age about thirty, height about five-ten, black hair and moustache. He put his hand out: 'Bob Knox. I'm a Royal Marine, rank of captain. Actually – in confidence – Special Boat Squadron, and it's the Squadron's business that brings me here.'

'Our researches tell us that you were a troop commander with 22 SAS in the Dhofar campaign. Where you (a) distinguished yourself in various actions and (b) acquired fluent Arabic, now a business tool when flogging Bentleys to Arabs.'

'You've done some homework. Except for the "distinguished" bit.' Charlie shrugged. 'Mucked in like everyone else. But – sure, I was out there from '74 until we had them running, in '76. I was barely weaned then, mind you. But I did another stint after that lot, and buffed up the language.'

9

The SAS had played a key role in winning Sultan Qaboos' war against the communist 'People's Democratic Republic of Yemen' and 'People's Front for the Liberation of Oman', and Charlie Swale as a very young SAS lieutenant had enjoyed practically every minute of it.

'One *had* to learn Arabic, you know. There was a lot of chatting up, as well as soldiering. What's sometimes referred to as the "hearts and minds" campaign? And we had Dhofari irregulars with us, *firqats*, one had to be able to communicate.'

'Fairly rugged conditions, the mountain fighting?'

'Oh, I suppose so . . .'

Sooner be there than here. Right now, this minute, put the clock back . . . He'd almost started saying this aloud, checked himself as the words began to form. One spoke too often without thought – revealing too much, allowing the Achilles' heel to show. Looking down at his glass, deliberately not touching it, reflecting that the drink problem then had been the basic one of keeping water-bottles full. Military problems had been the only kind Charlie had been aware of, in that period. He looked up: 'We used to say – about the "hearts and minds" thing – "once you get 'em by the balls, hearts and minds 'll follow".'

Knox smiled. He was several inches shorter than Charlie and maybe twenty pounds lighter, but if he was SBS you could bet he was as tough as old scrap-iron. Young for the rank, too: since a captain in the Royal Marines was equivalent to a major in the Army. He'd accepted the offer of a Scotch, pouring it himself and making it about half-strength by Charlie's standards.

Charlie said, 'I didn't get a chance to forget the lingo, because, as I said, I was back in the Oman later for nearly two years, instructing . . . What kind of help are you looking for? Translation, interpreting?'

'Rather more.' Knox leant forward, forearms on his knees, hands clasped. He hadn't touched his drink since sipping it once and then putting it down. Watching him, waiting for an explanation, Charlie was vaguely conscious of something not quite right, slightly disturbing in some way. He lost the feeling as Knox said quietly, 'We want you with us on – well, on a rescue mission, you might call it. Guy to be extracted –

Middle East. Any chance you could take some time off, help us out?'

Traffic growled outside. Inside the room, silence. Charlie, staring at his visitor, wondered if he'd heard right, if he dared believe he'd heard what the guy had just said. If it was real, there could only be one reason for it, he realised – the fact his Arabic was as good as it was. That made a *little* sense: but even so . . .

Staring back at the pale, bright eyes, thinking, *It's a hoax* . . .

For a year now he'd felt like a pariah: he'd kept his head down, dreading chance meetings with old friends. He hadn't set foot inside the Special Forces Club, and in his own goldfish-bowl of a showroom in Bond Street he had a horror of some former colleague passing and spotting him: 'Charlie! What the *hell*—'

But they wouldn't need to ask. They'd all have known, a year or more ago. He could imagine it, in SAS squadrons all over the world: 'Hear about old Charlie Swale?'

He asked the Marine, 'Did they tell you why they threw me out?'

'Something about a drink problem.' Knox's glance flickered towards Charlie's newly empty glass and away again. He added, 'I didn't make the enquiry myself. Now my brief's to see how willing or unwilling, fit or unfit you might be. I'm being open about this – hope you don't mind, but there's no point being shy about it, is there?'

Charlie shrugged. The Marine went on, 'Enquiries were made, at higher levels, but as I'm to be the team leader it's been left to me to make this contact. I gather you're running a very successful business, and using your Arabic pretty well all the time. You look reasonably fit – give or take a few days' hard work – and you have experience of operating in mountainous country.' He drew a breath. 'Which seems to cover most of it. You can take it as read, there'll be no liquor around once we kick off, so if that's too much of a drag for you now's the time to say. Otherwise – what d'you think?'

He was still struggling with the idea that the Regiment must have recommended him to them. At least, they couldn't have

11

told them not to touch him with a forty-foot pole: which was what he'd have expected.

'Where's it to be? Libya?'

'You're interested, then?'

Knox's eyes shone in his dark face. Like blue glass, reflecting light. Charlie nodded: feeling primarily surprise, but also pleasure, as well as the beginnings of a whisky-glow. Despite some qualm somewhere . . . But this was reinstatement of a kind: if the SBS of all people – that secret, ultra-professional hardcore of Royal Marine commando underwater experts, long-range penetration artists – if they, having checked him out in Hereford, could pay him the compliment of asking him to join them on some clandestine mission . . .

'What about your business? Could you take a few weeks off?'

'Sure. I'm not totally independent, I have backing from the big boys down the road and they take a piece of the action. They set me up, more or less – I took the idea to them and they fell for it and luckily we've prospered. There's a guy who'd keep an eye on things for me; doesn't talk much Arabic, but for just a short absence – ' He checked the flow. '*How* long?'

'Tell 'em three weeks.' The eyes held his. 'What d'you do for exercise, Charlie, when you're working here in town?'

'Squash and swimming, at the Lansdowne.' He asked again, 'It is Libya, I suppose?'

'I don't know about pay,' Knox explained. 'That sort of thing's up to the powers in MoD, they'll want to find some precedent or – '

'I wouldn't be offering myself as a mercenary. I've been doing well lately, and – well, frankly, having been given the order of the boot – OK, having fucking well disgraced myself – '

'That's not how your people seem to see it.' Knox spoke evenly, talking facts, not concerned with judgements or palliatives. This was Charlie's feeling, hearing it . . . 'You ran into a personal problem that threw you, and took refuge in – ' he pointed – '*that*. Not commendable, but you'd just come out of a very tough spot, you'd lowered your guard – right?' He shrugged. 'Happened to better men than you or me. Your

12

blokes went by the book because they had to, but I gather you were spoken of rather warmly. Dhofar – Falklands – then that last effort . . . '

It held together: despite the degree of surprise, the suggestion of a magic wand. He *must* have talked to the Regiment – someone must have – since there was no other way he could have known about that last job. And the lingering sense of unreality: well, he thought he'd pinned it down, the irritation which in recent minutes had bugged him and which he hadn't been able to identify. It was this man's eyes, the coldness in them: that was *all* it was, and you couldn't pass judgement on people for how they happened to look. Charlie's overriding feeling was still – naturally enough, he thought, in the circumstances – an element of fantasy, fantasy such as in the past year he'd come to indulge in deliberately, letting his mind run loose after a few drinks – before a few more deadened it – treating himself to a mental replay of events so edited that he was not as criminally stupid as in fact he had been. That particular scenario he'd rewritten in his daydreams time and time again, right through to the fade-out of a happy ending.

Then one woke up: knowing that daydreaming was as near as one would get to any ending that wasn't sickening. But this, now – this was a new scenario altogether: could be a new *start*!

The cold eyes were on him, as if trying to read his thoughts. Charlie asked his visitor, 'Am I right that it's Libya?'

'As it happens, no.' Knox watched him reach for his own glass – empty – and then glance over, seeing the other practically untouched.

'Setting me an example?'

'Wrong again.' Knox shook his head. 'It's just that I have to drive down to Poole tonight.' He checked the time, and scowled. 'Starting in about half an hour, no later anyway . . . Charlie, one thing I have to put to you – I've been told to. In a nutshell, this won't be any frolic. It could turn out to be very tricky, in fact, and if we foul up or run into bad luck – well, we could get ourselves greased, or taken prisoner which might be rather worse . . . It's a job that has to be done, and *we* have to stick our leather necks out, but the point is *you* do not have to, it's only your business if you want to make

13

it so. If you don't, this is the time to tell me, I'll take my leave, and nobody'll know or think any the worse of you. OK?'

'Any worse than they think already.' Charlie shook his head as he crossed the room. 'Thanks for the warning, but you can deal me *in*, chum.' The neck of the bottle clicked against the rim of the glass as he added, 'And I'm grateful for the invitation.' Knox pushed himself up, stood at the window looking down into the darkening square, heard Charlie being careful with the water. He invited, without turning his head, 'Any questions you want to ask?'

'Same one.' Charlie joined him. 'Who's to be rescued, and where from?'

'You'll get all that in plenty of time, Charlie. For now, let's just say Middle East, leave it at that?'

'Second question, then. When do we leave?'

'Probably in about a week. I don't know for sure yet. But I'll need you full time from, say, day after tomorrow. For some sharpening up, get the muscles working ... Is one whole day – tomorrow – enough for you to tie up your business arrangements?'

'I suppose. At a pinch.'

'We'll kit you up, of course. None of us'll be using anything but civvie gear, incidentally. If we fouled up we'd be mercenaries and we wouldn't know who'd hired us, we would *not* be SBS – OK?'

'All right.'

'First thing now is for me to report back. Then I think we'd better have you down in Poole.'

'Right.'

'On second thoughts – no.' The Marine shook his head as he turned his back on the window. 'We'd better *not* have you down there. Security reasons, the chance it might link you with us, then they'd ask themselves *Why Charlie Swale?* Likely solution: Swale talks Arabic, that's his obviously outstanding asset, and he's dark enough to pass for an Arab, especially when he's been in the sun a while. So what's the SB Squadron's interest in Arabia?'

'D'you really think the *adoo* could be trailing a reject like me?'

14

Adoo being Arabic for 'enemy'. Knox agreed, 'OK, frankly, no. But as you were SAS, and left in rather unusual circumstances — well, you can't be certain. And they know where *we* hang out, that's more to the point. So, much as we'd like to entertain you *chez nous*, we'd better forgo the pleasure, if you don't mind.'

Charlie swallowed some Scotch. The glow inside him wasn't the liquor working, though, it was the feeling that suddenly life might have some point to it again. He didn't feel he deserved it, but it was there, as full of promise as a child's Christmas. Out of the blue: a buzz, a stranger's voice, and hey presto!

Except for Anne.

He said, 'Returning one compliment with another, you don't look so very non-Arab yourself.'

'Because I *am* part Arab. My mother was Egyptian. My father was in the RAF, a sergeant at that time, when I was born, 1957, and — well, I was dragged up in Scotland mostly. In the house of an aunt, my Dad's sister.' He paused, then explained, 'The old man was serving in Cyprus when they met. In '55 — '56 was Suez, wasn't it . . . He met her in '55 in Cairo, and they got married in '56. Later they split up, she remarried, I'd been in her custody but I was packed off to Edinburgh, and from Day 1 at nursery school I was known as Woggy Knox.'

'I can imagine.' Charlie glanced sideways at the Marine. 'You blokes get to the Gulf from time to time, don't you?'

'You're thinking of the Arabic.' Knox nodded. 'Yeah, I've kept it up. Made some holiday visits to Cairo too, in earlier years. Although my mother's people talk more French than Arabic . . . On which subject, shall we try our Arabic on each other now?'

At the window, Charlie saw Bob Knox emerge from the front of the building and run down the steps, vanishing into the square. He'd be on his way to Poole now — burning down the M3, no doubt. He was going to telephone at noon next day, to the Bond Street showroom; Charlie had offered him a card with the business address and telephone number, but the SBS man had produced an identical card from his own top pocket and said, 'Snap.' He'd certainly done his homework.

Charlie wondered whether, if he'd been putting an SAS team together for some clandestine operation that required Arabic speakers, he'd have even fleetingly considered recruiting a man who'd already once crumbled under pressure.

He was sure he would not have.

But in the SAS, of course, he'd have had the whole Regiment from which to pick and choose. In contrast, SBS was a very small outfit, about the size of one rifle company – 100, 120 men, no more – so you'd have only a very few guys speaking Arabic, and if some of them happened to be deployed in the Gulf and couldn't be hauled out of whatever jobs they were doing, obviously you'd have to scratch around, scrape the barrel.

Scrapings. He nodded to himself. Dregs.

He poured himself a drink. His Arabic was flawless. That was the key to this business, explained it all. You'd get quite a few guys with a reasonable command of the language, but not many could actually pass themselves off as Arabs.

Bob Knox could manage that, all right. As well as Charlie could. So that made two of them.

Have to start weaning oneself off this stuff pretty soon, he thought. Not tonight – having had a couple already, and also he'd have to take Paula out for a meal when she showed up – but tomorrow, maybe. Except that tomorrow he'd need to be a bit jolly, entertain the big-company characters down the road. They'd accept the fact he had to take a few weeks off – for urgent family reasons, he'd tell them – but he'd have to soften them up a bit, and you wouldn't get far with that bunch on cups of tea.

He'd give up the booze when the SBS started him on this physical training programme. That would be soon enough. For the time being, forget it.

Prowling the room, glass in hand, casting long shadows, waiting for Paula's buzz. He wondered how he was going to break it to her that he'd be dropping out of circulation for several weeks, and not tell her where he was going. The Paulas of this world didn't much like not being told things.

Some kind of yarn, then. Checking on outlets in Germany, to set up a supply network for importing Mercs. She'd buy that, he thought.

He wished he could tell Anne what was happening. He'd have loved Anne to know that he'd been reinstated. In his imagination he saw himself telling her about it: Charlie Swale, the *old* Charlie Swale, back on his feet and asking her, 'If *they* can give me a break, can't *you*?'

He could see the answer, too. That withdrawn, icy look, eyes about as frigid as that bugger Knox's.

He wondered where the action was to be. Knox's last words – in Arabic – had been, 'Better let your moustache grow, Charlie.' He'd touched his own with a fingertip. 'Where we're going it's rare to see a shaved upper lip.'.

Syria, Charlie guessed. Or Albania. Those were about the only countries apart from Libya where clandestine entry would be the only way in, where you couldn't just walk in as a tourist. Or even the Yemen . . . But maybe it *was* Libya; Knox had said it wasn't, but that didn't mean such a lot, Charlie reckoned.

The man who'd called himself Knox wasn't on the road to Poole. He'd driven his shabby Ford Escort via Hyde Park Corner into Knightsbridge, turned left just short of Harrods and was now parking it in the NCP garage under Cadogan Square. The Ford looked shabbier than ever squeezed between a White Range Rover Vogue EFi and a scarlet Mercedes 560 SEL. He used the exit in the square's northwest corner, into Sloane Street, crossed at the lights and walked south about a hundred metres. Then at the top of a flight of shallow, grey marble steps he faced yet another array of bell-pushes: he found the one he wanted, and waited a few seconds until a woman's voice asked, 'Who is it?'

'Leo.'

'Leo. *What* a joy.'

He heard the click of the lock releasing, pushed the heavy plate-glass door open and made sure it locked again behind him. Then through the foyer – past an elaborate flower arrangement and then the porter's desk – there was no porter on duty this late – to the lift.

Second floor. Flat 9. These were serviced flats, available by the week. The door of number nine swung open as he reached it.

'Leo, darling, how *wonderful*!'

He'd never set eyes on her until this moment, and yesterday when he'd spoken to her on the telephone he'd imagined her as young, slim, sexy. She was fifty-ish, a big woman, in a flowing bright kaftan that made her look even bigger – a tent effect. Hawk nose, thin mouth, eyes with a sharpness in them to match the nose, that bird-of-prey look ... It would require truly enormous wings to get the bird off the ground though, he thought. She'd shut the door, and added more quietly now, 'You're bang on time, but our friend's late. Want a drink?'

He shook his head. 'OK to talk, is it?'

'Clean as a whistle. I'm not just a pretty face.' She laughed; Leo didn't. She asked him, 'Did you contact those two?'

'Yeah, and it's settled. Thanks for lining them up, at such short notice.'

'It's been a rush, all right.' She gestured kitchen-wards: 'I've a bottle of fizz on the ice, Leo, but maybe we should wait until Eric—'

'Personally I wouldn't bother even then.'

'*Abstemious* mystery man, eh?'

Buzzer.

'There.' She swept past him, out of the sitting room into the hall. 'Swept' was a good description of the way she shifted her bulk around. Once it was under way you wouldn't want to be in its path, either. He looked round the large, bare room – bare despite its furnishings. Chairs and tables made no odds, it was a transient's pad, its lack of any atmosphere or personality not in the least alleviated by the scattering of a temporary occupant's bits and pieces. A door in the corner led to a kitchenette; two tall windows were draped in heavy green. He heard the woman's incongruously girlish voice from the hallway: 'Come on up, Eric my dear ... '

'Eric' looked exactly as he had in the photograph which Leo had been shown in Moscow. His own height, near enough – 1.80 metres or maybe a fraction under that – with black wavy hair, a squarish face with laugh-lines in it, and a pleasant, humorous expression. Smartly dressed in a dark-blue suit: silk shirt, knitted-silk tie ... Boris Pyotrovich Smotrenko, from the Soviet Trade Mission in Highgate.

A ladies' man, Leo guessed, getting a whiff of some perfume – after-shave, maybe – as they shook hands.

Smotrenko began quietly, confidentially, 'One question I have to ask, before anything else is—'

'Yeah.' Leo nodded. Anticipating the question wasn't difficult. He told the GRU man, 'On present indications, he's hooked.'

2

'And the other two?'

Leo nodded. There'd been a brief exchange between 'Eric' and the woman, a second confirmation from her that this place was clear of bugs. Which was more than could be said of Charlie Swale's pad now. Leo told him, 'They'll do. Here are the descriptions, by the way . . . ' Glancing at the woman as he delved into a pocket: 'I'd like that full run-down on their backgrounds now, OK?'

'No problem.' She went into the kitchen. Leo gave 'Eric' a sheet torn from a notebook, listings of the two mercenaries' heights, estimated weights, general appearance; this information would go to Moscow in tomorrow's diplomatic bag. Smotrenko folded the slip of ruled paper into his wallet, studying Leo with shrewd interest. Here in London he was Leo's control, getting his own directives from Gudyenko; and the big woman worked for him, of course. Leo told him, 'I believe we're OK with Swale. First because his brain's awash with whisky, and second – as forecast – he's over the moon at being invited to take part, and he's not looking the gift horse in its mouth.' He frowned. 'At least, *seems* not to be doing so.'

Smotrenko still watched him, said nothing. Leo added, 'So as of now, the signs are good.'

He couldn't be anything like sure of Swale yet. Tomorrow noon when he telephoned him, he'd know better. Then later the bug's tape would reveal a little more – maybe even a warning signal to abort.

Smotrenko said, 'It's not just a matter of selling the project to him now, of course. It's maintaining the deception, isn't it. You're aware we don't move you out of here unless you're a hundred per cent sure he's fooled?'

Leo nodded – expressionless, to hide annoyance. 'Eric' flexing his muscles, *his* power to abort the operation in some circumstances. As if one wasn't only too sharply aware of the need to keep blinkers on Charlie Swale. It was a point that had been made at least a dozen times, for heaven's sake. All part of Gudyenko's fail-safe mechanism . . . But he could understand 'Eric's probing – because this was his first operational deployment, officially Leo Serebryakov's training hadn't run its full course, and this 'Eric' knew it, was treating him as a fledgeling. Leo thought, *Well, fuck it,* let *him* . . . and told him quietly, even humbly, 'First of all I suggested that I'd take him down to SBS headquarters at Poole. Then I changed my mind – on grounds of security, the chance he might be spotted visiting us and conclusions drawn.'

'Drawn by whom?'

'People like us, I suppose.' He shrugged. 'God knows. But the point is that the first intention – taking him to Poole – will seem genuine to him if he remembers it, which with any luck he will. Then with the other two – '

A cork had popped in the kitchen; and the woman had said something. Eric prompted, ignoring her, 'The other two?'

'They believe I'm a Royal Marine captain, and I've told them the fourth guy will only volunteer his services if he believes we all are. This suits them, as it happens – ready-made cover for them, I dare say. But as I've described it to them, it's strictly an off-the-record operation, not ever to be ascribed to the SBS. If we were caught we'd deny any official connections, we'd be mercenaries, all of us. And of course we need Swale for his own special skills, notably his Arabic. He's fluent, by the way, I've tested him and I couldn't fault him. But they've swallowed all that, and tomorrow I'll have a longer session with them, teaching them how to talk like Marines – calling themselves Bootnecks, that sort of thing, and naval slang, and – well, they're on their guard, naturally, at this stage, but they're dazzled by the money. D'you have it, by the way?'

'I do.' The woman brought glasses of champagne on a tin tray. 'I'll give it to you in a minute. Five thousand pounds each, other half on completion, right?'

She didn't know, and Leo guessed Smotrenko wouldn't either, that the mercenaries wouldn't be calling for any second payment. He told her, 'I'll need some cash myself, for current expenses.'

'Such as?'

'I had to give those two a hundred pounds each on account. So OK, I'll take that out of the money they get now. But also I have to hire transport, and tents, food and other things. Having given him a reason for staying away from Poole, he'll accept that the same applies to any other Royal Marine establishment, training facilities – and he knows we're passing ourselves off as civilians, so civvy equipment won't surprise him. Rations, everything. But I've got to take them somewhere or other for some training: if I didn't, he'd start wondering, wouldn't he. So – cross-country work, rock climbing, get him moderately fit.' Leo shrugged. 'Get *myself* fit, too.'

Eric handed the woman his empty glass. '*Proshu.*' She smiled, edged into the kitchenette to get the bottle. Leo continued, 'I thought Wales, to camp and do this running around. Swale will feel at home – it's home ground for the SAS, it'll make sense to him . . . No thanks, no more for me . . . Can you tell me how long we've got?'

'You fly from Heathrow on Sunday. Flight BA 570, takes off 0855. Check in at least an hour before that, of course.'

Logistics as well as leg-work were her department.

'Have you got our tickets?'

Return tickets for a fourteen-day holiday. Nobody would be returning, but she didn't have to know this either. She said, 'Will have. You can collect them here Saturday evening, any time after eight I'll be here. Unless of course I hear from you or from Eric before that – if anything went wrong, or – '

'You know my ticket's to be in the name of Donald Campbell, and Swale travels as Christopher Sharp?'

23

'Yes . . . You'll need to be back Saturday night anyway, won't you, for the early start. Your flight arrives Istanbul 1440 local time: then a few hours' wait for the connecting flight to Ercan. You're advised to take a taxi from the airport; the boat'll be waiting for you at Kyrenia and they'll be looking out for you.'

From there on, he'd be on his own, except for orders that would come by radio. Orders might have reached the crew, in fact, before he and his team arrived on board. The crew would be a freelance team originally with Fatah-Abu Mussa's crowd, the people who split with Yasser Arafat in 1983 when Arafat had begun to talk in terms of moderation and the Syrians and others turned against him. They were to speak French and English and carry Israeli papers, and the boat would be registered in Tel Aviv, or would appear to be.

The big woman said, 'I suppose you must know where you're going then. I don't, I'm not even looking at maps, in case I guess . . . But make sure there's nothing compromising in your luggage. Yachtsmen taking a holiday cruise don't need much more than shorts, towels and suntan oil . . . Incidentally, you're going to say you'll be cruising north into Turkish waters, right? Well, you'll be glad to hear the boat's a Turkish type, known as a *gulet*, built in Turkey at a place called Bodrum.'

'And does the tour company have a name?'

'Bluewater Cruises. Israeli, new business just starting up. Agent here in London — ' she curtsied, massively — 'is little me, but head office is in Jaffa. I'm having brochures printed, should have some for you when you come for your tickets. You answered a holiday ad in the *Sunday Times*, by the way, that's how you got on to it — same with the others, eh?'

'Was there an advertisement?'

'Sure was.' Emptying the bottle, splitting what was left between her own glass and Smotrenko's. 'Don't despair, Eric, there's another . . . '

'General Gudyenko's in good shape, I hope?'

Leo nodded. 'He's in excellent health. And his mind — the combination of range and capacity for detail — '

'Must have a high opinion of you, to have put this mission

24

in your hands.' The GRU controller paused, inviting comment. He added when none came, 'Kicking you straight into the deep end, huh?'

'My training's virtually complete. OK, I'd've been left to hang around for another year maybe, then the examining board – which to all intents and purposes *is* the general – but I wouldn't have gained much. Also, it happens that my training, languages, preliminary field experience – everything, this far – could've been designed to fit me for this job.' His cold eyes held the older man's. 'The general *will* have given it some thought, you know.'

'You don't say.' The smile was perfunctory. Leo put in quickly, 'I'm sorry if that sounded – well, precocious.'

'A little.' Smotrenko's smile was genuine, this time. He asked, 'You're what, about thirty?'

'Right. But if I'd been much older I couldn't have played this particular role, you see.'

The role of an SBS captain, he meant.

'And – ' the woman joined them, having eased the cork out of a second bottle – 'with those looks, you *must* be a Georgian. Would I be right?' Her smile clung to him. 'Georgians make the best lovers in the world. So I've *heard*, I hasten to add, I couldn't swear it from my own very limited experience, unfortunately.'

'Eric' laughed. Leo's imagination boggled, at the implication that he might do anything to broaden her experience. Like coupling with a hippo . . . He'd thought of dossing in this flat for the night, but with her bulgy eyes glistening at him he was having second thoughts. A good – and very practical – alternative would be to go back to where the two mercenaries were holed up in Clapham, drop in on them unexpectedly and use a couch there, spend the whole morning with them, preparing them for the charade, their impersonation of SBS Royal Marines.

It would be the best possible use of his time. The big woman leant over with the bottle: 'Georgian – is my guess right?'

He nodded. Covering his glass with his palm. 'I was born in Tbilisi.'

Between the Black and Caspian seas in the summer of 1957 Leonid Ivanovich Serebryakov had first opened baby-blue eyes on the lush, exotic landscape. Even as a toddler he'd shown signs of being exceptionally bright – to the surprise of his railwayman father, less to that of his mother who was a computer technician from Krasdodar. The schoolboy revealed a particular flair for languages and was also something of an athlete, which pleased his father, who'd been a sprinter in his own youth, and when the time came for military service Leo was picked for Spetsnaz special-force training. He was good at it and enjoyed it, up to a point, and appreciated the honour of having been selected for it, but he had his sights set higher than on soldiering, even the Spetsnaz kind of soldiering, and with some string-pulling from his mother's family – a favourite uncle had recently been promoted major-general – he found himself inducted to the Military-Diplomatic Academy.

He'd already achieved good passes in English-language studies and had set himself to learning Arabic – because there'd been a tutor handy, and being attracted by something so completely different, and the willing tutor having suggested to him that fluency in such a tongue might be a useful adjunct to his swarthy complexion. Then General Gudyenko's recruiters from the GRU Training Centre for 'illegals', talent-spotters for whom the Mil-Dip Academy was a natural poaching ground, got hold of him, and from his first short interview with the general himself Leonid's fate was sealed. He didn't know, on this evening in London at the flat in Sloane Street, quite how hermetically it had *now* been sealed, but this of course was a very much later development, all of twelve years later. In those fledgeling days under Gudyenko's wing he was returned to a Spetsnaz unit for a further year's specialist training – he was commissioned *mladshi leitnant* before the end of the year – and then set to advanced 'saturation' training in English language, politics and current affairs, with Arabic as a sideline.

The Training Centre's courses were invariably tailor-made, individual programmes to suit the candidate's talents and expectations, and the same flexibility extended to location, as the Centre had no premises except for Gudyenko's own office and staff accommodation. Leo Serebryakov thus spent two years in a private *dacha* forty miles outside Moscow, sharing

26

the little villa in its insulating birchwoods with two male instructors – one of them an Englishman – and an Iranian girl who taught him much more than Arabic. That – the Arabic instruction – was his relaxation. For two years, seven days a week, he lived in English. No word was ever spoken, in daylight hours, in any other tongue. English newspapers, magazines and books were his only reading-matter, BBC programmes and English-language tapes the constant background. Walls were covered with maps and with frequently varied photographs, maps of counties, road and rail and underground systems, street plans of London and other cities. His menus were English: bacon-and-eggs for breakfast, frequent cups of tea with milk and sugar instead of glasses of real tea. Flat beer in pint tankards, fish-and-chips . . . Every aspect of current British life was dinned into him: he knew the footballers and the cricketers, pop stars and gossip columnists, actors and actresses, tv shows, films and plays, politicians, trade unionists, civil servants, and the political and economic machinery which these people tended, manipulated or obstructed. He supported Chelsea . . .

'Tell me – ' Eric watched the bubbling liquid rise to fill his glass – 'how you explain here in England your otherwise rather conveniently – at least, I *imagine* it's convenient – Middle Eastern appearance?'

Leo was watching the big woman top up her own glass. She seemed to lick her thin lips as she did it, and he thought that in the circumstances they both drank too much. He asked Eric, 'Don't you know my background?'

'Why should I? I don't have to explain you. My function is only to – well, smooth your path, if it needs smoothing. You know this, surely?'

'I thought they might have briefed you on background.'

'Why should I be given information I don't need?'

'Since you put it like that – ' Leo smiled at him – 'the best answer I can give you is "good question".' He winked at the woman. 'Huh?'

She laughed. 'You walked into that one, Eric.'

'I'll tell you the basic answer, anyway.' He didn't have to, but there'd be no point in antagonising this character unnecessarily. It was well on the cards that he might have to

27

work with him again, one of these days. Boris Smotrenko was the GRU Resident here in London and might remain so for years – MI5 permitting. Leo confided, 'The guy whose skin I'm in had an Egyptian mother. French-Egyptian actually. My Dad met her out there – Cairo – when he was in the RAF in Cyprus in 1955.'

'So to all intents and purposes you're a *very* true Brit.'

When his parents had separated – Sergeant Campbell posted back to the UK, his Egyptian wife having no wish to go with him and the sergeant only too glad to leave his mongrel offspring with her and get the hell out – the deserted wife took her son home to Cairo, to a family which had disapproved of the marriage in the first place. Their reception of her and the child lacked any warmth: she'd defied them, and now she'd come back to sponge on them, with her halfcaste brat.

There *was* a Sergeant Campbell – a technician, communications – and he did leave an infant son with his Egyptian wife, did later obtain a British divorce. The boy had been christened 'Donald' by the RAF chaplain on the base, and having been born on British sovereign territory to a British father he was entitled to British citizenship. This made it easy for his mother to obtain a passport for him, when he was sixteen, through the embassy in Cairo. She'd remarried, to a man who offered escape from drudgery in her parents' home, and her new husband objected to having the kid around, so it was a stroke of luck that at this time an aunt, widowed sister of the sergeant – who was actually an ex-sergeant by then – had renewed an invitation to young Donald to come over and live with her in a civilised country and decent environment. She was a regular church-goer and supporter of moral causes; she'd strongly disapproved of her brother, of his marriage and then of his running out on it, especially of his having left the child to be brought up in heathen surroundings and no doubt moral turpitude. She'd long felt that to some degree she shared in her brother's guilt, should have accepted responsibility at a much earlier stage for the bairn's welfare and salvation, and she'd entered into a stilted correspondence with her former sister-in-law. It culminated now in an enthusiastic acceptance of her offer, and she immediately bought a one-way air ticket – ensuring first that it couldn't be redeemed for cash in Egypt – and mailed it to Cairo.

Donald Campbell spent seven months in the ice-cold, granite house outside the Scottish capital. The aunt hadn't expected him to be as dark-skinned as he was: and in the extreme cold his swarthiness turned to an unhealthy grey. Not, she insisted to her pastor and neighbours, that such physical characteristics bothered her; what she found unbearable was the boy's attitude – a slyness and an underlying hostility. Dislike was mutual, and the boy was returned to Cairo, where his stepfather said – holding up the British passport – 'Such an article has a value. And *he* won't have further need of it, unfortunately . . . '

He'd had certain undercover groups in mind as likely purchasers, but the intermediary to whom he entrusted the sale of the passport, a man he knew to have the right sort of contacts, tried his luck at the Soviet Embassy first. Which in the long run saved the GRU's forgers a job, and into the bargain was real, flawless, needing only a substitution of photographs. It went into stock for a couple of years, and when the Training Centre began to process young Leo Serebryakov the Centre's computer matched the passport to the new recruit.

When it expired, ten years after its date of issue, Leo was working in Beirut, on his first foreign posting but still in training and with years more of it ahead of him. The document was renewed without any awkward questions being asked, with his own up-to-date photograph in it now. From there on he was home and dry, he *was* Donald Campbell. With a father who'd emigrated to Canada and wouldn't want to be reminded of his existence, an aunt whose attitude was now much the same as her brother's and who in any case wasn't likely to be around much longer, and a mother who was effectively *incommunicado*, Leo was on as good a wicket as an illegal could have hoped for.

He'd been unable to discover what might have happened to the original Don Campbell. He'd asked, in the Centre, and had been told, '*You* are Donald Campbell. There's no other.' He thought it was possible they'd had the boy killed.

According to the records in the language college in Beirut where he lectured in English to Arab students and in Arabic to other nationalities including Brits and Americans, he'd got the job through his mother's relations in Cairo. In fact it had been set up by a dapper, multi-lingual Russian who lived in Paris and directed language courses for students throughout Europe. His primary value to both the GRU and the KGB was as a talent-spotter; a lot of potentially suitable raw material passed under his scrutiny every week.

Leo worked in Beirut for four years, taking local leaves and one longer break each year in Moscow. When embarking on these trips he claimed to be visiting his mother in Egypt, but in fact reported to a safe house in Cairo where he changed identity. Donald Campbell had thus never visited Moscow in his life, although Leo Serebryakov spent a couple of months there annually – taking written and oral examinations and undergoing political indoctrination as well as technical training. In his third year of this he began to see quite a lot of a girl called Nadia Zhenskinova who was an interpreter and translator on General Gudyenko's staff and with whom he found he had much in common. He'd learned early in his apprenticeship that in this line of work no one had any private life or secrets, and it was no great surprise therefore to be told by a senior GRU instructor that the friendship between himself and Nadia had General Gudyenko's approval. He took note of it, knowing that it would be in his own best interests – as well as being his natural inclination, up to a point; but this was in the last week of his fourth Moscow visit, and on his return to Beirut via Cairo he found a surprise awaiting him: De Gavres, the Parisian educational coordinator, had made arrangements for Don Campbell to spend two years at Stirling University in Scotland, on an exchange posting as a lecturer in Arabic.

So there'd be no early wedding. Although he felt sure the Centre would have begun work on a cover for Nadia's background so that when she did join him she'd be something other than a citizen of the USSR. They'd prefer him to be married, he knew, by the time he finished his training and went into the field. Husbands in this kind of work were routinely checked on and reported on by their wives – and vice versa – and when she had children they'd be left in Moscow with foster-parents, effectively hostages against any possibility of defection.

During his two years in Britain he travelled extensively, adding first-hand observation to knowledge acquired at the *dacha* and later in Beirut and Moscow. He visited the house in which Don Campbell had spent seven miserable months: it was occupied by strangers, and he found the aunt's grave in a nearby churchyard. He tried – as anyone in his position surely would have done – to trace his father, but the trail went cold at the point where he'd emigrated to Canada. Ministry of Defence records dug out from some satellite establishment outside London showed nothing later than the date of the sergeant's discharge and the fact he'd taken a lump-sum gratuity, not a pension. But Donald Campbell was now on record as having tried to find his lost father, there'd be correspondence in some file and it was proof – if proof were ever needed – of his identity. He visited most major towns and cities, and allowed an element of Scots accent to infect his speech. He possessed a driving licence, had his name and circumstances in the Inland Revenue and DHSS computer records; Don Campbell existed, and could prove it.

He'd still had six weeks' lecturing to do at Stirling when a cable arrived from Cairo telling him that his mother was seriously ill, asking him to come immediately. It was signed by a Dr Ibrahim, which meant that he was wanted urgently in Moscow. The university authorities were sympathetic; they suggested that as his time was so nearly up he might as well call it a day and return to his post in Beirut – after seeing his mother on the road to recovery . . . They'd recall their own man, and it would save one return fare London/Cairo. Leo had an open return ticket, and he left on a flight from Heathrow in less than twelve hours from receipt of the cable. Standard procedure then: the safe house, switch of identity, papers and appearance, Aeroflot flight from Cairo International to Sheremetyevo, where he was met by Nadia. She'd come in a large Chaika with a uniformed GRU driver; she whispered as they embraced, 'They have a mission for you, a very important one. It will mean the end of your probationary

31

status, Leo, the general himself has decided this. Aren't you proud?'

His cold eyes penetrated the bubbling exterior, probed the source of all this warmth, *her* angle on whatever the hell this was all about. He smiled: 'Then maybe you and I—'

'No "maybe" about it, darling! The general told me this morning, when you come back he'll not only attend the ceremony himself, he'll provide the *champanskoye* as his wedding gift!'

Gudyenko conducted the initial briefing. The only other person present was a Colonel Dmitry Arkeyevich Vetrov, head of the British section, whom Leo over the years had come to know well. He was a small man, fair-haired and pink-faced, very meticulous and thorough once the broader sweep of Gudyenko's mind had put him on the right track.

Gudyenko growled, 'You got here fast, Leonid Ivan'ich. Just as well, I might add . . . You won't be here long – as no doubt Nadia Zhenskinova will have told you, we've a job for you, an important one. I've decided to let you run it, and you'll do so under my personal control.'

Only the top GRU 'illegals' were controlled by the general himself, a handful of men and women with brilliant track-records and in the key locations. Leo began to murmur his appreciation of the honour, but Gudyenko cut him short.

'In your studies of the British scene, in particular of their armed forces, have you learnt what the letters "SBS" stand for?'

'Special Boat Squadron. Royal Marines – equivalent of our naval infantry but all commando-trained – and their SB Squadron is a small cadre of underwater swimmers, canoeists, parachutists, etc. They're similar to the Army's Special Air Service except that they possess those additional skills.'

Gudyenko nodded. 'You're about to join them. You'll return to London shortly, travelling as Donald Campbell as usual – from Cairo onwards – but with another identity up your sleeve, that of Captain Knox of the SBS. You'll be instructed here by specialists and you'll have a lot of reading to do, background stuff about the Marines and their SBS, and so on. In London your first and crucially important task will be to recruit a former SAS officer, an individual whom the

SAS dismissed because of – oh, drunken behaviour mostly. But you'll read his file in a minute.'

He'd glanced at Vetrov, who nodded, patting a folder. The general continued, 'As Captain Knox of the Royal Marines you'll present yourself as team leader in an operation that's being mounted to extract a British civilian whom Intelligence sources have indicated has been moved into Syria from the Lebanon. This person was kidnapped in Beirut several weeks ago, by the Hezbollah. His name's Stillgoe, he's a journalist but we believe was also involved with British and/or US Intelligence and had information which he'd been on the point of taking out of the country when the Hezbollah snatched him. So the British will want him out – or the Yanks will, or both – and when they hear he's being held somewhere in reach of the Syrian coast they'll be tempted, won't they?'

'I suppose they would be.' Leo asked, '*Have* they heard it?'

'Arrangements are in hand. They haven't yet, but they will – quite soon. It *has* to be quite soon – for reasons which I'll explain; also in the context of a further dimension in our planning, on which I may brief you later, but not now . . . What matters as far as you're concerned, you as Captain Knox of the SBS, is that not only has the information reached London, you've been ordered to take an SBS team into Syria, find Stillgoe and bring him out. You need this SAS man – former SAS man – in your team because you're short of Arabic speakers in the SB Squadron, and this person – whose name is – '

Vetrov supplied it: 'Swale.'

'Swale is fluent in Arabic. He's also likely to want to be recruited by you, our analysts tell us. You'll see their comments in his file.'

Leo nodded, waited. Vetrov's nose was running and he kept wiping it with his knuckles.

'The strategic background is that President Assad has seemed in recent months to have some softening of the brain. Since the American bombing of Libya, to be precise. To some people in Syria – and elsewhere, but it's Syria we're concerned with – our own closest friends in the area, he's appeared to be back-sliding. Consequently these people have deemed it necessary for some actions to have been taken without Assad's own knowledge or approval. So far as these aspects are concerned we're not directly or very closely involved, of course; I simply record the fact that it's been worrying many of his own people as well as some Lebanon-based groups such as the Hezbollah, Islamic Jehad, *et al*. You have the so-called "Popular Fronts" – those of George Habash and Ahmed Jibril – and Naif Hawatme's Democratic Front, to name only the more prominent. None of these are soft in the head – as you'll be aware, of course, you'd know it maybe better than I do . . . *Our* concern matches theirs primarily in the indications that Assad is flirting or contemplating flirtation with the West. Who naturally would be pleased to do business with him, political or otherwise, as typified now by his intention to buy French weaponry; and as he's been our most reliable ally in the Middle East for years now – well, Syria's our anchor, and in nautical terms we can't afford to let it drag . . . Consequently, plans were being formulated, contingency plans aimed at short-circuiting such tendencies, and now rather suddenly we find the necessity is upon us. Which is where you step in, my lad.'

The general looked at Vetrov. 'Anything important I've left out?'

'Well.' The colonel suggested, 'Perhaps the fact that those concerned people in Syria are with us as partners in the project. Also that the draft plan envisaged the provision of some form of bait, and this hostage – Stillgoe – happens to be as suitable as any we could have wished for?'

Gudyenko nodded, turning back to face Leo.

'At a certain stage, control of the operation will shift to Damascus. But this is detail, you'll get it all later . . . One reason, though, that the British may believe Stillgoe *has* been moved into Syria, without Assad knowing it, is that Assad has been trying to impose peace in Beirut by filling the place with Syrian troops. They're policing even Shi'ite areas, and sooner or later might find this hostage and release him. Assad's actually been calling for the release of all hostages, you know that? Another move towards ingratiating himself with the countries concerned . . . But now we come to the reason for our deciding here and now to implement the plan . . . ' He'd checked, frowning. 'You've a question?'

'Only that if the hostage's whereabouts are being made known to the Brits—'

'It's not. Not unless you'd call Syria a "location" . . . It's known to *you* – to Captain Knox of the SBS. And the former SAS officer will have no reason to doubt that the intelligence was received through official channels. Let me repeat at this point – absence of doubts of any kind in Swale's mind is a primary and essential basis to the operation, it's the one thing that's truly a prerequisite. He has to believe in you and in everything you tell him, and incidentally in the other members of your team.'

'May I ask what's to be the composition of the team?'

'Yourself, Swale, and two mercenaries.'

'Mercenaries?'

'They'll be identified for you by the time you're back in London. Men with military, commando backgrounds; they're being recruited now. You'll introduce yourself to them as Knox, and give them to understand that the operation has been sanctioned at the highest political level, but sanctioned only with the proviso that the action is officially *un*official, on no account to be attributable to British forces, SBS or any other. You alone are a serving Royal Marine, they have to know it but they're to keep their mouths shut. Except, you'll explain, you're recruiting this ex-SAS officer, Arabic speaker, and he's got to believe you're *all* SBS. Part of their contract therefore is to play-act as Royal Marines – as Marines working under cover, who'd pretend if they were caught that they were mercenaries, allowing only Swale to know the truth – that like you they're SBS . . . You'll explain Swale as the sort of guy who wouldn't otherwise volunteer, wouldn't want to work with mercenaries, has to be assured he's serving Queen and Country – which he *will* be, you'll point out, and you've got to have him, for his Arabic . . . Is something unclear?'

'But these others will be less particular about who employs them?'

'Possibly. After all, they're mercenaries.'

'And they've got to be hoodwinked, but also join in the pretence –'

'Exactly.'

'It seems a bit – unwieldy . . . Couldn't just I and this

35

Swale character see it through on our own, without that complication?'

'It wouldn't be realistic, might alert Swale's suspicions. SAS, like SBS, tend to work in teams of four or multiples of four. All right, in pairs as well – which they call "bricks", for some peculiar reason – but on a job like this one four is *much* more likely. There's at least one unavoidable departure from normal patterns – the question of transport, a detail you'll come to – and we don't want to pile one unlikelihood on another, Leonid Ivan'ich. It does complicate the deception, I agree, but we must accept it.'

Leo nodded . . . 'May I raise one other point? A week ago I was a university lecturer, Don Campbell. Now I'm to be the same face but I have a new name and I'm an officer in the Royal Marines. Presumably I'll have a passport in that name of Knox, but – '

The general had raised a hand, palm-outwards, stopping him.

'You'll have your own passport, you'll remain Donald Campbell. You'll represent yourself as Captain Knox only to Swale and the other two. If you ran into some former acquaintance, what would it matter? You'll be in civilian clothes, you're the Donald Campbell they know. You could offer some excuse, if necessary, for being in England instead of at your mother's bedside in Egypt. She died before you reached her, maybe, you just got back . . . But none of those three, although they'll be travelling with you, need see your passport – or your air ticket. And you won't be returning to the UK: on completion you'll be taken to Damascus and from there fly back home to us. In due course, obviously, you'll have to return to your British residence, but when that time comes no one will know you as Knox. Only Swale and the other two will have known you by that name. This is as it *would* be, incidentally; SBS personnel are highly secretive, their names are never made public. If you're back in England in a year's time, say, you'll be Donald Campbell formerly of Beirut and of Stirling University, nobody will ever ask you more than – ' the general put on what was supposed to be a girl's high-pitched voice in English – '*Where have you been hiding from me, Donald dearest?*'

He smiled, politely. 'But Swale and the others?'

'Oh, I'm sure you've guessed.' The general began to cough; reaching for his glass of water, he croaked at Vetrov, 'Tell him, anyway.'

Vetrov's pink face turned to Leo.

'There'll be no British hostage at that location. Only a camp of refugees, old folk and children and cripples, victims of Israeli barbarism. These innocents will be massacred, shot down by the submachine-guns of the SBS. You'll be equipped with Uzis, by the way, Israeli weapons, and you'll have landed from an Israeli boat. So Swale will believe ... So, in fury at discovering they've come all that way for nothing, the bird either flown or never there – well, as I say.' Vetrov panto-mimed the blaze of machine-gun fire. 'You yourself will take part in the atrocity and Swale must see you doing so. He's to be left behind, having seen his three companions go berserk and murder these wretched people ... A firefight will then develop, Syrian troops rushing to the scene. Swale will be shot in his legs but left alive, *kept* alive, to bear witness to the crime and to the fact it was perpetrated by a team of the Special Boat Squadron of the Royal Marines – with whom he was himself serving. He'll describe his recruitment by a man called Knox; the British will deny the existence of any such person, but (a) they would, would they not, they'd fudge their records however they wanted, and (b) what's a false name or two, in these clandestine games? You see why it's so important that he should believe you *are* an SBS officer. He has to *know* you were all three SBS, so he'll be ready to swear to it at his trial in Damascus.'

Gudyenko came back into the briefing.

'Assad will be forced out of his dreams. Deposed, if necess-ary. He'll be our guest in Moscow at the time, so ... ' He shrugged. 'The entire Arab world, even hitherto pro-Western states, will turn their backs on Britain and her American friends.'

Leo sat motionless, holding the general's bleak stare, think-ing it out. Initial concern – a quick visual appreciation of the physical problems of stage-managing an atrocity of that size – faded into the broader perspective, the inevitable tidal wave of world reaction.

He let his breath go. 'It's – huge . . . '

'Sure it is.' Gudyenko raised a forefinger. 'And an extra dividend now – with the need to move fast, as I was saying, to carry out the operation within the next couple of weeks – you'll have been reading your English newspapers, the trial of the Jordanian, Nezar Hindawi?'

Leo nodded. 'Tricked an Irish girl into carrying a bomb for him, to sabotage an El Al flight from Heathrow.'

'The trial hasn't far to go. Three weeks or so, we're told.' Gudyenko frowned. 'We're also advised that there's almost a certainty of conviction. Regrettably, involving the Syrian ambassador personally, and several of his former staff. With this outcome, it's predicted that there'll be at least a withdrawal of ambassadors, possibly a complete closure of embassies, with of course considerable damage to the Syrian reputation world-wide. To an extent, of course, there's a mitigating factor from our own angle, it should fix Assad's flirtatious tendencies – even with the French, much as they want his money. Want *anyone's* money . . . But still the damage would be enormous, particularly in the Arab world but also in all the non-aligned areas. And we're speaking of our close ally, so it rubs off on us and our own best interests, naturally. But this operation should counter all such effects. The world will see the British and their SBS as terrorists of the most unpleasant kind: they'll ask *Who are these people to accuse others of terrorist activity?* D'you follow? Evidence will be convincing and horrifying. Photographs – you can imagine. And this fellow Swale, you see – his having taken part in the atrocity, then his public testimony – well, it won't be just allegation, it'll be solid *fact*.'

3

On the Tuesday night Charlie was alone when he let himself into the flat. He and Paula had dined early at an Italian restaurant, after which he'd driven her to her own pad in Battersea and kissed her goodbye. She hadn't been too happy, unfortunately. She'd spent last night here with him, and she'd wanted to do the same tonight – to make up, she'd said, for the fact he was swanning off somewhere or other. She'd obviously had doubts of his story of a business trip to Germany, and he'd had the SBS business in his mind, hadn't been able to hide his elation, excitement, well enough to concentrate on her and her disbelief, persuade her that he wasn't taking some other woman off somewhere or other.

He wished he could have convinced her. He was very fond of her, genuinely so, and the last thing he wanted was to hurt her. He'd have liked to have had her with him now, too, in any other circumstances. But Bob Knox had telephoned on the stroke of noon to say he'd pick him up at the street entrance to his flat at 0600 Wednesday morning. Knox would be driving a white minibus and he'd have the other two members of the SBS team with him, also camping gear; they'd be spending the next few days in Wales, tuning up.

'Did you settle your business affairs, Charlie?'

'Sure. No problem.'

He'd even clinched the deal for the pale-blue Rolls. It was being brought down from Manchester, reputedly spotless and with only just over 7000 miles – 'genuine' miles – on its clock. The Saudi kid was going to have to dig deeply into his oily pocket but he'd be getting what he'd asked for. In more ways than one, Charlie guessed.

Knox was telling him, 'We're grateful, Charlie, I was told to pass this on to you. You're exactly the right guy for the job and we know we're lucky that you're willing to help us out. The question of pay, incidentally, is being referred to MoD, and with any luck – '

'It doesn't bother me.'

'Has to be settled, all the same . . . Listen, about equipment – d'you have any gear of your own that you could use in Wales?'

'I'd say so. Yeah.'

'Boots, particularly?'

'Boots, definitely.'

'That's fine. I'll have some gear for you anyway, but I'd anticipated getting you down here so we could have kitted you out on the spot, but – well, as I explained – '

'I remember.'

'0600, then.'

This had come as a relief. He'd been half expecting a let-down, imagining Knox having reported back to his SB Squadron's CO at Poole and being talked out of including Charlie Swale in his team. Knox would have had to admit that Charlie had sunk several strong whiskies in the short time they'd been together, that he was obviously a heavy drinker and therefore unreliable. And maybe the report on him from the Regiment might not have been all *that* warm. The Colonel was a hell of a good guy, but facts were facts and they were all on record. And surely the SBS would have been able to dig out some other Arabic speaker, even if it had meant recalling someone temporarily from the Gulf.

So hanging up after Knox's call he'd felt – *jubilant*.

But it wouldn't do to have Paula with him when they came by in the morning. OK, so he'd wake to the alarm and he could have been downstairs, leaving her tucked up, but they could be early, Knox might buzz and ask to be let in, or she might insist on coming down to see him off. Checking that it was *not* some girl he was taking off with. Then she'd have seen three SBS men and a van loaded with camping equipment and there'd have been a lot of explaining and lying to do.

He'd told her, 'I have some paperwork to fix before I turn in, and then I want to *sleep*. Know what I mean? Seriously, this deal's important, I hope it'll produce a lot of business.'

Paula wanted to be married, he knew that. She was in her late twenties, she was no career girl and she was worried about not staying irresistible for ever; and he was presentable enough, he supposed, and making money, and they got on well both in and out of bed. There was also something Anne had told him once — that he liked women, didn't only *want* them, and that they sensed this and found it reassuring.

The existence of Anne, of course, was the one factor that put the idea of marriage to anyone else right out of court. He might have to spell this out to Paula some time. But one of the snags with liking women was that you were averse to hurting them.

And *that* was a joke. If you liked black humour.

Maybe Anne — maybe after this business was over, if he could tell her about it —

Cloud cuckoo land. Anne wouldn't even speak to him when he called her on the telephone. He'd tried three or four times, since she'd moved up to London from her parents' house — she had a flat just off the King's Road now, which he guessed her father must have bought her — because when she'd been living down in Wiltshire she'd been closely guarded by the parents, who were nice enough people but seemed to regard their former son-in-law as some kind of wild beast, and when she'd moved up to London he'd thought he might have a chance.

He'd soon discovered that *that* had been wishful thinking: and he knew it now, had to live with the fact that he'd put himself beyond the pale. He topped up his glass.

He was out of bed at five, had a hot bath followed by a cold shower, and dressed in old khaki drill pants, khaki shirt, sweater and training shoes, threw a few other items into a grip before he fried some eggs and bacon and made more coffee than he needed so as to take the rest along in a thermos. He'd given the drink problem a lot of thought while in the bath – at night it never seemed to *be* a problem – and he reckoned that if he kept drinking tea and coffee it might stave off his longings for the hard stuff.

He thought it should be easy enough once they'd embarked on the operation itself. Although he didn't recall a time in his adult life when he hadn't enjoyed a drink or two, he'd never missed it when he'd been in the field. Obviously he was deeper into the habit now than he'd been before, but he hoped the same thing might apply.

Mightn't be too easy in a tent in bloody Wales, though. Particularly with a rain-belt moving in from the west. End of the weeks of Indian summer, finally.

Door-buzzer. Ten minutes early, for Christ's sake . . .

'Yes?'

'Bob Knox, Charlie. Can I come up a minute?'

It turned out that Bob wanted a pee. Charlie, glad he'd had the sense not to have Paula here, suppressed the natural comment of 'Should have gone before you left home' and said instead, 'You're a bit early, Bob. Luckily I'm ready.' Then they went down into the cold early-morning air, dew dripping from the trees, a white C-registered VW minibus parked there with two men in its rear seats.

'Charlie Swale – Pete Denham – Smiley Tait . . . '

Tait was smallish, dark, harsh-looking. A tough egg, Charlie thought. About thirty-two, thirty-four maybe. Charlie wondered whether that total lack of expression was defence or hostility. Neither, probably. Or both. The other Marine was younger by about five years, and also dark-haired, but pale-faced and of heavier build. Bob Knox climbed into the driving-seat; Charlie slung his grip up and the heavy-set younger man grabbed it, tossed it into the back. Then Charlie was in and had shut the door, leant back to shake hands with the Marines as the VW rocked away from the kerb. His own hand felt soft as the others grasped it in turn: it was a reminder of his civilian status, the soft year he'd spent. Denham's expression was friendly: 'Welcome aboard, Charlie.' West Country accent. The other one had nodded, with no change of expression: he muttered, 'Likewise.' Charlie asked them, 'Driven up from Poole this morning?'

'Not much on the roads this time of day.' Knox shifted gear. He and the others were dressed much as Charlie was – drill trousers or jeans, sweaters . . . 'And with luck we'll make good time down the M4 now. Might even be in camp by lunchtime.'

Small-talk had petered out soon enough. It was too early for conversation, and Tait was asleep – anyway had his eyes shut – within minutes. There'd been no word spoken from the Hyde Park Corner underpass all the way to Windsor, where the castle looked beautiful in the sun's first light. Knox was driving at a steady seventy-five to eighty miles an hour.

Charlie turned from admiring the castle as it fell astern. 'Tell me, Bob. Do these two blokes know where we're going and what for?'

'Going to Wales.' Pete Denham answered the question. He'd been leaning forward with his chin resting on his forearms on the back of the front seat, between them. He added, 'To run up and down some fucking mountain. Right, Bob?'

'About right.'

Charlie began, 'I meant—'

'The answer's negative, Charlie, they do not. They know as much as you do – Middle East, extract a guy, bring him home. No one has to know any more than that until we're a lot closer to the target than we are now.'

'All right. You're the guv'nor.'

It surprised him, though. If it was true and they weren't just keeping *him* in the dark. This would be quite understandable: he thought that in Bob Knox's place he wouldn't trust Charlie Swale any farther than he had to. But he'd have guessed the Marines would know it all, that they'd have worked out a plan and discussed it between them in all its detail. If you couldn't trust your own guys to keep their mouths shut, for Christ's sake –

'It's not a matter of trust or distrust, Charlie. Only that the job's quite straightforward as far as we can see from here, there's no detailed planning that anyone can do – apart from logistics, which are well in hand – until we're out there and we can see the lie of the land. So there'd be no advantage in discussing it.'

'You must be a mind-reader.'

Leo shrugged. It had been obvious what Swale would have been thinking. Leo had thought about this question of not giving any of them any detailed information about the job, because he'd realised that from his SAS experience Charlie would have taken it for granted that all the members of a team would have been in on the planning right from scratch. He'd decided that he could take a chance on Charlie's knowing next to nothing about SBS procedures; and if that turned out to be an incorrect assumption, OK, so this was a one-off, this was how they'd decided to handle it on this particular occasion. Charlie seemed to have swallowed it, anyway. Leo was hunched behind the wheel and apparently concentrating on the road ahead but he was searching his mind for any hurdles which he might *not* have foreseen, in the context of pulling the wool over the eyes of Charlie Swale. He'd passed the Swindon turn-off before Charlie broke the silence with another question.

'I was thinking, Bob — you said your parents married in 1956 — right? The year Nasser took over the Canal and we and the French invaded? Your father must have stuck his neck out with a vengeance, getting permission to marry an Egyptian girl just at that time?'

'The Suez crisis was at the back end of the year, Charlie, wasn't it? I think it was November when the paras went in at Port Said. And the wedding took place in the spring, you see — when the Canal takeover was probably no more than a gleam in Nasser's eye.'

'And by the time we moved in you'd already been conceived, I dare say.'

'I must have been, actually. But I remember now, it was July when Nasser grabbed the Canal.' He shrugged. 'Oddly enough the events around that time have always been of some special interest to me.' He smiled briefly. Thinking that drink or no drink, Swale wasn't all that slow on the uptake. He'd remembered what Leo had said about his parents' marriage, the date of it and the date of Leo's alleged birth, and had noticed the incongruity of an Anglo-Egyptian romance flowering at that juncture, and he'd remembered to ask about it. Despite the smell of last night's whisky on his breath. It might be taken as a warning, not to underestimate Charlie's powers of observation and recollection, not to assume he'd be all that easy to fool.

He glanced at him. 'OK, Charlie?'

'Fine. Like me to take over for a spell?'

'No, thanks, I'm happy.' He edged the van back into the left-hand lane. 'We put in some spare gear that ought to fit you. Tracksuit and so forth.'

'Very kind of you. And on that subject – what about equipment – weapons for instance – when we take off?'

'It'll be out there, waiting for us. We'll be on a scheduled flight out of London, you see.'

'*Will* we . . . '

He'd assumed they'd be taken out in a Charlie 130, a Hercules, to some NATO base. He was staring at Bob's profile, astonished at this idea, an ordinary commercial flight . . . Bob explained, 'It fits in, there's no reason not to. Won't be the first time we've done it this way. Depending on destination and timing and what we do or don't have to take with us. Actually there are advantages from the security angle this way, and as I said, everything we need will be out there ahead of us, we'll take nothing you wouldn't have in your luggage on any Mediterranean holiday.'

'Buckets and spades and snorkel masks?'

No smile . . . 'Sailing holiday, say. Shorts, T-shirts, warmer gear for cool evenings, that kind of thing.' A shrug. 'Suntan oil and a disc camera, if you like.'

Echoes of the big woman's advice, night before last, when she'd pointed out that security precautions on all the Middle Eastern air routes were likely to be more stringent following the Libyan-mounted terrorist assault on British women and children on the Akrotiri base. Unnecessary advice, he'd thought, although he'd shown no such criticism in his manner; but it had all been thrashed out in Moscow, where *he'd* expressed concern at the notion of 'SBS' personnel travelling as tourists on a scheduled commercial flight, and Vetrov's deputy, a major named Pavluchenkov, had sneered, 'You'd rather we hired a Hercules for you, from the Royal Air Force?

Or sent a Tupolev to pick you up in London?' As for the large woman, he knew she'd only been airing her views because this was as far as her knowledge went – as far as the destination on the tickets which it was her job to buy. Beyond that point she had no information and no responsibility.

She'd shown real disappointment when Leo had told them he wouldn't be spending the night in Sloane Street, that he'd decided to move in with the mercenaries. In fact this had been well worth while, and had also provided him with the opportunity to recover the bug he'd left in their flat. Identical to the one he'd planted in Charlie Swale's place – self-contained, sound-activated, the size of a packet of cigarettes only flatter, when anyone started talking it began its silent recording.

He'd asked the woman, in a quick follow-up to cover the embarrassment over where he did or didn't sleep, 'What about giving me the detail of those two guys' backgrounds now?'

'Certainly . . . '

'You said – ' Smotrenko dipping his oar in again – 'one of them was a paratrooper?'

'That's Tait.' She'd nodded. 'Sergeant in the paras. Left the Army because he had a big win on the football pools.' She'd smiled. '*There's* capitalism for you. He'd always dreamt of running a pub, it had been his great ambition, what he'd thought he'd do when he retired. But he'd have been a brewer's tenant, never dreamt he'd be able to buy a place of his own. Reading between the lines I'd say it was a rotten buy – cheap. In any case it flopped, totally, and our friend lost his money.'

'Not so surprising.' Leo said, 'Impression I have from my one meeting with him is he has a face like a lump of stone. People who go into pubs want to be made welcome, not glared at. If he was the guy behind the bar you'd drink up and get out quick, I'd guess.'

'Anyway, he's had work as a barman since then.' She added, 'Also as a delivery driver, and other jobs. But from his paratroop NCO background he'd worked as an instructor on survival courses, and from that he was recruited by an organisation called Action for Animals. You know – they attack mink farms, fox farms and so on?' Leo had nodded; she explained, 'Well, there's a hardcore of thugs who spearhead the attacks. The organisation rides on the backs of people who really care about animals, but there's this nucleus of activists who aren't so nice, certainly don't give a shit for our little furry friends . . . Training in commando tactics is a must for them, and that was Tait's job.'

'Was?'

'It wasn't full-time employment, and he's not on that payroll now anyway, he's on ours.'

'How did you get on to him?'

'Through — friends.' She glanced at Smotrenko, who nodded. Back to Leo, then: 'People who have connections with the AFA . . . ' She shrugged. 'An organisation of that kind could have other uses, couldn't it? When a group's adept at taking out farms, laboratories, whatever — most of which are guarded now, protected electronically and so on — well, they could be switched to quite different targets, couldn't they. Missile sites, airfields, for instance?'

Smotrenko cut in: 'What about the other man?'

'Denham met Tait in AFA, but before that he was a Gunner, attached to a commando brigade so he did commando training. He was discharged after a scandal involving a girl soldier, a gang-bang rape charge. In his case rape wasn't proven, they acquitted him but they still got rid of him. He was *there*, you see . . . He says he was innocent, of course. But he was unemployed for a while, then in some mercenary expedition. Temporary jobs then, and he was introduced to the AFA, where he met Tait. Tait never went on any raids, only instructed the men who did, but Denham took part in some, including one where a farm employee was nearly killed. This finished him — he says he didn't do it, but he was near and saw it happen . . . Like the gang-bang, huh? He went back to bar-keeping, which like Tait he'd done before. It was Tait whom our contact recruited, and he introduced Pete Denham.'

'A primary consideration was that neither should have any police record.' Smotrenko stared at her. 'One presumes Denham's rape case never came into any criminal court?'

'Right, it didn't. A military court cleared him. And Tait has no record at all.'

In fact they were ideal for the job, Leo thought . . . Changing up, with his foot hard down then as he swung the van out

47

– he'd been boxed in, a truck overtaking another, cars speeding by on the outside – he thought about the three of them and their acceptance of him as team leader. Easing the VW back into the middle lane, shrugging mentally, knowing that his ability to deceive, manipulate, and personally to survive, float clear, lay basically in his detachment from his fellow humans, the feeling he had of being as 'different' from all of them as if he'd just come from Mars. And a rootlessness that matched this, which had been brought home to him recently in Moscow when General Gudyenko had made some remark about his – Leo's – being brought 'home' from Damascus when his work in Syria was finished. He'd thought, *Home?* Other men had homes, he didn't. Not even as a child: and he'd felt no kinship or empathy with either of his real parents.

He wondered if this detachment showed, if it puzzled these people. He'd seen no signs of it – not as he had for instance in the flat on Sloane Street, Smotrenko's instinctive hostility, his resentment of some quality which he must have sensed. Very much like a dog's hackles rising . . .

And Swale – earlier that same evening, Swale's wary puzzlement?

He thought that now, having had two nights and a day in which to think it over, Swale seemed to have settled, accepted him well enough. Because Swale *wanted* to. So that seemed to be all right – so far.

They stopped for a snack and for petrol at a Trust House Forte service station not far from the Severn Bridge. They drank fresh orange juice and ate open sandwiches, then bought newspapers. Leo took the *Daily Telegraph*, Tait the *Sun* and Denham the *Daily Mail*. Charlie bought only a Mars Bar, murmuring as he stalked out, 'Bugger the news, it's always fucking awful.' Both the mercenaries chuckled, glancing at him and then at each other, as if they'd begun to like him.

By early afternoon they had the tents up, on a hillside somewhere in the wilds of Wales. Leo had been to the farmhouse in the valley and made a deal, giving the farmer to understand that they were a cross-country relay team from some naval

48

establishment near Bath, here to put in a few days' workout prior to an inter-Services athletics meeting.

It was a well-sited camp. They had a wood behind them for shelter from the southwest wind, and a couple of hundred yards down the hill was a stream with clear, cold water in it. Eggs and milk would be available from the farm and there was plenty of fallen wood around for fuel. Sheep dotted the hillside: it wasn't exactly lush pasture. Above the camp the incline steepened to a ridge, then fell for about a thousand metres into a dip from which the land rose to a rocky summit. Leo said, pointing uphill, 'There's our training ground. Or some of it. We might as well get cracking right away – the old bloke said it's going to rain before long, and anyway this is Wednesday, so we've only the rest of today and Thursday/Friday, on Saturday we have to get back to the smoke. OK?'

Charlie said, 'Suits me,' and Denham nodded: 'Yeah.' Leo added, 'But look, I have a confession to make.'

They all looked at him, waiting for it. Smiley Tait so hard-faced that if he'd been a confessor you'd know you'd *never* get absolution. Denham's mouth slightly open . . . Charlie said – enjoying himself, although he knew it was going to be hellish toiling up that hill – 'I know what it is, Bob. You didn't care to mention it before, but you've got a wooden leg.'

Denham laughed. Leo was too intent on what he was about to say, on putting it over in a way that would sound natural and credible, to show appreciation of Charlie's humour. He told them, allowing himself to look slightly embarrassed, 'The fact is, I've spent most of the past six months at a desk. One's supposed to get out and take exercise, but – well, you get snowed under, there's never enough time . . . Consequently I'm not as fit as I ought to be: so—'

'Slobs of the world unite.' Charlie patted his own belly. 'You have nothing to lose but your flab.'

'So – ' Leo told him – 'I'm putting Smiley in charge of the training programme. I've told him to work us as hard as he likes.'

Tait nodded. 'Get changed, for a start.'

Charlie shared one of the tents with Leo, who told him while they were changing into tracksuits, 'Tait's a sergeant and a first-class instructor.' He added, 'Purely for information, Charlie; we don't use ranks much operationally.'

He thought, *Teach your grandmother to suck eggs.* Surprised that Bob should have bothered with that explanation. One special force was very much like another in those areas. He changed the subject: 'Back to London on Saturday, you said.'

'Right. Get there some time in the afternoon. Drop you at your place, then I'll have to return the VW and the tents, you see. We'll be taking off rather early on Sunday morning.'

'Next thing you know, you'll be telling me where we're going.'

'I thought I'd mentioned it – Sunday a.m. takeoff, I mean – in the van.'

'No. Up to now the only thing you'd mentioned was that we're going on a civil flight.'

'Well, I'm sorry, I'd meant to tell you. It'll be a very early start, actually. In fact I might shake down in your flat on Saturday night – unless it's inconvenient?' He finished lacing his trainers, and stood up. 'You ready?'

It was an easy jog up to the ridge, and then the downhill stretch was no effort. Charlie pounded along beside Tait, with Bob out to the left and Pete in front. Uphill again now, steeper than the first part and twice the distance, getting steeper as they went. Charlie saw Bob straining to keep up; feeling it himself too although he knew this was only a warm-up, a preliminary to the *hard* work. He was thankful he'd played squash regularly.

Slowing, stopping; stooped, hands on knees, panting, then looking up at the rock-piles towering against grey sky as Tait said cheerfully, 'Up we go, then.'

Denham led, and Bob – face darker than ever with the sheen of sweat on it – started up behind him. Tait glanced at Charlie, jerked his chin to point upward, muttered, 'Tomorrow you won't stop at all, you'll *fly* up . . .'

Leo said, in the tent at about 1 a.m., 'Just as well we've got these few days.'   .

'Yeah.' Charlie turned out the naphtha lamp and lay back,

pulled up the zip of his sleeping-bag. 'Two more days of pure bloody agony and we'll be tigers, huh?'

He began to snore almost instantly. Leo wondered how long it might have been since he'd turned in without a load of alcohol inside him.

The tape from the recorder-bug was OK. Leo had recovered it this morning when he'd got into the flat on the pretext of needing a pee, and he'd played it in the van while the others had been carrying tents and stuff up this hill. All he'd learnt from it was that Charlie talked to himself a lot, also to the woman called Anne, the absent wife; but there'd been no dangerous calls or conversations.

Conceivably, old Charlie could have known there was a bug in position, could have done his talking elsewhere. Not likely, but – yes, conceivable . . .

Leo envied him his ability to just flop down and switch off like that. Particularly as they'd be turning out at 0600 to start a cross-country run at 0615. But his own brain was active, muscles still tense, thoughts crowding through his mind while his pulses drummed and wouldn't slow despite his deliberately taking long, slow breaths, taking the beat from Charlie's soft, continuous snoring.

Why should General Gudyenko have told him about the leak that was being set up?

It wasn't necessary for him to know, didn't help either him or the operation's chances of success. It was fascinating – brilliant, actually – but in boasting of it the general had broken that most basic rule, the principle of 'need to know' on which he himself had invariably insisted. Out of pride in his own brain-child – if it *had* been his? If that was it, then the old man was past it, turning senile. This wasn't borne out by any other aspect of his performance, though. As Leo had told the GRU Resident on Monday evening, Gudyenko's brain was as sharp and all-encompassing as it had ever been.

It was tempting to see it as a compliment. If Gudyenko of all people wanted Leo Serebryakov's approval of his stratagem – and he *must* have wanted that, surely, even if only subconsciously, to have let such a special cat out of his bag . . . In the process, Leo recognised, the old guy had displayed a higher degree of trust in him than *he'd* have placed in any living human being.

Even – the thought amused him – in General Gudyenko.

Maybe the general did think of him as his personal protégé. At their final meeting, after all the detailed briefings at more junior levels and just before Leo had left for the airport and the return to London via Cairo, he'd said something to the effect that the successful completion of this task might well provide his – Leo's – 'pathway to the stars'. Extravagant phraseology – out of character for the man, unless he'd really meant it and had been seeking to let him know that he had great hopes for him?

Towards the end of the *first* briefing in Moscow, Leo had asked him, 'Swale will be put on trial, you said, by the Syrians?' Gudyenko, sipping water again, had left it to Vetrov to supply an answer: lamplight gleaming on Vetrov's pale hair and pink-skinned face – 'face like a baby's bottom' a junior staff officer had described it to Leo once – as he glanced up, clearing his throat . . . 'Yes. For complicity in the crimes to which he'll have testified. It will be a – a formality. No Western lawyers or diplomats will be allowed access to him, and at the trial's conclusion he'll be sentenced to death and executed immediately. No appeals or second thoughts or pseudo-legal ploys. Most essentially, no second thoughts from *him* on any of his own evidence.'

'What about the mercenaries?'

The general cut in again. 'Syrian troops will arrive too late to prevent the massacre, but in time to intercept the killers as they withdraw. Swale will have no doubt that you, Captain Knox, were killed with your two Marines. Yes, they'll be among the other corpses. You'll have disappeared – you could be in the litter too, for all he'll know, he may have been unconscious and he'll certainly be wounded, losing blood and so forth. In fact a priority at that stage must be to ensure he's kept alive . . . Your job will have been done, Leonid Ivan'ich, you'll be on your way home to us from Damascus.' The general broke off to nudge Vetrov: 'Better make this point to our friends – that the Syrians who intervene must have a doctor with them, maybe an ambulance, blood plasma or whatever the medics consider necessary. They'll move him out by helicopter, I imagine.'

Vetrov nodded, making a note. The general turned back to Leo.

'One last item I'll explain. So you'll understand the scope of it. It's a small touch which I hope you'll agree has some – merit . . . The matter I touched on before – leaking to British intelligence a report that the kidnappers of Stillgoe have transferred him into Syrian custody? Well, that's the sum total of the information they'll be force-fed with, but it'll be received as red-hot intelligence in their Foreign Office, who'll naturally pass it at once to SIS – am I right? Yes . . . And – here's the bottom line – friends of friends in London have a mole – isn't "mole" what they call an employee who breaks his trust?'

Leo nodded.

'It's being arranged that this person will be on hand to leak the fact that the British government did receive this report, did have the information in their possession. The revelation will be splashed on the front page of a Sunday newspaper when the political storm is at its height, the world recoiling from the evidence of the atrocity. Imagine – parliament recalled, Whitehall in a state of siege, government ministers protesting ignorance and innocence: then the headlines – *Foreign Office and Intelligence services were tipped off three days before the SBS team must have been flown out . . .* '

It was the icing on the cake, Leo thought.

But there was a bit of a worry now, too: the question of when it would happen. He *hoped* they'd be triggering it quite soon. Two factors governed the timing. Well, three: the third being unclear, only something Colonel Vetrov had muttered about having to plant the disinformation before Nezar Hindawi's trial ended in London. He hadn't explained why. Maybe, Leo guessed, they wanted the SBS action in world headlines and denunciations before that trial was concluded, maybe Damascus would then break off diplomatic relations and eclipse whatever the Brits tried to make of the trial's outcome. But in any case the trial was expected to run for another ten or fourteen days yet, so the point wasn't all that cogent; the considerations that did count were one, that the intelligence had to reach London a few days before the imaginary, non-existent SBS team would later appear to have been despatched to the killing ground — so the report would have to be allowed to drip through some time before this weekend, surely — and two, President Assad had to be out of his own country, isolated and insulated in Moscow. If for any reason his trip was delayed, the operation would also be set back, and from this there'd be certain inconveniences, worst of all the danger that Charlie Swale, this newly sober Swale, might have time to get his thinking straight and come up with questions, doubts, suspicions. There'd been no date given yet — nothing in this morning's *Daily Telegraph* for instance — for the Syrian head of state's forthcoming Moscow visit.

4

Thursday was hell, and not only because it rained hard all day. On Friday Tait worked them even harder, but Charlie found he'd broken through some kind of endurance barrier, begun to realise the worst was over and that he had plenty in reserve. On Friday evening at supper round the fire – a night cross-country yomp was to follow – Smiley Tait broke his customary silence to observe, 'We're twice the men we were when we got here, eh?'

The question seemed to have been aimed at Charlie. He agreed: 'You've done a great job.'

'There.' Bob Knox jerked a thumb towards him. 'Praise from a Pongo. What about *that*, Smiley?'

'Although – ' Charlie admitted – 'there've been moments when I haven't felt exactly brimming with affection for you.'

'Thursday,' Pete Denham said with his mouth full of pilchards in tomato sauce, 'Thursday was your bad day, weren't it.'

'Was it?' He scratched his head. 'Maybe you're right. If that was the day we circled Wales three times and still found time for forty thousand press-ups, then chased our tails round the fucking woods all night – '

'Fed you well though, right?'

'Oh, *cordon bleu*, Pete, absolutely.' Denham had done most

of the cooking. Charlie asked Bob Knox, 'What sort of rations are we taking to the Med with us?'

'None. Supplies'll be there for us to pick up.'

'You mean like manna?'

Knox stared at him, seemingly without comprehension. Tait murmured, 'Locusts and wild honey, withall.'

Charlie said, 'That was John the Baptist's field rations, Smiley.'

'Yeah. Right.'

Tait still wasn't exactly loquacious. But prolonged exposure at close range to that wooden stare of his had taught Charlie that it was not, generally speaking, an indication of scorn or dislike. It was simply that the muscles in his face rarely moved; and one could often read expression – amusement, annoyance, interest or lack of it – in his eyes. It was the other way about with Bob, whose eyes showed nothing at all while his facial expressions varied like anyone else's. At Charlie's mention of John the Baptist, for instance, there'd been an immediate reflex, visible in the fire's glow even in this fading light, as if he'd only that second caught on, that the earlier reference to manna must also have come from a biblical context.

Maybe he'd missed out on religious education, Charlie guessed. He'd never said anything about his schooling, but that offbeat childhood, his Anglo-Egyptian parentage, might account for it.

Charlie asked him, 'So it may not be the usual ratpacks?'

'Your guess is as good as mine, Charlie.'

'How about weapons?'

Pete had asked this. Bob said, 'Same applies. Laid on out there, waiting for us.'

'Would it be giving away State secrets to tell us what kind of weapons we'll be getting?'

Bob looked thoughtfully at Charlie. 'If you'll agree to make this the *last* question.' Charlie nodded. Bob told him, 'Uzis.'

'There you are.' Tait turned his poker-face towards Denham. 'So we'll look like we're Israelis.'

'Not necessarily at all.'

He'd said that rather too quickly and sharply, Charlie thought. The inference being that Smiley's simple assumption might have been on target. He thought yet again, *Syria* –

surely . . . Then, diffidently: 'Bob, apologies, but as it happens I do have one other question. Affecting me personally, no one else.' He fingered his moustache: it was almost luxuriant . . . 'Thing is, you blokes are underwater experts, and of course I'm not. So the aquatics side of it – I mean, you won't be expecting me to climb in and out of submerged submarines, I hope?'

Denham laughed, and began, 'Oh, Jesus—'

'No, Charlie.' Bob's loud answer cut across Pete's interruption, silencing him. 'Nothing like that, don't worry, we aren't planning on drowning you.' He looked up at the darkening sky. 'Smiley, let's get moving.'

Thanking his stars that he'd been fast on that ball. A few more words, and Denham could have blown it. Supposed SBS Marine expressing horror at the thought of being required to make a submarine exit and/or re-entry. In literally a couple of seconds that idiot could have destroyed all the careful planning, the whole damn thing. He could feel it still in his gut – that near-miss and the continuing danger. And Tait had caught on, he thought: he'd been gazing at him – Leo – and now he was watching his pal Denham, shaking his head very, very slightly in sad reproof.

On the Saturday morning they turned out at 0500 instead of 0600 and went for a marathon cross-country run before breakfast. This was the finale. Pete then fried up all the eggs and bacon that were left, and fried slices of bread to go with it; it was a celebration breakfast, he announced. Charlie was on the point of asking facetiously where was the champagne, then thought better of it. The subject of alcohol had been taboo, he'd suspected, with the aim of keeping his mind off it.

Actually they needn't have bothered. But he foresaw that there might be problems this evening, when he'd be alone in his flat with a cupboard full of Scotch and damn-all else to do.

Ring Paula, maybe. But he was supposed to be in Germany. There were others he could call: but it was a weekend now, and short notice. Also, he remembered, Knox had asked if he might come back up to London and doss down in the flat, after he'd returned all the camping gear to wherever it had come from.

Bob stopped the VW at the farmhouse and went in to pay the few pounds they owed. Then they were on the way and it was still only just after 0800.

The ultimate destination, Charlie thought, sitting back with his eyes shut while Bob piloted the van carefully through winding, narrow lanes, would be Syria, almost for sure. Because surely it had to be either that or Libya, and for some reason he believed in Bob's denial – in the flat on Monday evening – that Libya was to be the target. But also, Libya was so much in the news, and there'd been nothing about any Brit having been locked up there recently. OK, not in Syria either – which would in fact have been a lot more unusual – but Syria bordered the Lebanon, and the Palestine refugee camps were surrounded by Muslim extremists of various kinds. In the copy of the *Daily Telegraph* which Bob had bought on the way down here there'd been an article in which it was stated that terrorists of the numerous factions – Islamic Jihad, the Ayatollah Khomeini's followers, had been mentioned amongst others – were currently believed to be holding three Americans and three Frenchman, but there were also two Brits, one Irishman, one Italian and a South Korean missing, presumed kidnapped.

Maybe an intrusion via Syria, back-door entrance to the Lebanon behind the backs of that assortment of crazies, snatch some poor bastard and bring him out?

Emerging from his thoughts, he heard Denham and Tait discussing cricket, the British team's recent deplorable performances and their prospects in Australia. Denham talking volubly, Tait mostly in grunts.

They took a long time getting to the motorway, and then stopped for an early lunch when the VW needed petrol anyway. It was about 3 p.m. when Charlie climbed out of the van outside his flat and Tait slung his gear down to him.

'Thanks. And thanks for the torture, Smiley.'

'Any time.'

Bob Knox called down, 'What'll you do with yourself between now and midnight, Charlie?'

'I'm glad you asked.' He'd been thinking about it. 'When

I've washed the mud off and done a bit of essential shopping I'm going to jog round to the Lansdowne and swim up and down that pool until my arms drop off.'

'I'd stop just short of that point, if I were you. Otherwise – great.'

Tait looked pleased too. As if Charlie was a pupil of whose progress he was proud. Charlie raised a hand to him and Denham: 'See you boys at the check-in desk, then.' He watched the van pull away. Wondering *which* check-in desk: and deciding that after the swim he'd do a few circuits of Green Park. Jogging and sprinting – weekend crowds permitting. After all that rain this was a fine, if somewhat muggy afternoon, warm and windless; Londoners and the tourists who were still around would be out in swarms. But – it occurred to him as he ran up the stairs to his flat – it would be a damn sight hotter in Syria.

In Damascus, it was stifling; *too* hot, for October.

Hafiz murmured, mopping himself with the sheet, 'I hate to say this, but I have to leave soon. I have to force my body off this bed, out of this nice apartment and into my car which will be so hot you could roast a lamb in it.' His dark head turned on the pillow as he thrust the sheet away. 'You know, I don't *want* to leave this bed.'

'Then don't. *I* don't want you to.'

Saturday afternoon, in this Syrian capital which Hafiz called *Dimashq* and where the time was two hours ahead of London's. Liz was conscious of the time difference because London had so often to be in her thoughts and calculations; she was Information Officer at the embassy. And the man beside her on the bed, Hafiz Al-Jubran, was special personal assistant to the Minister of the Interior, Muhammad Gharbrash.

Labels – for two bodies on a bed in a half-dark, comparatively cool room, this cool because of shade trees close to the house's white stucco front and the depth of the iron-railed balcony with its overhanging, shading eave. In contrast, the temperature in the streets was well into the eighties. A glass door was open to the balcony, tall shutters semi-closed outside

59

it; an overhead fan circled, stirring a flimsy curtain whose primary function was to restrict the ingress of flies.

Hafiz kicked the sheet off. Sweat glistened on his dark, angular body. On her own too, Liz realised, feeling the fan's draught.

'Why and where d'you have to go?'

'To meet with some people. Government business, something I *have* to do, unfortunately, even though this is Saturday.' His hand moved, a forefinger tracing her jawline and, continuing past her ear, pushing back her streaky, medium-blonde hair. He professed to find her beautiful: which she didn't mind — even quite enjoyed — although she knew for sure it wasn't true. Not true that she was beautiful, or even pretty. Quite possibly true that from some peculiar viewpoint of his own he *thought* she was. It was also possible that he'd cease to think so quite suddenly, when the excitement of the affair wore off for him or when she decided she might be getting in too deep.

Like any threat of marriage. From which anyway she'd run a mile. She'd done it before and she knew she would again, but in any case marriage to a Muslim would be unthinkable, for entirely practical reasons.

Hafiz *was* beautiful. Fine bone-structure, large sensitive eyes: a mystic's eyes, their whites gleaming in the half-light and his dark face, and fixed on her now — each of them studying the other as if each might be wondering who — or what — the other *was*.

Which either of them might quite reasonably wonder, she supposed . . . She asked him, 'Why didn't you say before that you were going off somewhere?'

'I didn't want to think about it. Or have *you* thinking about it.'

'When will I see you again?'

'I can't be sure. As soon as I get back I'll telephone you — naturally. Or maybe before, before I start back, to let you know I'm on the way . . . It'll be several days, however, maybe a week.'

'You're going *now* — and for a week?'

'Not *necessarily* so long.'

'Where, Hafiz?'

He kissed the tip of her nose. 'You're so inquisitive.'

'Don't I have some right to be?'

'Oh, I suppose – since curiosity is a known female character-istic.'

'If I told you *I* was about to vanish for a bloody week – '

'Surely there's a difference.'

'Oh, is there?'

'This is my country, I have duties which can take me anywhere. You on the other hand are a foreigner, your workplace is here in the capital and you would have no reason – except to go sightseeing, or – '

'In practical terms you have a point. But not in principle.'

'OK.' He kissed her, properly, this time. Then: 'OK. For the sake of your *principle*, I tell you. My journey now is to the town of Homs. You know where that is, of course.' She nodded. 'You see – no secrets. And no lady friends there either, I swear it.' He kissed her again, then pulled away. 'It's on my mind now, you see why I didn't speak of it before. I have to go now, Liz.'

There was a back way out which he always used – hurrying, head down, a surreptitious exit to a car that would, as he'd said, be broiling hot although if he'd parked it in front, under the trees, he'd have spared himself most of that discomfort. She'd have preferred it if he'd been less secretive, less seemingly ashamed. Although she realised that for him there *would* be shame, if his affair with her became public knowledge; and from that point of view, she supposed, even his scuttling to and fro with his head down and those quick eyes darting from side to side might be thought an act of courage.

It didn't look like it. It seemed to Liz to be drastically out of character. One of the attractive things about him was his arrogance, a kind of haughtiness which appealed enormously to her. There could hardly have been a sharper contrast to this than the scurrying exit that wasn't far off an impersonation of Groucho Marx.

Not that she would have welcomed publicity, exactly. But discretion didn't have to appear quite so ignominious.

She wondered about his motivation, why he'd have wanted the affair with her in the first place and why he was continuing it now when his involvement with her did so obviously scare him. It wasn't a new line of thought: she'd have needed to be stupid or ludicrously vain not to have looked for some ulterior motive. Knowing herself to be quite ordinary, no *femme fatale* by any means and also damn near thirty, whereas he was twenty-four and really about the most attractive man she'd ever known, let alone been to bed with. Anywhere in the world, Hafiz could have taken his pick.

There'd been a hint or two recently, in the embassy; one in particular, an embassy wife, quite senior, who'd obviously been put up to it, a woman whom Liz liked and who liked her, speaking in an entirely friendly and private way but plainly not by chance or quite off her own bat, asking her whether she thought she was being entirely wise . . . 'In all the prevailing circumstances?'

'Circumstances?'

'Well, the Hindawi case, Liz, the trial at the Old Bailey?'

'I really don't see how my personal friendship with Hafiz could be affected by anything of that kind.'

'But all our positions here might well end up being affected by it. That's the general feeling. And if you're involved – *really* involved – '

She hadn't felt inclined to answer with the truth – that she was intrigued, flattered, maybe infatuated even, but not in any deep sense 'involved', that it wasn't anything she couldn't walk away from when or if she wanted to. Because this sounded cheap: casual, meaningless . . .

So what if the relationship *didn't* mean so damn much?

In the shower – cold – she told herself for the hundredth time that he couldn't have any political or intelligence motive. She had no information to which he wouldn't be entirely welcome, professionally he operated at a much higher level than hers, and he also happened to belong to an influential and well-connected family. One way and another Hafiz needed her, in terms of his career, reputation and future prospects, like a kick in the balls.

Maybe he just went for blondes. That, or one had to subdue one's natural modesty and admit to the possibility that one's personal charm, sex-appeal and intellect had deprived the young Syrian of his senses. She was smiling as she padded damp-footed into the bedroom, eased one shutter back by a few inches to let in some daylight. The swathe of brilliance stabbed through semi-darkness, spotlighting the armchair on which Hafiz habitually flung his clothes.

Something under it, on the floor. Greyish, crouching.

Rat!

She looked round quickly for some weapon. Nothing . . . Then as the blinding effect wore off and she focussed properly, she saw it wasn't a rat at all, but Hafiz's wallet.

And he was on his way to Homs. About two hundred kilometres up the motorway which British residents here referred to as the M5. She wondered as she stooped and groped under the chair how the hell she'd get it to him: or whether he'd realise he'd lost it and come back. Or maybe he wouldn't worry, maybe he could get by without it.

It was stuffed with Syrian pounds. And his driving licence . . . A cheque card – Commercial Bank of Syria. An ID card with his photograph on it, heavily overstamped, an official government pass. He'd be needing this lot, all right.

He might have stopped at his own house before leaving town, she thought, for a change of clothes or to pick up a suitcase – unless he'd had it with him in the car. Worth trying, anyway . . . She sat on the bed, picked up the receiver and dialled.

No answer. She visualised him at the wheel of his Citroën speeding north. She was about to hang up when a female voice asked in Arabic, 'Yes?'

Liz used French. Her Arabic was practically non-existent but educated Syrians like Hafiz's family spoke French, in which language she was quite at home. 'May I speak to Hafiz Al-Jubran, please?'

'He's not here. This is his sister. Who's that, please?'

'It's Liz Thornton, Hoda. I'm at the British Embassy and I met you once with your brother, if you remember?'

'Yes, I remember.'

Without much pleasure – judging by the sulky tone. And on the occasion of their meeting she hadn't been exactly effusive. Liz said, 'The reason I'm calling is that your brother was at the embassy earlier on, and apparently he dropped his – oh, what's the word – his *sac* . . . '

'Dropped what?'

'*Portefeuille?*'

'Oh – '

'Anyway, I have it, it's full of money and some other things, I think he might be stuck without it. Would you tell him, please?'

'My brother is out of town, Miss Thornton. But if you could get it to me, I could arrange for it to be taken to him. He's on a visit to Homs, but – '

'I suppose I could bring it round.'

'Would you be coming soon? Otherwise – you see, I know of another person who will be travelling in that direction, but – '

'Yes. All right.' She groaned inwardly: *Out into that Turkish bath again* . . . Resignedly: 'In about half an hour, Hoda.'

She put on a cotton frock with a hemline a bit lower than she'd have worn in England, and sandals, slipped the wallet into her bag and went down into the street. Her Mini had been parked in the shade but it was still greenhouse-warm inside. She got it moving quickly, with all the windows open, to let some air through – warm, sticky air . . . Swinging presently into Al-Qouwatly Avenue, then right up to the big roundabout – completely circular but still known as Umawiyya *Square* – and off northeastward, over the Tora River and then left, to pass the British and Swiss embassies on Ru Muhammad Kurd Ali. Most of the world's diplomatic representatives had their missions within about a thousand yards of this point.

Thinking about Hoda, who was a grumpy, charmless little creature. The one time they'd met, Liz had been made acutely conscious of her disapproval – just for being with Hafiz, presumably, the two of them obviously enjoying each other's company. Liz had thought, *If only you knew just how much we enjoy it, you surly little cow* . . .

And maybe she *did* know, now.

There was one patch of shade outside the house. She backed the Mini into it and left the windows open. She was only going to be a minute, but that was all the time it took to become oven-hot.

Hoda answered the door herself. Little pointed face, shiny black hair pulled back tightly over very small ears. She was

64

wearing a *jellabah* – a long, wide-sleeved, richly-embroidered gown which Liz guessed she might well have put on for *her* benefit, changing out of Western dress as soon as she'd put the phone down.

She opened her bag, and handed her the wallet. 'I hope it won't have inconvenienced him too badly.'

'You were kind to bring it . . . Will you – come in?'

She'd smiled, but it hadn't reached her eyes, or lasted more than a second. Liz said, 'It would be nice, Hoda, thank you, but unfortunately – '

'I should like it very much if you would. For just a few minutes, even?'

'Well.' Checking the time, and glancing back to the car . . . A cosy chat with Hafiz's kid sister was about the last thing she wanted, in the circumstances. 'The problem's one of time, I'm afraid. I came out of my way, rather, and – '

'Just for a moment? *Please?*'

'Well – literally five minutes, then.'

It wouldn't have helped matters to have refused, she thought. Following the squat figure – so totally unlike Hafiz's – through a courtyard and then from a tiled hallway into a wide, cool room furnished mostly with cane furniture, bright cushions on it, expensive-looking rugs on the polished boards: on the way through Hoda had offered her coffee, then tea, and she'd declined both: now the girl had turned to face her: 'Please take a seat. I want to speak with you about my brother.'

Liz wished to God she hadn't decided to be polite, or diplomatic, whatever, that she'd had the sense to say 'Sorry, can't stop' – and let her make the most of it. Too late now. She was sitting, Hoda also seated and facing her across the room, small brown eyes fixed on her intently . . . 'What do you want with my brother?'

'Want?' Liz smiled. 'Nothing at all. I came to return his wallet.'

'But he didn't leave it at your embassy, did he?'

'Didn't he?'

'You know he didn't. You should also know that your association with him could very easily become a disaster for him, Miss Thornton.'

She sighed. 'Hafiz is a grown man, Hoda, you're a young girl, and while I have no wish to quarrel with you I may as well tell you right away that I don't intend to be lectured by you. In fact I should be on my way, so — '

'You haven't realised that fundamentally he's *against* you?'

'Is he?' She smiled faintly. 'I'll tell you, Hoda, if that's true he hides it pretty well.'

'He is against you and the Americans, against *all* colonialist — '

'Heavens, we're into politics now?'

'I'm telling you the truth, Miss Thornton!'

'Well, I'd say the only surviving colonialists now are based in Moscow. But if that was what you were so anxious to tell me, OK, I've heard it. I'm an Information Officer, a PR girl if you like, I'm not a diplomat; so if you want to talk politics — which incidentally Hafiz and I do *not* discuss — '

'No, of course he wouldn't. But — ' Hoda leant forward — 'look, Miss Thornton, I don't want to be your enemy, and you're right, politics are not your business or mine. My concern is for Hafiz and his future — which is also the future of my family. We are not *new* people here, you know, in fact if you mentioned the name Al-Jubran in the north — for instance in Halab — '

'I don't doubt it, Hoda, but it's hardly a concern of mine, you know.' She felt she was humouring a halfwit now. 'Very nice for you and for Hafiz, no doubt — '

'I thought that if you were genuinely fond of my brother you might have shared some concern for his future. Which in some ways is bound up in the background of his family. In fact, the present situation might well affect *your* future too — adversely, I may say . . . ' She shook her head. 'Hafiz, my brother, has an important part to play in the future of this country. We have some problems, and he is the man who will solve them: in time, when it is all in his hands alone, he will create peace, unity and progress. By that time you will not be here: but you will hear his name, you will remember what I am now saying to you . . . But — Miss Thornton — as far as his — his friendship with you is concerned, this present situation could destroy such hopes, *ruin* him!'

'Wouldn't it be Hafiz who'd have ruined himself?'

'But *you* could stop this happening! You, alone, if you had his true interests at heart — '

'I'm not so sure that he'd go along with any such plan, Hoda.'

'You say this.' Hoda was leaning forward and getting shrill again. Liz had only made that last remark to needle her, and she'd succeeded. Hoda spat out: 'You don't matter to him *at all*!'

'Well.' She smiled. 'If you say not.'

'My brother is an Arab, he fights for the Arab cause. This is his life, it will be *all* his life, he knows this and knows that nothing else — including *you* — is anything but trivial, a pastime . . . Do you think he admires the English? I tell you, I could *prove* to you that — '

'Hoda — really — I've had enough of this.' The child was raving: crazed with jealousy, Liz guessed, using the political stuff as a smokescreen. *She*, maybe, at this moment hated the English — for her own personal reasons . . . Liz picked up her bag, in preparation for departure. 'I really *don't* want to seem rude, Hoda, but also I really *do* have to leave now. I did tell you I don't have any time to waste this afternoon. And I've got the message — you dislike me and your brother being as close as we are. I'll bear it in mind — '

'It could become a very great embarrassment for you, Miss Thornton. For you as an official at the British Embassy: you have no idea how very, *very* serious it could become!'

Liz was on her feet. 'We're in 1987, Hoda. It's not Queen Victoria on the throne now, you know.'

There was actually some slight element of truth in what she'd said, for all that. Liz had been well aware, right from the start of her affair with Hafiz, that she'd have to be discreet about it. So she'd been careful not to flaunt her relationship with the beautiful young Syrian, she'd made it easy for her superiors to look the other way . . . Hoda's voice broke through again: 'It's possible you misunderstand me. I wasn't speaking of the obvious embarrassments — scandal, the gossip and so forth. I was speaking of something entirely practical and — well, *immediate* . . . This is why I have forced myself to speak to you now, Miss Thornton. Otherwise I would not, *could* not.' Shaking her shiny head . . . 'It's not a *small* thing, you see, it's a matter – political, very sensitively political, in which my brother is closely involved. *Prominently* involved. And if it were to emerge suddenly – I mean this situation, the political issue, and also the fact that you are closely associated with him – you, an Englishwoman and embassy official – '

'Hoda – please, calm down, just tell me what – '

'I should *not* be telling you, but – '

'Telling me *what*, for God's sake?'

Then she saw it: thinking – wrongly – *We're into that bloody Old Bailey trial again* . . . Hoda blurted, 'Have you heard of an Englishman, his name is Stillgoe, captured in Beirut by the Hezbollah?'

Liz nodded. Failing to see what this could possibly have to do with her. Anyone who read newspapers would have read of Vernon Stillgoe who'd been kidnapped, snatched from a car on the airport road when he'd been on his way home from Beirut, heading back to London. She heard Hoda say, 'He is not in Lebanon now, he is in Syria. Can you guess who has authority over those who are holding him?'

She felt she might be dreaming this. It was how dreams sometimes went, switching from one form of nonsense to another. Hoda said – predictably, when one recognised the line of confusion – 'My brother, Hafiz, controls this person's custody, also his – ' her eyes flickered – 'his interrogation . . . Hafiz told me that in Beirut he was a British spy – did you know this, too?'

'No.' Liz turned away. 'But if you like I'll take your word for it. And I really do have to go now.'

'I think you don't *want* to understand! But I am breaking a confidence, to tell you these things! Because it is necessary you should hear, that there are such matters in which my brother is concerned – in comparison with which you are as *nothing* – which maybe is why he thinks it's of no importance that he fornicates with you!'

'Well, I'll see myself out – '

'What d'you think he's doing now in Homs?'

'Fornicating with someone else?'

Hoda had rushed past her. She was leaning against the door, barring the way with her short, squat body in its brightly-coloured gown, the intricate embroidery. She was loud again, insistent . . . 'Stillgoe might have been released, if he had been left in Beirut or anywhere in Lebanon. That's why we have him now. Not in Homs, but – in that district. This is why my brother – '

'Why he's shot off there. OK, I'll believe you. But it's no concern of mine, you see.' Liz told her again, 'Hoda, I want to go, please, d'you mind?'

'Do you think this would be nice for you, in the English newspapers? When these facts become known? That Hafiz Al-Jubran is the lover of a woman who works in the British Embassy?'

'I told you – it's not my business, nothing to *do* with me . . . But you know – what you just told me, you have to be crazy, really. I mean, your President has been working for the *release* of the people who've been kidnapped in Beirut!'

'It has nothing to do with President Al-Assad. And true – nothing to do with *you*. I have only been telling you so as to *prove* to you – '

'All you've proved is what I knew already – that you don't like my relationship with your brother. OK, message received, *out* . . . I mean *me* out, *now* – '

'If I *show* you proof – then will you believe me?'

Liz stared at her. Feeling slightly dizzy, and thinking *I'm Alice in crazyland, I'm on a trip* . . . She said with a pretence of patience, calm, 'You're asking me to believe that Hafiz is mixed up in some conspiracy against the President?'

'No, I said nothing of this kind!'

'Well, what exactly – '

'Hafiz knows many people, all the leaders. My family have very wide connections. We are not – not *new* people, like certain – '

'Yes, I know, you told me.' She gestured, towards the courtyard and the street. 'And really I do think I'd better leave, before you tell me anything else that you might afterwards wish you hadn't . . . Leave it to Hafiz to sort this out when he gets back, OK?'

Hoda had her back against the door. Biting her lips, staring at Liz: as if she was trying to make up her mind about something, finding it difficult. Whether or not to stand aside, maybe . . . And maybe she really *was* crazy . . . Liz forced a smile: 'Let's leave it now, think it over? I promise you this — if Hafiz agrees with you that it'd be better we stopped seeing each other — OK, no problem . . . '

And no move. She might not have heard. Liz kept the smile on. 'Hoda?'

Hoda let out a breath so suddenly that she might have been holding it for minutes. She said, 'Would you please wait — two minutes, please? So I can bring something from my brother's desk to show you?'

Liz told Tom Elwell, an hour later in his flat which was only a stone's throw from the embassy, 'When I heard her coming back I suddenly thought God, she's been to fetch a pistol, she's going to shoot me . . . ' She spread her hands: 'But wow, *relief*, it was a map, a large-scale military map, all grids and stuff. The bit that was supposed to impress me was a ring he'd drawn in what looked like red felt-pen around an area that has its centre in mountains twenty miles northwest of the town of Homs. The ring's diameter roughly *ten* miles.'

Elwell was Head of Chancery. Forty-three, and overweight. Hilary Elwell, who was as skinny as her husband was fat, had brought them a tray of tea and biscuits a few minutes ago, then made herself scarce. Elwell asked Liz — nibbling a biscuit, and with a clipboard in front of him on which he was making neatly tabulated notes — 'Are you sure of those figures, distances, as — what, approximations?'

She nodded. 'That kind of map has latitude and longitude scales marked not just at the sides like charts have, but more or less all over. As well as the grid, which I'm sorry to say doesn't mean a lot to me.'

'You could estimate distances from those scales, though?'

'From the latitude scale. It was shown on longitude 35 east, which is roughly fifty miles off the coast.'

'You sound like a navigator.'

'I've sailed quite a bit, I'm used to charts.'

'I see . . . Anything else to say about this map?'

'Yes. I could sketch it for you.' She concentrated, *seeing* it . . . 'Just inside the red perimeter there's a village, Ayn Al-Dariqhah. A road runs through it from the south and carries on up to Masyaf and beyond. East of the road's a valley, more or less north–south lying, with another mountain spur on its other side. Near the end of that spur there's a dot and the word *Qal'at* – "castle" – ruin, I suppose.' She added, 'No doubt a Crusader castle.'

'More likely Assassin, in that particular area, Liz.'

'Assassin?'

'Ismaili sect. They cooperated with the Crusaders, oddly enough. "Assassin" is a name derived from their drug-taking habit – *hashish*, alias *marijuana*.'

She smiled. 'We live and learn.'

'Go on, Liz.'

'Well, on the eastern ridge a road crosses where it's lower, in a sort of saddle, then slants across the valley to join the other one *en route* to Masyaf, and just where it passes over is where Hafiz had put a cross, and Hoda said that's where they've got Stillgoe.'

The ballpoint was scribbling fast. 'You believed her?'

'Yes. To start with, as I said, she was a bit hysterical, rattling on as if she'd had it ready like a script, with *leave my brother alone* as the crux of it. Then when I wasn't impressed she came out with the Vernon Stillgoe story, and when she saw I was thinking she might be making it all up she made the really hard decision – to show me this map. It really scared her, doing it, and she wasn't acting. Not *then*, although she might well have been earlier on. When she brought the map her hands were shaking so badly I actually held them for a while, to steady her, for Pete's sake . . . And once she nearly jumped right out of her skin, looking round at the door like a little frightened weasel, as if she thought she'd heard Hafiz or someone coming.' Liz nodded again, emphatically. 'I'm *certain* what she was telling me was the truth.'

'And why – I want to be sure I have it right, just as you saw it – *why* do you think she'd have been so eager to impart this secret?'

She frowned, concentrating again. Like sorting through a jumble of bits and pieces . . . 'I don't say she was *eager*. More that – well, her first blather didn't work – her family's importance and so forth didn't throw me – so then out came this stuff about Stillgoe – even a reference to Hafiz being in charge of his "interrogation", the implication being torture

71

so I was supposed to think "How could I possibly associate with such a fiend!" — at least I *imagine* that was what — '

'I suppose — ' Elwell smiled — 'the language problem — '

'No, we were talking French, both quite at home in it.'

'Ah.'

'I suppose the answer is she told me about it because her opening ploy had failed and she had it up her sleeve as a really strong card that would put me off her brother. To some extent reasonably, maybe, the argument that if it became public knowledge, world news — this thing about Vernon Stillgoe — it could be highly embarrassing for me to have — that Hafiz should have been my lover.' She didn't look at Elwell. 'Headlines in the *News of the World*, and all that. Awkward for the embassy as well as for me, obviously.'

'Yes . . . ' Scribbling again . . . 'In effect, therefore, she tried to convince you and failed, then in absolute desperation fetched the map — very much as a last resort, and frightening to her to be doing so.'

'Yes. Absolutely.'

'She must be quite desperately anxious to protect her brother from you. Might she have had any reason to believe that you were contemplating a permanent relationship?'

'Most certainly not!'

He nodded. Underlining a note he'd made. Then glanced up: 'Did you tell her you believed her?'

Liz shook her head. 'Not in so many words.'

'What did you say, finally?'

'That I wanted to go away and think about it. I said I was sorry she was so upset, but I'd have to think, work it out for myself. Incidentally she'd rushed to put the map back in his desk even before I'd crossed the hall. I was feeling quite sorry for her by this time, she was *so* nervous. She muttered things like regretting we had to be on opposing sides, and I can still hear myself telling her, "But we're *not*, Hoda . . . " Ludicrous, really.'

Elwell put his ballpoint down on the clipboard, and sat back. Open-neck sports shirt clinging damply to his rounded shoulders. He said, 'You did the right thing, coming straight along with this. In all the circumstances I appreciate it might not have been the easiest of decisions. But let me add, if I may, that I feel sure nobody will concern themselves now with – well, with the personal side of it.' He was avoiding her eyes . . . 'I'm being clumsy, I'm afraid. Forgive me. But I'm *not* interfering, I only want to suggest that – that *if* you concluded that in the aftermath of this imbroglio the complications might be – oh, uncomfortable for you, I'm sure you could assume that if you decided to apply for a transfer, the ambassador – '

'Yes. Thank you. I'll have to think about it, obviously.'

'And now – ' he tapped his notes – 'I'll work the gist of this into a telegram which I think should go to the Office right away.' (By 'the Office' Liz knew he meant the Foreign Office in London.) 'I'll have a word with the ambassador first, actually. And that won't be possible until later on this evening. But if we're to take this seriously – as we *must* – I suppose it should be transmitted as a DEDIP signal.' He frowned, moved his teacup back from the table's edge; she heard him murmur, 'If Stillgoe *is* in Syria, it could make for a most *awkward* situation . . .' Liz thinking *DEDIP, for God's sake: and I set this ball rolling!* That prefix on a signal meant that it was to be decoded only by a diplomat, not by cypher staff. It lifted the communication out of routine, made it potentially a crisis call . . . Elwell had stopped muttering to himself; struggling up out of his chair, he told her, 'It'll go out tonight, anyway. If I can't get to the ambassador I'll go ahead and bung it out myself . . . Liz, thank you very much.' He raised his voice: 'Hilary, are you there? Miss Thornton's on her way . . . '

Charlie had tried to jog and swim himself to a standstill, and hadn't managed it. He felt as if he could have gone on for hours. Which was the right way to be, he thought with a touch of smugness, when he got back to his flat at about six thirty. The pubs had been open for half an hour and on the way back he'd passed several, jogging on past their open doors and shutting his mind to thoughts of cooling pints of bitter. In the flat, he drank about a pint of cold water instead, then put the kettle on to make tea. Thinking, *If they could see me now . . .*

And as a reward for long abstinence, he reckoned he might

73

allow himself a tot of the Black Label before supper. Maybe. If by that time he felt any real need of it. In the back of his mind he was aware that he'd just made himself a promise, the 'maybe' wasn't effective camouflage.

Bath. Then sort out some gear for Syria. If it *was* Syria.

Crazy, to be virtually leaving, and still not know the destination. And to be travelling on a regular, civilian flight, for God's sake!

Might ring Harry, he thought, while he was waiting for the kettle to boil and the tub to fill. Harry was his older brother, a solicitor with a practice in Suffolk and a wife who strongly disapproved of Charlie. Charlie had described her and some of her ways of indicating this disapproval, one evening in camp, and his impersonation of her had made Smiley and Pete laugh. Those two had accepted him now, he thought; he found them easier to get along with than he found Bob Knox, for some reason.

Odd sort of guy, old Bob. Although it wasn't easy to put a finger on exactly *what* was odd about him. And since one was going to have to share the trials and tribulations of this trip with him it might be better not to look too hard for oddities. He'd probably be first class once they were on the job. SBS were, after all, *crème de la crème*, and they'd put this guy in as team leader, for God's sake. His action performance would surely be dazzling.

That conversation with the lads about Harry's pain-in-the-arse wife had been an offshoot of talk about SBS specialist skills – canoeing, underwater swimming, etc. Pete had asked him whether he'd done any boardsailing – which he had, mainly on that East Anglian coast during weekends spent with Harry and the dreaded Patricia . . . He *would* call the old sod, he decided – if only to annoy her. But also to impart the news of this business trip to Germany, so Harry would know he wasn't going to be around for a while.

Not that he came up often. Probably wasn't allowed to. But he always let Charlie know when he *was* in London.

'Charlie's not a *bad influence* on you, Harry, he's an absolute *disaster*!'

He'd heard this once, a penetrating hiss from his sister-in-law's kitchen. She'd meant that the two of them had been known to take a drink together, on occasion . . . Leaving his own kitchen, he murmured aloud, 'Silly bitch . . . ' He took his mug of tea and a handful of biscuits into the bathroom, lay in the steam sipping and munching, recalling that Anne had never liked that woman either.

Anne. Oh, Anne. Darling, incredibly lovely Anne, how the fuck could I have been such a total bloody disaster for *you*?

And for oneself, for that matter. But to have hurt Anne, of all people: and not just hurt – *savaged* . . .

And for what?

He'd got back to London a few days earlier than had been expected. He'd been out of the country, out of sight and under cover. Not Charlie Swale at all, not anyone, just a mud-stained, rain-soaked creature with no name, no face, no origins, no base other than holes in the ground which tended to fill up with water. Seven weeks away and out of contact, nearly three of them like this, isolated to such an extent it could have been more like three months than three weeks. What he'd done in that time he'd put out of his mind as soon as he'd been debriefed. You had to: certain things had never happened, there were places you'd never been to but still saw in dreams, faces you'd never studied even through high-powered binoculars. They'd pulled him out early because there'd been some disaster elsewhere that would have had repercussions so that if they hadn't extracted him immediately he'd have stayed there for keeps. This was explained to him after his extraction, and he'd thought cheerfully, *Anne wouldn't have liked that a bit* . . . They'd been married only a few months before he'd been sent on that assignment and she'd kept him company, a warmth in his heart, in the mud-holes.

So, in London several days early, he'd decided to surprise her. They had a cottage in the Welsh borders, but during his absence she'd sensibly lent it to some friends and gone to stay with her parents in Wiltshire. His plan was to turn up on the ancestral doorstep a couple of days earlier than she could have expected; he'd be clean-shaven, immaculate, with a very special present for her – a rope of pearls – in his pocket.

He booked himself in at the Special Forces Club, and called Trumpers for an appointment to get his hair cut in the morning. But before going shopping for pearls he needed to check with his bank, to find out how much he had on deposit, so as to know how high he could set his sights.

He was riffling through the phone book to 'Ll' for Lloyds, and getting near it when his eye was stopped by the name Liscomb. It was the married name of a girl who, until she'd tied herself up to an individual by name of Bill Liscomb, had been Sarah Dubisson. When she'd married this guy, who was in the City and a stuffed shirt but very well heeled, she'd told Charlie that her reason for doing so was that he – Charlie – had become engaged to Anne.

In fact they'd been engaged for about a year, while he'd been on his second tour in the Middle East; he'd been home for leave and they'd got engaged before he'd gone back. But before he'd met Anne, he and Sarah had been lovers for a long time, on and off. This was the crucial thing about Sarah – the fact that whenever he'd been off, someone else had been *on*. It was simply her way: she was very attractive, great fun to be with, and she had the morals of a stoat. If one wanted to enjoy her company one had to accept this as a fact of life – of *her* life; no one in his senses would have dreamt of buying into it. For Charlie, certainly, there'd never been any remote possibility of marriage to her, and from the time he'd met Anne he'd done no more than brush her cheek lightly with his lips. He'd done this much at her wedding to Bill Liscomb, whom he'd known slightly through Anne.

He was on top of the world that afternoon, with the prospect of reunion with Anne next day. He could see the delight in her eyes, feel her body against his, hear her whisper in her ear. None of which, in fact, he was ever to see, feel or hear again. He was intensely happy, excited, in tune with the whole universe and with most of its inhabitants. In fact he'd been under extreme pressure, entirely on his own, for a considerable period of time, and the sudden release of that pressure, sudden return to the luxuries of civilisation, would obviously have contributed to his state of mind and subsequent actions or reactions: such as seeing that name Liscomb now, realising it was a long time since he'd given a passing thought to the former Miss Dubisson, chuckling as he ran his finger down the column – and the next – looking for Liscomb,

William, knowing there was a third initial too which he'd recognise when he saw it.

Why not, for old times' sake?

It occurred to him that having been married to that pompous twit for a stretch of quite a few months now, and since Bill would surely be at his City desk at this time of day, a telephone call might well interrupt something. Knowing Sarah Dubisson, and that leopards don't change their spots . . .

She'd answered on the second ring. 'Yes?'

'Guess who, you gorgeous creature?'

'*Charlie Swale!*'

He put the empty mug on the side of the bath. Recalling that scream of joy and wishing to God, wishing for about the thousandth time . . .

As a retreat from reality he'd evolved this other version of subsequent events, his own short-lasting panacea of a daydream in which Sarah insisted that he should rush out and grab a taxi, hurry round to Eaton Square . . .

'It's too good to be true, Charlie, I can hardly *believe* it, it's been such a bloody age! Charlie darling, aren't you the answer to a maiden's prayers?'

She *had* gone on in that vein. Mentioning also that Bill was in New York and couldn't be back much before the weekend, poor darling . . . But at this point the daydream took over, switching the points so that memory ran on to a fictional branch-line where he heard himself telling her that he'd have liked nothing better than to see her, *but* . . . and waiting for the wails of protest and persuasion to die away before plugging on: 'Honestly, I can't, I don't have a bloody minute. I just thought I'd check on how you and Bill were making out. Still piling up fortunes for you, is he?'

Actually he thought he probably *had* started off with an attempt at stone-walling. The point at which the two versions separated completely was that in the daydream he stuck to his guns, chatted for a few minutes and then said firmly, 'I *must* go now. Goodbye, Sarah pet. Regards to old Bill . . . '

5

What he'd actually said to her — eventually, however much he'd procrastinated in the first minutes of that telephone call — was 'All right, then, I will. Just one quick drink, see how you're looking now you're an old married woman, huh?'

'Getting older every minute too, so *hurry*, Charlie!'

Grinning, he'd turned away from the phone, thinking *Well, why not, for heaven's sake* . . . Then remembered what he'd come to the telephone for in the first place, turned back to it and called his bank to get the figures on his account. In fact it was good news, better than he'd expected; he could visualise the pearls' glow against his wife's velvet-smooth, tanned skin.

Meanwhile a quick drink with Sarah would be fun. A laugh or two, and to get the dirt on that self-important clown she'd married. Poor devil . . . But one should not give up one's old friends, and there was no question of disloyalty to Anne — rather the opposite, it proved the strength of their relationship that one did *not* have to cut adrift . . .

A taxi materialised as he reached the corner, and miraculously it was free. Miracles continued, in the form of traffic lights that were all green, and within about three minutes he was paying the cab off in Eaton Square, gazing up at the windows of the Liscombs' flat and unintentionally overtipping. Profuse thanks surprised him, but it was too late to do anything about it: anyway, what the hell – just forty-eight hours ago he'd been flat on his belly on a rain-swept hillside, soaked to the skin and filthy . . .

He ignored the lift, took the stairs four at a time . . .

'Charlie, *darling*!'

In that second, it was as if someone had turned a switch to 'off'. None of this counted or was real; it was a hole in time and space. Clocks stopped, mind stopped, memory and identity all lost. He'd kicked the door shut behind him and the flimsy housecoat which was all she'd had on had slithered into a pool of yellow on the mat.

In a news bulletin on Radio 4 a few minutes ago it had been mentioned that President Assad of Syria had left Damascus for Moscow. Charlie had poured himself a small Scotch just as that broadcast had been starting, and now his glass was empty. Which only showed how pointless it was to be so niggardly, when it only left you needing a second one before you'd even sat down.

Bread and cheese would do for supper. Unless he made an omelet. Cheese omelet maybe, and there'd be bread and cheese available for Bob Knox if he needed it when he arrived. Sarah, Charlie remembered, had had smoked salmon in her fridge, and champagne, to which they'd got round eventually. He took the new drink back to his chair.

The odd thing was that he had absolutely no wish to see Sarah again. Despite the fact that she and that sod Liscomb had split up. Now, for instance, on this lonely evening with a sense of excitement in the back of his mind: it was conceivable that she'd be alone too – not likely, but conceivable – and he had no interest at all. He wondered whether if he could have explained this to Anne and she could have allowed herself to believe him it would have made any difference, even induced her to pause for thought?

You couldn't explain any of it, though, that was the frustration. He'd attempted explanations several times and got nowhere – trying to make her understand that it had simply *happened* – like falling down a manhole or walking into a plate-glass door. She'd laughed when he'd said that, as if she'd thought he was trying to be funny. But it was the truth that it had been utterly unpremeditated and – honestly – *unwanted*. There'd been a certain stretch of hours in limbo, and he could have wiped it from his mind, changed it in retrospect into a dream, into fragments of erotic fantasy as unbidden as any other dream.

Anne couldn't accept any of this, she'd refused even to consider it. As far as she was concerned it *had* happened, he'd done it and it was stuck in her mind permanently, as solid and ugly as a block of concrete, unforgettable and unforgivable. So although he couldn't deny that it had been entirely his own doing – his own *crime*, in the context of his relationship with his wife – it came to feel at times that it was she who was destroying what should have been indestructible.

Of course, the boozing didn't help. But that was the egg, not the chicken. He'd always enjoyed a drink but before the bust-up with Anne it had never been any problem. Then, it had become one in a biggish way. Worse then than it was now, even: as far as one remembered. Which was what had finished him with the Regiment – and now, he supposed, it wasn't much of an attraction to Anne.

Give it up? He'd managed without it for three whole bloody days and nights, after all!

Thinking about this – on his way back to sit down again – he'd stopped in the middle of the room and noticed that his glass was empty. Maybe he'd been distracted to the extent that he'd forgotten to refill it, just walked slowly across and back again . . .

But OK, he'd behaved like a total shit, let Anne down as he could never have thought himself capable of even contemplating. That was fact. But surely after a few months – a year now – surely *eventually* she'd –

Water. Just a splash.

– eventually remember, one might have hoped, how marvellous it had been up to that moment?

Maybe she'd set her sights on some alternative. It might account for her having put the lawyers to work now, after a long period of inaction. He frowned, sipping his drink and realising that this was a *highly* unattractive concept . . . But there was another thought he'd had a minute ago: something

81

connected with her determination never to forgive and forget.

Yes – got it. She'd started with this attitude, and she'd still been clinging to it when he'd last spoken to her. Or rather when he'd last *tried* to speak to her. But – *inshallah* – might not time soften her? Mightn't she tire of this – this *revenge*? Therefore, keep trying, don't be put off? Even though she'd now filed for divorce, she could call it off if she changed her mind, surely.

He stared at the telephone. Thinking, *As long as she hasn't fallen for some other guy . . .*

There'd be others after her, all right. Looking as she looked, being as she was, there'd always be contenders.

Call her – *now*?

But she'd hang up when she heard his voice. Or she'd say as she had last time, 'It's no good, Charlie, there's no point, please leave me alone' – and *then* click off.

It was more or less a reflex with her now, he guessed, and the telephone made it too easy for her. He reached for his glass, and it was empty. Carrying it over to the bottle he thought, *Go round there, see her?*

Then inconsequentially – pouring – *Might ring old Harry first*. But even there there was a deterrent, the fact bloody Patricia so often took their calls.

Hoda Al-Jubran went quickly across the hall to the ringing telephone. Steeling herself for the lie or lies she was going to have to tell her brother. This would be him, it was the time he'd said he'd call . . . 'Yes?'

'Hoda, it's me. What's the news?'

'It happened just as you said it would. She brought it round not long after you'd left.'

'And?'

'Well – she came round – she'd telephoned first, and I'd said – '

'Look, spare me the detail, I don't want to know exactly who said what to whom. I just got here, I'm tired, all I need to know is *did she believe you*?'

'Eventually, yes. It was very difficult at first, though, she didn't want even to hear what I had to tell her. But I knew how important it is to you that I should convince her – '

'And you did, you're certain?'

'I just *told* you!'

'So tell me what were her final words.'

'That she wanted time to think about it. About herself and you, she meant. But she was in a hurry to leave – '

'Ah. She *was*, was she.' He paused. Then: 'Tell me just briefly what you told her, Hoda. What information she took away with her.'

'What you wanted, that's all. That this person is now in our country and that you're in charge of him and of his interrogation.'

'Did she ask *where* in Syria?'

'I don't – think so . . . She may have, but – well, anyway, I told her not in Homs – where she knew you'd gone – but in that district.'

She couldn't see that it would have done any damage, showing her Hafiz's map. The essential thing had been to convince her that the story was true, that had been the point on which Hafiz had been so insistent. She knew – because she knew *him* so well – that he'd have hit the roof if he'd known about the map, but he would have been more furious with her if she'd been telling him now 'No, she did *not* believe me.'

'Did you give her any reason for having told her about it?'

'Exactly what you told me, that's all. I said she should leave you alone, she'd ruin your career, all that, and she took very little notice, so then I told her about this other business and pointed out that when it becomes public, and also that you're her lover, how terrible it would be for her. I don't think she'd have any doubts that this was my reasoning.'

'All right. Hold on, would you, just a moment.' He covered the mouthpiece. Thinking hard, wondering in particular what was making her so nervous: as if she was scared of him . . . He searched his mind for any other question he should have been asking: in order to be *certain* . . . 'Are you there, Hoda? Tell me this, now. Did she say anything – any little thing, please cast your mind back and think carefully – anything that might suggest she could have had suspicions we'd set her up for this?'

'No – I don't see how she could have.'

'You're positive?'

'Yes, Hafiz, I'm *positive*!'

It might have been an ordeal for her, he guessed. To be involved in it at all, but also having to take on a woman ten years older than herself and far more sophisticated . . . Needing the kid's help — because it had seemed far the best way to do the job — he'd taken her for granted, hadn't considered what a lot he'd been expecting of her. He said in a gentler tone, 'Don't be upset, Hoda. It's simply that I need to be sure. It's an important job you've done, a lot hangs on it. And obviously you've done it well, I'm grateful.'

'That's all right, then.'

When he'd rung off, he told the operator to get through to the Soviet Embassy in Damascus and ask for Major Feodor Vorontsev. 'He'll be there, he's expecting this call.'

Waiting, Hafiz lit a cigarette. It would be the briefest of calls to the Soviet attaché, no more than 'Feodor — Hafiz here. Just to let you know — the information will by now be on its way to London.'

He knew Liz Thornton well enough, he guessed, to be sure that it *would* be on its way. And then within minutes Vorontsev's head office in Moscow would be getting the same good news: although President Al-Assad, who'd be inspecting a guard of honour on Moscow's Sheremetyevo airport at about this time, would *not*.

Charlie pressed Anne's doorbell. He could hear music from inside the flat, but she might have left a radio on to fool thieves. The same applied to lights: he'd invariably used these simple dodges, as well as others, and during the months of their marriage the same habits would have rubbed off on her. He prayed, none the less, *Please be here, my darling*: and then added, *Alone* . . . Asking a lot, he knew it. Then he heard movement on the other side of the door: it jerked open, came up hard against the chain and Anne's face was behind it in the gap, her expression changing from wary interest to a kind of frozen *nothing* as she saw him.

Wrinkling her nose, and moving back a bit. Smelling the whisky, of course.

'What d'you want, Charlie?' Then her eyes widened: 'My God, you've grown a moustache . . . '

Blinking down at as much as he could see of her: he was so much taller than she was that he felt like a giraffe, peering down at that visible section of her fine-boned face, grey eyes, soft brown hair. He answered her question: 'See you, talk to you. Sorry to bust in without warning, but – '

'You *haven't* bust in, have you.'

It occurred to him that it might not be so much an anti-burglar chain as an anti-Charlie chain. And she wasn't thinking of taking the thing off, he guessed was what she'd meant by that last comment. He told her – accepting the fact she had him stymied – 'I'm leaving tomorrow. Leaving the country, that is. I only thought – well, you know, say goodbye, see how you are, that sort of – '

'I'm quite well, thank you. Are you going on holiday?'

'Well – not really . . . Couldn't I come in, Anne? Just for a minute?'

'I can't see what good it could do either of us, Charlie.'

'Would it do any harm?'

She stared back at him. He could read her thought: *You've done all the harm* . . . He said, 'I might be gone a long time. I do wish you *would* . . . '

It tailed off, unexpressed, withered by her stony lack of response. The music was familiar – Chopin, maybe, one of her favourites . . . 'OK. I thought I'd – you know, try . . . You know I'm sorry for everything, don't you. I suppose that's about all I'd have had to say if you'd let me in. And you've heard it before, so I dare say you're wise.' He began to turn away. 'Look after yourself. I'll be thinking of you. Actually I do that most of the time. 'Bye . . . '

'Charlie—'

He pivoted: keeping his balance . . . She was saying, 'If you promise you won't stay longer than ten minutes . . . ' The door had almost shut as she took the chain off, and now it swung open. Anne was wearing green slacks and a darker green alpaca sweater. Bare feet – accounting for her ultra-smallness – indented the new, deep-pile carpet. Various things passed through his mind as he followed her across an entrance hall and into a sitting room with soft lighting and some furniture and pictures that he remembered: the formality, being ushered in like this, and the strangeness of seeing his wife in a new setting, unfamiliar to him but already 'home' to her; also the pleasure in having found her here, and now at least to this limited extent a slight de-freezing.

Curiosity, he guessed. She'd want to know where he was going.

In case her bloody lawyer wanted to know?

'I've no whisky, I'm afraid.'

'Even if you had, I wouldn't – '

'I won't be a minute. Sit down if you want to.' She switched off the tape on her way out of the room. Going to put shoes on, he guessed. He wondered how it might have turned out if Bill Liscomb had not returned early – on Concorde, *naturally* – or if he'd telephoned to let his wife know he was on the way. That little omission might well have been deliberate, Charlie guessed. But if he'd done anything except what he had done – which had been to let himself into the flat very quietly, turn as white as the sheets in which she and Charlie had been entangled, then march straight to the telephone to call Anne . . .

Charlie had wondered once or twice since that frightful day why he hadn't killed the bastard.

He'd been right about footwear. Her feet were now in slippers with half-heels that gave her most of another inch . . .

'Sweet of you to let me in, Anne.'

'You've guessed why, of course.'

'You want to know where I'm going.'

'Bull's-eye.'

'You're in for a disappointment, then. Plain fact is I don't know.'

'You're leaving tomorrow and you don't know where you're going?' She frowned. 'That moustache doesn't do much for you, Charlie.'

'Don't you think so?' He was looking around the room. 'This is nice, though. Are you back in your old line of work? You said *a* job, but – '

'Flashman. That's what it makes you look like.' She suppressed a giggle. 'No, I'm PA to the head of an advertising agency.' She shrugged. 'Well, I suppose it is pretty much the same . . . Where are you going, Charlie?'

'I think – but this is only a guess – Syria.'

'A guess.' Gazing at him, her grey eyes slightly narrowed. She might have been wondering whether she still knew him *at all* . . . 'Mystery tour, no doubt. And that adornment for disguise. But I believe I read somewhere that they don't let tourists into Syria now.'

'That's true. Not Brits, anyway.'

He'd thought of giving her the yarn about a business trip to Germany, but it had stuck in his throat. Partly because he wanted her to know what was happening to him; but it was also a fact, oddly enough, that he'd never told this woman a lie. So how *would* it have been, he wondered, if bloody Liscomb hadn't sneaked in when he had? Could one have gone on down to Wiltshire, given her the pearls, revelling in reunion with her and ever after pretended to oneself it hadn't happened?

In a sense it wouldn't have. That wasn't all bullshit, the way he'd tried to persuade her that the slate could be wiped clean. He wouldn't have allowed it brain-space, she'd never have seen it behind his eyes or read it in his thoughts, and he would never have gone anywhere near Sarah again.

He didn't *believe* he would have – even without the dénouement, Liscomb's incredibly foul reactions. Although it was true that he'd never have admitted any possibility that he'd have acted as he had on that one occasion: so there did in the strictest honesty have to be a doubt, and it surfaced in his mind now because he was looking at Anne, from whom he'd never had any secrets large or small.

Well – that last deployment, the solo job, she'd known nothing about that. But he probably would have talked about it – about some aspects of it – in time, if they'd stayed together. Not names or places, but the experience itself.

'Tell me, Charlie?'

'If I do, will you keep it to yourself?'

'Heavens, no. The minute you're out of here I'll ring up the night editor of the *Daily Mirror*, give them the works!'

'All right.' He raised a hand defensively. 'Just does happen to be rather secret stuff.'

'Better *not* tell me, then.'

'As the man is wont to say, "I've started, so I'll finish".' He shrugged. 'In any case I *can't* divulge any secrets, for the simple reason I don't have any. There's a guy to be rescued from somewhere in the Middle East — that's all I know, it's only my guess that it could be Syria.'

'But — are you going alone?'

'By no means . . . Oh, it could be Libya. Or even, I thought, the Yemen. So you're not getting any State secrets, you see . . . No, I'm joining a team of the Special Boat Squadron — because they don't have enough blokes who talk Arabic. Know what I mean by SBS — Royal Marines?'

'But surely — ' She'd started, but did *not* finish, having seen — she thought — the answer . . . 'You're in one of the Territorial regiments, I suppose. I hadn't realised . . . ' Then frowning again, the doubt returning: he saw it, and she was right, they hadn't wanted him in the reserves, 21 or 23 SAS; she'd have known it, he guessed . . . 'So what have you got to do with the SBS, for heaven's sake?'

'The lingo — Arabic — is all they want. Plus being SF-trained, I suppose, but it's the Arabic they're in need of. What's so good about it from my angle is that they checked with the Regiment before they came to me, they must have been told something like "old Charlie Swale came a cropper, trouble with the sauce, but he's basically OK" . . . And it means a lot to me, d'you see?'

'I suppose . . . But it's still hard to — well, frankly, to *believe* they'd — '

'Fact is they *have*. And — ' his eyes held hers — 'I was thinking, Anne — if *they* can give me a second chance, maybe *you* could?'

Staring back at him: uncomprehending . . . Then: 'I can't see the parallel . . . Charlie, SBS are underwater specialists, aren't they? So how — '

'Short of guys fluent in Arabic, that's all. It makes perfect sense — that and the SAS experience, and that's *me*. OK — scraping the barrel, you're right, but there it is. This guy — team leader, Marine captain — came knocking on my door, knew all about me, asked would I help them out. And there you are. I've been in camp with them all this week, sweating my guts out, up and down Welsh mountains — and not a dram of whisky, let me tell you!'

'But you've been catching up this evening, Charlie.'

88

'I've – had a couple.' He blinked at her. As if her comment had surprised him. 'Won't be any where we're going. Old Bob told me – as a condition, and I accepted it. We take off tomorrow, and that's *it*.'

'You aren't making this up, are you?'

'Why would I do that?'

'Or someone's practical joke?'

He gestured, brushing the suggestion off. Then: 'I never did lie to you.'

'I suppose that's true.' Her grey eyes held his. 'But you would have. You'd have had to, wouldn't you?'

'Odd you should say that. I was thinking about it too. I honestly don't know – I mean whether I could have lived with it.'

'Half the world does, Charlie. Maybe three-quarters.'

'Never had much to do with us, did it.'

'It didn't, no. At least I'd *thought* – '

'Shall I tell you again – how much I'd like to put the clock back?'

'No, Charlie. Thank you, but – '

'I don't get drunk now. I drink, but – not real falling-down drunk. Honestly. And I don't – ' his arm scythed – 'you know – '

'No, I've no idea what – '

'Get sick.' The gesture illustrated it, showed her a pool on the carpet. He saw her eyes close, and went on quickly, 'All right, OK, I never did – around *you*, Anne, not – '

'Thank God – ' her eyes were open again – 'for small mercies.'

'All I'm saying – *trying* to say – '

'I know what you're saying, Charlie.'

'This lawyer business, couldn't it be stopped? So we'd have a – a little time, a *chance* – fresh start, just the chance of one?'

'No, Charlie, there *isn't* any chance of – '

'Not even think about it?'

'D'you imagine I haven't thought about it?'

'*I* think about practically nothing else!'

She was staring at him; for a moment he had the wild hope that she might be weakening. Then she'd shaken her head.

'I haven't gone through the misery of this past year just to start again. You might as well make your mind up to it, get your life going – fresher the start the better, I'd think, but just don't waste your time with thoughts of including *me* in it. You *must* understand this, accept it. I don't wish you any harm, Charlie, far from it, I just don't intend to put my own head on the block again – OK?'

He winced. Getting up, slowly, because she was standing now. He said, 'I'd hoped you might have remembered how wonderful it was. It was, wasn't it – I mean for you as well as for me, we *meant* the things we said in those days, didn't we?' She'd turned away. He muttered, 'I wouldn't have believed you could be so – so unforgiving.'

'*I* wouldn't have thought I could be so – '

'Hurt?' He'd supplied the word for her. Feeling as sober as he had on Wednesday, Thursday, Friday . . . 'You don't have to rub that in, I *know* it.'

'But it's spilt milk, Charlie, it's spilt milk.' She had her back to him. 'And your ten minutes is up . . . '

The telephone buzzed and the man slumped in the armchair stirred, pushing himself semi-upright and reaching over the desk to get to it. Muttering to himself: a crumpled-looking man in his fifties, in need of a shave, the whites of his eyes the colour of dirty laundry.

He knew what this was going to be about, anyway.

'Harrington.'

'Despatch from the FCO, Mr Harrington. Wants a signature, he says.'

'I'll come down.'

He'd been waiting for it, had dozed off again since the resident clerk on duty in the Foreign Office had called half an hour ago to say he was sending it over. But he'd been waiting for that call from the FCO anyway. He'd accepted the chore of duty officer last night as well, would have had to take Sunday's too if the message hadn't come through tonight. In fact he *would*: to cover the truth that this was the crucial night, the thing he'd been waiting for. It had been due to come some time out of working hours and during the weekend, and he'd provided himself with an excuse to be available as a stand-in by encouraging his wife to go on a visit to their daughter and son-in-law in Paris. It bored him to be alone in the flat, he'd explained, and he and the son-in-law didn't get on; so why not give some colleague a break. After all, he'd soon have all the free time he could handle: in a matter of weeks he'd be out on his ear, not retiring but *being retired* – early retirement with a matchingly reduced pension, of course. He knew what the young gentlemen had been saying, on the top floor: 'Eddie Harrington? Well, old Eddie's been rather running out of steam, you know . . .'

He shambled to the lift, descended in it to the entrance floor and signed for the brown envelope, took it back upstairs with him. His movements were slow, even ponderous, as befitted a man on the verge of retirement. Although he knew he could still have run rings – if he'd been given the chance – round those young so-called 'high-fliers' . . .

He shut the door, sat down at the desk and opened the envelope. He made his first note – on the back of another envelope, actually a gas bill which he'd had in his pocket – before he'd read anything but the figures at the top. Time of receipt – in the Foreign Office, not here at SIS. The FCO was where they'd look for their leak, *if* at some later time he was contacted as they'd said he would be.

And this was it, all right. Telegram from the ambassador in Damascus. Prefixed DEDIP, decoded by the resident clerk on duty, the one who'd called to say he was sending a copy round. He'd have made other copies, of course, for certain FCO officials. The head of the Middle East department, obviously, and the DUS who was *his* boss, and probably the head man too, the Permanent Under-secretary. And others: and the more the merrier, Harrington thought as he read on.

Vernon Stillgoe, kidnapped in Beirut several weeks ago, allegedly now in custody in Syria. Map-reference, for God's sake: nobody had said there'd be this much detail . . . Statement by Hoda Al-Jubran – brother Hafiz special assistant to Minister of Interior – in conversation with Elizabeth Thornton, information officer at the embassy. The brother alleged to be supervising Stillgoe's custody and interrogation. President Assad reportedly not privy to this situation. Ambassador requesting guidance as to whether to make representations to Deputy Minister of Foreign Affairs, the Minister having left for Moscow in company with President Assad. An alternative might be to request an interview with Vice-President Halim Khaddam, but with the report as yet unconfirmed, and not being in a position – without instructions – to name the source, this might not be considered timely.

Suggestion: an approach in Moscow to Assad?

Harrington added a few more notes to those he'd scribbled on the back of his gas bill. Then he replaced it in an inside pocket, and reached for the other telephone.

'I need to speak to Mr Bremner. At his home, or wherever.'

In the apartment on Sloane Street, feeling buoyant with relief because a late edition of the evening paper had carried the news of President Assad's departure for Moscow, Leo checked through the airline tickets which the big woman had had ready for him in envelopes bearing the logo of Bluewater Cruises. Outward and return flights to and from Ercan in the Turkish Republic of North Cyprus, via Istanbul, in the names of Campbell, Sharp, Tait and Denham. Charlie and Leo would travel as friends who'd booked together, and the other two would appear to be travelling as individuals, unknown to each other; as a foursome they'd have been an unlikely group. He noticed that the tickets had been rubber-stamped by a travel agency in Knightsbridge.

'I thought you'd set up your own business?'

'As a pilot scheme, sure. To see if it'll get off the ground. Obviously I don't have ABTA and IATA licences at this stage, though. These people are helping me out, we split commission. If they were asked they'd confirm they'd sold the tickets on behalf of Bluewater Cruises – head office in Israel, local agent my own home address . . . Which reminds me – here . . . '

Brochures. Leaflets, really, but professionally produced. Brilliant blues of sea and sky, and a photograph of a quite large timber ship with two masts, sails furled on the booms.

'Is that our yacht?'

She nodded. 'Pretty, isn't it?'

'Very nice.' He put the brochures away with the tickets, and picked up his one piece of luggage. 'Be seeing you, then. Thanks for your help.'

'Mind you're at the airport in good time.'

'Mothering me, now?'

'Being a good travel agent, that's all. Don't want you back on my hands after missing the flight, do I. It's Terminal One, by the way.'

'I know.'

'You'll have a long wait in Istanbul. On Sundays there's no connection to Ercan until the evening. You could take a look around the town, if you felt like it.'

'Yes, Mummy.'

'And Eric said to wish you the best of luck.'

'Tell him I look forward to renewing our acquaintance.'

'*I* wish you luck too, Leo. Or Knox, Campbell, whoever you are.' She beckoned. 'Here – just for luck . . . '

It was like being kissed by a giant grouper.

In the taxi on his way to Charlie's flat he put his mind rigorously to checking over detail, searching for anything he might have overlooked. He didn't *think* he'd forgotten anything. He'd given Tait and Denham a final pep-talk, impressing on them the importance of maintaining the fiction of being Royal Marines, SBS, and rubbing Pete Denham's nose in the fact that he'd come very close to blowing the whole thing in that exchange of remarks about underwater entry to and exit from submarines. He'd pointed out to them that they had to be alert for traps of this kind, and to think before speaking, no matter how trivial the subject might seem to be. He'd also reminded them of the terms of their contracts – balance of cash payable only on successful completion – and pointed out that success depended amongst other things on fooling Charlie.

It was remarkable, Leo thought, how easily people could be fooled – in this case, led by their snouts to end up not only unpaid, but dead.

He rang Charlie's bell, then waited. Too long a wait – he was beginning to worry, to think he might not be there, might have gone out on a bender, might even not come home tonight . . . A wave of near-panic then: seeing what risks were involved when you had to rely on someone with a built-in flaw like Swale's . . .

'Yup?'

'It's Bob here, Charlie!'

Virtually shouting, in relief . . . Last-minute nerves, he told himself. Better take a grip. Smotrenko's comment echoing in memory: *Kicking you straight into the deep end, right?*

Five nights ago he'd answered that identical 'Yup?' with his own introductory question 'Captain Swale?' and the reply had been – characteristically – 'Never heard of him'. They'd come a long way in the five days – thanks to Swale's instant acceptance, boozy lack of suspicion – but at that moment, Leo remembered, he'd reckoned the chances of success as no better than evens. One mischance for which he'd prepared himself as he'd travelled up in the lift had been that this former SAS officer might know serving SBS people, might ask his visitor, 'How's Johnny Smith?' – which could have been a trap. Alternatively he might instead have telephoned some 'John Smith' later: 'Johnny, what can you tell me about a colleague of yours, bloke by the name of Bob Knox?'

He'd been on guard against some such contact having been made before he'd called Charlie at his office on theTuesday; in that conversation his ears had been fine-tuned for any false note. Then a day later the tape from the bug had provided another check – as good as one could expect to get, ninety per cent clearance, say, enough anyway for Leo to have felt justified in telephoning Smotrenko with an 'OK' this afternoon.

A blast of whisky fumes met him in the doorway of the flat. He could see it in Charlie's face, too, and in his stance – upper part of the body inclined a bit forward and a slight weaving motion . . . Leo said as he walked in, 'Undoing the fine work of recent days, are we?'

'Ah, fuck off.' Charlie lurched away into the sitting room. 'Just had a few to remind me what it tastes like. What's more, young Bobby bloody Bootneck, I'm about to have another . . . You wan' one?'

'Maybe I will. Thanks.' Leo followed him into the room. 'We might drink a toast – happy landings . . . '

Colonel Vetrov knocked, opened the door without waiting for an invitation, sidled into his chief's large, functionally-furnished sanctum. He shut the door carefully, ensuring privacy from the staff in the outer office, before he advanced to the glass-topped desk.

'Excuse me, General. Word's just in from Damascus. Vorontsev's heard from his Syrian that the information's on its way to London.'

'That's good.' Gudyenko shut the file he'd been studying. 'And all's well in London meanwhile?'

'Yes. Smotrenko's confirmed they'll be flying out tomorrow. They'll get to the port rather late, probably about midnight. Cyprus time, that is.'

'So our wonderboy has put us into orbit.' Gudyenko added, 'The achievement's not to be underestimated, you know, he had some real problems there . . . Sit down. Let's see where we stand, roughly, the timing. With Assad safe under wraps here, Leonid Ivan'ich and his odd little party on their boat tomorrow night . . . Obviously it's the Syrians – and Vorontsev – who'll have to run it now – run our *molodyets* once he's out of our own reach . . . But – would you agree the action might take place Wednesday night, Thursday morning?'

Refreshing his memory, Vetrov realised, putting himself back on this wavelength. He'd have plenty more on his plate, the colonel knew very well, not just this one operation. He said tactfully, 'Thursday's probably more – realistic, General. It's not only the physical problems – factors such as the night landing, the distances that have to be covered, also in darkness – but as you'll remember, we have to time it with the receipt of the Stillgoe information in London. There must be time for reaction, for their people to have been readied and sent out. We don't want the risk of their being able to show that if the intelligence had been received at *this* time they couldn't have been on the spot by *that* time . . . But in any case the transit overland won't be fast. Swale has to believe he's with an SBS team, they wouldn't risk moving in daylight – eh?'

'Presumably Vorontsev and his Syrians are aware of these limitations.' A shrug. 'It has to be left to their judgement, anyway, nothing else would make sense – unfortunately. But – ' the general shrugged again – 'with Assad here all week there's certainly no need to rush it.'

'Does he – ' Vetrov queried – 'fly back on Saturday, to

Damascus? Or maybe Friday night – if the visit's only for *this* week?'

'How would that concern us?'

'Only that maybe we shouldn't cut things too fine at that end either. I'm thinking of Leonid Ivan'ich, getting him back here when he's finished. When Assad gets home, his return more or less coinciding with the event – maybe – or with the news of it breaking – well, there'll be political explosions. I suggest we should have our lad well clear of the scene *before* then.'

'Well.' Gudyenko's gesture was dismissive. 'That's – in the light of my orders to Vorontsev – *not* of consequence. Forget it.'

Vetrov frowned, worried that he might have missed something obvious. The Syrian end of the operation wasn't strictly his business; but Leo was, and there had to be some overlap. Gudyenko said, 'I never accept a risk when I don't have to. You know that.' His tone was gentle, explanatory. 'So I dislike half-measures if they impose such risks. Think of the massacre scene – the Syrians who'll float in to keep Swale alive, and so forth ... Ask yourself, Dmitry Arkey'ich – if you were one of them, what would your thoughts be if there was another survivor, not even wounded, whisked off to Damascus in a chopper like some movie stunt-man who's earned his fee ... Remember, some of those guys'll be walking around afterwards – with tongues in their heads, wagging. They'll remember – and talk – when the world's listening to the revelations from Swale's trial. Huh?'

Vetrov nodded.

'Now from the viewpoint of the same eye-witnesses, think of it this way – if there's no such mysterious person rising from the ashes, no survivor except Swale – and of course the Syrian soldiers who've put paid to the invaders?'

'Yes, I see.' Vetrov blinked. 'But – '

'You're thinking of the waste of that talented young man with his identity so well established, and all the years of work we've put into him.'

'Well, yes, I admit I – '

'Don't think of it as waste.' The general's hands moved

dismissively. 'Think of it as though he'd been designed, reared, *created* for this one enormously worthwhile purpose. Then it's *not* waste – d'you see?'

6

Flight BA 570 had been called; its passengers were pouring out of the departure lounge, out through the glass doors and around the bend into the first long straight. Charlie and Bob only strolling, knowing there'd be another wait before long.

Charlie had been up at five, to shower then fix breakfast for himself and his guest; they'd had a cab ordered for six fifteen. On the early side, but Bob had wanted to make sure of it, also to meet Tait and Denham outside the terminal building to give them their tickets and brochures. Those two were now solo, separate from each other and from Bob and Charlie; they were to get together as Bluewater Cruise clients on the ground at Istanbul.

Charlie had grumbled, 'So who gives a shit who knows whom?'

'As a group, we might look like — well, what we are. We don't want 'em to know we're coming, do we.'

'Or me to know where we're going.' He'd shrugged. 'Except it has to be Syria.'

Because he knew now that they were flying to Cyprus; and where the hell else would one go from there? Except maybe Syrian-controlled Lebanon. Bob had said, frowning, 'You'll know soon enough, Charlie': and picked that moment to mention that on the passenger list he was Christopher Sharp, not Charlie Swale. Charlie had checked his ticket: Bob pointing out, 'Same initials, you see. But they don't normally check passports against the list. You must put your real name on the card for Turkish immigration, of course.'

'But what does this achieve, for God's sake?'

'My ticket and passport aren't in *my* real name, Charlie. There wasn't time to get you a faked passport, that's all.'

'I asked why, what—'

'Covering tracks. We don't want reconstruction of our movements, anything to tell anyone how we got there. "Investigative journalism" for instance.'

Presumably, he'd thought, they knew what they were doing. The SBS were famed, of course, for their obsession with secrecy and anonymity. Anyway he had a rather sore head this morning and he wasn't straining it any more than necessary.

He'd bought a bottle of malt whisky and a box of Havanas. If they wanted him to look like a tourist, he'd told Bob, OK, he'd *look* like a fucking tourist. In fact when they'd first come through to the departure lounge he'd shied away from the Duty-Free emporium, protesting that he didn't need it, but Bob had pointed out that damn few yachtsmen would go on holiday without their iron rations. So now Charlie swung his plastic bag with the rest of them. He and Bob were clearly tourists – open-neck shirts, anoraks; reminding himself occasionally, *Christopher Sharp* . . . He could see Smiley Tait's striped sweater in the straggle ahead of them, and Pete Denham a few paces ahead of Smiley – flowered shirt, blue anorak over a shoulder.

Bob muttered, 'That pair could be Special Branch.'

A dozen yards ahead, a man and a woman behind a little counter were watching the passing flow. Pete Denham, level with them at this moment, was chatting up a red-headed girl. Jeans, skin-tight, and a well-filled T-shirt . . . Charlie met the official's thoughtful stare: his companion was studying Bob. Or seemed to be. Charlie said, 'She reckons you're pure Arab. Or *im*pure.'

'You're full of shit, Charlie.'

'What makes the world go round, old chum.'

*   *   *

Paul Salvesen — tall, grey hair receding — invited his guests, 'Who'd like to open the batting?'

This was Salvesen's house, Queen Anne and elegant, in a Chelsea backwater where on a Sunday forenoon nothing much was stirring, except for Salvesen himself and a manservant who'd opened the door to John Bremner and to Hugh Vestey, who as head of the Middle East department at the Foreign and Commonwealth Office was Salvesen's junior. Vestey was a counsellor; Salvesen, a deputy under-secretary, had overall charge of several such departments.

No sight or sound of Mrs Salvesen. She'd be asleep or in the tub, or breakfasting in bed, Bremner guessed. Guessing was a large part of his job: at least, of the way he did his job. He nodded to Salvesen, who'd now asked *him* to 'open the batting' by giving them his department's view of the report from Damascus.

Bremner had the Middle East desk in SIS. He'd been woken by the duty officer's call just after 2 a.m. and he hadn't had more than an hour's sleep since then. Salvesen's strong coffee had been doing him good, though; he put his cup down now, with his thoughts more or less collected.

'I suppose to start with we have to decide — or try to — whether it's genuine or whether it's disinformation. Basically the suggestion seems to be that there's an anti-Assad faction who may have got Stillgoe into their keeping in order to precipitate a political crisis. *Maybe* timed for Assad's absence in Moscow. And the Al-Jubrans seem to be involved in this. Well, they're from the north end of the country, that fertile stretch northwest of Aleppo/Halab. Definitely prosperous, influential, and were becoming more so — up to about the time Assad took over. Assad's an Alawi — as you know, of course, I'm only trying to muster what *I* know. Or rather what I *don't* know, is what it comes down to . . . The Al-Jubran clan may well have resented the flood of Alawis into the administration and senior army jobs and so forth. On the other hand, with this boy at the Interior Minister's right hand — and there's an uncle who's a prominent Ba'athist, big noise in the National Progressive Front — well, if they're lining up agin the boss, it's news to me.'

'Could be quite a recent development, John.'

Vestey had the look of a younger Edward Heath, Bremner had often thought. He tried not to let this prejudice him against the man. Vestey adding now, 'Since Assad seems to be off at something of a tangent – his peace policy in Lebanon for instance?'

'I'm only saying that we have no evidence to support it.' Bremner shrugged. 'OK, this neither proves nor disproves anything. Since Syrian independence forty years ago there've been more plots and counter-plots than any of us have had hot breakfasts. As you know, of course . . . But looking at it from the other angle – might it be an effort to disinform – we could start by asking ourselves what they'd hope to gain by having us believe it. And then – well, whether young Hafiz Al-Jubran's affair with Miss Thornton might have been promoted right from scratch as part of a deception operation. Mightn't be such a far-fetched theory, you know – in his position, and with the mix of political and religious differences, you could say he *was* sticking his neck out, rather . . . But as to what might have been the purpose behind it – I don't mean only Miss Thornton's romance, I mean the yarn about Stillgoe if it *has* been planted on us as disinformation – unless to have us rush in with protests, denunciation which they could then demonstrate to be a load of rubbish derived from our own resident Mata Hari?'

Salvesen put his cup down. 'Nuisance value only. Calumnies come readily enough without elaborate contrivances to support them.' He glanced at Bremner. 'Plenty in the pot still, make a long arm . . . Any *other* ideas?'

'Yes. With a stretch of imagination as well as arm – what if they hoped we might try to extract our man physically, by special-force insertion or with the help of agents already there? Could be aimed at bringing such agents to the surface – if there were any . . . We *would* like to have Stillgoe out, certainly – and they must know it. Which in fact makes this whole thing smell, just a little.' He left his coffee black, but spooned sugar into it. 'They've had him for nearly four months now. And they kidnapped him in circumstances which make it highly probable they knew he was doing a job for us as well as for his newspaper. He'd met his informant – a Syrian, military person – earlier that day, in East Beirut, and the Shi'ite extremists snatched him on his way to the airport. With rather important information in his head. Quite likely they'd had the Syrian under observation, observed the meeting, then when he made his dash for the airport they'd know he'd got what he was after. What *we* were after. Then they'd have sweated all they needed to know out of their own guy, and they've got Stillgoe as a very effective bait – which is how I'd guess they're now using him.'

Bremner paused, sipping coffee, then continued, 'Taking it a bit farther, I'd suggest this scenario's supported by (1) location, I mean access from the coast, and (2) the Syrian lass having shown our girl the brother's map. Sounds as if she did it quite cleverly, fooling Miss Thornton into believing she wasn't supposed to be letting her see it.'

Vestey nodded. 'Almost an invitation.'

'Which we wouldn't dream of accepting.' Salvesen was lighting a cigarette. 'They surely can't believe we'd be such idiots . . . *Do* you have such an agent or agents in Syria – as a matter of interest only?'

'No.' Bremner shrugged. '*Effectively*, no. But if they thought we had, or that the Yanks had – and they might be somewhat paranoid on this subject, in view of recent events – not to mention their own inbuilt duplicity . . . Bear in mind that if this *is* a disinformation exercise, nothing that Syrian girl said can be believed. It doesn't have to be a splinter-group setting us up, for instance, Assad himself could be calling the shots – even from Moscow . . . On which hypothesis, now you've got me going on this line of thought I'd suggest they *might* believe they had a chance of luring us in. And wouldn't they be right, truly? If we were convinced the report was genuine?'

'If – ' Vestey qualified – 'if it was thought to be both practicable and worth it on balance against the political repercussions.'

'Well, I wonder.' Salvesen's eyes were narrowed into the smoke of his cigarette. 'If it was so very desirable to have him out – and if such an operation could be carried out quietly and neatly, without any side-effects or other awkwardness – well, any Syrian protest would involve admitting they'd had him there to start with – as much an act of terrorism as was the kidnapping itself. And with this Hindawi trial hanging over them already – well . . . '

Vestey and Bremner began to speak simultaneously. Both stopped. Bremner offered, 'Go ahead.'

'Well, suppose it's a set-up. He's not there, but they think they can make us believe he is and chance our arm – what, drop in a team of SAS? Well, the Syrians could have let's say two of their five commando regiments deployed around the target area – at which they've so carefully pointed us – and they could drop their one parachute regiment behind our boys as soon as they'd moved inland. Eh? It could be a trap that even the SAS would have problems getting out of.' He nodded at Salvesen. 'Counter the stuff that's arising from the Hindawi trial, make *us* seem to be into the business of terrorism?'

Salvesen agreed. 'Distinctly embarrassing.'

'Actually – ' Bremner put in – 'and purely *en passant*, I'd say the SAS might walk out of it all right. The Syrian army did lose the Golan Heights, you know. Which I've heard it suggested a troop of Girl Guides could hold.' He shrugged. 'But as you observed just now, we wouldn't fall for it, would we. In the cold light of reason, I'm sure you're right, we wouldn't be that bloody daft.'

'Let's *hope* we wouldn't.'

'It really is quite viable, as a guess at what they might be aiming for.' Bremner suggested, 'I think you'd both agree, from your own appreciation of the current moves and tendencies in the area – notably the Soviet efforts to rebuild their influence. *And* maybe short-circuit this new pragmatism for which Assad is being credited? I'm saying that although it's nothing but guesswork, the guesses are by no means extravagant – *if* the Damascus leak was deliberate, this could well be the explanation, or near enough to it.'

'We've one thing established anyway.' Salvesen took a quick glance at his watch. 'Even if it's true that Stillgoe's in Syria, we'd advise against any military reaction.'

Vestey murmured, 'Oh, absolutely.'

'So let's consider what *diplomatic* response might best suit the circumstances. If we decide to accept that the report may be factual, say, but irrespective of whether or not it was fed to us deliberately. I'm talking now about the alternatives of approaches either to some quarter in Damascus or directly to Assad in Moscow.' Salvesen told Vestey, 'I'm seeing the PUS this evening, by the way, and I'd like to have something on paper for him. If you could see to that, Hugh? The main points, and our conclusions . . . So let's start with Damascus. The ambassador suggested approaching either the Deputy Foreign Minister or one of the Vice-Presidents. From your own knowledge of those individuals, what would your recommendation be?'

Anne Swale hadn't been able to get to sleep until after four, and she'd slept right through to – she reached to turn the alarm clock so she could see its face – after *ten*, for God's sake . . .

Charlie was still in her mind: as he had been before she'd dropped off, and maybe in her dreams, she suspected. Stumbling through to the bathroom: her head buzzing as if it had bees in it . . .

The *Sunday Telegraph* was on the mat outside the door. She brought it in, glancing at the front-page stories, thinking *Damn Charlie!*

By the time she'd bathed and had breakfast in her dressing-gown it was about eleven. She left the newspaper in a crumpled heap and went into the bedroom to get dressed: then a walk, she thought, fresh air . . . Charlie was either sick and hallucinating, his brain all whisky fumes so that he was confusing daydreams and the real world, or he was so desperate to impress her that he'd *invented* all that rigmarole about the SBS.

She knew in her heart that he had not. Charlie was no inventor.

Her mind wouldn't leave it alone. She didn't understand it, and it maddened her. She'd been trying to make herself think about other things, but it kept coming back, tormenting her. Hence the *nuit blanche*.

She walked out to her kitchen, re-arranged a few objects, came back again. Pausing at the music centre, then deciding that noise was the last thing she wanted. She was looking at the telephone a minute later, thinking *Call him? See if he's here still, whether he remembers any of that stuff?*

She shook her head. Whatever her reason for calling him, he'd take it as a sign of interest in him, a desire for contact.

She flopped down, leafed through the colour supplement, read part of an article in which she hadn't the least interest. A new thought was taking root, expanding while she read the same paragraph three times and still didn't get the point. She threw the magazine down, pushed herself out of the chair and found her old address book in a drawer under the telephone. Riffling through to the letter 'P' . . . She put the book down, and dialled.

Janet Prentice answered. Anne said, 'Janet, this is Anne Swale.'

'Anne . . . ' A second's pause: then, '*Anne!* How *are* you? What a lovely surprise! And *where* – '

'I'm in London. I've got a puzzle – bit of a worry, actually . . . Could I possibly speak to – '

'Bruce, you want. Yes, you're in luck, he's here, for once . . . Anne dear, it's lovely to hear from you, and I *would* so like to see you again . . . Oh, here he is, hold on . . . '

Bruce Prentice asked, 'Can this truly be the beautiful Anne Swale?'

'Colonel Bruce, I *am* sorry to – '

'That's the worst possible start, my dear. You must not be sorry, because I'm tickled pink to hear from you. Janet just yelled that you have something on your mind, though, so let's get to it and see if I can help.'

'You're very kind.'

He was. He was a brilliant soldier, so Charlie and Charlie's former friends had maintained, and he was also – like his wife – outgoing, wholehearted.

'A question, actually, Colonel Bruce . . . Have you or the Regiment been contacted recently – or at all – by the Royal Marines wanting to know something about Charlie?'

A silence. Then: 'As the question strikes me here and now, the answer would have to be a straight "no". Frankly, I can't imagine in what circumstances it might occur.'

'He's going on some operation with the Special Boat Squadron. They need him for his Arabic, apparently. As you know, he's fluent – and he's kept it up, he uses it in his business. The SBS thing is somewhere in the Middle East, he said he thought

106

Syria but wasn't certain, they hadn't told him. But apparently they'd checked him out with you – I mean with the Regiment – before they approached him.'

'He told you this himself?'

'Yes, last night. He came here, to tell me he's leaving today – just turned up at my door, begging me to let him in. I suppose you'll have heard we're separated. I'm getting a divorce – I've my own flat here, and a job, but he's tried several times to talk me into trying to start again – which I will *not* do – and last night he was trying the same thing. His line was that if the SBS would take him on, having checked with you – which they told him they'd done, he said – then why shouldn't *I* give him another chance?'

'Well, I wouldn't presume to advise you on the personal issue, Anne. But the SBS bit – I can fairly definitely assure you it's not true. For one thing, if we had been approached by the Royals on that subject, I'm afraid it'd have been a thumbs-down . . . I'm sure you'd understand this, Anne.'

'It's why I'm telling you about it. It's so extraordinary. I've been awake all night, and – '

'He's made it up, that's all. Can't say I'd blame him for wanting to get back into your good graces, but – '

'The answer can't be as simple as that either, Colonel Bruce. Charlie's a drunk, but he's no liar. He never was, I'd stake my life on it. I haven't any doubt at all that he *believed* he was telling me the truth – which means he *has* been recruited for whatever this is. He'd been in the Welsh mountains all week, he said, training with this SBS team!'

'Any names, or other detail we could check on?'

'Only that he thought they were going into Syria. No, no *names* . . . He said maybe Libya or the Yemen but he guessed Syria. He made the point about it being only his guess, so he wasn't giving out any secrets, he didn't *know* where they were taking him.'

'Did he say where in Wales, so we might check whether – '

'No, I'm sorry – '

'Anything else, then?'

'They needed him for his Arabic, since they're short of Arabic-speakers. And they'd checked with you. And – oh, yes, the man who came to his flat to recruit him was a captain in the Royal Marines and also the team leader. During the week in Wales he'd had nothing to drink, he said, but he was full of whisky last night – I said something about it, and his excuse was it was his last night in civilisation, there wouldn't be any where he was going.'

Colonel Prentice said, 'Excessive indulgence in the hard stuff can change a person, Anne. Can you be so certain he wasn't fabricating?'

'Yes. Yes, I *can*. But I just thought – another thing... When he said there'd be no drink out there he said that "old Bob" had made that a condition of his going with them. He hadn't mentioned that name before, but I took it for granted he was talking about the same man, the recruiter.'

'An SBS captain with first name "Bob". That might be a start, there can't be many captains in that little outfit. Of course, *if* there's any truth in this –'

'Colonel Bruce, please believe me – he was *not* making it up.'

'All right. All right, Anne. You know the guy, after all. As a matter of fact my own somewhat different view of him leads towards the same conclusion, when I think back a bit. Certainly I'd say so of the man as he *was*. If the drinking hasn't changed him –'

'It has, but not that basically.'

'Very well, then.' A pause ... 'First, I'll have to check with some of our own people. No – on second thoughts, some other poor fish can handle that. *I'll* check with the Royals. Meanwhile, if you have a minute to spare, and could bear to do it –'

'Of course, whatever –'

'Second thoughts again – no. I'll do this, I'll start with it. Give me his telephone number – d'you have it, I mean Charlie's? I'll take this head-on – if he's still there, of course ...'

There was no answer from the number she'd given him. Just past noon, now. Prentice hung up, then telephoned his adjutant.

'Jimmy. Have we had, or do you know of anyone else

108

having had, any enquiry from the Royal Marines about your old chum Charlie Swale?'

'From the Marines . . . No, Colonel. Nor have I heard of anyone else being asked – good lord, he's not trying to join the Royal Marines, is he?'

'Not exactly. But look, ask around, will you? Find out – confidentially – whether anyone's had any such approach. Anything from the Royals, or anything from any other quarter about Swale. If you get any positive result, call me back at once – all right?'

The third number he wanted had to be looked up in a classified directory which he kept under lock and key, but within a few minutes he was talking to the Officer Commanding Special Boat Squadron.

'Charles, this is Bruce Prentice.'

'Well, hello . . . I just got in, this minute. What can I do for you, Bruce?'

'Answer a couple of questions. No, *three* questions, I think . . . First – have you ever heard of a former officer of my regiment by name of Charlie Swale?'

'No, I have not. Next question?'

'Do you have any special deployment to the Middle East – probably Syria but could be elsewhere in that area, and by "special" I mean the kind of antics in which you specialise – but something that's afoot now, today?'

'In a word – no. But any more questions of that kind, Bruce, I'd suggest you waited half an hour so we could both get to another line.'

'May do that later.' The secure line, he'd meant; it would have involved both men going to their respective headquarters. 'Or someone else might. Maybe not, but the feeling gets stronger with every "no" you give me . . . Will you be at home later in the day, Charles?'

'From now until about two thirty, then I'll be back here maybe seven or eight. Of course if it's something urgent I could stick around.'

'Well, let's try the last question. Do you have a captain in your outfit whose first name is Bob? Robert, maybe, but called Bob?'

'Let me think . . . '

Five seconds was all he needed.

'No. There's your third negative, Bruce. *Now* how's the pricking of your thumbs?'

'Very prickly indeed . . . Look, if I need to bother you again, it'll be before two thirty, well before. Otherwise forget it. Meanwhile, many thanks.'

He rang off, then tried Swale's number again; and again, no answer. He looked up another one in the classified directory. Two rings, a receiver was lifted and a male voice confirmed the number. Prentice asked, 'Duty officer, is that?'

'Yes, who's calling?'

'My name's Prentice. Colonel Bruce Prentice. I'd like to be put in touch with Mr John Bremner, if that's possible.'

The young executive who'd taken over the daytime duty from Edward Harrington reached for a directory, began leafing through it one-handed. 'If you'd hold on just a moment, Colonel . . . ' Prentice waited, guessing he was being checked on, the SIS duty officer making sure that John Bremner wouldn't be averse to talking to him. The check was fast: the young voice asked, 'Is there any urgency, sir?' Prentice noticed the step-up, that 'sir' . . . 'I ask because he's at a meeting – in London but not in this building. Would you like to give me a number where he could call you back?'

'Could he get to a protected line, wherever he is?'

'Hang on, sir, I'll see.' Another check: and again, a quick one. 'Yes. He could.'

'Then give me fifteen minutes to get to one myself.' He gave him the secure line number at the regimental HQ, and checked the time. 'I'll be there, hoping to hear from him, by – say twelve forty.'

The balance of opinion here, John Bremner thought as he listened to the two Foreign Office men chewing over the pros and cons of diplomatic moves in Damascus and/or Moscow, was that an approach might best be made to the Syrian head of state, at present a guest of the Soviets. If this decision was endorsed by the PUS, whom Salvesen would be seeing later in the day, the ambassador in Moscow would be briefed to implement it.

Or to *try* to implement it. Bremner had certain misgivings

on that score; if the circumstances and company had been different he'd have been ready to place bets by now. But he also knew that these FCO people might well, in their wisdom and entirely proper caution, decide on the alternative of recommending no action at all – euphemistically, to 'adopt a wait-and-see policy'.

But Moscow would be the best hope, in the present view, on the principle of going straight to the top and also because if the Damascus Report – in more than an hour's thinking and talking the words seemed to have earned their capitals – was to be accepted as genuine, one might also accept that Stillgoe was being held in Syria without the President's knowledge, so manoeuvres in Damascus might be complicated by not knowing who was or was not in the conspiracy.

Hugh Vestey was saying, 'He has his Foreign Affairs minister with him, unfortunately. What's his name – Farouk al-Sharah. Could be an obstruction – unless we decided to trust *him*. But I'd still prefer – '

'No argument.' Salvesen turned his gaze on Bremner. 'You've been sparing with your comments, John.'

'Hardly my field, the heights of diplomacy. I'd agree that if there's to be *any* approach, Al-Assad's the guy to nobble. But that's hardly my problem, of course. Also, I do feel pretty damn sure this is a con-trick. The more I think about it, the more it smells. And I'd chance my arm a bit beyond that point too. OK, if our ambassador is able to get to Assad, I'll eat these words; but my guess is Moscow could well be pulling the strings off-stage, and if so they'll make sure nobody from the West gets within a mile of him.'

Salvesen frowned. 'May we hear your reasoning?'

'For what it's worth.' Bremner nodded. 'As far as thinking the report's been planted on us – fairly subtly, less obvious than actually panting the news across a steaming pillow – well, we've looked at it from several angles, but to my mind the only approach that tells us anything worthwhile is the question of what the Syrians might stand to gain if it was straight up and they do have Stillgoe there, or by conning us. We concluded that if it's the latter there could be mileage in it for them if we swallowed the hook and rushed in where angels fear to tread – which they could be justified in hoping for – but that there's no dividend for them – as far as we can work it out – if it's genuine. So, as one's bound to accept – unless one's KGB or some such – that two plus two equals four whereas a zero amounts to zilch, I see this as disinformation.'

'Reluctantly – ' Vestey nodded – 'I believe I'd back that horse.'

Bremner looked back at Salvesen. 'The political background – breaking your own recent analysis down into my own kind of simplistics – seems to me to support the likelihood of Soviet involvement. As you said, they're working hard to regain their lost influence in the Middle East. After all, what have they got as of now – Assad, who seems to be turning soft on them, and Gaddafi who's as much of a pain in the arse to them as he is to the rest of us. But the Soviet talks in Helsinki with the Israelis, for instance: propitiate the Jews with a few promises – and as a sweetener let Scharansky's relations out under the wire – simultaneously reassuring the Arabs by announcing that nothing was achieved . . . Then the other moves you've mentioned – attempts to dissuade Assad from his Paris visit, and pressure on him to make this Moscow trip . . . Well, if they could pull *this* one off – con us into some crazy rescue attempt?'

Salvesen stirred: his movement suggested a readiness to bring this meeting to an end . . . 'With all that in mind – as hypothesis – we have to consider the likely or probable effects of an approach to Al-Assad. Whether we should react even to that extent. After all, if we're assuming the report is fictional, the obvious course would be to ignore it. What d'you say, Hugh? Sit tight – '

A knock at the door had interrupted him. 'Yes?'

The manservant came in, a folded slip of paper in his hand. 'I'm sorry to interrupt, sir. Telephone message for Mr Bremner, from his duty officer, who said it was very urgent . . . '

Bremner read the note. He told his host as the door shut again, 'Someone's anxious that I should call him back. On a protected line, though.'

'In my study.' Salvesen pushed his chair back. 'I'll show you.'

He rejoined his Foreign Office colleague a minute later,

commenting, as he sat down and offered Vestey a cigarette, 'You've had dealings with Bremner before, of course.'

Vestey nodded, using his lighter. 'Only quite recently, I can't say I know him well. He transferred to our friends from Box Five – well, as you'd know.'

'Rather given to – er – flights of fancy, would you say?'

'Well – he does·have a considerable reputation, for the accuracy of those – those flights. One or two notable bull's-eyes, in fact. And one heard that this was the basis of the JIC sub-committee's decision to recommend his being moved over, they felt that our friends needed his particular talents.'

'Well, that's – interesting.' Salvesen checked the time. 'Very . . . Nevertheless, Hugh, I'm still inclined to the view that our policy for the time being should be to hold our horses, let his people ferret for a lead to Stillgoe's present whereabouts. Eh?'

'He could be dead . . . '

'He could, yes. Or he could be in Syria. Meanwhile if there were some opportunity for an exchange of views with Assad in Moscow, preferably away from the microphones, I'd see no reason not to take advantage of it. Simply to inform him that such a report seems to have been pushed our way, that we have no strong belief in it, but wanted to bring it to his attention for as much or as little as it may be worth. *Not* revealing the source – since that might blow back on us, later if not right away . . . Would you agree?'

Vestey said yes, he would. If the Al-Jubrans were stirring up trouble for the present administration, wisdom suggested it might be better not to alienate them at this early stage. He and Salvesen talked on, desultorily, for several minutes, on this and related subjects; effectively the meeting was over now, but it might have seemed ill-mannered for Vestey to have left before Bremner finished his telephoning.

When he came back, Salvesen asked him, 'All well?'

'Well – no . . . ' Going to his own chair, resting his hands on the back of it, leaning slightly forward . . . 'No, I'd say – *un*well.' His expression – surprise, even alarm in it – increased the MI6 man's resemblance to Charles Dance, a likeness Salvesen had noticed earlier. Bremner told them, 'You may find this difficult to believe. *I* do . . . That was Colonel Bruce

Prentice of 22 SAS Regiment – calling with a bizarre account of – well, it centres on Syria, of all places. Yes, nice timing, eh? It seems a former SAS officer has left England – *probably*, he was leaving today and he does seem to have left – in company with people whom he believes to be from the Special Boat Squadron, Royal Marines. They recruited him – an SBS captain with the first name "Bob" did – because he's fluent in Arabic, and the operation they're engaged in is to the Middle East, this guy thought most likely Syria. He told his ex-wife all this, last night, and she telephoned Prentice – her husband's former commanding officer – less than an hour ago. Since which time Prentice had done some checking and discovered (a) there's *no* current SBS deployment in the Middle East, (b) the CO of the Special Boat Squadron says he has no captain in it with the name of "Bob", and (c) according to the ex-SAS officer, name of Swale, the SBS had checked on him at SAS headquarters before they recruited him, but in fact the SBS have never heard of him.'

Bremner pulled the chair out, and sat down. 'So *now* where are we?'

About halfway, Charlie reckoned, adjusting his watch to Turkish time, with the airliner somewhere over Jugoslavia. He glanced at the man beside him.

'Bob, tell me this. This fortnight's package deal your tame travel agent's fixed up for us. If we get on with the job, in and out smartly and no snags, how do we spend the rest of the time?'

'Acquiring a tan, Charlie.'

'Come again?'

'Cruise. Up into Turkish waters. What we've paid for. We just relax and enjoy it. Turkish wine's cheap and good, and Scotch is five quid a bottle, you'll have no worries at all.'

'I see. Our chauffeur-driven *bateau* stooges around and picks us up again, does it. And what about the extra hand we hope we'll have with us by then?'

'He'll go straight on his way to London. No problem, it's all organized.'

Charlie frowned. 'You say "no problem", but if you happen to get greased, who knows what to do?'

'The *gulet*'s crew. They'll be in radio touch with the other party to the rendezvous . . . Want another of those, Charlie?'

Brandy and ginger. Like pushing a dummy into a fractious baby's mouth.

To Anne, they were a phalanx of unfamiliar faces – plus Bruce Prentice's once-familiar and still well-remembered features, and the girl who'd greeted her and was back in the room now – nine of them including herself, all settling into chairs around the table after a series of introductions, murmurs of '*most* kind of you to have come, Mrs Swale' . . .

Bruce Prentice had flown up from Hereford by helicopter and called for her at her flat in an official car, whisked her to this building off Whitehall, into this high-ceilinged room in which she was now trying to fit names to faces. The names she'd heard and registered included Bremner, Salvesen – tall, greying hair, seemingly chairman of the meeting – and Vestey – pale face, almost a rhyme, 'pasty Vestey' as an *aide-memoire* – and a Royal Marine major whom Prentice called Charles. Balding, an amiable expression: Prentice had arranged for him to be here, and he'd come by helicopter too, from Poole. There were also two dark-suited younger men, with the hushed manner of church ushers, and this girl – quite nice-looking – who'd introduced herself as Verity MacDonald and was now beside her, operating a tape-recorder.

Bruce Prentice was on her other side. And the one on his feet, since she'd put names to all the others except the Marine called 'Charles', had to be Bremner. He had a look of Charles Dance, she thought, tuning in to the sound of her own name, hearing ' – Mrs Swale, who's nobly come along to tell us at first hand exactly what her husband said when he called at her flat last night . . . '

Bremner had ignored the speed limit and taken liberties with traffic lights all the way from Chelsea to Century House, where he'd drafted a summary of facts and theories so Verity could word-process it when she dashed in, she and his two executive assistants plus some others who were in the office now, having been recalled from their weekends at home. He'd put them all on to research tasks – airline flights and passenger lists, and checking that Swale wasn't in his flat, and that his brother — name and telephone number obtained from Anne Swale — hadn't any idea where he might be, and alerting Special Branch, who'd put a watch on air and sea ports and had a man on his way to Cyprus now. There'd also been some calls to be made to various places in the Middle East and to the sovereign bases in Cyprus, and while all this had been happening Bremner had crammed down two ham sandwiches. Then they'd packed into his car and he'd driven fast down to Whitehall, beating Salvesen and Vestey to it by a whisker.

Those two would have been enjoying a decent lunch, he guessed.

He finished, 'After that, Mrs. Swale, we won't detain you. We're grateful for your cooperation. For having come forward in the first place, particularly.' He heard Salvesen's bleat of 'Hear, hear,' then looked over Anne's head at Bruce Prentice as the SAS colonel made a move to intervene.

'Colonel Prentice?'

'I'd just like to put a few points on record, save Mrs Swale having to explain the background. If I may?'

Salvesen said, 'By all means. If Mrs Swale — '

She nodded, then sat with her hands folded in her lap, not looking at any of them while Prentice explained that she and her husband were separated, that his visit the night before had been unexpected and uninvited; then that his service with the SAS had included deployments in the Dhofar and in the Gulf States, as a result of which he spoke fluent Arabic. His service there and elsewhere had matched up to the highest standards of the SAS; his leaving the Regiment and then the Army had been brought about by personal problems which had led to a degree of alcoholism, contributing to the break-down of his marriage.

'I think that gives you as much of the background as you'd need.' He looked down at Anne: 'All right?'

She smiled her thanks; appreciating that his little speech had been mainly for her benefit, breaking the ice for her. She launched herself straight into an account of Charlie's call at the flat, everything he'd told her, as well as she could recall it. It seemed so little, *too* little to justify this Sunday assembly of high-powered people; although at one stage she became aware of having created a stir when she'd quoted Charlie as having told her that the operation involved 'rescuing some guy' from some place in the Middle East. At that point Bremner and the tall man, Salvesen – and then Vestey too, late on it but doing a double-take – looked sharply at Colonel Prentice, who spread his hands as if in apology. She'd faltered, now forged on again, dredging up every scrap that she could remember.

Finally there wasn't any more. She said, 'That's about it. Not very much, I'm afraid.' Verity stopped the tape, and Bremner said, 'Your contribution has been invaluable, Mrs Swale . . . I wonder – if we could steal another minute of your time – whether there may be any questions, while we have you with us . . . '

'Well, yes.' To her surprise, it was one of the young ushers who half-rose, half-bowed towards her. 'Just one question, if I may . . . When your husband was serving with the SAS, Mrs Swale, would you have expected him to discuss with you an operation on which he was about to embark?'

For a moment she felt like a witness about to be torn to shreds by Counsel. But she could see the point of the question, that it could be highly relevant. She told him, 'He always talked about – well, what it was like, how he felt, and so on. Without any details such as obviously would have been secret. But I suppose not *before*, either – where he'd be going or what for . . . I suppose really the answer to your question must be *no*.'

'His coming along and talking about it was a surprise to you, then.'

'His visit was a surprise anyway, it's hard to separate the two elements. What he *said* surprised me – which is why I telephoned Colonel Prentice. But – he did make the point that he was only guessing at Syria, so he wasn't revealing secrets – meaning conversely I suppose that if they had told him, he'd have kept his mouth shut . . . But also he had his own reason for wanting me to know. Leaving the Regiment really shattered him, and the fact – he *thought* it was a fact – that they'd given him a good reference as it were, to the SBS – well, he was very happy about it and he wanted me to know.'

The young man nodded. 'Thank you very much, Mrs Swale.'

'Excuse me.' The other lad now. 'Sorry – and this may seem an unnecessary question – but there is the possibility that he'd been *instructed* to give you that information . . . But one gets the impression that you quite unhesitatingly believed – believe now – that he was telling you the truth. Is that the case?'

'Yes, it is.'

'Might he not – conceivably – have been selling you a false bill of goods?'

'Not knowingly, no. I'm convinced he believed what he was telling me. He's an extremely forthright person – no liar, he'd be a truly rotten actor.'

Prentice had nodded agreement. The questioner glanced at Bremner, murmured, 'Thank you, Mrs Swale.'

'Right.' Prentice got up from the table. 'I'll run Mrs Swale home, then I'll come back.' Addressing Salvesen: 'If you'll excuse us. Actually I doubt if you'll need me again, but I'll remain available just in case. Having come all this way.' He nodded to the Royal Marine: 'See you presently.'

The Marine – his name was Charles Hislop – had confirmed, in answer to Salvesen's questioning, that there was no current SBS involvement in or near Syria, and that there'd been no approach to Charlie Swale.

He added, 'There'd have been no question of headhunting outside the Squadron anyway.'

'Ah.' Salvesen nodded. 'Major, I had no opportunity earlier on to thank you for joining us, at such short notice.'

'Since it's my Squadron's name that's being taken in vain . . . '

Bremner brought the subject back to Anne Swale's evidence. 'That was the first I've heard of Swale having said the objective was to rescue someone. Either she didn't tell Colonel Prentice, or he forgot to pass it on. So it's not in these notes, but it should've been.'

'Tightens the link with the Damascus Report, clearly.' Salvesen asked, 'Are we agreed there must be a link?'

Vestey nodded. 'Surely. One and the same conspiracy.'

'So what light might either throw on the other?' The DUS looked at Bremner. 'Can you develop your earlier theory now?'

'I'm convinced it's a set-up. Theorising, I'd say quite possibly Soviet-inspired. Plain fact being that a pseudo "SBS" team has left — I *think* they've already left — for a destination in or near Syria. We can take it as fact because in my view Swale does have to be believed.' He glanced at the assistant who'd been the second to question Anne Swale. 'You were right to consider the possibility he might have been primed with it — even believing it himself — but on reflection that won't wash, will it. Whoever's running him could hardly count on his spilling it to the wife, from whom he's separated. And he certainly couldn't reckon on her then passing it on to us via Swale's former CO. So we can forget *that*, I suggest . . . But as to the pseudo team's destination, I'm betting heavily on Cyprus. It's so much the most likely place — OK, places, plural — that Special Branch have a man on his way out there — ' Bremner checked his watch — 'in the air by now, flight to Larnaca, photograph of Swale in his briefcase.' He nodded to Prentice. 'Courtesy of the SAS, who were rushing it to Heathrow and please God *should* have made it to a rendezvous with this guy in the departure lounge. Otherwise he won't get away until this evening, which may be too damn late.' He shook his head. 'Could be too late even as it is . . . Anyway — the next logical step in our reasoning on this might be to ask what anyone would expect to gain by the deception. But hang on, I'll come back to that. First let's consider this — that what we know now, through Swale's leak to his wife, indicates that the Damascus Report was *not* planned disinformation, that it may have been a fortuitous leak giving us detail that even Swale didn't have.'

Salvesen frowned. 'I may be missing the point. If you've made it.'

'I'm leading to it. But I'll start again . . . Take it as read, Swale was telling his wife the truth as he sees it — he was about to leave for foreign parts in company with at least one individual whom he believed to be SBS, with the object of rescuing "some guy" — whom we can assume to be Stillgoe, target area therefore Syria. As he'd guessed, and as the Damascus Report alleges. But leaving that report aside for the moment, let's try to answer two questions. One, why would some group want to impersonate an SBS team and go into

Syria? Why in so doing would they take on the enormous complication of having to delude Swale as they have done?'

Salvesen murmured, 'Your questions, you answer them.'

Bremner nodded. 'But that task — convincing Swale — just *think* of it. Among the problems they'd have had to face must be that they can only travel out there on a civilian flight, regular or charter.' He looked at the Royal Marine. 'Imagine having to sell that to a former SBS man, Major.'

'You wouldn't. No one in his right mind would buy it.'

'So it's lucky for them that Swale may *not* be in his right mind.'

'Hardly luck, if they picked him for it.'

Bremner smiled agreement. 'Another factor is that being ignorant of SBS ways of going about things, and wanting to go along with them anyway, he'd adopt a "when in Rome" attitude and simply accept it all. On top of which it's conceivable that the planners may have underestimated some of the problems, just had the luck to get away with it. *So far*, they've got away with it: let's hope to God . . . ' He checked himself, and went on, 'But anyway — answers to those questions, now. Or attempts at answers . . . To question one — well, they sure aren't doing it for our comfort. The aim has to be to drop us in the shit, have the world see us as involved in some — well, some thoroughly invidious situation. A frame-up, in fact. And at this point I'd refer back to our conclusion this morning — conclusion reached on the basis of the Damascus Report alone, remember — that there might be a Soviet involvement in an attempt to lure us into Syria. It'd be a trap, and we saw it as a strong enough possibility to warn us off any such physical intervention.'

Salvesen nodded. 'Check.'

'Well, we also asked ourselves whether they'd really expect us to fall for it, and we concluded they might *if* they appreciated the value we put on getting Stillgoe out. But suppose they decided we *wouldn't* go for it, that we'd be too canny? Then might their solution not be to ensure that an "SBS" team went in anyway — *their* team?'

'For the sake of argument, we might accept this, I suppose.' Salvesen added, 'With a fairly hefty pinch of salt. Seems rather far-fetched to me, anyway — despite awareness that there are more things in heaven and earth, etc . . . But where would it get us in relation to your second question? What's Swale's part in this scenario?'

Bremner steepled his fingers, stared across them at the DUS . . .

'If the scenario's more or less as I've outlined it – and far-fetched or not, I'd say it has to run pretty close to it – well, consider *this*. What if the pseudo "SBS" could take in with them a British special-force officer, who after they'd got in there – ' he paused, frowning, wanting to get it right first time – 'look, I'm thinking aloud, putting it together as I go – '

'They'd leave him behind, wouldn't they.'

The Marine had suggested it. Everyone except Bremner looking towards the door at that moment as Bruce Prentice arrived back. Bremner was staring at the SBS man: approvingly again, appreciating a mind that *saw* things, as his own did . . . 'Yes, that's it. If I were planning this, Swale would be destined to fall into Syrian hands. Captain Swale, SAS – nobody's going to believe *ex*-SAS . . . Imagine it – they've nabbed him, and he believes he went in there with the SBS, he's sure of it. Anyone's guess what they've been up to. An attempt at assassinating Al-Assad, something of that nature?'

'No, surely.' Vestey piped up. 'Swale would know they'd had the rescue mission as their objective, wouldn't he?'

'Nobody has to believe him. And it's what happens after they get into Syria that would count. Which is up to *them* – and whether he likes it or doesn't, by that time Swale's part of it.'

Salvesen muttered, 'Oh, Lord . . . ' Glancing round then at another interruption. One of Bremner's aides, the one who'd asked whether Charlie ordinarily discussed SAS business with his wife, had left the room at about the same time as Prentice had taken Anne Swale away, and now he was back, virtually on Colonel Prentice's heels. He was offering Bremner a file of notes, and the MI6 man was scanning them swiftly . . . 'Nothing?'

'Afraid not.'

Charles Hislop was talking quietly to Prentice, bringing him up to date on progress. Bremner nodded to the young man: 'All right. Thanks.' He looked up at Salvesen as the DUS asked him, 'One point in connection with your admittedly very frightening scenario, John. If persons unknown *were* sending in this team impersonating Special Boat Squadron, why would they have alerted us by leaking the Damascus Report?'

'I think you could take your pick of two answers. One, they did *not* leak it – not deliberately. This would mean that Stillgoe *is* there, of course: in which case I admit I don't immediately see the tie-up ... So forget that, and we're left with the situation as I've guessed at it – our heads already in the trap, nothing we can do but wait for it to be sprung. Then screams of protest, world headlines and not an Arab alive prepared to give us so much as the time of day thereafter.'

'And the leak *was* deliberate, you're assuming, so – '

Bremner snapped his fingers. '– so it's on record here. We were told – by the ambassador in Damascus – we've spent the whole day trying to sort it out. Could *you* go before a Select Committee – or even face a mob of probing journalists – and swear you'd never heard of it?'

'But – heard of what, exactly?'

'Of the reported fact of Stillgoe being in Syria. Where by that time an allegedly SBS team will have intruded and – well, God knows *what*.'

The DUS sat speechless, absorbing it. Vestey muttered, 'We'd be saying no, we did not send in the SBS or anyone else. But we'd also have to admit we knew Stillgoe was there, within reach of the coast.'

'Exactly.' Bremner nodded. 'Who's going to believe for ten seconds that HMG had *not* sent those people in?'

'We could be barking up an entirely imaginary tree.' Salvesen – searching for a straw to clutch at. 'It's pure hypothesis, you must admit.'

'Yes, I do admit. But it also happens to meet the questions that otherwise seem unanswerable. I'd be delighted if someone would come up with an alternative scenario, one that fits and *doesn't* give me the shivers. *Sure*, it's guesswork, but – look, that use of Swale, for instance – ' he nodded towards the SBS man – '*his* guess, not mine – it'd be savagely effective, and I can't think of any other reason they'd want him.' Turning

122

to Vestey — 'But Hugh — a minute ago you said something about Stillgoe being "within reach of the coast". I think we should bear in mind that although the Damascus leak probably *was* deliberate, we may not have been meant to know the precise location. Seems a bit odd, I know, but this was the view expressed in the ambassador's report, wasn't it. And he has the girl there — Miss Thornton — I mean he has the story straight from the horse's mouth, we've no business ignoring it.'

'So what deduction — '

'Logically, that the report wasn't supposed to include information that might put us in a position to take any preventive action, surely.'

'So the point's academic, unless we *were* contemplating a military response.'

'Since we've ruled out any such — yes . . . ' Bremner shrugged. 'The snag is, of course, that if we take no action — well, we're on to a hiding to nothing, aren't we.'

Allowing time for comments from any of them, he reached for the notes his assistant had left with him. Prentice had nodded, agreeing with that last observation; the Royal Marine, who'd been jotting down notes from time to time, looked thoughtful as he made another.

'May as well tell you — ' Bremner, starting up again — 'what we and others have been doing in the last few hours, in the hope of stopping these people short of their target . . . These are lists of flights from British airports to destinations in and around the Eastern Med. Quite a few such destinations would put them in reach of the Levantine coast. From Heathrow, for instance, flights to Larnaca in Cyprus at 0935, 1445, 2100. Cyprus is still busy with tourists at this time of year, incidentally . . . Or, they could be flying to Istanbul and from there to Ercan in Turkish Cyprus. Flights 0855 and 1236. From Ercan they might use Famagusta for embarkation — don't ask me embarkation in *what*. Kyrenia could be an alternative, up in the Turkish half, but it's on the wrong coast, isn't it, not at all convenient. Same applies to Paphos in the south — too far west. Not that this has to rule either of those places out, but — '

'Isn't there some kind of airfield at Paphos?'

He nodded to Bruce Prentice. 'Was. Abandoned, now. Anyway — it doesn't *have* to be Cyprus, you see. Beirut, maybe — or Damascus, Athens, Cairo. Or charter flights — not so many now, admittedly — to such places as Crete or Rhodes. But Special Branch and/or Five have covered the lot now, and the name Swale — all we have to go on, isn't it — doesn't appear on any list at all. Myself, I'd bet on Cyprus, but . . . ' he shrugged — 'anyone's guess . . . And all right, they could have left via some continental airport — if they'd had any reason to suspect we might be on their trail. This takes us into the area of private charter aircraft — hire companies, flying clubs. Our colleagues aren't overlooking any of it, but so far they've drawn blank; and as I see it, we'll either get our clue *now*, or never. My own people have been alerted, of course, and Special Branch have a man on his way out to Larnaca. He'll check there, and Famagusta and Kyrenia, and also follow up any leads from RAF Intelligence. We've asked for their help, and from the Army at Dhekelia. From Akrotiri they'll be checking on any reports of foreign bodies on their own doorstep at Limassol, and I hope also Paphos. Liaison with harbour masters, and so on. From Dhekelia they should cover exits from Larnaca and Famagusta. Somewhat needle-in-haystack, mind you, hell of a lot of yachts around to confuse the issue. But there we are . . . Oh, Special Branch were getting a warrant, they'll have been into Swale's flat by now, in case he left a diary note or anything. But that's it. Unless we strike lucky in the next hour or two — ' he dropped his notes on the table — 'well, frankly, short of military intervention of some kind — and let's not forget they may be smarter than my scenario gives them credit for, this entire act could be aimed at forcing us to react . . . '

He'd checked his own flow of words. Vestey said, 'If our ambassador in Moscow can get to Assad — which he surely will unless there *is* Soviet involvement in this business — '

'Yes.' Salvesen looked like a man having a bad dream. 'That "unless" is certainly valid. Although failure to contact him might not be *proof* of Soviet involvement. Assad's own posture, in the shadow of the Hindawi trial, for one thing . . . ' He shook his head and glanced at Bremner. 'If you're right in your guesses and we can't get through to him, just sit and twiddle our thumbs in the hope that sooner or later contact *should* be established . . . ' A pause, as if seeking words, solutions. 'Well. You're right — a hiding to nothing.'

Bremner had nothing to add. He'd said it already. The DUS looked at Prentice and at the Royal Marine beyond him. He said quietly, carefully, rather as if he was aiming to play down the import of the question, 'To enable us to make recommendations that take into account whatever options may be open to us — especially as they don't at this stage seem to be exactly numerous — how would you advise on the practicability or otherwise of some kind of physical intervention?'

Prentice murmured, 'Your shout, Charles.'

'Well.' Hislop's calm eyes held Salvesen's. 'If we could get out there fast, and if these people's boat — or ship, whatever — can be identified — ' he glanced at Bremner — 'which let's hope may result from the steps you've taken — '

'But then surely — ' Prentice suggested — 'we might ask the Greeks or the Turks to arrest them, in whichever harbour — '

'Hardly.' Bremner explained, 'Very sensitive toes all over Cyprus, one needs to tread warily. I'm sure the FCO would advise extreme caution?' They both nodded; Bremner added, 'Apart from the Graeco-Turk confrontation, with assorted Blue Berets on the *de facto* border between them, we have Athens tending to support Damascus, the whole place alive with Syrians on holiday, PLO on leave or otherwise, Israeli spooks — well, my God, you name it!'

'I was about to say — ' Hislop continued — 'we'd stop them at sea. In international waters. No problems of trespass, and no tracks or traces. We'd intercept, take Swale away from them — I don't know what you'd want done with the others — '

'What if identification of their boat isn't possible, Charles?'

'Well, at a pinch, with cooperation from the Crabs — '

Prentice translated, 'Royal Air Force.'

'Nimrods, for surveillance, then to spot the target and guide my blokes to it.' He looked at Prentice. 'Or if Nimrods weren't available, maybe the Cousins might help. *Saratoga's* there now, isn't she — with E-2s on board — '

Salvesen said, 'Sounds as if you're about to save our bacon, Major.'

'Well.' The SB man qualified, 'If we can get out there in time. It'd mean moving *extremely* fast.'

7

In the Joint Operations Centre in the Ministry of Defence, Charles Hislop spoke quietly, privately, into a green telephone – a protected line – in the corner near the door.

'All right, Harry. Get on with it, set it all up on those lines, and I'll get back to you as soon as I can. But Harry, listen now . . .'

He glanced round into the space behind him, at the half-dozen men around a narrow central table, and had his glance met by an impatient stare from the major-general who this evening was Duty Operations Director; he was currently occupying the red-upholstered, metal-frame chair that was officially reserved for the Minister. Between him and the end of the table another chair had just been vacated by an SAS major, the duty Special Forces Adviser; he was returning to it now, scanning a computer readout. This was the Special Forces section of the JOC, which comprised a number of component offices separated by partitions which in a full-scale emergency, anything like a real war, could be taken down, converting the whole area into one big Ops room.

This was effectively a ways-and-means conference. The political considerations had been taken to higher levels by the Foreign Office DUS, Paul Salvesen, and meanwhile from here the military conclusions would wind up as proposals for submission to the Minister of Defence and Chief of the Defence Staff. Hislop checked the time – 1802 – as he turned back to resume his private conference with his own second-in-command, a hundred miles away on the Dorset coast.

'Harry, assume it's on, except for the signal to go. You said the boats are loaded? Right, get the truck away – *now*. The rest of the gear can follow with the lads, by helo . . . Yeah, two Wessex, they'll be coming up to you from Eastleigh. Have the team ready, Harry, geared up and briefed – OK, as far as you *can* brief them . . .'

Some would be on the base already – those who'd had the weekend duty – but others would be at their homes nearby, would at this moment be taking leave of wives, children, girlfriends. Knowing from experience that they might be gone for a few hours or for several weeks: and knowing not a damn thing else . . . Two two-man crews for the Sea-Rider inflatables and two four-man boarding parties, making twelve ranks in all.

Despite the fact the use of the Squadron hadn't yet been ordered.

It would be, though, it couldn't *not* be, Hislop thought. The threat plainly had to be countered – even the civil servants had seen that much; and just as plainly it was a job that only the SBS was equipped to handle. He'd been sure of it when he'd left that last meeting. Salvesen had been dashing off to see his Permanent Under-secretary, and the PUS would as likely as not have been in touch with Downing Street by now; while Hislop had got straight through to Poole, issued a Warning Order and told his 2 i/c to call an 'R' Group – R for reconnaissance – which was the meeting now in progress down there.

The major-general murmured, as he rejoined *this* meeting, 'You're trying to be in two places at once, Hislop. Might be more productive to conclude our business here first?'

'I'm sorry, sir.' Looking over other men's heads at the teletext tv monitor on its bracket at the far end of the room. Nothing of relevance on it at this moment, no report of any fracas on some Middle East airport for instance. Hislop added, running his eyes over the computer displays lining the right-hand wall, 'Fact is, though, we could be too late already.'

He looked round at the SAS major: 'What was that, Frank?'

'Your point about asking the Cousins for help in the air. Obvious question comes back – what's wrong with Nimrods?'

'Nothing at all, I hope. Except we're told – that signal in your hand – there are only two machines out there. If we can have them both full-time, and guaranteed air-worthiness – fine. But we *must* have it round the clock. Also – well, frankly the Hawkeye's capability – look, we might have to track them a long way over, and if there's any Syrian air about it could be a lot easier – safer, I'd imagine – from the kind of stand-off position the E-2s could operate from?'

'Aren't we talking about an interception in *international* waters?'

'We are, sir.' He nodded to the general. '*Aiming* for that. But we're starting late even if we could start this minute.' He nodded towards the telephone he'd been using. 'Why I'm trying to have my chaps on the top line. The opposition have had about a day's start on us, and the Syrians claim thirty-five miles of territorial water, which doesn't leave a lot to spare between Syrian and Cypriot. In places, none, there's an over-lap. Obviously we'd rather stop them in deep water . . . Which brings me back to the fact that the air's vitally important, Nimrod availability may be uncertain, and we know the USS *Saratoga*'s there with Hawkeyes embarked.' He paused for breath. 'All right, I know, I'm looking for belt and braces, but we can't intercept them if we don't locate them!'

The general half-smiled. 'We'll try it on, anyway.'

Meaning he'd pass the request with the rest of this meeting's proposals to the Minister and the CDS, who if he agreed would most likely make a scrambled transatlantic call to the chairman of the Joint Chiefs at the National Command Center in Washington. From there on, if the Cousins looked favourably on the idea, the 6th Fleet's commander would get orders directly from the Pentagon.

Hislop added, 'Obviously our request for Nimrod patrols still stands. To start at daylight tomorrow morning. And who knows, with a bit of luck we might get an early sighting. In which case we won't bother them.'

'Question here that needs answering – ' the Special Forces Adviser ticked the next line on his agenda – 'is what action's to be taken, following interception, in regard to (a) Swale's companions, (b) their boat.'

The general glanced at Hislop. The point had been touched on earlier, but they'd lost it in some interruption. 'What's your view on this?'

'Only that once we've snatched Swale, if this afternoon's assessment of enemy intentions is accurate they're knackered, aren't they. Plan's defused, we can call it a day.'

'Allowing the rest to sail off into the sunset?' The DOD showed surprise. 'What if the appreciation's wrong and they could do it without him? And other British nationals in the team, for all we know?'

'If there were, they'd be removed with Swale, but – '

'If I might make a point?'

A middle-aged civilian: thickset, balding, sporting a Gunners' tie. This was the Secretariat Officer, the basics of whose function amounted to liaison between this Ministry and the Foreign Office.

The general nodded. 'Go ahead, Mr Bennett.'

'Well, they're terrorists, potentially highly dangerous, and I'd have thought – well, isn't it likely they'll resist the boarding operation?'

Hislop nodded. 'Very likely.'

'I'd have thought that gave us the answer. They're our committed enemies, and if they show fight – I'd have thought you'd deal with them appropriately. In the course of the action their boat might well be sunk – right? – so there'd be no mess, no repercussions, and no threat remaining. Eh?'

The DOD stared at Hislop, inviting comment. 'The final decision won't be made in this room, of course, but – '

'Well.' It might have been, to all intents and purposes, if the Minister had been present. Except he'd probably have wanted to take advice. Hislop hoped the ratification wasn't going to take all night: his hope was that Salvesen's chief *would* have gone to Downing Street, to cut some corners . . . He answered the general, 'Mr Bennett's point's logical enough – kill them, destroy their boat, threat eliminated and no backwash. But we aren't in that line of business, frankly, it's very important that we don't act like terrorists ourselves –

the way these guys are trying to *make* us look, in point of fact.' He added, 'OK – if we're shot at, we shoot back. And we aren't trained to miss. Then we'd end up with bodies on our hands, and in that event you're right, we wouldn't leave signatures, we'd – well, common sense, isn't it . . . But apart from that contingency, which might be forced on us, the alternatives on which I'm asking for a directive are should we remove Swale – and any other Brits, certainly – and let the rest go on their way, or should we arrest them all, take them and their boat into one of the sovereign bases? Dhekelia, I suppose. If we want to take the thing apart and establish who was behind it?'

A quarter-hour later the JOC meeting's conclusions were on their way to the Minister, with copies to Chief of the Defence Staff, Commandant-General Royal Marines and Chief of the Air Staff.

If the Minister didn't like the proposals, if he developed cold feet and sent the plan back – well, you could forget it, Hislop thought, everyone could run home and put their heads under the bedclothes.

Back at the green telephone, waiting for his secure-line reconnection with Poole, he checked the time. A few minutes short of six thirty.

'Ah, Harry . . . It's sewn up here, now, except we have to wait for approval from above, which with luck may not be long coming . . . Listen – on the equipment side, if you haven't thought of this already – they might have to scuttle whatever kind of craft these people are using, so better take along PE and accessories.'

'PE' being plastic explosive, 'accessories' such items as igniters, Cordtex and timers. Cosgrave noted that down, although he was fairly sure it would be on the list already. Adding a note against it, the name of Marine Hall . . . 'We're about done here, too. Most of 'em are in, the boats are on their way – '

'Who are you giving Ockley as his number two?'

'Colour Sergeant Kelso, sir.'

'Couldn't be better. Ockley there yet?'

'Here beside me.'

'Tell him I'll meet him at Lyneham. Any particular problems there?'

He couldn't think of any: except not having much idea what the task was. He said, 'I suppose when *you* fill in the gaps – '

'Exactly. Listen – got a photographer on the team?'

'Sergeant Wilkinson?'

'Right.' Photographs came in handy, sometimes, as evidence in post-mortems, reconstructions of events . . . 'All right, Harry. I'll have the helos sent up to you now.'

Harry Cosgrave – he was a captain, as were most of the men present – hung up the phone and went back to his chair at the top end of the battered old dining-table which stood centrally in the shabby conference room. Giving them the gist of what the CO had been telling him – which still left a lot of detail unanswered . . . The CO had obviously been immersed in the business all day, but Cosgrave had had his sketchy briefing in somewhat disjointed telephone calls and he still felt that he was flying blind.

But then, instant reaction to crisis calls was the name of the game, and by no means unusual.

Cosgrave said, 'CO'll be meeting the team at Lyneham. Ben, you can throw out any gear you think's superfluous in the light of that more detailed briefing, to come back on the truck that's taking the boats up.' He looked down the length of the table: 'Mr Henderson, check what's down there for weapons, will you?'

Blackie Henderson, the Squadron's sergeant major, Warrant Officer II, knew the answers without having to consult his notes.

'SA80 Individual Weapons for all ranks. M79 grenade-launcher, one per boat, ditto LAWs.'

SA80 IWs were submachine-guns, 4.85-mm, still quite new on the scene. And an LAW was a light anti-tank weapon, disposable. When you'd fired it you'd drop it over the side. *If* you fired it: if the boat they were going to intercept made that necessary.

Cosgrave was reading through the rest of his scribbles, which dated from the CO's first two calls and weren't all that legible. Discussions on other points were in progress around the table; the officers present speaking for Intelligence, Signals, Operations, Logistics, Admin. Plus the sergeant major at the other end, painstakingly recording it all in longhand, and Ben Ockley who'd been the last to arrive and whom the CO had nominated as team leader. He'd been reading the script over Blackie Henderson's shoulder, and he was coming up to Cosgrave's end now, pulling up a chair beside the 2 i/c. Movements loud, echoey on the bare floorboards. This was a prefabricated building, single-storey, nondescript enough to be mistaken for a youth-club headquarters in some run-down city centre. Maps covered all the wall space, doubtless also covered a lot of cracks and blemishes.

'Drybags over DPMs?'

Drysuits, and DPM stood for Disrupted Pattern Material, camouflage-pattern khaki-green overalls. At the moment, Ockley was wearing old drill trousers, sweatshirt and anorak, with a very scruffy pair of trainers on his feet. Straight from a relaxed Sunday evening at home with his wife and baby daughter.

Cosgrave had nodded. 'But fly out in uniform. Can't guess how long you may be at Akrotiri, but allow for two or three days. Weapons – you just heard. Three magazines of SA80 per man, and three anti-personnel grenades.'

Checking his notes . . .

'Oh, one set of PNG in each boat, also starscopes.'

'But touch wood the interception will be in daylight.'

'Let's hope.' He agreed, and added, 'But we're also giving you VHF in the boats, just in case you need it.'

Night interception by para drop with Sea-Riders wasn't all that simple. Not even with the aid of PNG, passive night goggles. The lightweight kind they'd take with them would extend night vision up to about 800 metres – if the lenses could be kept dry – but even then there could be problems.

Ben Ockley, Cosgrave noticed without any great degree of surprise, wasn't allowing those or any other problems to upset him. There was a glint of enthusiasm in those deepset, wide-spaced eyes, and – Cosgrave guessed – *joy* inside that tough skull . . . He hoped the CO was being wise in giving Ockley this break. He could follow the reasoning: the fact it was high time Ben had a chance to prove himself – having been unlucky on a few previous occasions – and that he was a first-class soldier, natural leader and – another essential quality in the SB Squadron – a fast thinker on his feet. So why *not* give him the job? The answer – Cosgrave's anyway, but the CO must also have taken it into consideration – was that Ben had about as much political acumen or finesse as a bull-terrier.

It wasn't a bad analogy. Looking at him analytically you could well imagine that if he'd been a dog he'd have been one of that breed. And at that, one of the sort you'd keep on a chain, muzzled.

Actually he looked exactly what he was – a cold-eyed, hard-headed, extremely professional young officer, whom you wouldn't want to run into on a dark night, or even in broad daylight, if you weren't on his side. And it could be argued that the CO had picked just the right job for him. The task was simply to lead a para drop into the sea, intercept a boat – guesses were that it would be some kind of fast launch – grab a Brit out of it and bring him back. The whole task to be performed at sea and with any luck out of sight of land: thus with no sensibilities to offend, no foreigners to annoy. In this respect it might be said that the CO hadn't so much picked the man for the job, as the job for the man.

Not that Ben was stupid. Not in the least. He was from Preston, Lancashire, and at Manchester University he'd won a good degree in Maths and Physics. It just happened to be a fact that the sort of jobs the Special Boat Squadron was asked to carry out, in peacetime, did very often call for those qualities of diplomacy which Ben Ockley lacked.

Or maybe – Cosgrave wondered privately – disdained?

'I'll have Sticks Kelso with me – right?'

'Yes.' Cosgrave nodded. Other consultations were in progress around the table. 'I suppose you'll give him the second boat. That'll leave you the choice of Sergeants Hosegood or Wilkinson to have with you.'

Ockley dug in his pocket for a coin. 'Heads it's Hosegood, tails Wilkinson.' He span the coin, caught it and slapped it down. 'Hosegood.' Cosgrave had pushed the list of names towards him; Ockley added, glancing at it and not making any great effort in the selection, 'And Marines Hall and Judge. Leaving Sticks burdened with Sergeant Wilkie, Corporal Laker and Marine Teal. Serve him fucking well right.'

The sergeant major said, grinning, 'Boats' coxswains are Sergeant Hattry and Corporal Clark. Crewmen Marines Deakin and Kenrick.'

Ockley pretended to shudder. 'My God.' He scraped his chair back. 'I'd best go and get 'em sorted.'

Get some food into them, he was thinking, letting the flimsy door slam shut behind him. That list of names was in his head, but they weren't just names, they were men with faces, brains, personalities, quite exceptional individuals every one of them and *his* guys now, the team who'd pull off this simple job like the pros they were, and who'd better be fed now because God only knew what time of night they'd get to Lyneham; the RAF could be counted on to have shut down their kitchens, and it was a yomp of about a mile and a half across that great sprawl of airbase to the canteen, where if you were lucky and it happened to be open they just *might* not have sold the last Mars Bar . . .

'Hey, Sticks!'

Colour Sergeant John Kelso. Still known as 'Sticks' because when he'd joined the Royal Marines at the age of sixteen he'd been enrolled as a Junior Bugler, drummer-boy, for which the traditional form of address was 'Sticks', and the sobriquet had – so to speak – stuck.

Kelso had halted, swung about, saluted. 'Sir!'

A big man: well over six feet of hard-packed bone and muscle, heavy brows, thick moustache, close-cropped hair like a bristly cap on his rounded cranium. But for all that a surprisingly thoughtful set of features, a lot of intelligence looking out through the tough exterior. Looking *down*: Ockley was only five-eight.

A grin . . . 'Coming along for the ride, are you, Ben?'

'Thought I might. Have the lads all reported in?'

'Ready to go. Except Marine Hall.'

'What's up with Hall?'

'Just landed. Been windsurfing. I told him he can shift in the helo, sent him in to scoff with the rest of 'em.'

'Eating now, are they?' *Might've known* . . . 'Helos are

135

said to be on their way. When they arrive we load up and sit tight, wait for the word . . . Look, one thing -- Sarbes. Make sure the batteries are all good, eh?'

SARBE was an acronym for Search and Rescue Beacon. Each man would have one slung round his neck or fixed to his drysuit; they were essential life-savers. He added, 'I'll check stores and weapons myself before we leave.'

'Thought you might . . . Are we likely to be told what the task is, before we go?'

'You bet. CO'll be meeting us at Lyneham.'

He went to his own quarters, in this large base of which the SBS occupied only a minor section. The light was fading rapidly. He had to shift into uniform now, and pack the kit he needed. He'd been at home when the call had come, with Mary and the kid, Julia, who was now eighteen months old and a midget duplicate of her mother, who was − frankly − beautiful, and who had her head screwed on well enough not to have fussed at all, not to have cried or even told him to 'take care' or any of those standard expressions of anxiety. In fact the opposite, she'd looked and sounded glad for him, for the chance he was being offered and which he'd been longing for. She'd clung to him for a few moments with her face hidden against his shoulder; it was all she'd needed, about fifteen seconds in which to get her act together.

Charles Hislop, waiting in the JOC for a ministerial decision, which he hoped to God *might* come accompanied by the Chief of the Defence Staff's endorsement, avoiding yet more waste of precious time − took a call from John Bremner of MI6. Bremner was telephoning to report that checks at various Mediterranean airports had produced no results, as yet. At some places, he'd admitted, local cooperation was often not as wholehearted or efficient as one would have liked; this wasn't new, it was about par for the course, you could be sure of results only if you had time to put your own people in; and time was the one commodity everyone was short of, right now.

Hislop said, 'Only hope is to concentrate on Cyprus. And move *now*, and *fast* − when I'm allowed to, for Christ's sake.'

'Absolutely. If you're to have any chance at all of stopping them at sea.'

'That *is* the point. Because if we miss out — well . . .'

'Right.' Knowing as well as the SBS commander did that an intrusion on land would never be sanctioned . . . Bremner said, 'Special Branch, incidentally, have sent out *two* men, to Larnaca. One'll go north, the other'll coordinate enquiries in the Greek half. We've some problems, potentially, with the Greeks, you know, wouldn't be wise to expect much help from them. Specially in relation to Syrian affairs.' He paused. 'I gather your deployment hasn't been approved yet?'

'Waiting for it now, John. I thought this call might have been it.'

'I'll clear the line, then. Will you let me know, when — '

'Someone will.'

Availability of aircraft had been confirmed. A Hercules C130 was being made ready at Lyneham now and another would be provided at Akrotiri, would be ready for takeoff by the time the SBS team arrived. And Nimrod surveillance of the sea between Cyprus and Syria would be laid on — if the request was confirmed before midnight — from first light tomorrow. Also, if the decision was to go ahead, the CDS or his deputy would explain the situation to the Cousins in the hope that the *Saratoga*'s E-2s, little brothers of the AWACS, would be available if asked for.

Some of this information was still showing cryptically on one of the computer monitors. Impatient, and bored with seeing it there, Hislop was reminded of civil airport lounges, long waits at Heathrow and Gatwick with his wife and young sons and the seemingly unchangeable legend on the flight-departure screens: *Delayed. Wait in lounge.*

He knew perfectly well that a decision like this couldn't be made at the drop of a hat. But even so . . .

The door banged open, and the duty SF Adviser burst in. Seeing his expression, Hislop felt a surge of relief even before the SAS man told him, 'You're in business, Charles.'

Hislop's Gazelle helicopter from the east and the two West-land Wessex bringing the SBS team up from the south were converging on Lyneham when flight CY 327 from Heathrow

137

landed at Larnaca in southeast Cyprus. The two Special Branch inspectors, Jimmy Hayward and Ken Fellows, had brought only cabin baggage and were consequently among the first passengers to get out through Customs and Immigration. Pushing their way out through the throng they were already sweating, in suits which in England they'd thought of as lightweight. Hayward himself was about a stone *over*weight, and feeling it.

'Looks like our guy there, Ken.'

Pointing – at a young man in jeans and T-shirt, but with a somewhat military style of haircut, who was holding up a square of cardboard. He spotted them too, in the same moment that Hayward got a clear sight of that board, their names on it. He led the way over.

'I'm Hayward, and this is Inspector Fellows. You'd be from what I believe is known as the sovereign base?'

'From Dhekelia, yessir. Sergeant Ross, RCT. I've two cars here. I was told one of you may want to go up to Kyrenia?'

'Me.' Jimmy Hayward nodded. Actually he didn't *want* to go there, he'd far sooner have stayed in the Dhekelia base with people who spoke his own language, but he and Fellows had tossed for it and he'd lost. 'Do I get driven?'

'If that's what you'd like, sir. In that case we'll have to go into Dhekelia first, that's all. On the other hand, long as you've a valid licence – '

'I can drive myself.' He wiped sweat off his forehead. 'OK.'

Instant decision – because this was a rush job and he didn't want to hang about. Ordinarily he'd have preferred to drive himself, anyway. Now, he almost changed his mind: he wasn't a globe-trotter by any natural inclination, tended to find foreigners irrational as well as incomprehensible. Maybe he should have been opting for a driver, who'd know his way around ... Ross had turned away, though, shouldering a path towards the exit, checking with Fellows, 'You'll be coming into Dhekelia with us, sir – will you?' With him and the other driver – a private soldier who climbed out of a black Ford Escort and told Hayward its tank was about full, road-map on the seat ... 'Thirty-five kilometres to Nicosia, then near enough twenty to Kyrenia, sir. North from here into Larnaca town, then it's sign-posted – follow your nose, can't go wrong.'

Accepting that instruction at its face value, nodding. Later, he'd remember it. He peeled off his jacket, tossed it into the back with his case. 'Bloody hot here. This time of night, too?' Easing himself under the wheel . . . 'Always like this in October, is it?'

'It was warmer last week.'

'*That's* a comfort.' He asked the sergeant, 'D'you know if they've picked up our bloke's tracks, or spotted his boat?'

'Wouldn't know, sir.' Ross looked blank. 'Guy on the run, is it?'

'No matter. Thought they might've told you.' He looked at Fellows. 'Can't be any news, Ken, there'd 've been a message. I'll push on.'

At Lyneham, Hislop left his pilot to get the Gazelle refuelled, and crossed over to the terminal building, the passenger-processing section. RAF Lyneham is a huge establishment, acres of buildings and service roads as well as the sprawl of airfield on which tonight the only signs of activity were those surrounding three parked Hercules C130s – illuminated from their interiors, light flooding the areas around them, cargo loading or off-loading in progress. One of them would be the Hercules which he'd requisitioned for the transit to Akrotiri. The Crabs obviously wouldn't send it out without utilising its full cargo capacity.

He must have passed through this place a hundred times, he thought, in recent years. He identified himself at the entrance and was directed through to find his men in one of the other rooms – again familiar, from countless arrivals and departures, hour upon hour of waiting. But on previous occasions this space had always been packed with Royal Marines and others, and tonight with only a dozen individuals scattered around – some on the benches, others chatting in small groups – there was an unnatural emptiness, a spooky feel about the place.

Crabs having a slack period, he thought as he walked in. A few Marines' heads turned casually, their expressions brightening then as they recognized him and scrambled to

139

their feet. A voice called, 'CO, sir!' and Ben Ockley strode over quickly to meet him.

'Evening, sir.'

'All set, Ben?'

'*We* are, sir. Crabs aren't hurrying any more than usual.'

In fact the loading was an intricate job that had to be done exactly right. The loadmaster's expertise lay in positioning the weights at precisely the right points; then the cargo had to be rigidly secured. The internal layout of a Hercules for cargo and personnel was extremely flexible, and every combination of loads was different from the last one; the fact was that the job could not be rushed, and Ben Ockley knew it as well as Hislop did. But it was a tradition, almost, to grouse about the Crabs; also, Hislop knew that if his SB detachment arrived in Cyprus an hour too late there'd be nothing for it but to turn them round and bring them home again. With ensuing disaster in the Middle East — 'disaster' being by no means too strong a word for it.

He raised his voice . . . 'Gather round me, so I don't have to yell, and I'll give you the background to this deployment.' Stopping in the middle of the room, clear of the benches, beckoning them in closer. Ben Ockley was beside him: he was a few inches shorter than Hislop, but — well, you could see it in his eyes and mouth, it would take twice his weight and five times his guts to stop him . . . Beyond him, closing in as ordered, was Geoff Hosegood: Hosegood was twenty-nine and he hadn't been a sergeant all that long. He had — Hislop taxed his memory — *two* young daughters now. Close to six foot, lean, with a floppy-looking dark moustache and a somewhat humorous expression . . . During the Falklands war, Marine Hosegood had been one of a team who'd gone into mainland Argentina to sabotage Exocet missiles; he'd been advanced to corporal soon after his return to the UK and qualifying as SC2 — swimmer-canoeist second class — and he was now an SC1 and one of the Squadron's most useful NCOs.

Overshadowed, of course, by Colour Sergeant Kelso, who'd just halted face to face with Hislop, at attention for a brief moment of mutual greeting but now relaxed again, that friendly look spreading across a face that was already darkening with stubble. Kelso had joined at sixteen and left in his mid-twenties when he'd been a sergeant; he'd left in the expectation of earning big money on the oilrigs, being then married to a girl who'd known how to spend every penny of his Royal Marine pay before he'd got it. He'd left the rigs when he'd seen oil prices falling and companies shedding workforce, and not being willing — then — to swallow his pride and rejoin the Corps he'd become a policeman. There, his pay vanished even faster, life became impossible in other ways as well, the marriage fell apart and John Kelso woke up to the fact that *this* was where his home was. Figuratively speaking: he had another as well now, and a new wife about whom he was quietly crazy.

Beside this outsize character, Sergeant Ray Wilkinson looked small, although he was a perfectly respectable five-nine. In his early days in the Corps he'd declined to allow his name to be put forward for a commission, but he'd certainly never wasted his talents. An accomplished artist, he was also a specialist in camouflage techniques; he'd earned himself a private pilot's licence, had ski'd for the Navy and was a skilled photographer.

Hislop asked him, 'How's that small boy of yours, Sergeant?'

'Mutinous, sir.'

Hosegood murmured, 'Must be in the blood.'

Another sergeant here was Bert Hattry, who was to cox one of the boats. A heavily-built man with a wide face and clipped moustache, his speciality inside the Squadron was communications — radio. He was also Squadron snooker champion. The other boat's coxswain, Corporal 'Froggie' Clark, was small, rather ugly, battered looking. A genius with outboard motors . . . Then, next to him in the circle, topping him by an inch or two, Marine 'Romeo' Hall. Hall was specialist in explosives and electrics, demolitions, and in the dismantling of booby-traps. Twenty-five now, he was engaged to a Bournemouth girl, but rumour had it that there was a paternity suit threatening from even nearer home. Physically he was similar to Ben Ockley: no more than average-sized but — as someone had expressed it recently about Ockley — 'twenty-eight pounds to the stone'.

141

Marine Dave Judge was a Londoner born and bred, and black, in Royal Marine logic and tradition therefore known as 'Chalky'. He was twenty-four, and a skilled mechanic with an HND.

Then there was Corporal 'Doc' Laker. Stocky, ginger-haired, younger looking than his twenty-five years. Andy Laker had done a medic's course with the Royal Navy and then a period on secondment to the National Health Service, working in the casualty department of a big hospital. Public school educated, he'd wanted to become a doctor but hadn't been able to make it academically. His uncle, a surgeon, had told him he should have arranged to have been born fifty years earlier; in those days he'd have been snapped up by any of the famous teaching hospitals purely on the strength of his performance as a Rugby scrum-half.

And Marine Teal. Tall, broad-shouldered, nicknamed 'Ducky'. Don Teal had been an apprentice jockey until at the age of eighteen he'd started growing so fast that he'd been obliged to dismount and rethink. He was twenty-three, and this would be his first operational deployment with the Squadron.

Beside Teal in the circle forming around the CO was Marine 'Wee Willie' Deakin, a Judo black-belt instructor, crewman in Hattry's boat on this outing. He was twenty-four. So was the guy behind him, Frank Kenrick, although by appearances Kenrick could have been several years older. Dark, craggy-faced, an Aberdonian whose forbears had all been trawler-men.

Charles Hislop's mild glance surveyed them all. 'Right, then, we'll start. At least, soon as someone's shut those bloody doors, we'll start . . .'

8

Leo, in the crowd straggling towards the terminal building at Ercan — in north Cyprus, about five kilometres east of Nicosia — felt an earlier nervousness returning. Which in itself was worrying: he knew that a trained observer saw the symptoms of anxiety, looked for them . . .

Maybe, he thought, he was reacting psychologically — superstitiously, more like — to the stroke of luck they'd had at Istanbul, where there'd been a *really* nasty moment or two. As if for good luck you'd have to pay sooner or later with the other kind.

Which was rubbish. The Turks wouldn't check the same passports twice, in any case.

Light from the terminal flooded across the apron. Baggage trucks were on their way out to the aircraft from which this crowd had just disembarked, back there where converging avenues of runway lights speared southeastward into surrounding darkness. Flashing reds and greens as decoration . . . Warm, sticky air; Turkish soldiers fondling rifles stared balefully at the passengers trooping past them. Leo wanted to be out of this, out on the boat and clear of land where he'd be able to breathe freely, think straight; being herded like this gave him a sense of claustrophobia which exacerbated lingering anxieties — especially about Charlie, the area that hadn't been checkable and which he'd therefore been forced to accept as an element of risk: the chance Swale hadn't been fooled at all, might have run straight to Special Branch last Monday night or Tuesday morning and ever since then followed their instructions.

Special Branch's, or someone else's.

The crowd was squeezed here, driven through the bottleneck into the building's even muggier heat. More armed soldiers loafing, watchful and vaguely hostile.

There *was* a passport check ahead . . .

He looked round, checking on the others' positions in what was now more or less a queue. Charlie was behind him, with two other people between them. They'd been together but – well, typical of Charlie, stopping, inviting some Turkish peasant to precede him . . . Leo couldn't see Tait at the moment, but Denham was in sight not far ahead, in company with the redhead and her boyfriend – skinny, pale, giggling drunk. Pete was helping them, carrying some of their stuff as well as his own while the girl steered the lad along. Meanwhile there was a delay – the Turks were dealing with their own nationals first, that side of the mob moving along quite fast.

He put his case down, rested the Duty-Free bag against it. Watching Pete with his arm round the girl, either whispering into her ear or nibbling it.

In Istanbul, over several rounds of drinks in a taverna to which their cab driver had delivered them, Charlie had asked Leo again, 'It *is* Syria – right?'

By that time they'd 'done' Istanbul. The driver had taken them on a guided tour – with stops for his friends to try to sell them carpets – of St Sophia, the Blue Mosque, the Topkapi Palace and the Mosque of Sultan Suleiman the Magnificent. He'd had other places of interest up his sleeve, but Charlie had dug his heels in: 'Bob, look. I'm as keen on bloody culture as the next guy, but we don't want to overdo it . . . If Mustapha here'd take us to some suitable *estaminet*, I'll buy us a Coca Cola – huh?'

He'd had plenty on the flight from Heathrow. Leo hadn't tried to ration him. Charlie Swale was a lot easier to handle when he'd had a few.

This time, after a glance around, Leo had finally answered

that question. 'Yeah. You guessed right, of course. Sorry I had to keep you in the dark this long, Charlie.'

'Why did you?'

'Because you drink a lot. You might've gone on the piss and blown it.'

'Bloody hell, Bob – '

'I apologize. But I couldn't take the risk. Anyway – you know now, OK?'

Charlie Swale, Leo thought as the queue began shuffling forward, was too ingenuous to be a double-crosser.

Unless he was very, *very* sly.

It was still a possibility. For instance, if he'd left the bug in place and called them from his office – Special Branch, or whomever . . . Now, he'd be their guide. They wouldn't want to spring the trap prematurely, they'd want to trail their quarry to the final destination. The real scoop would be to catch them on a boat loaded with weapons and crewed by PLO killers carrying fake Israeli passports.

He caught his breath. There was a plain-clothes hanger-on beside the uniformed man at the head of the queue. Short-legged, pot-bellied, doughy complexion, dark suit shiny with wear. He was checking his list as each passport was flipped open, held for a second, snapped shut again. No rubber-stamping here, they'd be checking the stamps already applied in Istanbul.

The redhead's boyfriend had an arm latched over Denham's shoulder. Mumbling to himself as he fumbled with the other hand for his passport. Then he was through . . . And the girl, who'd passed through ahead of them, was coming back – taking his arm, the stout guy in the baggy suit asking some question as she did so but aiming it – apparently – at Pete. Who was taking no notice, leering at the girl, not aware he was being spoken to. But she fielded the question for him, called to the official, 'Sure, the Deniz Kizi!'

'All? All togezzah?'

The boy waved his free arm: '*Sure*, together!' Wanting corroboration from Pete: 'Right, mate?'

The Turk sniffed in distaste at the stink of *raki* in that waft of breath, and turned his back on them. The uniformed man gestured to the girl, wanting the nuisance removed. The queue

145

advanced. Tait had his passport checked, stalked on through. Then Leo: the straight routine, no speech. Clear of the desk he moved on slowly so Charlie could catch him up, but not so slowly as to make it obvious they were together.

Just in case . . .

The one in uniform took Charlie's passport and thumbed it open. The other man asked him, 'You Deniz Kizi?'

'Never heard of him, old son.' He took the passport back, slid it into a pocket. The Turk shrugged, rolling his eyes upward – sick of it, giving up. Charlie murmured, 'Gracias, Senor.' There'd been no reference to any passenger list. Denham told him a few minutes later when they were getting into the taxi, 'Deniz Kizi's some hotel. My bird's booked there with her little feller.'

Hayward had made good time to Nicosia, and he was expecting to pass quickly through the town – since there was so little traffic at this time of night – and with luck get to Kyrenia in not much more than thirty or forty-five minutes. So far he'd enjoyed the drive – a good road, the satisfaction of making swift progress, and the rush of cooling night air with the scents of the Mediterranean in it – herbal, spicy, a fragrance that might make a fortune for anyone who could have packed it into aerosols.

Then he saw the barrier across the road ahead. And a guardhouse, lights blazing, Greek police backed by soldiers. Frontier post, the demarcation line between Greek and Turkish Cypriots. There'd be a Turkish checkpoint up the road, he supposed; between them the frontier was policed by a multi-national peace-keeping force from the United Nations Organisation. He took his foot off the gas, dimmed his headlights as he braked gently. He had plenty of ID – passport and other documents – but didn't intend to show his Special Branch card. There'd been no time for any request for permission for a British policeman to nose around outside the perimeters of the sovereign bases; he'd gathered, back in London, that such permission might in any case not have been easy to obtain. So he'd be on private business; he'd come to look up a friend, a yachtsman, who'd said he'd be calling in at Kyrenia at about this date.

He wound the window down, nodded to the Greek cop. 'Evening.'

'Pass?'

'Pass*port*. Sure . . .'

The man took it gingerly — maybe he couldn't read — and handed it to a colleague before stooping again to the open window. Dark-brown eyes, small hooked nose . . . 'Pass, you have?'

'I didn't know I'd need any special — '

'UN pass.' The Greek tapped the glass of the windscreen, for some reason. 'No UN pass, no go here tonight. Not have pass?'

'No one told me anything about any UN pass. But—'

A stream of Greek: and both of them shrugging: helpless, or uninterested, or both . . . Hayward tried, 'Look, I *have* to get to Kyrenia. To meet a British citizen who should be there but won't be for many hours, I could miss him if—'

'I excuse me.' Polite enough, but adamant. 'Sir is cross only with UN pass. *Sorry.*'

Follow your nose, can't go wrong, that RASC lad had said. Hayward felt like a clown himself, for not having known, not having made it his business to find out. Frustration and anxiety piling on tiredness: and the importance of this mission, the fact he might be wrecking a whole lot of other people's efforts if he did *not* get through to Kyrenia. OK, so Swale was most likely *not* there, but Christ Almighty, if he was, and now he missed him . . .

He took a grip on himself. It wouldn't help to get excited. 'All right. How — where — can I get a pass?'

'Hah.' Smile. One hand pulling back the other sleeve by an inch or so at the shaggy wrist; a finger tapped a gold-plated watch. 'Office close, all sleep. Morning, sir get pass. *Sorry.*'

From the airport the taxi had headed west to start with, about five kilometres into Nicosia's eastern fringe and then through the Turkish sector of the town, the Renault threading its way quite fast through empty streets. Charlie having no way of knowing, of course, that at one stage he was passing within two hundred metres of the Greek-manned checkpoint where

Inspector Jimmy Hayward of Special Branch was slumped behind the wheel of his Ford, a cigarette glowing brightly as he smoked it too fast – despite trying to make himself relax, accept the fact he was here till dawn at least. The need for diplomacy, for *not* throwing one's weight around or even trying to, had been stressed hard in London: so here he was, keeping the profile low, playing it cool, going quietly mad . . . Switching on the car's inside light to study once again the photograph of the man they'd sent him here to find in order to identify whatever boat he might be on: and not for a moment dreaming that the faint, distant squeal of tyres he'd just heard had come from a Renault taxi in which Swale was sitting beside the driver, pushing his foot into the taxi's floor in a subconscious effort to slow it as it approached the *next* corner . . . Jimmy Hayward was staring at – and memorizing – this photo of a large, strong-looking guy in Army captain's uniform. Dark, short hair, wide-set eyes, straight nose, cleft chin. He looked as if he'd need to shave twice every day. Height six-two and weight – according to a note on the back of the print – about fifteen stone. He'd been smooth-shaven when this had been taken, but in London someone had said he'd recently grown a moustache. Not that you'd count on this: experience had taught one that men on the run sometimes grew beards and/or moustaches simply in order to shave them off again as soon as an updated description had been circulated.

This fellow might not, technically speaking, be on the run, might not know there was anyone after him. If this was the case it should make it easier to pick him up.

Except that whatever boat he was in had probably already left Kyrenia, Famagusta, Limassol or Paphos. Or some damn beach or cove . . .

Hayward wondered whether bribery might work with these people. They were foreigners, so he guessed it might. But there was always the risk of it blowing back in your face; and in the circumstances and with the difficulties of communication . . . For instance, that bugger had said they didn't have a telephone that he could use, but from right here where he was sitting he could see the bloody wire!

He swore: added quietly, grimly to himself, *Much as I can*

fucking stand . . . Pushing the door open he got out, strutted towards the guardhouse. It was a strut, he knew it, he was too short-legged for the weight he was carrying. A policeman swung round to face him, and in the road beside the barrier a soldier also turned, not exactly levelling the carbine at him but damn nearly.

'Look here.' Voice well up, to give the bastard a better chance of understanding him. 'I must insist on using your telephone. You do have one in there – right?'

Charlie, in the front passenger seat of the taxi – the other three were crowded in the back – fingered his moustache. He hadn't become used to it, and since Anne had commented on it unfavourably he'd actively disliked it. She was right: he'd never bothered to grow one before, for the simple reason he didn't need it.

Except as camouflage, Bob's idea that it might help him to pass for a Syrian if he had to.

They were leaving Nicosia, driving out of its top-left corner with about twelve kilometres to go and a range of mountains to get over before running down to the coast.

He asked the driver, 'D'you speak English?'

'Speak very good!' The car swerved a bit, then straightened. He added, 'Little, little.'

Charlie laughed. 'Better than I speak Turkish, anyway. What do they call you – Mustapha?'

Heading due north now. He'd felt the swing on that long bend but he was reading the stars too, a clear sky making this no problem. The driver was protesting that his name was not Mustapha, but Ahmet. They'd been climbing, but the road as it bent to the north had levelled out again. They'd have climbed about five hundred feet, he guessed; there was a gleam of water off to the right, some lake . . . 'And where d'you live, Ahmet?'

'Me live?' He pointed, right ahead. '*Girne*, me.'

'What's that, a village?'

'Kyrenia, you say. *Girne*, Turk man say.'

'Ah, well, we live and learn . . . But this is a good deal for you, then.'

'You England?'

'Right. London.'

'Hah! Me brother, London!'

'Small world, Ahmet . . .'

Not a word from the rear. They could be sleeping. Comatose sardines. The road had begun to climb again, and at the top swung right. Charlie had meant that the driver had got himself a good deal with this late-night job that was also taking him to his home. But the chit-chat had run its course. He was waking up to the fact that the SBS thing was about to start, play-acting about finished, reality at the foot of these mountains. His thoughts switched back by six — nearly seven — days, to this total stranger Bob Knox issuing that astonishing invitation: *We want you with us . . . Guy to be extracted, Middle East . . .*

'There's the coast. See? Kyrenia, must be.'

Bob leaning forward, pointing in the dark. Way down, maybe as much as a thousand feet down, white buildings decorated a black shoreline, linked by lights and clusters of light, a concentration of it at one point, an indentation in the coast, black land against the flat gleam of the sea. The road descended through woods here, with a scent of pine and herbs, tangy air cooling now. Charlie asked as the cab swept round a sharp bend and trees shut off that view, 'Will we know where to find our boat?'

'Shouldn't be much of a problem. They'll be looking out for us, they knew we'd be on that flight.' Bob added, 'Anyway, it's a small place, and we know what the thing looks like, don't we.'

They were in the little port ten minutes later. A *very* small harbour, busy semi-circular waterfront, lights shimmering in the still water and yachts' masts motionless against the stars. The taxi's doors opened into a thrum of voices, music, restaurants still busy and noisy, their lights spilling down stone steps to the quay. From across the water a diesel rumbled, some craft's generator . . . Townsfolk and tourists strolling, staring at the newcomers. The driver asked, 'You ship here, you saying me?'

Charlie, Tait beside him, was looking up and down the crescent of moored boats, seeing nothing that resembled the one pictured in the brochure. These were all small and made of GRP, nothing like the sixty-foot timber vessel they'd been promised.

A dark mass dominating the eastern side of the basin had to be some kind of old fort or castle, its upper edge a clearcut horizontal blackness against the lighter background of the sky. He called over to Bob Knox, 'Show the man the picture, Bob? May know where she's tied up?'

'Good idea. Hang on . . .'

Bob was counting out money, peering through the half-light at innumerable scruffy little notes. Charlie strolled back, handed the driver his own copy of the brochure. 'This is our boat, Ahmet. Have you seen it?'

'Hah!' Admiring it: tilting the brochure to the cab's interior light. '*Gulet*!'

'*Gulet* is right.' Bob confirmed it. 'Turkish name for that kind of ship.' Ahmet was distracted now, Bob having got a handful of paper money together for him: he'd put the brochure down and begun to count it.

'Bluewater Cruise?'

The question came in a shout from a short, dark guy in jeans and T-shirt, the word 'SALOME' printed across his chest. He'd come running. 'Bluewater Cruise?'

Bob read the name on the T-shirt. 'Is that our *gulet*?'

'*Gulet*, sure!'

He was about five-three or -four, late twenties maybe, bouncy like a gymnast; introducing himself as Joseph, the *gulet*'s captain, he told Bob his ship was at anchor outside the harbour. Shaking hands, Charlie asked him, 'You're Israeli?'

'Israeli. Sure.' He had no specially Jewish look about him, Charlie thought. Maybe they didn't, in Israel. They were collecting their gear from the taxi, Ahmet wishing them 'Happy holiday', other tourists flowing by. Charlie heard Bob ask Joseph as they set off eastward along the quay, 'Any news yet – about when we sail?'

'Morning. Sun-up.' Waving a hand northward. 'OK!'

The dinghy was an inflatable, bright yellow, with its controls in the pointed bow, room for one passenger on a wooden seat beside Joseph – Charlie got this, as he had in the taxi, since he took up more space than any of the others – two in the seat behind, and Pete squatting uncomfortably in the stern with most of the gear on top of him. Joseph was the last to leap on board; then they were puttering across the dark harbour, land noises fading astern.

Charlie leant back, twisting to look at Bob. 'How come this chap – crew – all right, they're Israelis, but how did you get hold of them? Presumably they know what it's all in aid of?'

Leo put his mouth close to Charlie's ear. The boat was approaching a mole which sheltered the harbour from the north; they'd be passing close to its eastern end. Charlie heard, ' – as much as they *need* to know. But – they want our help sometimes. Technical, for instance. Example – what we were talking about the other day, getting in and out of dived submarines? Well, if they want instruction in such techniques – OK, no problem. Then if we want a *quid pro quo* – like *this* – huh?'

It made sense, Charlie supposed. Although he was surprised at Bob's telling him so readily. After all the reticence: and it would certainly put a cat among the pigeons if the UK's friends in Arabia got to hear of it. It didn't occur to him, of course, that he'd just been fed a ration of disinformation intended to be regurgitated later in a Damascus courtroom.

From a white-painted light structure on the end of the mole Joseph had altered course northwestward. He was slowing the motor, although it hadn't been at more than half-throttle. Keeping noise and wash down, letting the people sleep in the darkened yachts inside.

'See!'

Ahead of them two craft lay at anchor. The nearer was a big, expensive-looking yacht, and beyond it was the stubbier, sturdier shape of the Turkish-built *gulet*. Like a big *caique*, really; according to the brochure it was sixty feet long and sixteen in the beam. Riding to their anchors, with the breeze coming from the northwest both ships were stern-on to this approach. On the *gulet* a single masthead light was burning, and Charlie saw a crewman cross the open stern deck, in silhouette against light seeping from inside – from the wheel-house, deckhouse, whatever . . . Then a torch flared, and its beam steadied on a ladder, steps hooked to the port-side bulwark. The inflatable curved in towards it, slumping in the water as the power cut off, then thumping against the high, timber side. Joseph grabbed hold of the ladder and tossed a line up to where the torch-holder grabbed it; he jerked his head, telling Charlie, 'OK . . .'

He grasped the ladder's sides, and climbed up.

It wasn't a crewman, it was a crew girl. Dark face, wide-apart eyes, a lot of dark hair tumbling loose over the shoulders of her white sweater. A lot of white here and there: teeth, eyes, in the shifting torchlight. A *big* girl . . .

'Welcome aboard.' She was making room for him to climb over on to the deck. 'My name is Leila.'

Voice American-accented over French intonation, and low-pitched. But like any travel company's courier, he thought. He shook her hand, noticing as he did so the bulge of thighs in tight denim shorts. First impressions by torchlight . . . 'I'm Charlie.'

'That way, Charlie . . .'

To make way for Bob, whom she was greeting now, on the narrow side deck. Tait came next, and Denham began passing gear up to him. No room there for anyone else to help, but Joseph swarmed up without using the ladder's steps – sailor-fashion, monkey-fashion, the little guy *was* a bit ape-like – and took the line from Leila, to secure the inflatable alongside. Bob asked him, turning from her, 'That's not the boat we're to use for landing, is it?'

'No.' Leila fielded the question. Guiding him on to the after deck where Charlie was. It was a wide, open space with seating – plastic cushion-tops on wooden lockers – around the curve of the ship's stern. She said, 'We have a larger boat for you, with a sixty-horsepower engine. You wouldn't make a secret landing in that bright yellow one, would you.'

'Exactly why I asked . . . Listen – you've had word, we're to sail at sunrise?'

Charlie left them to it, went inside for a look at what was, as he'd guessed, the wheelhouse. But it was also the galley and messing space. The wheel and the engine controls were in the port forward corner, high up and with a stool for the helmsman to sit on, and windows at that level extended across the width of the compartment. On his left as he entered was a bar – or counter – with a narrow working-space the other side of it, between it and the ship's side where there was a stove, sink, lockers. The starboard part had a cushioned bench around three sides of a low table. Dining area, Charlie noted. And right ahead of him in the centre of the forward bulkhead, on the helmsman's right when he was up on his stool, double doors were latched open above steps leading down into what had to be the accommodation space – cabins, whatever.

He looked round at the others crowding in. Bob introducing Tait and Denham: Pete clearly fascinated by Leila. Four litres of booze were now on the table in their plastic bags; Charlie said, retrieving his cigars, 'If this is how the SBS deploys, I was in the wrong racket.' Looking at the girl again, in the light now, and confirming that she was quite stunning, in a savage sort of way. Reminiscent of photographs one had seen of Israeli girl soldiers, some of them very eye-catching and sexy as well as commando-trained. They'd have put the best-looking ones nearest to the camera, of course; but Leila could well be one of those. He thought this placed her fairly accurately, that he'd hit the nail on the head as far as *that* one was concerned; a rider to the thought was that either in battle or in bed she'd take some handling.

A scrawny guy appeared now, edging his way through. Smiley Tait backing to let him by. A man of forty-plus, three-quarters bald and with a yellowish complexion, he was wearing a filthy vest and ragged pants striped like pyjamas. Leila said, 'This is Max. Engineer, also cook.' She switched into French. 'This one's their officer – Bob, his name's Bob. The big one there's called – oh – '

'Charlie.' He nodded to them. 'Bonjour, Max.' She was introducing the other two: Denham still unable to take his eyes off Leila, and Max nodding, licking his thin lips – like a lizard when it's swallowed a fly, Charlie thought, having watched lizards doing so on hot rocks in the Dhofar. Max looked sick, but his arms and shoulders were roped with muscle. Leila told them, 'Four cabins are down there. The nearest on the left is mine. Two of you must share – each cabin has two bunks. You can sleep late, no reason you should wake when we pull up anchor . . . Lavatories also down there – one each side, and each has a hand-shower . . . Anything else you want to know?'

'No jacuzzi?'

She didn't seem to have much sense of humour. Charlie tried again: 'Where do the other crew bunk? Or are there more than we've met?'

'Only those two. Mostly they sleep on deck.'

'Joseph's the captain – right?'

'For sailing the ship – sure. But for telling him *where* to sail it and what to do when we get there, that's me.'

'Except this is my operation, Leila.'

'When you leave us, Bob, *then* it's your operation.' She smiled: the first time Charlie had seen her do it. Wide mouth, full lips. In that peculiar way, *very* attractive. But the smile was telling Bob *Let's not fight this, you won't win it* . . . 'Midnight day after tomorrow.' She glanced at her watch, and corrected this: 'Midnight *tomorrow*, since we are now into Monday. Midnight Tuesday.'

'Tuesday – the night after this next one.' Bob nodded. 'All right. But leaving at daybreak?'

She nodded. 'Senseless to be in such a place as this when there is no need. We will start a little *before* daybreak, be away from the land before light. I've let it be known on shore we go to Fetiye.'

'Turkish mainland . . .'

'A mainland port of entry, a place a cruise *would* go to. But this is my business, Bob, you leave it to me, you'll be put ashore right place, right time, OK?'

That was a reprimand, of sorts. Charlie cut in, 'You talk good English.'

'Also Yiddish, French, small bit Arabic. Only a few words German.'

She'd taken his comment as a statement, not as a compliment. Gesturing towards the cabins: 'Why don't you change your clothes, take showers if you want. Max will fix a meal now.'

The Hercules thundered eastward. Well into its six-hour flight: over the Adriatic or thereabouts, Ben Ockley guessed.

He worked his arms and shoulders out of the sleeping-bag, pushed himself up on an elbow in the very cold rush of air – reaching for his thermos flask, for coffee. Looking round for

155

anyone in reach who'd like some: but only Froggie Clark was nearby, and he was asleep, his bag jammed between the seats and the stack of cargo and only the top of his head visible. Ben set his mug down on the jumpy, resonant steel plating, and reached again, this time to dip one-handed into the white cake-box with which he'd been issued by the Crabs, this being the standard packaging for their in-flight snacks. Breakfast in bed: with a choice of a ham sandwich, an apple and a chocolate biscuit bar, also some kind of chemical cold drink in a plastic container. Sandwich in one hand, hunched on the other elbow, he stared around at the cavernous, noisy hold.

There was a short line of nylon-web seats against the side of the fuselage, but nobody was using them now. The cargo, only a very small part of which was SBS gear – which was at the back end anyway – was stacked centrally on the bed of steel rollers and securing clamps, leaving only just room for a man to squeeze by between it and any seated men's knees. Now, on this side, there wouldn't be room: anyone wanting to go aft, Crab crew heading for the tented Elsan-type WC for instance, would have to mountaineer over seats or cargo. In fact the SBS men, all experienced C130 customers, were up on top of the stack, having found themselves places where they could spread their bags – on ledges or in hammock-like nests in the covering that shrouded the outlines of crates, cartons and weirder shapes. Within seconds of being allowed out of their seats and seatbelts after takeoff they'd swarmed up the stack in competition for the best spots, dragging their sleeping-bags with them; it had looked like a kind of mass levitation, that swift and apparently effortless upward swarm of men who were ultra-fit.

The Sea-Riders were at the after end of the hold; Ben had seen them loaded. Their side blisters were deflated, of course, but the rigid, deeply V-shaped hulls took up a lot of space. With them were their outboards, 140-horsepower, bulky as well as heavy, extra gas-tanks (empty now) and the containers of weaponry and other gear.

As soon as they touched down at Akrotiri that lot would be transferred to the C130 which would be standing by for the para-drop interception. Before anything else was done, it would all be moved over and put in its right place in the other plane, and the boats would be prepared – inflated, their outboards and radios fitted, containers secured inside them, parachutes attached on the special harness that would float them down to hit the sea even-keeled. Drysuits would be unpacked: everything would be set ready and in place for instant takeoff.

Then, the team could indulge themselves in breakfast, showers, whatever home comforts the Akrotiri base might be offering. Shifting into DPMs *before* breakfasting, Ben noted mentally. Then there'd be no hold-up at all when the whistle blew.

He hoped there wouldn't be long to wait. As far as the waiting period and the reconnaissance operation were concerned there were basically two stages foreseeable. One, a Nimrod would take to the air at first light to patrol the waters on the east side of the island and watch for any small craft – especially high-speed craft – making for the Syrian coast. (The approximate landing zone was known, through an Intelligence report which had supplied the coordinates of Swale and company's inland destination.) Two, ground reconnaissance was in progress with the object of identifying the boat or ship, so that the surveillance aircraft would then have a specific target to locate and track. From the SBS point of view this would be a great advance: you'd know what you were doing then, wouldn't be running any risk of dropping on the wrong target.

At night, that could be a problem; by day the likelihood of any such fiasco would be much reduced. For other reasons as well, technical ones, it would be far easier to do the job in daylight.

To get a chance at all, though – day *or* night – that was the gamble, just to be in time. Charles Hislop had pointed out in his briefing at Lyneham that they might already be too late, that the other side could have been on their way *then*: by now, could be in Syria . . .

'It's up to you.' He'd looked round the circle of faces. 'If we're there too late – well, won't be your fault or mine, we couldn't have moved any faster than we have. But if luck's with us and we get out there with a fighting chance, there'll be a hell of a lot resting on your shoulders. The issue is

157

tremendously important. I'll say it again now: we want them all – however many, which as yet we've no way of knowing. We want them stopped, arrested and brought into Dhekelia with their boat. And that's your objective if all goes perfectly . . . *But* – the key to the whole thing is this fellow Swale. If he's removed, the bomb's defused, as it were. Obviously the best result would be to snatch him – and any other Brits there may be on board – and bring him back in one piece. But if for any reason that's not on, then you're to kill him.' Hislop had added, 'That's an order, Ben.'

Charlie took a long time getting to sleep. Maybe his system wasn't accustomed to being laid to rest cold sober. His mind was still active anyway. And with sobriety was even a touch of hangover, from the steady intake of alcohol throughout the day, both airborne and on the ground at Istanbul. To which oddly enough Bob Knox had raised no objection, although in London a week ago he'd warned that there'd be no drinking once they'd started.

Maybe this didn't count as having started. Maybe *now*, having embarked. Nobody had touched any of those Duty-Free bottles tonight, or suggested doing so.

Knox was an odd character, though. In some ways, *out* of character. One recollection which still irritated had been his condescending to have a drink in the flat last night, last night before departure, because he'd wanted to toast 'happy landings'. It had been so phoney that Charlie had gagged on it mentally even though he'd been three parts pissed at the time. It might have come out of some tv drama – intrepid hero posturing – but in real life the sort of people who were involved in this kind of thing tended *not* to pose in front of mirrors.

Charlie assured himself, not for the first time, *He'll be all right on the night* . . .

Touch wood. Rapping the side of the bunk. Thinking for some reason of Leila about six feet away in hers, and stirred by the visual imagery . . . Smiley Tait had growled – in the passage-way outside these cabins – 'Some hard lady, that one!' Charlie had concurred, adding quietly, 'Israeli army, Smiley. I'd bet on it. And most likely commando-trained.'

'Could be.' Tait had pushed open the door of the cabin he was sharing with Denham, and tossed his gear on to the lower bunk. 'She'd break either your neck or your balls, soon as look at you.'

Meat balls, Max had offered them for their late snack, and with them an oily mixture of aubergines and tomatoes. Leila had sat with them while they ate, and Charlie had asked her whether she'd been born in Israel. She'd glanced at him sharply, her look asking *What's it to you?* before relaxing, nodding.

'And would I be right in guessing you're – ' he'd hesitated, not wanting to have her think he was suggesting she was all that butch – 'well, all Israelis of military age, men and women, do time in your armed forces, don't they?'

'It's necessary, for our survival as a nation.' Then she'd changed the subject, before he could pin her down as a commando, prove to himself and Tait that his hunch was right: she'd said to Bob, 'When we're out at sea, we can get the stores up. Check out your weapons and so forth. Rations, all that . . . And the boat, you'll want to have it in the water, give it a trial, huh?'

Bob agreed, he'd like to do all those things. She assured him, 'The motor is excellent, no problems, we had it running last week and Max did a servicing routine on it after. The boat is French, purchased recently in Marseilles.'

'So if the Syrians found it – ' Pete Denham chipped in – 'they'd be looking for Frogs.'

'They might.' Leila shrugged. 'If they're simple-minded. It's what we were told you wanted, that's all.'

'As the French tried to do to us in New Zealand.' Charlie recalled this. 'When they sank the Greenpeace ship. They'd bought their inflatable in London.'

'So anyone would know this was the Brits getting back at their old friends.' A glance at Charlie. Huge eyes, golden-brown and the whites very bright and clear. '*So* smart.'

'Israelis would be smarter, no doubt.'

'Don't you know it?'

'The answer is – ' Charlie admired her arrogance – '*not* to let it be found.' He looked at Bob. 'If it was, how'd we get off the beach?'

Bob had answered rather testily: 'Steal some other boat. Or something. Fucking *swim* off.' Leaning back almost horizontally from the table, reaching towards Max with his plate, wanting a refill. Charlie meanwhile persevering: '*We* might swim off, if the R/V position's not too far out.' That was another question, but he decided it could wait . . . 'But the guy we hope we'll have with us by then may not be in such great shape, eh?'

'Oh, shit, Charlie.' Bob swung back with his second helping. More salad than balls, this time. 'One, no reason they'd get our boat. Two, you're right, we can't know what shape he'll be in. That's one reason for using an inflatable, not canoes. *You're* another of the reasons, incidentally . . .'

When he woke, it was a major effort to fight through to consciousness, remember where he was and what for, and how he'd got here. Memory rebuilt itself in pieces; and what stuck, like solids left high and dry when the sludge had filtered away, were his doubts about Bob Knox.

In the half-waking state, it scared him, while remaining out of reach, not clearly definable. An impression, an amalgam of small doubts. The only thing he could say for sure was that he disliked the man.

Disliked or distrusted. If there was any difference. OK, both.

But – hold on, now. *Think* . . .

One: you couldn't expect to like everyone you worked with. Two: it was a two-way thing, like all relationships. Bob had *his* doubts, his distrust of Charlie Swale. Because of the drinking: maybe for other reasons too, but it was a *mutual* wariness.

So forget it. There wasn't a bloody thing you could do about it anyway.

That suggestion of light in the circle of the port-hole could be a reflection of shore lights, he guessed. It still felt like the middle of the night. The air coming in was decidedly cold, chilling a sweat which had sprung out when he'd begun – half-awake – to worry about Knox. He pushed at the brass ring to shut it, wondering at the same time whether that might not be a first suggestion of the dawn. If this ship was still lying the way she had been – and this was the starboard side – well, that would be the east, all right . . . Confirming it, he heard someone on deck – bare feet or soft shoes padding overhead, up the strip of side deck – and remembered Leila saying that the intention was to move off before sunrise, get away from the coast before the light came. Maybe their moving around up there was what had woken him out of his deep sleep. And if you can't beat 'em, join 'em . . .

He groped for the light switch. Then climbed off the bunk, pulled on trousers and a sweater and went up through the wheelhouse on to the stern deck.

There was a reddish glow on the horizon; from port-hole level only a high, colourless reflection of it had been visible. The white yacht was still with them, fifty or sixty yards away, two white anchor lights halo'd in the damp salt air. Charlie glanced around, checking to make sure he was alone here, contemplating having a pee over the side – they'd all be up at the sharp end, from where he could hear the rhythmic *click-clacking* of chain cable being winched in. But at that moment a diminutive, dark figure came hurrying aft, ducked into the wheelhouse and then stopped, turned – doing a double-take, looking back to see who this was lurking in the stern . . . Joseph. But he didn't waste time or words; he went inside, got up on the stool and must have pressed a starter button. Right under Charlie's feet the *gulet*'s diesel engine rumbled into life.

Hayward's Ford Escort rolled into Kyrenia only a neck behind the sunrise. The sun was fresh up out of the sea, blazing like fire in windows at the western end of the waterfront.

He'd got his call through to Akrotiri – finally, but not easily. Initial delay had resulted from the Greeks advising him to contact the Swedish UN contingent, which had led to a lot of talk, promises of help next day. So then he'd returned to his original intention of contacting the Akrotiri base. Again there'd been delay, he'd had to leave it to some NCO to find Ken Fellows and get him out of bed, to ring him back. Even this had only been possible because by sheer luck Hayward had remembered the name of an individual to whom Ken had been due to report on arrival; until he'd dredged up this name

161

he'd been having problems convincing the military exchange operator that Ken — or even he himself, for that matter — existed. Admittedly this had been taking place at around 0300, an hour when people tended to be not quite at their sharpest. But Ken had come through eventually, promised to do his best, and after another hour had crawled by — Jimmy Hayward back in the car, despairing, chain-smoking, certain that even if Swale had ever visited Kyrenia he'd be a hundred miles away by now — after this further age a military officer had arrived on foot, spoken at some length to the police sergeant — not the same one, the watch had by this time changed twice — and then approached the Ford.

Hayward had wound down the window. He'd had hopes at first sight of this character, but had then been forced to the conclusion that it was only another Greek. Doing a round of the guard-posts, or something. Now, hopes soared.

'Mr Hayward? Are you the guy who's busting a gut to get to Kyrenia?'

'Right! You're — American?'

'Canadian, sir.' He was a lieutenant, unshaven, bleary-eyed, but friendly. 'I'm from CANCON, sir — Canadian Contingent, that's to say.' He pointed. 'We live right there in that hotel.'

It was plainly visible, about a minute's stroll from here. And this sector was Canadian-controlled, apparently. So why the hell that Greek bastard had wanted him to waste time with the Swedes . . . The Canadian said, 'Here's your pass, Mr Hayward, all signed and sealed as they say. And you need to display this plate — right here . . . OK?'

It came out of his greatcoat pocket, a plate like an ordinary car number-plate, for display behind the windscreen.

'You'll have no problems now, sir.'

'I'm more than grateful.'

'Entirely welcome, sir.'

The barrier swung up. And down the road he had no problems with the Turks at their checkpoint. Clear of the town, he put his foot down — to save a few seconds, having wasted hours.

On the waterfront in Kryrenia, a woman swathed in black was washing the steps outside a restaurant. He asked her if she could tell him where he'd find the harbour master's office, and she straightened to an upright position on her knees, her black eyes taking in this short, stout foreigner in his crumpled suit before waving a wet hand towards the west side of the harbour.

He set off that way, walking, with the new sun already warm on his back. Feeling overdressed in a suit and hard-soled shoes, as well as unwashed, unshaven, tired and hungry. There was a jetty on that side of the basin; a small ship tied up there was either half loaded or half unloaded. Signs here and there of the day's work starting: not with a rush, exactly, but there were some fishermen sorting nets, a boy loading lobster-pots into a bright blue rowing boat.

It was an attractive little port. He knew that in different circumstances he might have appreciated its charms more keenly.

He couldn't find the harbour master's office. There was a customs house but it was locked, apparently empty. That ship, with ropes from a crane dangling into an open hold, wasn't going anywhere in any hurry, and none of the yachts around the quay seemed big enough. Pleasure-boats, smart little toys, nothing that matched up to what he imagined would be the Swale party's requirements.

Still snooping round for the harbour master, he noticed masts outside the harbour. They were motionless: a yacht presumably at anchor. Seeing some steps nearby, he climbed them to get a view over the top of the nearer clutter.

She was big, all right. You didn't have to know anything about yachts to see there'd be plenty of room in that one. And she'd have a fair turn of speed, he guessed. Also – staring out at her, feeling his stubbled jaw and jowls – it intrigued him that she was alone out there, shunning the company of the lesser fry inside the harbour.

Shunning close inspection by sneaky coppers?

He started back down the steps. Maybe that lad with the blue boat would row him out.

9

The drab-patterned bulk of the Hercules was parked a few hundred metres – sprinting distance – from the transit block in which the SBS team were to be accommodated. The Hercules that had brought them out from Lyneham had landed about three-quarters of an hour ago, dropping thunderously into the glare of the rising sun, condensation showering on the Marines' heads – six men each side perched on their nylon seats, seatbelts clamped shut, the sleeping-bags in which they'd spent the journey rolled and in the straps on their bergens. With steep changes in height in the C130s you always got the rain-showers, whether you were going up or coming down, condensation gathered on the ceiling and then ran off in streams. It was how the Crabs got their laughs, Geoff Hosegood had suggested. Ben Ockley had allowed himself a brief look at the base and its environs, standing to look out of one of the small ports in the fuselage in the minute or so before he'd had to sit down and fix his seatbelt. Nothing seemed to have changed much in the past four or five years: a few extra buildings here or there maybe, but the sight of it was so familiar it was almost a home-coming, the sovereign base sprawling among its low surrounding dunes and the long jut of land towards Cape Gata to the southeast. The land rose there, he remembered, ending in a cliff a couple of hundred feet high at the Cape itself, but the peninsula as a whole was low and flat, with a salt lake in its centre glittering now like a great tinted mirror in the day's first light. The base area was billiard-table flat: an expanse of airfield and runways, brick barrack buildings and family quarters, workshops, hangars, stores, recreational amenities, sports grounds, the entire spread of it spiked and studded with masts and antennae of all kinds. The Hercules had banked then, giving him a slanting view of vividly blue sea curving up the peninsula's east side: rocky coastline in the south, then shingle and black sand edging Akrotiri Bay all the way around the curve to Limassol where the tourists played. He'd turned, sliding down into his seat, clicking the belt shut and donning his green beret to keep his head dry.

It had looked more attractive from up there, he thought, than it did down here at ground level. Especially since the flight lieutenant who'd been assigned to the team as RAF liaison officer and who'd met them – together with an NCO from something called 'Movements' and a truck for the transfer of their gear from one aircraft to the other – especially since this Flight Lieutenant Morgan had given a negative answer to the question Ben had asked as soon as his boots had hit the tarmac: had there been any news, sightings, reports from any of the Cyprus harbours.

'Damn-all.' A shake of the head. 'Up to half an hour ago, nix.'

So much for the hopes of instant action, expectations of the target being identified at first light, pinpointed and held on a Nimrod's Searchwater radar screen. He'd even worried about it, during the last hour or so of the incoming flight – whether he'd be justified in sacrificing half an hour to let the guys eat some breakfast, whether he'd be wrong to allow it or even crazier not to accept that small loss of time in order to get a meal into them before they dropped. Because they wouldn't be taking much in the way of rations, only snacks to keep them going for a few hours on the water . . . He was still talking to this liaison character – tall, thin, face like a chicken's – when they'd heard the mounting roar of an aircraft taking off, and then seen it as it lifted – from a distant part of the airfield, a Nimrod soaring gracefully into the bright dawn sky. The flight lieutenant had said with an air of satisfaction, 'There – your surveillance operation under way. Not bad timing, eh?'

'That's the start of it?'

'Well, yes . . .'

'It's light now. The surveillance was supposed to have been effective as from *first* light.'

In other words, that Nimrod should have been on station now, not just starting out . . . He made a quick calculation: distance from here to the patrol area between Cyprus and the coast of Syria maybe a hundred and twenty miles; and Nimrods flew – or *could* fly – at upward of five hundred m.p.h., maybe nearer six hundred. So all right, they hadn't lost all *that* much time on the job. Maybe . . .

The Hercules, unfortunately, wouldn't get there quite as fast. Not *half* as fast. All the more important, therefore, that there should be no time lost here on the ground. When the word came, he wanted to have his team airborne within minutes.

No reason they should not be. The C130's engines were being kept warmed up, and the gear was all loaded now: boats rigged, the outboards' gas-tanks full, drysuits unpacked and laid out ready for their owners to climb into them during the air transit.

Neither the boy with the boatload of lobster-pots nor the old sailormen picking weed out of their nets had any interest in Hayward's proposal that they might ferry him out to reconnoitre the big yacht. In fact the way they stared at him gave him an impression that in their eyes he might have been suggesting something illegal or improper.

He'd given them up, was heading eastward along the quay-side when a female voice called a question to him: 'Why'd you want to visit those buggers anyway?'

Female Australian. She was in the stern end of a rather smart little yacht – yellow hull with a red stripe round it – on which there'd been no sign of life when he'd passed twenty minutes earlier. The girl was blonde, tall, tanned, and about the age of his own elder daughter. Bikini pants – white –

were just visible under a man's checked shirt hanging loose, unbuttoned.

Hayward crouched on the edge of the quay, held Swale's portrait out towards her.

'I'm looking for this fellow. If he's here at all, he'll be on some boat. My guess is it'd be a biggish one, so when I saw that thing outside there – '

'Might he be a pooff, by any chance?'

The question surprised him. He frowned. 'Most unlikely. No, he can't be.'

'Doesn't look it, I'll say that.' She shrugged. 'Not that you can always tell, not straight off.' She jerked a thumb seaward. 'Reason I asked is *that* lot are as queer as you'd ever get. Owner's a Frog – real old queen, plus what he calls his "crew" . . . Millionaire, I heard.'

Hayward withdrew the photograph. 'You've saved me a trip.'

'Might've had yourself a ball, eh?'

'Well, thanks.'

'That guy's supposed to be here, but you're not sure, and you don't know him very well – right?'

'Right. Anyway, I take it you haven't seen him. If he's here, he'd've got here yesterday.'

'You a copper, then?'

'I'd have to be, wouldn't I.'

'That or bloody Mafia.' She smiled at him. 'What's he done?'

'Nothing – yet. I'm here to – well, *stop* him doing it. He's with a crowd he wouldn't be with if he knew who they were.'

'I hope you find him, then.'

He nodded. 'Thanks.'

'You said he'd've got in yesterday, but I don't recall any-thing come in, not yesterday.' She waved an arm seaward: and she had no bra on, under that loose-hanging shirt. Becoming aware of the degree of self-exposure, she pulled the shirt together, secured one button . . . 'I mean, wouldn't pitch up here in a bloody dinghy, would he.'

'He'd've come by air. The boat would've been here waiting for him. For him and these others.'

'Oh, I get you . . .' Thinking about this, she brightened. 'So

168

he'd 've come from the airport by taxi, wouldn't he. Maybe Ahmet brought him. Or he'd know who did. I mean, it's not a big place, this . . . How did *you* get here?'

'Car. I drove up from Larnaca.' He asked her, 'This taxi —'

'Hey!' She'd spun round, staring seaward. You could see the yacht's masts from here, over the top of the mole. Turning back, blowing her cheeks out . . . 'I must be bloody *stupid*. There *was* another boat out there. Came — well, you could be right, at that, I didn't *see* her come . . . Big sort of *caique* thing, know what I mean?'

'No, but I'd like to.'

'Yeah, she was on the anchorage last night, I'd swear to it. Could've moved about sundown, I suppose . . .' Slapping her forehead: 'Look, I'm sorry, I only just woke up, and last night we —'

'A sort of *what* did you say it was?'

'*Caique*. Only bigger, fifty feet or more . . . Look, hang on a mo'.' She turned away, ducking to push her head and shoulders into the narrow cabin entrance. Hayward had a different view of her now . . . Warning himself that the fact there'd been some other ship here didn't mean it had had Swale on it; in the last week there could have been fifty or a hundred boats in and out without Swale on any of them. He heard a male voice from inside, a low grumbling tone, and allowed himself to wonder what *he*'d have to grumble about. Then she was out again and the right way up, flushed under the dark tan and telling him, 'She was there on the anchorage last night, he reckons. So she's not gone long or far yet. For what good *that* does you.'

So Swale might have been here last night. Might have left eight or ten hours ago, or *one* hour ago. Might even have been hidden in the offshore mist when he'd been catching glimpses of seascape from the mountain road.

He asked her again, to get it right: '*Caique*?'

'Yeah, that's it. But you want to ask Ahmet about your bloke?' She pointed. 'Up there, and to your right off the quay, either first or second corner. Small caff place, he'd be having his brekker and you'd see his cab — Renault, shit-coloured thing — well, like two-tone. OK?'

'Thanks!'

Running – for a hundred-to-one chance. But there'd be a consolation prize too: if he did not strike lucky, *he*'d have breakfast . . .

The Renault was there, unmistakable. And it was parked outside a café – which called itself a restaurant, according to the sign in English. Hayward pushed through the dangling bead curtain, the fly-restrainer. He was in a large, rather bare room in which there was only one other person, a small, dark, balding man hunched over a Turkish-language newspaper and his breakfast. The aroma of strong coffee was so alluring that for a moment he almost forgot what he'd just come racing up the alley for. He also saw and smelt fresh bread, smelling so good that he knew it would be still warm from the oven. The cab-driver was loading a piece of it with clear honey, spooning it on directly from a glass bowl and then stuffing his face so that the stubbled cheeks bulged with it.

'Ahmet? That your taxi out there?'

Staring: eyes wide, and incapable of speech, fortunately knowing this and not attempting it. The proprietor – could have been this one's brother – appeared from the back, wiping his hands on a rag.

'Have breakfast, you like?'

'Please.' He'd just about have sunk to his knees and begged for it, if he'd had to. 'Coffee, bread and honey, same as his.'

'No problem!'

The other one swallowed, and croaked, 'Taxi, you? Airport?'

'No. Thanks, but . . .' He pulled a chair back from another table, a few feet away, and sat down, took out Swale's photograph. 'I'm looking for this man. He's British. A friend – I have an important message for him . . . Did you bring him here in your taxi – last night maybe?'

Ahmet had begun to push food into his mouth again, holding the print in the other hand. It would soon be sticky with honey, Hayward guessed. This ceased to bother him when he saw a slow nod beginning.

'Airport – him in taxi, me. Sure . . .'

'Last night? You brought him *here*?'

'Night, sure.' Ahmet reached to show him the face of his watch, pointing at the figure twelve. 'Taxi me here, this sir.'

170

He touched the portrait again. 'Taxi airport for Girne. Kyrenia *you* saying.'

'You drove him here from the airport at midnight. Did you bring him to a boat?'

'Hah?'

He remembered the Aussie girl's word for it. '*Caique*?'

'*Gulet*.'

'Sorry, chum, I don't – '

'Wait, you.' Ahmet pushed his chair back and went to the doorway, looking back to gesture at Hayward to stay where he was. His breakfast happened to be arriving at the same time.

'OK?'

'Fantastic!'

The taxi door slammed, then Ahmet pushed in through the rattling beads. The proprietor was withdrawing, waving his hands in the air and muttering, 'Fantastic, fantastic ...' Ahmet placed a brightly-coloured pamphlet in front of Hayward. It was an advertisement for some holiday outfit, Bluewater Cruises. On the front was a photograph of a timber-built craft, two-masted, rather old-fashioned looking with its high bowsprit. Ahmet's forefinger jabbed at it: '*Gulet*. No *caique*, no. *Gulet*, him.' He waved towards the quayside, then pointed at Swale's portrait: 'Come for *gulet* in taxi me. Un'erstand?'

Breakfast on board the *Salome* – fruit, bread, rolls, Turkish honey – had been cleared away, and Max was washing up. The *gulet*'s diesel was pushing her along at about seven knots.

'You wanted to see this, Bob.' Leila spread a chart in front of him. 'We are here – steering this course – which will bring us *here* – Anamur Burnu. We anchor a few hours, and you can land if you want. Try out the boat? Tonight we go east along this coast – while you sleep, your last good night for sleeping – and maybe stop again a short time in this bay.'

Bob read out the place-name: 'Ovacik.' He pointed to the first anchorage, Anamur Burnu. 'We'll land this afternoon, anyway. Stretch our muscles. All right, Charlie?'

Tait grunted approval. Bob asked Leila, 'Might get ashore tomorrow as well?'

'I don't think so. Depends on progress tonight, but we may not even stop.'

'Straight to the target area?'

'Not so straight. This way – as if we were going into the Gulf of Iskenderun. We've come from the west, we're cruising around this coast – a Turkish *gulet* cruising in Turkish waters. Close inshore, most of the time.' She pointed upward. 'Up there a Turkish flag. We have Turk registration also, Marmaris is our home port.'

'I thought Jaffa – or Tel Aviv – '

'In Turk waters we're Turks, believe me . . . But you see, this leaves only a short passage before it's dark tomorrow.' She nodded at Charlie. 'You're wondering who would be looking for us. You're right – *nobody*. I hope . . . But naturally there is surveillance of such a coast, by Syrians, maybe also from Cyprus by the – ' she'd checked herself – 'by *your* people.' She asked Bob, 'Officially, your people wouldn't know of your coming, would they?'

'Certainly not.'

'So.' She pulled the chart away. 'Now I'll ask Max to bring up the Uzis so you can practise with them. We won't be so far from shore again as we are now.'

Max threw beer-cans over the side for target practice. The SBS marksmanship wasn't impressive, Charlie thought. Smiley Tait was good, and he himself was up to about that standard once he got his eye in. Bob excused his own lousy showing on the grounds that he'd never felt at home with an Uzi, they didn't suit him.

They were in the *gulet*'s stern then, in shorts in the burning sun, cleaning and oiling the stubby little Israeli weapons. Bob said, 'With luck we won't have to use the things anyway. Just grab this guy and sneak away with him.'

Charlie was preparing one of his Havanas. Nobody else wanted one. He'd cleaned his Uzi and put it down beside him; there were still two magazines to be filled. He said, 'Question time now, Bob. I see no reason to be kept in the dark any longer, so let's be ready with some straight answers.'

'I didn't realise you felt you *were* in the dark, Charlie.'

Tait winked at him. Charlie nodded. 'Yeah. Pull the other

172

one. And try this for starters: who's this guy we're hoping to extract?'

'His name's Stillgoe. Vernon Stillgoe. Ring a bell?'

He gave it a moment's thought. Denham muttered, 'Ah, *that* bloke . . .' Charlie got it: 'Newspaper man, kidnapped in Beirut a few months ago.'

'Right. But he was also doing a job for MI6 or someone. He was supposed to make a contact on their behalf, meet a Syrian who had some information which London badly wanted. Whatever it was, it should still be in his head now and they still want it.'

'Good.' Charlie nodded. 'Second question. Maybe Smiley and Pete already know the answer. Question of how we withdraw and get back on board this vessel once we've got him. Because as I mentioned before, you could get yourself greased before you'd passed on this rather valuable info, eh?'

'I haven't told any of you yet. Obviously would have before we landed, Charlie.'

'No time like the present, is there.'

'It's very simple.' Bob told them, 'Fifteen miles offshore on two-seven-zero degrees from Ras el Hassan, one hundred hours after we leave the *gulet*. If for any reason we find we can't make that deadline it's postponed forty-eight hours.'

'Why not twenty-four?'

'Because then our friends would have to hang around more or less in the same place all that day, which would be asking for trouble. With a two-day interval they can clear out and then come back.'

'Not bad thinking.'

'But we should make it in the hundred hours. That's four days plus an extra four hours of darkness. So if we push off from this ship midnight tomorrow, the R/V time will be 0400 Sunday morning.'

Tait growled, 'Still have to steam, won't we, with only nights to move in. Snatch the guy in daylight, will we?'

'Evening of the third night. Gives us the rest of that night plus the last one for getting back to the coast and off it. We'll be pushing it, sure, but we don't want to be hanging around there, do we.'

'Ras el Hassan's marked on the chart, I suppose.' Charlie

173

went inside, brought it out and spread it on the deck, and the other two crowded round to see. Leo said, 'Just north of the Tartus oil terminal . . . Have *you* got any questions, Smiley? Pete?'

'I'm just hoping it's a decent outboard she's got for us.'

Tait was thinking of those fifteen miles to be covered, westward from the headland, with no kind of fallback if it turned out to be as unreliable as outboards tended to be. Denham nodded agreement: 'Yeah, Jesus . . . Long way to bloody paddle.' Charlie said – his cigar was burning now, and Tait had given it a critical glance, doubtless with his mind on physical fitness – 'I have one more to ask, Bob. Not as vital as the others, just my naturally enquiring mind . . . The signal – radio message these people had yesterday, day and time for the landing . . . Who and where might that have come from?'

'Best answer I can give you there, Charlie, is some Israeli source. I'd guess the Mossad, either from Haifa or Tel Aviv but more likely Haifa. The Mossad don't miss many tricks, you know, you can bet your life they have ears to the ground inside Syria. There's a lot more sense having them watch over this end of the operation than someone a couple of thousand miles away, wouldn't you agree?'

'I suppose. Personally, I'd rather have my own people running things.'

'I'm only guessing, Charlie. I was told the signal would come to the *gulet*, that's all. And as this is an Israeli crew, it seems a reasonable assumption.'

'OK. But one *more* question, while we're at it. This Stillgoe character – kidnapped in Beirut, now he's in Syria. How come?'

'Ah.' Leo nodded. 'That's a *good* question. All I can tell you for sure is that Intelligence – meaning presumably SIS – got the buzz that that's where he is. But I gathered, rather off the record this was, that he might be in the hands of some revolutionary Syrian group. In Beirut he might have been freed, you see – by Syrian troops, the peace-making force that Assad's put in there. On that basis one might assume Stillgoe's in Syria without Assad's knowledge or connivance. Consequently when we snatch him back we'll be taking him from

174

this gang, not challenging the Syrian state as such. Which could go some way to explaining (a) why this somewhat tricky operation was authorised, (b) why it's being run in such an offbeat way . . . D'you reckon?'

Charlie nodded. 'And I'm glad I asked.'

He was thinking, as he tapped ash over the ship's side, that that explanation really did begin to make some sort of sense.

In the Special Boat team's office/ops room at Akrotiri, Geoff Hosegood snatched up the telephone.

'Royal Marine office, Sergeant Hosegood!'

Ben Ockley and Ray Wilkinson watched him from across the room, where they had Admiralty charts spread on a trestle table.

'Yeah, he's here. Who wants him?'

He put his hand over the mouthpiece. Ben was on his way over. 'Inspector Fellows, Special Branch, calling from Dhekelia.'

Ben took the receiver from him. 'Ockley here. Inspector Fellows?'

'That's me. News for you, captain. The boat we've all been looking for left Kyrenia either not long after midnight or just before dawn this morning, and we have it identified. It's a timber-built craft described as a *gulet* – that's Turkish – and it's something like a Greek *caique* only bigger. Length about sixty feet, timber construction, beamy, two masts, has sails but wouldn't use 'em much, motors around on its diesel. Ought to be easy to spot, because although there are lots of 'em up on the Turkish mainland coast you'd hardly ever see one down here. My colleague Inspector Hayward has a picture of it – photograph on some tourist brochure – and he's on his way south now, to Akrotiri and he'll come asking for *you* – maybe you'd have 'em look out for him. He called me from the Canadian UN billet in Nicosia; he'd hoped he'd be able to fax the picture from there but they don't have the facilities, so he rang me and I told him to get it to you, quick as possible if not faster. He ought to be with you by midday, maybe eleven thirty, I don't know about the roads.'

'This *caique* thing – *gulet* – left Kyrenia at dawn?'

'That's what the harbour master there believes. It was at

175

anchor outside the port, he's not certain but he *thinks* it was there all night. Certainly was around midnight when Swale and his friends arrived by taxi from the airport – party of four, by the way, and the boat has a crew of three including a woman . . . But it *could* have sailed soon after they embarked.'

'Anyone mention what speed it might make?'

'No, I'm afraid not. But if Hayward's with you by noon – well, he could call that harbour master, *he* should know.'

'He's done a good job anyway, by the sound of it. Will you be passing this to London?'

'Yes. My next call.'

'Fine, so I don't need to. Thanks a lot, Inspector.'

He hung up, joggled the phone until he got the exchange. 'Would you put me through to Flight Lieutenant Morgan, please?'

Waiting: glancing round at the others in the room, half a dozen of them. Ray Wilkinson asked him, 'Identified the boat and it's sailed from Kyrenia?'

'Right. Type known in Turkey as a *gulet*, resembles a large *caique*, runs on diesel although it has masts and sails. So it might make – it's a heavy, beamy craft apparently – say anything from five to ten knots . . . Try this on the chart, Ray – departure from Kyrenia 0500, or alternatively four hours earlier, 0100. On the speed question let's split that difference, call it seven and a half knots. Try all the permutations, see where the thing could've got to – bearing in mind its target's on that section of coast. And that they'd want to get there after dark.' He took his palm off the mouthpiece. 'Morgan, listen. We've identified the boat, and a photo of it's on the way to me by road from Kyrenia. That's the first thing – the guy bringing it is a Special Branch officer, Inspector Hayward, he'll be here by noon or earlier, asking for me by name. Would you see he's met by someone who'll steer him this way? Thanks. Second point: I don't want to stray far from this telephone or from the Hercules, but I could describe the boat to your off-duty Nimrod pilot before he takes off. Any chance you could persuade him to come over? You will? Well, listen, what time's he due to take off? Yeah. If you'd find out. I'd like to get this picture copied when it arrives – you'd have the

176

facilities, I suppose. Right, fine. And the pilots had better have a copy each, obviously — or copies, plural. How many crew does a Nimrod — hell, *that* many? But right away, lacking the photo as yet, I could give the one who's on the ground a good idea of what he'll be looking for, so — '

Listening again, to Morgan's slightly singsong tones . . . He nodded: 'That's terrific. Yeah. I'll be down there waiting.' He hung up. Sticks Kelso was in the doorway, filling it, and Hosegood had been giving him the news. Ben told him, 'Swale's with three other guys, plus the boat's crew which numbers three and includes a woman.' He glanced over at the chart table, where Ray Wilkinson was laying off courses and radius rings, driving himself nuts with so many alternatives. Ben said, 'Morgan's coming for me, on wheels, we're going to the control tower so I can talk to the Nimrod that's on patrol and tell its pilot what he's looking for . . . Sticks, if the balloon goes up, get 'em out to the Herc and I'll meet you there.' Kelso nodded. Ben, at the door, looked back at Hosegood: 'Geoff, tell the rest of the lads what the form is, will you. They might as well know *some* fucking thing's happening.'

10

Then *nothing* was happening. By midday on Tuesday it was looking more and more likely that they'd missed out, that Swale and company had to be in Syria by this time. Ben wasn't saying so, or consciously allowing his gloom to show, but according to the Special Branch man's information the *gulet* would by now have been at sea for thirty, maybe thirty-six hours.

If she'd left Kyrenia around midnight Sunday, she'd have been off Cape Andreas at about the time the first Nimrod had been starting its patrol sixty miles to the south. He studied the chart, asking himself how *he*'d have handled it if he'd been skippering that thing.

You'd use the hours of darkness in which to get as far east as possible. But when the light came — and since obviously you'd intend making your landing in Syria after dark — you'd round that Cape Apostolos Andreas in a hairpin turn to the southwest. In no kind of hurry, at that stage. Hug the Cyprus coast, drift around — maybe with the sails up, even if they were flapping like washing on a line; you'd present a picture of innocence while the Nimrods were burning up taxpayers' money watching the international maritime boundary, not the inshore holiday cruising grounds. The *gulet* would have cruised around in that bay, using all the daylight hours of yesterday to drift about forty miles southwest, and with darkness you'd have turned her east, slipped across — somehow without being picked up by the Nimrod — and dropped Swale and his buddies off, probably in an inflatable, not far from the edge of Syrian territorial waters. Thirty-five miles was no great distance, if you had a decent outboard. The *gulet* would have started her run eastward — sails down, diesel churning out maximum revs — at about the latitude of Famagusta, which as it happened was right opposite the probable Syrian landing zone.

It made depressingly good sense, to Ben Ockley.

Kelso muttered, joining him at the chart, 'Reckon they got by us, do you?'

'No.' Outside, jets screamed off the tarmac. 'I reckon they're hiding out somewhere. Christ knows what for, but — ' he checked himself — 'look, another possibility is they could've gone westabout. So they'd be passing south of us here — could've rounded Cape Gata maybe a couple of hours ago. Aiming to be off Cape Greco at dusk.' He showed him. 'See? Sixty miles from there to a drop-off in inshore waters around midnight, thereabouts . . . But no, I do *not* think they could've got by us, Sticks. We need faith, bags of it, right?'

Ray Wilkinson had just come up the stairs, and joined them. Using a towel, having been limbering up outside on the tarmac, sprints and press-ups, with some of the others. Filling in time, as much as staying fit. He'd caught Ben's last comment, and agreed, 'Sooner or later they'll show. No call for alarm . . . Except I was wondering, Ben — might get some Yank assistance on the recce job, if they're so willing?'

There'd been a call last night from the Special Forces Adviser in the JOC, to say that the Americans were ready to help if called upon, the 6th Fleet had been given orders to that effect, from Washington. But a later signal from the Task Group Commander on board the carrier *Saratoga* had qualified this. Every effort would be made to comply with any request that might be made, but the *Saratoga*'s E-2Cs, Hawkeyes, were certain to be fully employed in the next few days, not only with routine surveillance commitments but also in tracking a Soviet Black Sea Fleet squadron now deploying southward from the Dardanelles.

Wilkinson evidently hadn't seen that message. Ben told him, 'Soviets have a *Cresta* and two *Krivaks* transiting south towards the Kaso Strait. This end of Crete. That Task Group's been told to keep tabs on them, as well as whatever else they're into.'

Sticks commented, 'Hawkeyes is all we'd fucking want, right?'

'What we fucking want, Sticks, is patience.'

'Ah, well.' The colour sergeant winked at Wilkinson. 'You got loads of *that*, Ben.'

Geoff Hosegood announced during lunch — the Marines all ate together at one end of the mess room — 'My guess is zero hour'll be 1600.' He looked round at them all. 'How about a sweepstake? Quid a go, fifteen-minute intervals, nearest takes the pot?'

'Neat idea, Geoff.' Bert Hattry pushed half an orange into his mouth, dabbed at his moustache. 'Local time or Zulu?'

'Local, bloody hell. Be dark here, 1600 Zulu!'

'Zulu' meant UK time; operationally, once they got off the ground it was the time they'd keep. *If* they got off the ground . . . But even 1600 local time would be getting a bit close to the end of the daylight hours. The scene of projected action was at least two degrees of longitude to the east of Akrotiri, so they'd be flying into the dusk, into a night-time interception. A lot better than *no* interception, but it would mean taking on problems one could more happily have done without. Ideally you'd hope for a daylight sighting, well outside Syrian waters.

'Geoff, if you're running this sweepstake, you'd better be clear whether "zero hour" means receipt of a sighting report, or time of origin of the report, or the time the Herc takes off. I'd suggest takeoff, then there's no argument, you'd have a dozen witnesses to it.'

'Yeah. Right. Herc's wheels leaving the ground.'

They'd all brightened. Everyone wanted in on the sweepstake, convincing themselves in the process that the question was 'when', not 'whether'.

*   *   *

Ben was out near the parked Hercules, in mid-afternoon, when he heard and then saw a Nimrod take off from the other side of the field and circle away, climbing, to fly east. Checking the time, he saw it was 1530. That would be 8 Kilo 6, to whose skipper – Doug McPhaill – he'd talked from the control tower yesterday. 8 Kilo 6 would be taking over from Foxtrot 2 Bravo at 1600; the flight to and from their beat took them only twenty minutes each way but they were allowing thirty and working four-hour watches round the clock. Although the standard Nimrod patrol plus transit periods would have been six hours, Morgan had said. In fact there was a spare crew – or spare crew members, including pilots – so at intervals they were getting longer breaks as well.

He jogged back to the transit block, and found most of the team in the office-cum-ops room. There was continuing interest in the sweepstake, the list which Geoff Hosegood had pinned up with names and times on it, a name at each fifteen-minute interval from 1400 – long gone, now – to 2215. It would have been bad luck to take it beyond that time, Hosegood had reckoned, and he'd extended it that far only because it would give each punter three chances. For instance the first slot, 1400, had been allocated to Tony Hall: 'Romeo' Hall, as his friends called him, would get his next chance at 1645 and a third maybe at 1930.

Hosegood wasn't present to see his time expire, he was taking a turn of guard-duty on the Hercules, in company with Frank Kenrick. Whose own chances came alive at 1622½ when Corporal Froggie Clark's expired. At about that time Ben happened to be at the window when Foxtrot 2 Bravo roared in to land; and twenty minutes later Russell Haig, the Nimrod's skipper, dropped in.

'Still hanging around then, Ben.'

'Regrettably. Since you didn't find our *gulet* yet.'

'No. No . . . Actually I came in the hope of finding a cup of Bootneck tea. Since I'm now getting a few hours' break from the excessively boring task you've lurked us into.'

'But really you've come to gripe about it, right?'

'I can tell you, today's turning out to be a bloody marathon . . . No, not exactly *gripe* . . . Any tea going?'

'Wee Willie' Deakin told him, 'Wetting it now, sir.'

'How very hospitable.' Haig, who was a flight lieutenant, sat down and swung his legs on to a spare chair. He was a large, shaggy-headed man of about Ben's own age; they'd met yesterday, when he'd come for a description of the *gulet*. Both he and Doug McPhaill of 8 Kilo 6 had reproductions of the brochure illustration now, of course. As had other pilots from this base, and also the *Saratoga*'s, by this time. Haig said, 'Not to *gripe*, Benjamin. But since you mention it, some of my crew *are* beginning to wonder whether your mystery ship's ever going to show up. All that rush to get into the air yesterday, and now – well, to coin a phrase, fuck-all . . . Thought I might sound you out, so I could keep my chaps in touch, to some extent.'

He'd put it nicely and he was a likeable character, but the question still irritated.

'It's been a trying day for us too, Russell.'

The flyer blinked at him. 'I honestly don't think *we*'ve fucked up. It's not impossible, nobody's perfect, etc., but our track record's quite impressive. Impresses *me*, anyway. One might even say "astonishes". And we've had near-ideal conditions. I don't believe it could've got past me – or past Doug either. Sorry to be annoying, and all that.' He took his mug of tea from Deakin. 'Thanks . . . I mean, frankly, Ben, facing facts?'

'Facts.' He nodded. 'I'll give you some facts. Like – well, the *gulet* started out from Kyrenia – *fact* – between midnight Sunday and sunrise Monday – *fact* – couldn't therefore have been farther east than Cape Andreas when you began your surveillance – that's fact three – and its destination was – *is* – a beach on a fairly limited section of the Syrian coast. That's also a fact – supplied by Intelligence and accepted by my CO, by the Chief of the Defence Staff, and I'd guess by the Chief of the Air Staff as well. To whom you might care to refer if you or anyone else wants to know how urgent, vital, etc. it is to locate these sods and stop them.'

He shook his head. 'Ought to be putting this on tape.'

'Why not.' Haig nodded. 'Then you could play it to Doug when he gets down. That won't be for a while yet, incidentally, he's out there on a six-hour stint this time. My kite's off at 1700 – another guy driving, thank the Lord . . . Any minute

183

now, in fact.' He checked the time. 'As I said, it's a marathon . . . But look, Ben, I believe you, I accept your logic *and* the importance of the task. Well, obvious, isn't it, you wouldn't have been rushed out here otherwise . . . But I still ask, where *is* the bloody thing?'

'If you want guesses . . .' Ben reached for the chart, and pointed at the southern bulge of the Turkish mainland. 'Could be thereabouts. Supposition by courtesy of Colour Sergeant Kelso.' He pointed at him. 'That little fellow.'

'How do, Sergeant.'

Sticks bowed.

Ben said, 'Could well be hiding up there. That bay, for instance. But there'd be a lot of ins and outs a chart this scale couldn't show; and I suppose they wouldn't let you trespass in Turkish airspace, would they . . . Any case, the guy from Special Branch said there're shoals of *gulets* in Turkish mainland harbours, so we wouldn't know one from any other . . . Incidentally, how's your radar likely to perform on that kind of target?'

'I wouldn't expect any problems. We'd get a distinctive profile, from 5000 feet, thereabouts.'

'You wouldn't need to go right down, then, which might scare them off?'

'Right, we wouldn't. That's sort of what it's all about.'

'If it's so good, why can't they make the prototype AEW Nimrod arrangement work?'

'Something else entirely, Ben. It's not the aircraft that doesn't work, it's the gear. We're Maritime Surveillance, "MR", that early-warning stuff's infinitely more complex . . . But tell me – why would your *gulet* want to hang around on the Turkish coast?'

'Picking up more people, maybe? Four's a small group, for whatever they're up to, we'd never go in in such small force . . . Could be a matter of timing their arrival in Syria – if they were feeling too exposed at Kyrenia? But that's another thing we don't know, whether they've any suspicion we're after them. Could be they're circling westbound, so they'd enter your surveillance area from the southwest. Could be *anywhere* – which is why I arranged to have that picture fax'd to the *Saratoga*, off-chance one of their planes might spot it.

Incidentally, one answer might've been to borrow an E-2 from the Cousins, to cover the outfield, but – '

'You wouldn't have had a prayer. That's why my Nimrod's taking to the air right at this moment – filling a window in the E-2s' tracking schedule. Soviet cruiser and two destroyers, no less.'

'But – Christ's *sake* . . . Look, what about *our* job?'

'They asked could we help, and it happens we can just fit it in. *Just* . . . three-hundred-mile transit each way and two hours' patrolling. When my plane gets back it's me back in the saddle – quick fuelling and off again, before old Doug falls out of the sky . . . But – ' Haig rapped the edge of the table for luck – 'maybe he'll have found your target for you by then.'

In London, where no news was looking more and more like bad news, attempts were being made in various localities to limit potential damage.

In a public telephone box outside Gloucester Road tube station, for instance, a young man who looked as if he might have been an insurance salesman had dialled a number and was listening to it ringing, ringing . . .

Finally satisfied, he hung up, recovered his 10-pence coin, left the kiosk, edged out between a car and a delivery van and slid into the front passenger seat of a BMW that was double-parked with its engine running and a girl with orange hair behind its wheel.

'OK, Jill, she's not home yet.'

'The flat, then.' She had the car moving. 'And then we're up, up and away, right?'

'If we don't get lucky here. Or if one of the others hasn't meanwhile. I'll phone in before we go.'

'Nice day in the sticks is what *I* call lucky. How about the Mermaid, that's *really* nice.'

'See, won't we.'

Two minutes later she double-parked again, for long enough to let him out. Residential road, but it was full of cars, both sides.

'I'll circle the block, OK?' She added before he'd shut the door, 'Don't try *too* hard . . .'

The hallway was deserted. No porter; they didn't even have entry-phones. After a glance at the lift, which was practically antique, he loped up the stairs.

Second floor, flat eleven . . . He rang its bell and stood waiting, nursing his briefcase. Ready to trot out his sales-spiel. Just in case: it would be rotten luck if she'd arrived home in the few minutes since he'd telephoned, but you had to allow for the unexpected.

But she was *not* back yet, evidently, from her long weekend in Paris with the daughter and son-in-law. She was due back this evening, hubby had told a colleague . . . The third key fitted. He went in, pushed the door shut with an elbow while he was pulling on some gloves and simultaneously taking in the *ambience* . . .

Depressed middle-class. Depress*ing*, anyway. The carpet was worn, the green wallpaper might have looked quite smart a hell of a long time ago. Sporting prints: might be good ones, might not be. Sad, really: if you'd had time to stop and think about it. The vague question in that thought, as he moved out of the hall, was which came first, the chicken or the egg?

What he was looking for was a desk.

There was one in the sitting room, but it was small, rather delicate, and a moment's inspection confirmed that it was the wife's. Personal correspondence, trivia, no business or trade stuff. Silver-framed snapshots of children, and two china dalmations. So much for the *salon*.

Bedroom. Frilly, with some fairly hideous Victoriana on the walls. The masculine corner – heavy chest of drawers serving as a dressing-table – had no paperwork on or in it. Group photograph of a cricket team and some family snapshots under glass. The top drawers were full of socks, mostly grey or brown, and the shirts in the next one down were nearly all white. Below that, cardigans and pullovers – fawn . . . He hadn't touched anything, except with a gloved forefinger.

Spare bedroom. Twin beds, one of them with a stuffed animal on it. The daughter would come over sometimes, of course.

Study?

Until he'd opened the door it could as easily have been a broom-cupboard. A little cell containing a desk, two chairs

186

and a wooden filing cabinet. On the desk a scarlet clip (Habitat?) held items presumably scheduled for attention. Some bills, a handwritten letter from a Paris address, a typed one from a London house agent saying the undersigned would be glad to call in order to make an inspection of the property and advise regarding valuation if Mr Harrington would telephone to arrange a mutually convenient time.

Retiring to the cottage near Rye, presumably.

Thinking, while shuffling expertly through other letters and memos, that he'd hardly have telephoned to arrange a mutually *in*convenient time.

Long brown envelope, crumpled, bearing the Gas Board's logo. On the back, ballpoint notes in a neat, cramped hand. A date and a time, letters DEDIP in capitals, and some Arab-type names: *Hoda Al-Jubran, Hafiz Al-J., Elizabeth Thornton – info officer, Damascus . . .* Then after some lines of really minute writing, *Hafiz J. allegedly supervising custody of V. Stillgoe.* Letters and numbers followed: a map grid, the world geographic reference system. Then: *Assad believed not privy to this. Head of Chancery's conclusions following interview Miss T. . . .*

Jackpot. And the brief had been spot-on. Amateur here, and a one-off; he wouldn't have had the imagination to foresee that anyone might take an interest.

8 Kilo 6 floated northward on the thrust of her four Rolls-Royce Speys, five thousand feet over a deep-blue sea with a haze in the distance at horizon level and a lot of small stuff down there, all of it pictured electronically on the 24-inch tactical display over which Frank Cornwall presided, reporting from time to time whatever the computer-controlled system suggested might be worth a mention. Frank was tactical navigator; just across from him, with damn-all to do in present circumstances, was George Binnie, the routine navigator. You could say it was the routine navigator's job to get the plane to the scene of action, and the TACNAV's to fight the battle when it got there. In some Nimrod crews, the TACNAV was the aircraft's commander; it just so happened that McPhaill and Haig, both pilots, commanded the two Akrotiri-based Nimrods.

On Doug's right Harry Denniston, his co-pilot, was flying the ship at this moment; and behind them Peter Stuart, flight engineer, was in one of his fretful moods, muttering darkly about fuel consumption.

Stuart was an old woman, Doug thought. OK, so they'd taken off with the fuel load they'd been carrying for the four-hour patrols, having learnt only just before takeoff that they were going to have to stay up this time for six. Because Haig's Foxtrot 2 Bravo was swanning off to Crete to play footsie with the Cousins. But the fuel load was still adequate, in view of the fact that one invariably took on an ample margin over and above anticipated requirements. You had to, to allow for diversions or other emergency situations that might arise. And, to have played it by the book and demanded a top-up at that stage would have delayed the takeoff, delayed relieving Foxtrot 2 Bravo, which had to be brought back with a bit of time in hand to prepare for the long haul westward.

On the port side forward of the beam the long neck of mountainous country reaching in a northeasterly slant to Cape Andreas was clarifying fast, edges hardening as 8 Kilo 6's course converged with it. Near the top end of the patrol line Cape Andreas would be only twenty-five miles away; then three minutes' flight farther north – fifteen miles, at this cruising speed – you'd begin a wide turn to starboard to end up returning southward on a flight-path ten miles to the east of this one, right on the edge of – and at times actually inside – the thirty-five miles of coastal water and airspace which the Syrians claimed as their own.

Doug said into his intercom, 'Search at extreme range to the north when we get to the top, TACNAV.'

'Sure.'

'It'll be all yours by the end of this next lap.'

He meant that the light would have gone, the only useful sensors electronic.

The 2100 slot in the sweepstake was Sticks Kelso's. 2107½ came and was gone, and Ducky Teal – who'd been reared to become a jockey, but stood eye to eye with the colour sergeant – murmured, 'Ah, now, *here* we go . . .' Because his name was down against 2115. Kelso said amiably, 'You can forget it, lad. You all can.' He tapped the list, told Hosegood, 'Better extend this lot, Geoff, there'll be another round.'

Hosegood turned down the corner of a page in the paperback he'd been reading.

'*You* extend the fucker. I'm for early kip.'

Interest in the sweep was wearing thin, now they'd all missed out a couple of times. But it was the continuing disappointment that was *really* wearing.

'Geoff.' Ben spoke from the window, where he'd been rooted for some while, staring out across the runways. 'You want to turn in, my advice would be to take your bag out to the Herc.'

Hosegood stared at him across the room, fingering that floppy back moustache of his. 'Yeah. Maybe I will . . .'

'And take the sweepstake list with you. Extend it to midnight, why not, but that's where you'll want it when the Herc's wheels leave the ground.'

All looking at him: seeing the bull-terrier glint in his eyes, a force of certainty compelling them to believe . . .

'Between now and midnight, it's *got* to show.' He turned back to the window. Knowing – because Russell Haig had spelt out the projected schedule of Nimrod movements – that Foxtrot 2 Bravo was now twelve minutes overdue. Haig's Nimrod should have landed at 2100 and immediately commenced refuelling, for takeoff with Haig at the controls at 2130 in order to relieve 8 Kilo 6 over the sea at 2200. But no aircraft had landed, runway lights hadn't been switched on, even, the only light out there was the glow seeping from the interior of the Hercules.

It was fifteen minutes past the hour now. Sticks joined him at the window. 'Good thinking, that, Ben, to kip on board.'

He heard the words without taking them in. Still thinking about Foxtrot 2 Bravo. He didn't know how fast a Nimrod might be able to refuel, but after a flight of that duration he guessed its tanks would be fairly low. This switched his thoughts to Doug McPhaill, who by 2200 would have been out there for six hours. Haig had said, *Quick fuelling, then off again before Doug falls out of the sky* . . . but now it looked inevitable that 8 Kilo 6 would have to turn for home without being relieved on the surveillance job.

Kelso asked, 'Problem?'

'Yeah. Nimrod should've been down by now. If the one on patrol doesn't get relieved – and it can't be without the other lad getting back and refuelling first – well, can't stay out there with empty tanks, can it.'

He went to the phone, called an extension and asked for Flight Lieutenant Morgan. They kept him waiting for a few minutes, then transferred his call to the control tower, where he got not Morgan but Russell Haig.

'Benjamin . . . '

'Why aren't you on the point of taking off to relieve McPhaill?'

'You noticed.'

'It's a crucial time. And we aren't here for fun, you know. Where's Foxtrot 2 Bravo?'

'Ben, you're going to hate this, but she's about four hundred miles west, still tracking Soviets. Those ships altered course to the north of Crete instead of holding on through the Kaso Strait. He was supposed to've been relieved by a Hawkeye at eight, but – '

'Christ.' There was a silence on the line. 'So – *we* have to lose out. This entire operation – *infinitely* more important than—'

'There's been a very high-level exchange of signals, Ben. And he should be leaving them in the next few minutes, we're expecting confirmation now that he's on his way. That's why I'm here.'

'If he started now – four hundred miles – '

'We'd have him down at 2230, roughly. Then refuelling – '

'What about Kilo 6's endurance?'

'Doug *should* turn for home at 2200. He's bound to try to stretch it, knowing him, but – well, when he fuelled, the expectation was for a four-hour patrol, you see.'

'So – so whatever happens there's going to be at least one hour with no surveillance. Right when the *gulet*'s most likely to show.' He drew a hard breath. 'That's it, then. All I can do is call London, tell them what's—'

'They *know*, Ben. MoD are spitting blood. Go ahead, if it'll help you, but it won't change anything. And we're going to do our best to – Ben, hold on, just a second?'

He felt sick. Sweating, and pulses racing. Aware of a lot of eyes on him, a mix of sympathy and anger and his own feelings of incredulity, desperation . . .

'Ben. F 2 B's on her way back, ETA 2225. Fuelling crew'll be standing by and so will I and my crew, we'll be out there by 2320 latest. Doug's being told to stay with it as long as he reasonably can. We *might* be able to reduce the gap to not much more than one hour. I know, I'm *sorry* . . .'

McPhaill's eyes shifted to the digital time display: 2210, and the seconds ticking over as fast as always. Holding 8 Kilo 6 on her course of due north, and roughly midway up the length of the beat. He'd just brought her round: having told Akrotiri that he reckoned he could make the fuel last long enough to stay on the job until 2240, if he finished at the bottom end with a short run home. He'd turned early, therefore, abbreviating the run south so he'd be in a position to do just that.

His engineer didn't like it at all. Stuart had insisted that 2220 was the very latest they could afford to remain on patrol, and even that was taking more of a risk than anyone in his right mind would take, with an extremely valuable aircraft and a crew whose costly training didn't include much long-distance swimming. He'd put it in this semi-humorous way, Doug recognised, because he had to be aware that his nagging must have been getting on his skipper's nerves.

'If it looks as bad as you're projecting, I'll break away sooner. Cut the corner halfway down, maybe.'

He glanced to his right. Denniston was upright in the co-pilot's seat but he hadn't said a word in the last ten or fifteen minutes. Switched off, or asleep, or both.

Five minutes now to the top, the final turn to starboard. It was a bit over the odds, McPhaill thought, to bounce you with a six-hour stint instead of the routine four, and then on top of that expect you to bat on. On the other hand he was aware that the absence of Foxtrot 2 Bravo meant that some real wally on the staff had let the Marines down very badly, and he was personally concerned to go as far as he could to minimise the damage.

'What've you got now, TACNAV?'

Cornwall made a sound like a man snapping out of daydreams.

'Ah – nowt that's new, skipper. Same bodies continuing southward, no changes of courses or speeds. The two *from* the south have gone into Famagusta, and the ferry's off the screen.' He was talking, McPhaill thought, like a man who for some time hadn't given the picture much attention, was now catching up, refreshing his *own* memory ... 'On the Syrian coast we have the tanker that came down from the northwest: she's now off Baniyas. That's the boy we looked at, if you remember, Cuban registry ... No, as you were, correction – that one's stopped, right inshore, close to the oil terminal, must be at moorings. Our lad's still twenty-five miles offshore, southbound. Destination Tartus, could be ... Now, northern sector: no, not a damn thing ...'

'Make sure of it. We're coming up to the turn, then it's home, sweet home.'

The Routine Navigator, George Binnie, commented drily, 'That couldn't be a reference to Akrotiri, surely.'

'I don't know.' Denniston stirred, a hand coming up to adjust the position of his throat microphone. 'After seven hours, Akrotiri's OK by me.'

'Good sleep, Harry?' McPhaill put the Nimrod into the turn. Maybe anticipating the moment just a little. Denniston admitting that he might have dropped off, for a spell. He'd heard all the earlier chit-chat though, knew what was happening. He'd evidently been thinking, too; he said, 'Bootnecks'll be going mad, won't they, until Foxtrot 2's back on the job.'

At 2228 George Binnie broke a silence, asking Cornwall, 'Didn't we have *four* southbound widgers under us last time round, TACNAV?'

'Uh-huh. Three.' Pause ... 'Here – *three*, OK?'

'Lap before that, then. Or even the one before *that*. Quite a stretch farther north. What's your log say to that?'

'Hang on.' Adjusting scale, Doug guessed. It wasn't what was happening three laps ago that mattered, it was what was down there *now*. He heard Cornwall say, 'If there were four, still are four ... And lo and behold, we do still have ... No. No, we have three.'

'So what's this?'

'Tanker. I just told the skipper – '

'I suggest he's number four and he split from this cluster some time back. Long enough to have displaced himself eastward by – Jesus, *twenty miles?*'

'That'd mean the tanker *is* this fellow close inshore. But if so . . . Well, *can't* be, but . . .'

He'd be getting a verdict from the computer: from the computer setup, there were actually three separate computers in the assembly. Working fast and – despite that 'can't be' – anxious now, Doug had heard the uncertainty in his tone for the first time ever, in that moment. He didn't interrupt with any questions or urgings, he left it to the TACNAV to sort it out. Knowing he was more than capable of doing so, knew his job backwards, had always been right on top of it, with all the answers and always bull's-eyes. Anyone could make mistakes: but from this cliché Doug would have excluded Frank Cornwall, and at this stage he still didn't believe the guy could have fouled it up, was still expecting him to have it sorted, verified, within seconds.

8 Kilo 6 was already five miles farther south than she had been when the Routine Navigator had stuck his oar in.

Cornwall blurted, his voice suddenly high-toned: 'My God, course is one-two-eight, speed is – ten point six knots, it *did* split from—'

'Radar profile?'

'It's – our target, skipper. The *gulet.* Jesus, I can't see *how* I—'

'My course to take a look at it?'

Stuart, engineer, broke in: 'If we divert now, let alone go down to—'

'All right, protest noted. TACNAV?'

'Come left to zero-zero-seven. But that's in Syrian—'

'Range?' 8 Kilo 6 banking as she turned. 'Co-pilot call base, tell 'em we have the *gulet* – position, course, speed – computer confirmed, I'm going down to double-check.'

'Skipper – sorry, but—'

'Twenty-three point two miles.' Cornwall, answering the range question. 'Course should be zero-zero-six.'

'I want to pass two hundred metres clear at one hundred feet.' The way he always did it, on a level flight-path, to look

193

as if the aircraft just happened to be passing close, so there'd be at least a chance the target wouldn't know *it* was the centre of attraction. Doug told his engineer, 'Our esteemed staff have already dropped those guys in the shit, *I'm* not dropping 'em on some bloody tanker. If we have to we'll land at Larnaca, right?'

'How long is it since they threw you out of the Army, Charlie?'

Denham asked the question. He, Charlie and Bob Knox were in the *gulet*'s wheelhouse as she closed in towards the coast, showing navigation lights because if the Syrians had her on radar a darkened ship would arouse more suspicion than a lit one. Charlie told Denham coldly, 'They didn't. I was chucked out of the SAS, more or less, so I went back to my old regiment. I couldn't stand it, so I resigned.'

'And they let you go, just like that?'

'Yes, Bob.' Staring at him . . . 'Just like that. What you're implying is maybe they weren't sorry to offload a piss-artist. You're right, too, I was *really* into it at that stage.'

Knox's dark shape shifted. 'So damn touchy, Charlie –'

'Hey!' Smiley Tait called from outside, the stern. 'Hey – Bob –'

They'd all heard it at that moment. Joseph at the conning position lowering himself in an attempt to see upward through the window, the other three rushing to join Smiley outside. Then it was almost on top of them, a roar mounting to climax in an explosion of noise – close to starboard, not overhead as it had seemed it would be – a hurtling shape visible for about two seconds, then the glow of jet-trails fading, soundwaves reverberating away into the enclosing night.

'Bloody near hit us!'

'Same one, maybe.' Bob added, 'Nimrod, obviously from Akrotiri.'

'It *could*'ve been a Nimrod.' Charlie was still staring after it. 'But unless you saw a lot more than I did –'

'I'm only guessing, Charlie. It was something *like* that.'

'Whatever it was –' Leila, coming from forward, ducked into the wheelhouse – 'I don't like it.'

They'd seen a Nimrod earlier in the day, when they'd been a long way north and steering as if to pass close round Cape

194

Andreas. They hadn't stopped at Ovacik, after all. Leila had wanted to push on farther east so that when they turned it might look as if they'd come from Iskenderun, and later she'd taken advantage of the chance to join up with three other boats steering a similar southward course, one a motor-cruiser and the other two under sail, all three flying the Swiss flag, evidently some kind of holiday flotilla. They'd seen another earlier in the day, up north, apparently making for Kyrenia, about a dozen identical sailboats straggling down from the Turkish west coast. There was a Swiss holiday flotilla based at Marmaris, Leila had said, although she didn't know if this might have been part of it. Charlie suspected she'd been counting on finding company of this kind, to disguise the *gulet*'s approach to Syrian waters; she'd made sure they had a lot of time in hand, and as they'd closed up on the Swiss she'd twice told Joseph to reduce speed, first to six knots and then to three. At dusk they'd been in a close group crawling south when they'd seen the Nimrod circling from west to east, and about three-quarters of an hour later they'd heard it — assuming it was the same one — pass overhead somewhere. Soon after this they'd altered course to southeast and increased to full speed. There'd been a tanker ahead, distantly visible stern-on to them before the light went, but it must have been drawing rapidly away ahead of them even after the increase to about eleven knots.

That tanker had appeared from the northwest and crossed ahead of the little flotilla an hour or so earlier. But they'd seen no other ships or ships' lights since the change of course and speed.

Charlie suggested, 'Might have been Syrian. Unless it was a different Nimrod to the one we saw before. Could've been a Mig-25, d'you reckon, Bob?'

Denham agreed. 'Nimrod wouldn't be swanning around here, would it.'

Tait said, 'Could've been Syrian and still not seen us. *Or* a Nimrod. Who gives a shit — *I* don't.'

But the *gulet* was turning, broad white wake bending as she swung to port. Leila called, 'Bob, here, please?'

She had the chart spread on the table and she'd been working on it.

'Look here.' Charlie followed Bob inside, peered over Leila's tanned shoulder. 'We can't know what that airplane was doing, but maybe it reported us.' She pointed at new pencil markings. 'We were steering as if for a legitimate approach to Tartus – but then to turn off before we'd come so far. D'you see? And to be gone before anyone on shore began to scratch his head too much . . . But now, I think we put you off closer to Baniyas – here. This beach is only a little more than eight kilometres north of the other one. No big problem for you, I think. And you see, ten forty now, you leave us a half-hour early, that will help, huh?'

11

The C130's hold, with only the two black-hulled Sea-Riders as cargo, seemed not only cavernous but incredibly noisy, an empty steel drum thunderous with the roar of engines. The cargo door had been shut, the hydraulically-operated ramp angled upward towards the tail: and when that thing was next lowered it would be to eject a dozen men and two boats into the night.

The boats were on the centreline, on the track of steel rollers which allowed for the loading and unloading of very large weights of cargo. They were held there by braced steel-wire strops, with their snouts pointing towards the exit in the aircraft's tail.

Ben was up front conferring with the navigator and the pilots. They'd been checking 8 Kilo 6's signalled position of the *gulet* – first report at 2222 and the second at 2231 after McPhaill had confirmed the identification visually. Position, course and speed matched, near enough exactly, the information which the CO had provided in his briefing at Lyneham less than forty-eight hours ago. Hislop had brought maps and a chart with him, the maps showing the grid-reference location of the inland target and the chart reflecting this so you could see where Swale's party would need to land – where you'd choose to land yourself if that was where you had to get to.

From the position 8 Kilo 6 had given, extending the *gulet*'s course of 128 degrees at the given speed of ten and a half knots, you had them getting in close to that bit of coast at just about midnight. That was where you'd have expected them to land, it was where their course was taking them, and midnight was about the time you'd have aimed for yourself: it made sense, you could accept it.

The main difference between the present reality and the scenario as it had been projected was that the intention had been to stop the *gulet* well away from the Syrian coast, and with any luck in daylight.

Luck hadn't been exactly plentiful, so far.

Still sitting, waiting, engines thundering . . .

'What's keeping us?'

The navigator yelled into his ear, 'Nimrod landing — Fox 2 Bravo . . .' He saw Ben's expression, added 'Landing *now*, chum!' Then he turned away: the co-pilot had punched his shoulder and was holding out a radio headset, gesturing towards Ben . . . 'Tower!'

He pulled the phones over his ears, said into the mike, 'Ockley here.'

'Ben — Russell . . . Listen — I'll have us chasing after you within minutes. Won't need to be up long so I'll cut short the fuelling. You may have dropped before I'm on the scene, otherwise I'll try to guide your pilot. But listen, you have Sarbes, don't you?'

'Yes.'

'So if you need guidance when you're on the water, we can communicate.'

'*Right!*'

Having taken over the *gulet*, what was more, he could report the situation and London would know all about it within minutes.

'Good luck, Ben.'

The Sarbes, search-and-rescue beacons, had a speak function as well as the automatic one. On auto they'd transmit bleeps on the international distress frequency, but with the switch to 'speak' you had two-way voice communication with aircraft up to ten thousand feet, provided they were more or less overhead.

He passed back the headset. And the Hercules had begun to move. The navigator grinning at him, raising a thumb . . . Ben went back aft, rolling the chart as he went; it could be stowed in one of the containers in the first boat. He had Hislop's map inside his shirt; it was actually a strip cut from a larger map, rolled into a tube and protected in a condom with its open end knotted. Sticks had the same. Condoms supplied by Marine Tony Hall who'd thus justified – as if he hadn't before – his nickname, 'Romeo'. The maps would be of more use than the chart, in inshore waters, as they showed more coastline detail than the chart did, landmarks such as new oiltanks and other recent installations in that area. Oil from Iraq was pumped across Syria to that coast, to terminals and refineries in the Tartus – Baniyas area.

Preparing to give his team a last-minute briefing, Ben was thinking that despite the problems imposed by darkness, it was essential that the interception and boarding should be completed quickly and efficiently, so that the Sea-Riders' powerful outboards could then remove them from the vicinity of the Syrian coast as rapidly as possible. The drop was going to be much too close to that coast to feel any kind of complacency about it. Fast interception and a quick, neat boarding: if it took more than minutes, the gulet's ten or eleven knots might not get her away quickly enough, it might well be necessary to sink her. If her crew and passengers had had the sense to stay alive – it was up to them, how they reacted when they were stopped and boarded – they could be brought back in the Sea-Riders.

You had to sit, now, for the takeoff. The aircraft had halted, done a half turn. Noise and vibration worse again as engine revs built up, and the loadmaster – a burly Crab NCO – was ordering the Marines to their perches along the sides of the fuselage. Grey-painted metal and plastic, patches of multi-coloured wiring and other gear . . . Some of the team were already in drysuits, others hadn't yet pulled them on over their DPMs and such equipment as they were carrying on their bodies during the drop. Most of it – the SA80 individual weapons and ammunition, and grenades, and such gear as Laker's medical bag, Hall's kit of explosives, Ray Wilkinson's Nikon, two starscopes and several pairs of binoculars, were in the containers inside the boats. In fact there were two categories of equipment: 'first line' consisting of the gear that was ordered — weapons, compasses, Sarbes, divers' knives, water-bottles, first-aid packs, a ration-pack — and 'second line' varying according to individual choice. It might include extra rations — 'nutty', alias chocolate, etc. — energy tablets, spare knife, maybe a handgun. The DPM suits were elaborately furnished with pockets internally and externally for such items.

The Hercules began to roll again. For real, this time. Launching itself down the runway, engines at full blast. Geoff Hosegood, pausing in the application of black camouflage cream to his face, held up his left arm, drawing back the sleeve to expose his diver's watch; Froggie Clark shouted over the din, 'Gotter be Doc's — right?'

Hosegood pursed his lips, shook his head, eyes on the watch. Nobody caring now, because there were plenty of other things to think about. The sweepstake had served its purpose, but it had become a triviality. Anyway, Laker hadn't won it: he'd been down for takeoff at 2245, which extended to 2252½, and it was a few seconds past that now. 2253 . . . Hosegood grinning, pointing at Chalky Judge, who raised both fists in a gesture of victory and then continued with what he'd been doing, tightening the straps of the holster on his right leg, his diver's knife. And the wheels *had* left the ground . . . Ben unclipped his belt and got off the seat; the loadmaster looked displeased, but this was no time for humouring Crabs. He told the team, pitching his voice up to beat the noise: 'Thirty minutes. *Thirty*. Then — ' — pointing at the tail-end, and downward.

Actually it would be nearer forty before they dropped. The transit was a distance of one hundred and forty miles and then there'd be a minute or two for manoeuvring into the dropping run. They'd jump from one thousand feet, which meant about half a minute in the air although it always felt a lot longer than that. But from a thousand feet he doubted whether on this moonless night the pilots would have much hope of actually spotting the *gulet*. And there was no Nimrod out there to direct them, as there should have been. So the drop would in a real sense be 'blind': except that he'd done the chartwork, and based on the data supplied by Doug McPhaill you could reckon on ending up ahead of the *gulet* and inshore of it. The Sea-Riders would be dropped two thousand yards apart and would then close in at speed on their target.

With a Nimrod calling the shots, of course, you could do it a lot more accurately. You'd know precisely where the target was right up to the moment of the drop.

He was in his drysuit, applying cam-cream. They were mostly finished with their individual preparations by the time the Hercules had levelled at its transit height of two thousand feet. If they'd had to they could have jumped in three minutes, let alone thirty.

Plenty of time for briefing, therefore. Ben sat on his own Sea-Rider's stern, with an elbow on top of its outboard, and beckoned to them to gather round close enough to be screamed at . . . Sticks Kelso right in front of him, on the bow of the second boat: leaning forward, elbows on rubber-encased knees. The others packed in around them.

'We'll be dropping a couple of miles short of where the *gulet*'s likely to stop to send her boat ashore. Her course is 128, reciprocal of that's 308, we'll drop a mile apart – Sticks on the right . . . Weather forecast is clear sky – no moon. Moon later but not now. Low swell, wind northwest two to three. Coxswains'll wear PNG – should have a half-mile vis from the tops of the swells. We'll use VHF to synchronise the approach. Usual drill then, you know it. If they don't stop and we have to use the LAWs, aim for the wheelhouse, OK?'

Kelso had pointed at Ducky Teal, to handle his boat's light anti-tank weapon. Chalky Judge already knew it would be his job in the first boat. Ben went on, 'We're not here to kill anyone. But *one*, if they resist, or *two*, any attempt to send up flares – because we'll be bloody near that coast – then we don't risk *our* lives, right? Geoff, I want their radio smashed as soon as we board . . . But any threat to us or to the completion of the task, don't mess about, use your SA80s, it's what they're for.'

Sticks glanced around at the faces ringing them, then looked back at Ben and nodded. Ben yelled, 'You know what Swale looks like. If all goes well we'll take him with us, but otherwise he's to be killed. I'll do it, but if I'm not in a position to for any reason, someone else must.' Sticks nodded again. 'But the outcome we *want* is the *gulet* stops – or doesn't, but anyway we board and take it over, crew and passengers surrender. We'll secure them – ' he mimed it, crossing his wrists behind his back – 'in the *gulet* if we have the time, otherwise in the boats. Point is we must be out of Syrian water by sunrise. If time allows we'll take the *gulet*, but she's slow so maybe we'll have to sink her.' He looked at Romeo Hall. 'PE in the bilges, three locations. She's heavy-timbered, need to blow her bottom out.'

Hall nodded. It wouldn't be any problem.

He'd about finished. Thinking that they were going to need the extra petrol they'd brought. The regular tanks would give these outboards a range of sixty to eighty miles, but they'd have used some before they boarded, and the run to Dhekelia would be about a hundred. Result of having to start so close to the Syrian coast . . . 'Sticks, one more thing. I had Russell Haig on the radio from the tower just before we took off. He's most likely in the air by now, chasing out after us. He suggested he could guide us – if we need it, which maybe we will – by Sarbe voice comms when we're in the boats. So listen out, OK?'

Sticks raised a thumb.

'That's it, then. Questions?'

There weren't any. Fortunately. Briefing in a loud scream wasn't the easiest way to do it. But that last-minute call from 8 Kilo 6, the proximity to Syria and the absence of Nimrod guidance had changed the basics of the operation quite considerably.

2316 now: about a quarter of an hour to go. Coxswains and crewmen checking their boats and the boats' fittings for about the fiftieth time. Ben took a look round too, at the Sea-Riders and the containers in which some items' stowage had to relate to that boat's crew. For instance, Judge's explosives were in the first boat – Ben's, Bert Hattry as coxswain and Deakin as crewman – while Doc Laker's medical outfit had to be in the other – Kelso's, coxed by Froggie Clark.

Each man's Sarbe was inside his drysuit, on a lanyard.

Sticks was going from man to man checking Sarbes. Back in Poole – which at this moment could have been some place on the back of the moon – there was a poster on the wall in the sergeant major's office, a photograph of an extremely attractive tennis girl in the shortest of short skirts, walking away from camera with a racket in one hand and the other hand's fingers up under the fringe of skirt, reconnoitring to touch a pair of minuscule pants; below the picture was the advice *Don't chance it – CHECK!*

Sticks was checking. Although each of them would have checked already.

2325: the Hercules was losing height, and the two halves of the team were separating, mustering round their boats.

Radar monitoring and the satellite communications link was via Dhekelia now. On radar they had the Hercules approaching the Syrian coast and Foxtrot 2 Bravo on her way out from Akrotiri. Foxtrot 2 had climbed to its transit height of five thousand feet while the C130 was at this moment descending towards the thousand-foot mark from which the Marines would jump. The Nimrod had a long way to go before it could make any useful contribution, and obviously the jump couldn't be delayed.

In London, in the Special Forces section of the Joint Operations Centre in the Ministry of Defence, a warrant officer spoke into a microphone in front of him on the long central table. 'Any movement over Syrian airfields?'

An RAF staff officer had asked for this information, after a question from Charles Hislop, and there was an interval before the answer came. Hislop mentally counting out the seconds, visualising the interior of that Hercules, his men ready in their drybags around the Sea-Riders; seeing also the fat, lumbering shape of the aircraft as a blackness blacker than the surrounding night, gleam of restless sea below and distantly – though not distantly enough – pools of light marking towns and settlements, ribbons of light along new roads and motorways, and – *maybe* – airbase runway lights switching on, Migs rolling forward . . .

'Negative.' The voice came from nearly two thousand miles' distance, by surface measurement, but in fact had travelled a lot farther, bouncing off an orbiting communications satellite. 'Negative, Syrian air.'

'That's something.' The Duty Operations Director — a rear-admiral — glanced at Hislop. Charles Hislop running a palm over his bald head, seeing in his mind the C130's cargo door opening, the ramp's initial jerk before it began to hinge downwards, descending steadily then until the tail-end of the aircraft was open to the night. Hislop had jumped from Hercs enough times himself to know exactly what it looked like, felt like.

He murmured to the SF Adviser — who happened also to be a Royal Marine major, formerly a member of the Special Boat Squadron — 'Why wouldn't the Syrian airforce react, I wonder?'

'Maybe they guess the intrusion'll be over before they'd get there.'

'Or — ' the admiral suggested — 'they guess the intruders might be Israelis and they don't want to lose their Migs.'

Two miles to the west, Eddie Harrington flung himself over on the bed again. In the other one his wife snored softly in deep, enviable sleep. While he stayed wide awake in nightmare.

Not because he was in the doghouse with *her*. He was: she'd been in bed when he'd got home, she'd half-lowered her book and asked him coldly whether he couldn't have been back at a reasonable hour on her first night home? He'd begun to tell her: he'd had this meeting . . . She'd cut him short: 'You could have telephoned me — *some* time during the evening, couldn't you?'

It was the truth that he'd been obliged to attend an after-hours conference. It had been on purely routine, domestic matters, and he hadn't got away until about eight thirty. He'd wanted to get home early, not having seen her since Friday morning and knowing she'd be expecting him to hurry, to be agog for a blow-by-blow account of her weekend in Paris. But that had been just too bad; and he hadn't telephoned because he hadn't expected the meeting to take anything like that long.

Too bad. And from bad, to infinitely worse.

He'd thought about taking a taxi, but at theatre time they were never easy to find in that area, weren't always that much quicker anyway, so he'd decided to go as he usually did by underground; in fact he'd only covered the first thirty yards before a taxi had taken *him*.

He'd jumped clear, sure it was going to hit him: its headlights had sprung up to blind him as it had swerved, wheels mounting the pavement. He'd cannoned back against the wall and the cab had stopped, slewed slantwise across the pavement, its lights dimmed then and two men jumping out of the back – he'd thought, to see if he'd been hurt . . . They'd grabbed him, flung him inside – half-stunned, flabby with shock – and the cab had bumped down into the road, driven on. Passing Century House.

Struggling up: astonished and very, very frightened . . . 'What the *hell*—'

'Shut up, Eddie. Sit still, and look at this.'

Holding it so a street light caught it as they passed: the brown gas-board envelope on which he'd made those notes. And which when he'd last seen it had been on his desk in the flat.

'Who put you up to it, Eddie?'

'Who are you – where'd you get – '

'To the first question, never mind, to the second, where d'you *think* we got it? But *I'm* asking the questions, Eddie, and there's really only the one that matters: who put you up to it?'

'Up to what?' He'd begun to move, and met with immediate restraint. They were young, strong, and he was neither . . . 'Where're you taking me?'

'Well, it depends. If you don't answer that question we'll end up some place very quiet and private, what you might call unfrequented. If you *do*, we'll drop you at your door and you can live as miserable as you like ever after. The other way, Eddie, you'll be the victim of a hit-and-run. Saw how easy it could happen, did you?'

'Look. I haven't the least idea what—'

'End up dead that way, Eddie. Can't have you on the loose when you're trying to kick us all in the balls, can we. We know the background, old son, let's not hang about. We won't waste time and effort sweating it out of you – no, honest, I can reassure you on *that* point. The deal is, you can tell us or we kill you. Let's try again: who put you up to it, you fat old creep?'

'Christ—'

'Sorry. Sorry. Didn't mean to—'

'If you're from Box Five—'

'Box of five *what*?'

'You *must* be, but—'

'Answer the question, Eddie.'

'If I told you – if I *could* tell you – how would I know you'd – '

'Let you live horrible ever after? Well, you'd have to take my word. There'd be a condition too – you wouldn't tip 'em off. We wouldn't 've been near you, no one would, all you'd say is you can't go through with it. If you said we'd been on to you, you'd get the old hit-and-run bit after all. From us, that is. Oh, and you'd have to put it in writing, Eddie – what you were doing, who was paying and how much – all that stuff, and over your autograph. That's the deal if you want it, Eddie. Do you?'

'I'd be free – I mean, retire, and my pension – '

'Not my business, Eddie. One thing we're *not* is the DHSS.'

The other one laughed. Harrington began, 'The person whose name you want – '

'Name, address, occupation, family detail: and your connection, how he got on to you, how he'd 've known you'd do it.'

'What'll happen to him?'

'Happen?'

'Might he be left – well, free, and – '

'You've an enquiring mind, Eddie, haven't you.'

'Why I'm asking – '

'I know why you're asking. Question of what he might do if he got to know you'd shopped him. Right? Yeah, well, you'd have to cope with that one yourself, Eddie. Man tries to betray his own country, he can reckon on losing a little sleep, eh?'

* * *

Above the black opening in the end of the hold a red light came on, a warning glare just as the loadmaster shouted, 'Stand by!' The loadmaster would have been reacting not to the red light but to the order in his headphones, from the cockpit. Six Marines crouching with their hands on the first Sea-Rider's sides and their heads up, eyes fixed on that light. Ben Ockley at the bow, port side, Bert Hattry opposite him: behind Ben, Romeo Hall, and Chalky across from him. In rear, Wee Willie Deakin and Geoff Hosegood. All six in more or less the athletes' *on-your-marks-get-set* position: six taut faces streaked with cam-cream garish in the light's red stain.

It went out. A green one flashed on and the loadmaster bawled, 'Go!'

The six ran aft, taking the boat with them on its track of rollers and launching it ahead of them so that it reached the end of the lowered, down-slanting ramp before they did, tilted over, flew out into the darkness before their own dives took them after it, bodies seemingly suspended in the black frame for a motionless fraction of a second and then snatched away in the howl of wind and the roar of engines.

The green light went out.

Sticks Kelso, Ducky Teal, Ray Wilkinson and Andy Laker, and at the stern Froggie Clark and his crewman Frank Kenrick, moved the second boat up to where the first had started. Hanging on to it so that the aircraft's lurchings wouldn't send it charging out on its own, while Froggie clipped its static line to the runner on the jackstay.

Red light.

Six rubber-suited men crouching with their boat. Knowing the first six would be plummeting into the sea at about this moment.

Red light out. Green on: and the loadmaster's yell. The same rush then, the Sea-Rider hurtling aft into the oblong of night sky, bodies tumbling out behind it, right and left.

Gone. The green light went out. The loadmaster was reporting into the mike of his headset on its long trailing lead that the drop had been completed. The ramp was rising, hydraulic rams sliding over to drag up those tons of steel and shut the door behind departed guests.

A small blue light was switched on automatically when the Sea-Rider hit the water, slamming down even-keeled at a distance which Ben, splashing in a second later and releasing himself from his harness instantaneously, then surfacing and looking for the boat, judged to be about ten metres. In fact it was at about twice that distance, the apparent proximity an illusion which he remembered now from previous drops. By the time he got there Geoff Hosegood and Wee Willie were already inboard, had extinguished the blue light and cleared away the parachute gear. Bert Hattry heaving himself in over the bow. Ben came aboard in a rolling motion over the port blister, hearing the drone of the Hercules' four engines fading westward and knowing that Sticks' team would be on their way down by now – and Chalky Judge conveniently creating a balance with his own arrival from the other side. Hattry was at the outboard, stripping it of its protective plastic bag and plugging in the lead from the gas-tank, then opening the tap and feeling for the toggle on the lanyard. Hall, last to come aboard, slithering in over the quarter. Wee Willie had one container open and was getting out first essentials when the outboard fired at the first pull, revving high to start with, Hattry then at his controls amidships, throttling down . . . Wee Willie was passing out the SA80s but he had Bert's PNG headset ready for him, for as soon as he could handle it.

The loom of a light, triple flashes, was from Ras el Buri and bore 055 degrees. Ben had had this lighthouse's range and bearing from the dropping point, from the chart before they'd taken off. The chart had flattered it with a visibility of twelve miles, and they were inside that range now, but chart-data visibility was for a height-of-eye of fifteen feet and it was a very different matter from wave-level in a Sea-Rider.

The boat was swinging, rocking around to point northwest; as she got on to that course and gathered way she began to bump, her bow meeting the swells head-on. It was an easier motion than the general tossing around, you could use both hands instead of having to keep one for holding on with.

'Starscope, Ben.'

He reached back to take it from Wee Willie. *Star Tron* nightscope. He put its strap over his head and crawled into the bow, and the next thing was to get the SA80 hooked to one of the fittings provided for that purpose on the blisters. Then in action you wouldn't lose it over the side if you had to let go of it for some reason – like being shot or having to grab a neighbour before *he* went over. Bert Hattry was steering one-handed, using the other to adjust the headset of his passive night goggles, and Geoff Hosegood had taken the wrappings off the VHF radio and was tuning it. There'd be nobody in range to communicate with yet, but there would be in a minute; the range of the set was virtually line-of-sight – daylight sight. The Sea-Rider's bow lifted as she climbed a long, low swell. Pole Star clear and bright fifty-two degrees to starboard; so Hattry had it about right: when the *gulet* appeared she should be more or less right ahead.

Bert Hattry was using his coxswain's seat now, a kind of saddle roughly in the middle, but with the PNG on too he was half-standing from time to time, and whenever they were lifted on a swell, to get a longer view forward. Ben similarly occupied – kneeling, using the starscope as the boat rode up another ridge of black water. Still throttled down, not much way on while they waited for the others, but in any case expecting the *gulet* to be coming to *them*.

Nothing in sight. Dark night, and the immensely long lines of the ridges approaching, rushing under. More movement on the sea than he'd expected. All the guns were clipped to the blisters now, and Wee Willie was passing the LAW to Chalky when a voice from the radio, distorted but recognisable as Ray Wilkinson's, squawked: 'Sticks calling Ben. No see *gulet*, can you? Over.'

'Tell him negative, steer three-zero-zero, twenty knots, *go*.'

Hattry opened his throttle while Geoff passed the message. Plunging into a dip, no hope of seeing anything at all, the *gulet* could have been fifty metres away and you wouldn't have seen it until you lifted again. Like now . . .

Nothing, except the black curve of the sea. Sky slightly less black, thanks to the stars. Polaris still where it ought to be. Levelling out a bit now, the motion slightly more violent but less vertical movement in it because of the speed building, speed carrying her from ridge to ridge . . . Ben was wondering if he'd taken too much for granted, expecting as he had to find the *gulet* just where it should have been if it had held on with unchanged course and speed. It might have reduced speed as it approached the coast, or stopped to launch its dinghy farther out than one had expected.

Not that one could have done anything about it. That Nimrod report was all he'd had to go on.

But if it had sent its boat in from say twenty miles offshore – no reason not to, in conditions as good as these – one might guess they'd have picked a landing place farther north. In relation to the inland target this wouldn't make a lot of sense, but it was a possibility; and if that *was* what was happening the dinghy might be on its way inshore now, somewhere higher up this coast.

Split the force, send Sticks north at high speed to cover that possibility?

It was the improbability of Swale and company choosing to add about ten kilometres to their overland transit that decided him against it. Also, the conclusion that he might be panicking for no good reason. Visibility with the PNG would be only about half a mile, if that, and the *gulet* could be not far at all from where he'd anticipated it would be, no more than a mile or two behind the schedule he'd imposed on it.

He had the chart – for offshore detail – and the map, for landmarks, pictured clearly enough in his mind. He knew he must be nine and a half or ten miles off the coast, and within about half a mile north or south just about opposite the landing place which he and Charles Hislop had agreed they'd have chosen. And this patch of sea where the Sea-Riders with a mile between them and visibility of half a mile were covering a width of two nautical miles, four thousand yards, as they advanced, was where the *gulet*'s course and speed as established by that Nimrod should have brought it by midnight.

And it was now – the glow of his diver's watch-face told him – ten minutes *short* of midnight. Ten minutes at 10½ knots: ten and a half over six: one point seven five.

So no problem. Swale's ship still had one and three-quarters miles to cover; with vis roughly half a mile, the effective distance before sighting would be as near as damn-it one mile – since at twenty knots the gap was closing fast anyway. One mile at twenty knots – three minutes. But *two* minutes, if the *gulet* was herself making ten.

Two minutes, then. Brainstorm concluded.

The Sea-Rider was hardly noticing the swells now as she banged across them in a fast thumping rhythm, white wake peeling away astern. He thought of calling Sticks on the VHF and telling him the *gulet* couldn't be far ahead. Deciding against it: he had the starscope up, trying to hold it steady enough for a search across the line of advance, when Wee Willie yelled, 'Aircraft!'

He'd heard it too. He shouted to Hattry to slow down, knew he didn't have to tell Geoff to keep Sticks informed. It was 2351 now, and Foxtrot 2 Bravo could have been airborne by 2330, could therefore be overhead now. He got his Sarbe up out of the neck of his drysuit, knowing it well enough by feel to thumb one switch to 'speak' and the on-off to 'on'. Half expecting Russell Haig's voice to boom right out of it at that moment, but getting nothing except static.

There was no send/receive switch, as long as the thing was switched on the line was open both ways.

'Foxtrot 2 Bravo, d'you hear me? Ben calling Foxtrot 2 Bravo!'

Engine-noise had dropped, and the boat had only steerage-way on, bashing around again . . .

'Foxtrot 2 Bravo – '

' – you loud and clear, Ben, you receiving me?'

'Fives, Russell. Go ahead, where's my target?'

Fives meaning five out of ten, reception not too bad.

'Bad news, Ben. I've two on the screen, the *gulet* and its boat. *Gulet* bearing from you now is zero-seven-zero distance six point four, course three-four-zero, speed ten. The other – '

Steering northwest . . . He knew the answer now. Disliking it intensely . . . Hosegood talking on VHF in the background of sea-noise and the outboard's slower hammering, telling Sticks to mark time . . . Haig's voice crackly with static but audible enough: ' – leaving, it's dropped them off. Second contact is a dinghy, nine miles from you on zero-seven-four, speed fifteen, course zero-nine-zero. It's getting close to the beach, I can't promise to hold the contact much longer.'

Nine miles away, and already close to shore. Visualizing the coastline and the bearings and distances, he knew he hadn't a hope of getting to it before it beached. So that was that, and –

211

Haig's voice in a stronger burst: ' – in the bay south of Ras el Buri – getting right into it . . .'

Ras el Buri was the headland with the triple-flashing light on it, this side of Baniyas, and the bay was about two miles south of that light. It meant they were on the point of landing about six miles north of where he'd decided they ought to land. As more recently suspected – and the idea rejected . . .

Wouldn't have been able to do anything about it, anyway. Too bloody late.

'Foxtrot 2: are you *certain* it's them?'

'Affirmative. Had it at long range on our way over, saw one split from the other, and – ' Cut off. Static crackled wildly, faded with voices audible in the background: then sharply, clearly out of it: 'Have to leave you, Ben, Syrian fighters scrambling from Al Qusayr . . . Hear me?'

'Yeah. Fours . . .' But simultaneously he'd woken to a chance he still did have. 'D'you hear *me*, Foxtrot 2 Bravo?'

'Fours. Make it quick.'

'I'm going to catch them on that beach. Out.'

The airfield at Al Qusayr was only about ninety kilometres away. No distance for Migs . . .

'Geoff! Tell Sticks to take station astern of us when we cross his bows in a minute. Speed forty-plus . . . Bert – steer for that light, full speed, *go!*'

By aiming straight at the light on Ras el Buri, you'd clear the nearer headland by about a mile. When he had it in sight he'd turn in towards the beach, on this side of it. There *was* a chance: even if Swale and party were already landing they'd have to cache their boat, which couldn't be done all that quickly. Especially if they tried burying it in a shingle beach. So – nine miles at forty knots – fourteen minutes, say. Call it fifteen, you weren't making that speed yet . . . Coming round, Polaris crossing the bow and coming to hover on roughly fifty, fifty-five degrees to port as Hattry aimed for the light and the speed mounted, bow lifting, the deep-V'd hull beginning to take the battering of the swells as she hit them with increasing frequency and power.

Hosegood yelled, 'Message passed!'

A steady crashing, bouncing from ridge to ridge: you

tightened your gut to counter the punching impacts. He shifted back . . . 'Change over, Geoff . . .'

Wanting to explain to Kelso what he had in mind. Hall shouted, 'There, on the beam!'

White patch in the black background: the other Sea-Rider also working speed up while this one steered to cross ahead of it. Coming up on to the plane now, skimming the swells instead of hitting them . . . 'Ben calling Sticks, over!'

A roar of noise struck the ear that was close to the set; and they'd be getting the same hurricane sound out of their end of it. Sticks' voice then – as if his mouth was full of water – 'Go ahead, over!'

'Steering for the lighthouse – Ras el Buri. Hear me? Over!'

'Check, Razzle Barry, over!'

'Two miles south of it – headland, no name, enclosing a north-facing beach. The *gulet*'s dinghy's there now, *gulet* withdrawing northward. I'll land south of the headland, cross it to hit them on the beach. When I turn inshore, you stop, lie off, *wait* for me . . . Got that? Over!'

He'd switched to 'receive' but for a few seconds he wasn't getting anything. Then it came alive with the other boat's noise: and finally Sticks' voice again: 'Roger . . . Roger, Ben. Good luck. Out.'

Not liking it . . .

This felt like fifty knots, nearer than forty. Flying . . . Trying to keep a balance, kneeling, while using his starscope trained over the bow, back-up to Bert Hattry's PNG. Hattry had a better range of vision from up there on his padded seat. But he'd be keeping a more general lookout – for flotsam, for instance. If you hit a log at this speed, that would be *it*.

He checked the time, saw four minutes had gone. Ten to go: maybe nine, to the point where he'd turn in towards the land. He was already looking for the headland – careful not to look straight at the flashes from the Ras el Buri light, which would be blinding; it was the light itself now, not just its loom fanning the sky. When he spotted the headland he'd steer directly towards it and then hug this south side of it; the chart showed rocks inshore not so far to the south. Shingle beaches all along, with offshore rock in patches not infrequent. He'd have Hattry take the boat in slowly and stop

213

about a hundred metres off; he'd get out then and swim. Himself and one other. Wouldn't matter which: whoever was best placed to slip over. None of these guys was any more proficient than any of the others.

There were still about five miles – seven minutes – to go when the outboard seemed to explode.

The Sea-Rider jarred savagely as it hit the next ridge, only impetus carrying her forward, no thrust now at the stern. It had *sounded* like an explosion. Hitting the next sea and the next, all but stopped, down from well over forty knots to nothing, burying her snout in the next swell, stern rising: Chalky was back there, he and Bert Hattry swinging the engine forward to get the shaft and screw up out of water, Ben wishful-thinking that they were surely right, prop must have hit some submerged object, something solid but in neutral buoyancy and far enough below the surface for the planing hull to have passed over it. Lucky, at that: if you'd hit it squarely, there'd as likely as not have been men dead.

Count your blessings, therefore. A spare screw could be fitted in about one minute. As long as the shaft wasn't bent: which please God –

'Screw's intact!' Chalky's voice yelling as the other Sea-Rider crashed past them, swerving in a sheet of spray and a blast of noise – falling note, doppler-effect as it swept by, Froggie shutting his throttle on the turn, and the wash of its passing throwing this lot around . . . Hattry shouted, telling Ben, 'He reckons crankshaft or a piston!' Sticks' boat was circling to manoeuvre itself up close to this one, and Ben was praying *Oh God, no* . . . Because that would be the finish of it, absolutely.

Chalky had swung the outboard back into its upright, functional position. He reached for the lanyard, telling Hattry as he leant back to give himself some room, 'If it's either, we're fucked.' He tried the lanyard, drawing it out slowly: winning a few inches, then no more.

Seized up, solid.

'Crankshaft or piston.' Yelling his verdict to Ben. 'Could be either. Sold us a dud, didn't they.'

It was a brand-new outboard, of a make chosen after enormously painstaking research and long experience. Since its delivery to the Squadron it would have been prepared and tuned by expert engineering staff, put through its paces on a Sea-Rider at Poole and then pampered with further maintenance to ready it for operational deployment. Chalky was right, they'd been sold a dud. The manufacturer unfortunately wasn't here.

But Swale was almost certainly on that beach.

Even though a few minutes had been lost. With a few more yet to lose. There was still a chance. He told Hosegood, 'I'll have Sticks put me on the beach, then he'll come back and tow you in. Sit tight here.'

He unclipped his SA80 from the blister, and slung it. The other boat could tow this one at – well, easily, say fifteen knots, loaded. Two and a half hours then, to get clear of Syrian waters. There ought to be about four and a half hours of darkness left; so you had two hours in hand. You wouldn't need that long: only long enough to get (a) ashore, (b) into a position overlooking that beach, (c) Swale's head in the nightsight on this weapon, at any range up to three hundred metres, at which distance an SA80 in the right hands had killing accuracy.

Foxtrot 2 Bravo's report had been relayed by Satcom and received in the JOC in London. The Duty Operations Director had leapt up as if the Minister's red chair had stung him.

'Intending to *land*?'

Hislop was seeing it in his mind's eye, understanding Ben Ockley's dilemma in the suddenly changed situation: the *gulet* having changed course, dropped its passengers prematurely and in the wrong place. The question he needed to answer was what *he'd* have done if he'd been out there with the responsibility for decision, immediate, there and then.

Pack up, admit defeat, head for home comforts?

Knowing that Swale, the vital target, was almost surely on that beach, and that if he could get there really fast he'd have a good chance of completing the task in a matter of minutes?

He told the admiral, 'He's got his man within reach, and he knows how much is resting on it. I'd be disappointed in him if he *didn't* have a shot at it.'

The admiral re-settled himself on the ministerial seat. Accepting Hislop's expert view – with which the SF Adviser agreed, after a moment's hesitation – but still looking extremely worried. Computer screens along the right-hand wall were static, displaying the information most recently demanded of them, and there was a background mutter of telephone conversations.

'Syrian Migs crossing the coastline westward, south of Tartus at ten thousand feet.'

The report had been made by an RAF warrant officer who was manning an open line from Dhekelia. A protected line, 'open' in the sense that it was being manned constantly at both ends.

'Show of strength.' A wing commander submitted to the DOD, 'If that's the right description. They've been careful to give our guy time to clear out. I'd guess they'll make a sweep and then go home again.'

'Sea-Riders at high speed make a bloody great wash, don't they?'

The admiral was thinking of their being seen from the air, the phosphorescence of their churned wakes visible even on the darkest night.

Hislop nodded. Adding, with an eye on the RAF man for confirmation, 'But hardly from that height, and the Migs'll be looking for intruding aircraft, I'd imagine, not for small boats. Even if they saw the wakes they probably wouldn't regard it as anything to take notice of.'

The airman agreed. The fighters would have been scrambled because Foxtrot 2 Bravo's visit to Syrian airspace had been the second intrusion and they'd have felt some gesture of defiance had been called for. They'd sat still during the Hercules' brief visit, but the repeat performance had seemed like one too many. Even now, though, they'd hardly be seeking confrontation.

'Joe, what was the last reported position of the *gulet*?'

The SF Adviser consulted a computer that was right beside him, and told Hislop, 'Six miles off Baniyas, steering due north at six knots. Before that it was heading northwest at ten. The alterations indicate it could be the intention to put in to Latakia at first light.'

The DOD asked, 'Do we have much interest in the *gulet* now?'

'No immediate interest, no, sir. Except it might be intended to pick up some or all of Swale's companions at some later stage. Must admit, it gripes one slightly to see them getting away with it.'

The *gulet* had certainly made a nonsense of the surveillance operation. Obviously there'd been some kind of cock-up, for 8 Kilo 6 to have only picked it up when it was just about nudging the Syrian coast. Whether this had been caused by human error or equipment failure was something for the Crabs to look into, but whatever answer might emerge from a post mortem, that failure – compounded by the earlier blunder at a higher level – was why Ben Ockley was having to stick his neck out now. Hislop had no way of knowing at this stage, of course, how much more exposed that neck had just become as a result of a piston disintegrating in one Sea-Rider's outboard.

The admiral was lighting a pipe. 'Might get a crack at the *gulet* some other time, Charles. Now we have it identified as a terrorist conveyance and with luck they don't know we have. Did you say you'd passed details of it to the Americans?'

'Ockley did that, from Akrotiri.'

The SF Adviser murmured, taking the chair beside Hislop's, 'And now he's paddling on a Syrian beach.'

'Not for long, with luck.'

'But it'll be a long time before we'll hear any more, won't it.'

Because the Nimrod was out of it, now, and with the Syrian airforce stirring could hardly go back in there.

12

The headland was flat, low-lying, not a lot higher than the beach which it sheltered from the south. Elevated enough to give him a view of the crescent of shingle, dayglo white of the surf and the beach itself like a dog's bite out of the low coastal belt. He was already fairly sure he'd got here too late.

Andy Laker was somewhere between Ben and the sea, making his own recce of that area, a distance of roughly four or five hundred metres separating them.

There were some fishing boats at the top end of the beach, pulled up there out of the sea's reach. Maybe in expectation of autumn storms: and the locals would know . . . Beyond them, on rising ground between the beach and the coast road, was a cluster of shacks, no doubt fishermen's homes, but with no lights showing anywhere in or around them they could have been deserted.

Sand would have been preferable. You'd have had tracks to look and feel for, which you did not have in shingle. He considered checking the shacks at close range, but decided against it. Might set dogs barking – there were nearly always dogs around – and there'd be nothing gained, he guessed; Swale's lot wouldn't have holed up here, they'd surely have pushed on towards their target – for whatever their purpose was – using the hours of darkness that were left.

There'd be a moon later. Some time after 0300. Until now he'd ignored this, not having expected to be hanging around for anything like that long in Syrian territorial water, let alone on the Syrian coast.

He didn't intend to be here when it rose, either. The thought of it added urgency to the imperative of getting the team and their Sea-Riders the hell out as soon as possible.

Lights fringed the coast road. A power-line followed the line of the road and new motorway; it was shown prominently on the map with pylons at intervals. So you could guess there'd be electricity to those shacks. Road and power-line linked Tartus to Baniyas, with a couple of smaller settlements and coastal villages in this stretch of about sixteen miles; one village was only a few hundred metres from this beach, a stone's throw to the south and with a hill behind it.

He'd heard aircraft passing over, high and flying west, Russell Haig's Migs maybe. Haig and his Nimrod would be back at Akrotiri by now ... Darkness here, away from the surf, was total, the shacks and boats visible only because the flow of light from the direction of the road was behind them. To his left, the surf's brilliance, and the shingle rattling in constant movement. He was crawling in dead or very dry tall grass that rustled as he moved through it. Thistles in it too. A scent of lusher vegetation, almost a greenhouse odour, could only be from a distance, on the breeze. And a black mass straight-edged against the background of stars in the north was Marqab Castle, *the* coastal landmark in this area, a massive Crusader ruin two miles south of the centre of Baniyas. It was built on a rocky hill that ran seaward in a ridge terminating in the headland, Ras el Buri, where the triple-flashing light was.

He was moving in the direction of the road. Doc Laker had begun his recce about four hundred yards from where they'd landed, after the swim ashore from Sticks Kelso's Sea-Rider. They'd split up there, at one possible exit from the beach that Swale and company might have taken; the other way they might have gone would be this way, eastward, directly inland, over the road and the coastal strip and straight on into the foothills of the Alawis.

They'd be more likely to have gone south, he thought. The

easier route. And where Laker was prospecting was a likely area in which to have cached a boat. Close to where they'd have landed, the nearest higher ground, sand instead of shingle and this scrubby grass for cover. You didn't need a very large hole for an ordinary inflatable and its engine, the boat deflated of course and a plastic bag to keep sand and stuff out of the outboard. A hole like that could be dug and filled in again in minutes.

Stopping again: to watch and listen from this higher ground. But there was no movement, and no sound. At least, no scrape of a spade in sand, no voices. If they'd landed here – which they must have done – they'd now be yomping into the hills. They'd get to the mountains before daylight too, probably. To them, not through or over them. They'd reach their destination, that map-reference, on the second night, maybe not much before the following dawn. It would be rough going in places, and steep, that second night, and since the former SAS character was reputedly an alcoholic you wouldn't expect him to be in prime condition.

Marines might yomp it a lot faster, in fact.

Bloody well ought to, anyway. And having failed to catch the bastards here, that would be the way to go about it – head straight and fast for the target location, be there ahead of them. With a team of eight you could stake out the area well enough to give them a real Bootneck welcome. Then back to the coast in one good night's yomp; you'd know the route by then and you'd have taken out that whole party and covered all tracks. God knew, you'd been trained hard enough and long enough for just that kind of operation.

Nice thought – while it lasted. He could imagine just how the CO would react, if by some kind of mind-reading act from London he could read Captain Ben Ockley's fanciful thinking on a Syrian beach. Hislop would shut his eyes, clamp his jaw tight in a few seconds' tense exasperation, a hand smoothing that tonsured scalp as his eyes re-opened, the bland expression returned . . .

Marvellous guy. Terrific record in the Squadron's recent past, and doing a great job as its CO now. He'd still throw a fit.

Circling around the top of the shingle beach, low in the thistle crop and hearing a vehicle or two rushing past from time to time along the coastal highway, he decided that while he was here, as close as he'd now come to those boats, he might as well take a look at them. Whatever information sprang from recces on forbidden coastlines, it was all grist to the mill, all of interest and maybe one day of *vital* interest. And there was time in hand: Kelso would have taken five minutes to get back to the immobilised Sea-Rider, a few more to take it in tow and maybe ten to bring it inshore, actually to a waiting position just *off*shore on the far side of the headland. And it would only take him – Ben – about five minutes to get back there, collecting Doc Laker on the way.

Anyway, nobody'd be kept waiting very long.

Plenty of reasons *not* to go chasing after Swale. No authority to land in Syria was the obvious one: he shouldn't be here now, shouldn't even have a toe on this beach. In fact he knew he could justify having taken this much of a risk, when there'd been a good chance of catching them. If that outboard hadn't fallen apart he probably *would* have scored. One shot, Swale dead, three terrs with no place to go.

Might still be achieved?

In the mountains: not tonight, probably, but maybe the night after or the following day . . .

So what about withdrawal?

Another para drop. Boats with crews only, for a rendezvous at the original beach, the one Swale should have landed at if he'd obeyed the rules . . . Boats away now, so that by moonrise they'd be well clear and by sunrise in international waters. You could be sure there'd be a Nimrod over at dawn, looking for the team as it withdrew. Hattry could talk to it over the Sarbe voice link; effectively he'd be talking to Dhekelia, Akrotiri and London as well as to the Nimrod, asking for a replacement outboard to be flown out. It could be at Akrotiri by this next midnight. As could the two Sea-Riders, if they got into Dhekelia in the afternoon and were transferred by road. In fact you wouldn't want the pickup off this coast before Friday night: might even settle for Saturday night, allowing an extra day for completion and withdrawal to the coast, spending a day lying-up somewhere if you finished sooner. They'd have bags of time for setting up their end of it.

He'd got to the fishing boats. Feeling his way around the first one, he found it was about sixteen feet long and constructed of heavy timber. There were holes to take crutches – rowlocks – but no oars. The oars would be locked up in one of those shacks, he guessed. It would be a very heavy boat to row, in any case, you wouldn't move it very fast. The transom was knotched deeply, for propulsion with a single oar, but there was no scarring of the timber as there would have been if an outboard had ever been fitted. And being so heavy it would take a lot of moving, without a trolley – which wouldn't be any use on shingle anyway. You'd need at least two men each side to get it down to the water.

He was beginning to think he was wasting time. Some vague notion of being able to withdraw this way. He told himself to forget it: he'd be withdrawing in about twenty minutes, by Sea-Rider under tow.

Imagining Hislop's sigh of relief, and some comment like *Must say I didn't believe you could be* that *much of a fucking idiot, Ben . . .*

Except that he *had* pointed out, quite forcefully, that Swale's death or removal was of huge importance. If you were in his position and you went around stressing points like that you'd have to expect to be taken notice of. Nobody was going to feel they had any right to say, 'Oh, what the hell, let's pack it in . . .'

This second boat was glass-fibre. Twelve foot, roughly. Intact, as far as he could tell; there was a little water in the bottom which wouldn't have been there if it was not. Crawling to the stern, he ran his hands over a strong transom with a metal plate where an outboard would clamp on. The outboard itself would be wherever the other boat's oars and crutches might be, he guessed.

You'd shift this one easily enough, two men could drag it down to the water without much trouble. But you'd have to (a) locate, (b) steal the outboard. And, the boat wasn't big enough for eight men, not over any distance or in even a moderately disturbed sea.

Time to go back, anyway. Having wasted at least the last

223

ten minutes. Out of reluctance to accept failure, leave Swale alive with God only knew what consequences.

Halfway back he paused, listened, whistled, heard the same signal repeated from the right. From where he was crouching now, that was the direction of the corner of the beach, the tidemark closest to this higher, grass-covered spit. He heard Laker call quietly, 'Over here, Ben.' Then two or three more words, he thought something like 'found their boat'. Probably something quite different, though. Joining the Doc, and not really wanting any further delay now, he asked him, 'Say you've *found* it?'

'Right here.' He'd grabbed Ben's arm, guiding his hand to loose, recently excavated sand and stones. Sand and shingle . . . 'Feel down there.'

A foot or so deep, digging down through loose sand, his fingers touched wet rubber. Laker's whisper asked him, 'Got there?'

'Yeah. How come you – '

'The outboard's a metre to your left. Probably all one hole they dug . . . I just struck lucky. Guessed they wouldn't have lugged the stuff farther than they needed to, and this is just up from where they'd very likely have beached. So I groped around for a while and then found the diggings.'

The outboard was there, all right, and so was the fuel tank, separately bagged. He remembered that according to Russell Haig the inflatable had been making fifteen knots on its way inshore.

He sat back on his heels, fixing this spot in his memory.

Also, plumbing his own thought-processes, wanting to be certain he wasn't raving mad . . .

'Marvellous, Doc. Well done.'

It had changed things dramatically, this find. He was back to contemplating the possibility of seeing the task through, killing Swale, *not* crawling back to Cyprus – and then to Poole – with his tail between his legs.

'Yes. Hang on a second.' He told them, 'Drybags can go home in the boat that's being towed. But let's be sure we have all we want out of the containers now. Not LAWs, not the M-79s either. I want to travel as light as possible, and we're after

224

one guy, not a bloody regiment. Don't leave any second-line stuff behind, though – especially rations . . . Bert, if you blokes have any spare I'd say our needs are greater than yours, OK?'

He turned back to answer Kelso's question. He'd sent Laker down here to flash a message to him to bring the boats inshore, while he himself had gone to suss out those fishermen's shacks. There'd been no dogs. He'd noted the positions of doors and windows and checked there were no telephone or power lines. It was knowledge he'd need when he got back here in a few days' time. If there'd been wires he'd have planned on cutting them, and you'd cover exits to prevent interference while you carted that boat down to the water and – maybe – even found its outboard.

'Right, Sticks. Answer is, we *can* now finish the job . . . Bert, listen – '

Various jobs were in progress in the Sea-Riders – preparations for the tow, extracting gear from containers, stowing the drysuits . . . Ben told Hattry, 'You shove off as soon as we're ready. Four in the one boat – if you meet trouble, cut the other adrift. There'll be a moon in about ninety minutes, but you should be well out by then. By sunrise you'll be in legit waters and you can bet there'll be a Nimrod around by then, you can give them the update by Sarbe. Hey – heads down . . .'

Helicopter: coming towards, up-coast from the south. He'd heard it and now its belly-light was visible, flashing red.

The Syrians had several helo types in their armoury. Including – this passed through his mind at the first sight of it – Mi-24 gunships.

But why the light? Surely if they were on an offensive – or defensive – mission, they'd hardly be advertising their approach?

Crouching, heads down, immobile, ears filling with the noise as the helo pounded straight at them. It wasn't an Mi-24, wasn't anything like it. This was a Gazelle, its sound clearly recognisable when your brain relaxed enough to take it in. 'Syrian Air Defence Command' did have French-built Gazelles; they specialised in Migs but they had a few others, such as these.

Dark figures on black rocks; the Sea-Riders might look like extensions of those rocks. It was at any rate better than being on the water at high speed with a spreading wake: half an hour ago you'd have been spotted for sure.

Over the top – noise at its peak – now . . .

Passing on over and away northward. No change, no alarm. The decibels from the hammering rotor fell away as rapidly as they'd mounted: out of nothing in the quiet night, back to nothing now. He could hear the sea again, slapping and sucking through the rocks.

'Let's get on with it . . . Bert, I'll have the spare tank out of the one you're towing. You'll still have plenty. Someone give Doc a hand, he knows where to bury it. Bert, tell the Nimrod by Sarbe, for info London, that we're going into the mountains to grease Swale. Having missed out here for reasons which you can explain. I've a grid reference for where Swale's heading and we can get there first, take them out then yomp back here, push off either Friday or Saturday night, depending on how quick we've been.'

'You say "push off".' Sticks cut in, low-voiced: 'Eight guys, in –'

'Two boats. The Swale lot's inflatable with its outboard, plus a GRP twelve-footer that's up on that beach. It's light enough to tow easily. And they came ashore at fifteen knots, with the bigger load we should work up to maybe ten. So, maximum four hours and we're out there sunrise Saturday. Got it, Bert?'

'Ben.' Sticks again. 'Suppose it's less easy than you think, and we can't make that schedule –'

'Then twenty-four hours later. If not first light Saturday, Bert, Sunday.'

'Right.' Hattry offered, 'Rucksack here if you want it.'

For some of his gear. He had too much slung round his neck and weighting the DPMs' pockets. Several of the team had brought their own light packs to hold second-line equipment inside the containers. Hall had one for his explosives; Laker had a specially fitted bag, of course, for his medical kit. The team was more or less ready to move off now except that he – Laker – and Teal, who'd gone off with the spare tank of petrol, weren't back yet. Waiting, Kelso drew Ben aside.

'We're not equipped for this, Ben, are we. Rations, for one thing. Clothing – be cold up there, right?'

'We'll travel too fast to get cold. Really fast yomp, flat out. We've a ratpack each, plus whatever else, and we can forage, maybe . . . Christ, we've managed on short rations before this, haven't we?'

'And trainers – for fast yomping over mountains?'

'Turning wimpish on us, Sticks?'

It was a joke: but neither of them was even smiling. He could see the whites of Kelso's eyes in the dark: and behind him the shadowy movements of men making their final preparations, the white flickering of the surf and its sound, boats moving against the rocks, crewmen fending them off. High time Laker and Teal got back: although digging a hole with divers' knives and bare hands in that stony ground might be slow . . . 'Come on then, Sticks, what else?'

'Well, like – not *your* fault we fell short, was it. We could pull out now, and – well, Jesus, Ben, this is fucking *Syria*!'

The politics were scary, all right. Too much so to spend time on. In terms of having to come to an immediate decision, however, he'd considered it – the motivation, whether he was dragging them into this for his own sake, out of aversion to accepting failure. And there *was* a touch of that: but no more than a touch, the real issue was that he'd been given a job to do, had some notion of the consequences of its not being done, and reasonable certainty now that it still *could* be done. The bottom line was that he'd be wrong to pull out, wouldn't honestly be able to justify it to himself later if he did.

Recalling, in that context, the CO's words: *If you're in there with a fighting chance* . . .

'It's what we're here for, Sticks. OK, slight extension of the plans, but – "local initiative", remember *that* item?'

Kelso's grunt indicated acceptance. Maybe. Ben asked him, 'Any *practical* contribution to make now?'

'Yeah.' A nod in the darkness. 'Sea King or something to meet us first light Saturday, or Sunday. We could have some guys hurt, or the Swale bloke with us, might need lifting out.'

It was a good idea – if they had any helicopters to spare.

Wessex, maybe; he was fairly sure there weren't any Sea Kings on the Cyprus bases. He called to Hattry, 'Bert – Friday sunrise – or whenever – out in the middle, see if they'd lift us out of the boats in a Wessex or some such. Might have to be two Wessex – or two trips.'

Two minutes later Laker and Teal were back. By this time Ben had decided on yet another burial party: they'd take the grenade-launchers and one of the LAWs when they moved off in a minute, bury them above the beach where they could find them when they got back here. In case of Syrian interference at the embarkation stage. Hattry would have the other LAW in case of need during his withdrawal now. The brief appearance of that Gazelle didn't necessarily presage trouble, but you couldn't take anything for granted.

'OK, gather round.' He had his own map out, and the blue torch carefully shaded. Sticks had a copy of the same map too – or rather the piece of map, as supplied by the CO for navigational purposes. Ben explained the route they'd take now: the roads to be crossed, four to five kilometres of flat, low-lying coastal strip, skirting the nearby village and passing wide of another before coming to a river which they'd follow in a curve to the left around a 2000-foot hill. Up-river south-eastward then, into the Alawi foothills and leaving the river, crossing an east – west-lying road: a steep yomp to a ridge, then, and down into a valley with a smaller watercourse in it. There'd be enough moonlight by then, he hoped, to make the climb possible, and it would save a long detour. From that valley it would be all upward, up a spur of the mountain range.

'Two and a half hours of moonlight before dawn. Unless the moon's behind the peaks.' He hadn't checked on that kind of detail, hadn't thought of the moon, or anything like this . . . 'Meanwhile, we *might* run up behind the Swale bunch. Odds are against it, obviously, but it's not out of the question. After all, we're heading for the same place. So – well, if we do, we'll make a job of it, deploy around them and make sure we get them all – and no shooting, right?'

In the mountains, four and a half hours later, he lay hearing men's snores around him and guessing that somewhere in the hills to the west the Swale team would also be lying-up. Even if they'd come by Syrian invitation they'd still be acting like intruders, maintaining Swale's belief in them for another day or two.

And they'd be equipped for it, no doubt. Sleeping-bags and proper rations, warm clothing for cold nights in the mountains.

He'd hoped to run into them: for that much luck. He'd deployed his team like beaters spread out to flush game, and before departure from the beach he'd told Hattry, 'If we did strike lucky, we'd lie-up tomorrow, get back here and shove off tomorrow night. Not likely but they should have a Nimrod airborne just in case.'

Making the most of the final moments of contact with an outside world. Once the boats pushed off and the team moved inland, whatever you'd forgotten would *stay* forgotten . . . This thought had given rise to another.

'If we didn't show up – well, on Saturday – they might consider sending a Nimrod over to contact us by Sarbe. If they thought it could be risked. So we'll be ready to switch on if we hear anything coming over. Not bleeper, obviously, it could be Syrian: voice only, OK?'

'Doubt they'd send one inland, Ben.'

'So do I. And I'm not asking them to. Contingency, that's all. If we were stuck, and they'd want to know whether we'd greased Swale?'

'Right.'

Sticks had said when they'd been moving off – Ben looking back to see the fast-fading white trace of the Sea-Riders withdrawing seaward – 'Not likely they'd send Crabs over. Not even for you and me.'

'They'd want us out, though, wouldn't they. If we got caught ashore here, we'd have put ourselves in Swale's place, in a way. Even if we'd killed him they'd have us instead – genuine articles, eight for the price of one!'

'You did think of that, then . . .'

Dawn blazed behind the mountains, a golden furnace silhouetting that jagged frieze. The sun's warmth would be welcome when it got over that rock barrier; although the low night temperature hadn't stopped several of them falling asleep almost instantly after tucking themselves into rock angles and crevices fifteen or twenty minutes ago. Three were on watch: two higher up the slope, right and left, well hidden but with wide fields of view, and Ray Wilkinson fifty yards downslope where he could see over the ridge into a connecting valley. In daylight you'd see how effectively they'd merged themselves into the rockscape; Ben would be checking this before he went to sleep himself.

If he could. His mind was active, restive. The uncertainty, so many unpredictables ahead: and Sticks' comment a few hours ago, *You did think of that, then,* and his earlier protest, *This is fucking Syria!* mentally regurgitated brought a flare-up of anxiety so acute it was almost panic: panic disguised, in that moment, as fresh clarity in his thinking. Himself alone, without authority or sense, leading a team of Royal Marines – armed, and in a sense uniformed – into territory that even he, Ben Ockley, could recognise as politically ultra-sensitive. The quality of *outrage* shocked him as dawn flamed brighter, spreading up from behind the black rock-masses; he was wet – cold – only sweat-damp at first but now his whole body running wet inside the lightweight DPMs, sweat cold as a film of ice. Urging himself – teeth clenched to stop them chattering – *Hang on, think this through again . . .*

Like handling a threat of panic under water. One had learnt in the very early days of training to take a grip on the mental processes: to hold the breathing steady and hold the *mental* breath as well while the false fears faded . . .

Rather the same procedure now: starting with the basic that his orders were to take out the former SAS guy. Who'd been only a short jump ahead and on his way to a known point on the map, a place which this team could surely reach before he did. Hislop had stressed how vital it was that Swale shouldn't be left alive in Syria: and it had been obvious, back there on the rocks, that there was still a good chance of ensuring that he was *not*. So you came down to the general sanction – imperative, in some circumstances – for a decision of the kind they called 'local initiative', allowing one to go beyond the limitations of the brief. And it was, clearly, arguable that they'd have been wrong to have given up.

Contrary to Sticks Kelso's reactions. But the team leader

was Ockley, not Kelso. Kelso had sounded his warning out of a sense of duty, also concern for Ben as much as for the issue itself, and he'd have had in mind Ben Ockley's reputation as a man who faced complex challenges with his head down and hooves pounding. Ben himself was fully aware of this image of him in some of his brother Bootnecks' eyes. He'd had it in mind when he'd been down there on the beach. But he'd also registered the thought — as he did again now — that you couldn't let yourself be pushed into making a wrong decision just because making the right one might seem to reflect some of the damn-fool yarns they'd put around.

Six or seven kilometres northwest and a few hundred feet lower, Charlie unrolled his sleeping-bag into a deeper shadow of overhanging rock. Any danger of being spotted here, he guessed, would be from aircraft or helicopters. There'd been one helicopter – a Gazelle, and too close for comfort, particularly so soon after the close pass by that plane which he still thought had been a Nimrod, not long after they'd left the beach . . . He squirmed out from under the rock. The sun was showing now, not just the brilliant fire surrounding it but the crimson ball itself, its rim pushing up in a cleft of the mountain range, flushing the surrounding peaks and ridges with colour that was only slightly less intense.

Smiley was brewing tea on the portable, Israeli-made naphtha stove which Leila had provided. Safe enough now for that dim blue glow on the brightening hillside.

They'd trekked a long way south from where they'd landed, staying parallel to the coast but inland of the road, and making diversions around villages, until Bob had concluded that they were on the line of march which they would have been on if Leila had landed them where she'd been told to land them. Bob hadn't liked the change of plan at all, had considered it unnecessary, being sure that the low-flying jet could have had nothing to do with them or with their objective.

Charlie had asked him, 'Why should the Syrians be so slack about watching their own coast?'

'Watching a small timber sailboat, on a coast that's dotted with fishing villages?' He'd glanced critically at Charlie, as if wondering about his ignorance . . . 'Syria's enemy is Israel, and Israelis come in Fast Attack Craft or even destroyers. They don't come here, anyway, they attack PLO bases in Syrian-controlled areas of the Lebanon, don't they.'

The gear Leila had provided was all Israeli Army stuff. Not uniform as such – she'd equipped them with greenish-coloured cotton fatigues and heavier camouflage-pattern smocks and caps, the sort of gear you could buy in army surplus stores – but it was Israeli-made, as were the Uzi submachine-guns, ration-packs, sleeping-bags, and that naphtha stove. She'd told Charlie, 'My government gives all this for nothing. Israel is generous to her friends, you see.'

'Even to the extent of buying the inflatable for us in Marseilles.'

'As I told you, it's what we were asked to do.' She shrugged. 'Maybe *not* so stupid. A little confusion?'

It might have the reverse effect, though; a French team would *not* leave a French-made boat around. In that sense, you might be putting a *British* signature on that beach. And why any Syrian should (a) find the boat or (b) believe Frenchmen would risk their necks to extract a British hostage – if you believed that, he thought, what *wouldn't* you believe?

Tait poured tea into Israeli mugs. There was adequate cover here, broken rock all over, and no reason for anyone to pass this way. Animals wouldn't graze on rock, and there was a perfectly good track winding through the valley, skirting the bottom of this hill and continuing west through a densely cultivated area where the river widened in its approach to the sea.

He lay back, resting an elbow on a bunched-up end of his sleeping-bag and sipping the hot tea.

'What's the form from here on? Do we get to where they're holding this guy tonight? Village, whatever?'

'The rendezvous is at an old castle – a *qal'at*. This country's littered with such relics.'

'In a dungeon, is he, real Crusader stuff?'

'I doubt it. Not so easy to dig dungeons out of solid rock. It's one of hundreds of such places, just an ancient ruin: and he's not necessarily *in* it, just near it.'

'Day *after* tomorrow, you said.'

'We won't make it in one night, Charlie.'

'Twenty-five kilometres?'

'Mountains. How many mountains have you climbed in the dark?'

'Since you ask – three or four.' He shrugged. 'But OK, we get there tomorrow night, not tonight. In time to recce before sunrise?'

'Yes. But *we* don't recce, *I* do. The easy way, as it happens, I have someone to meet there, an agent.'

'Agent . . . ' Tait and Denham were staring at him too; evidently they hadn't heard about this either. Charlie asked, 'What kind of agent?'

'Syrian, maybe on the SIS payroll. I don't need that kind of information, any more than you do. But he'll point me to where they've got Stillgoe, I'll have a look around and then rejoin you three, and we'll decide how we're going to do it.'

'Spring him after dark, presumably.' Charlie was less pre-suming it than querying it. Some of the SBS arrangements puzzled him. Two nights just to cover twenty-five kilometres, for instance. OK, with some rock-climbing included: but they'd be passing *through* the range, surely, not over it, and they'd have some moonlight too . . . He added, 'So we'll have some dark hours left for the move out. And if we can get him out really *quietly* – '

'Exactly, Charlie. That's more or less how I'm hoping this guy will have set it up for us.'

'Never mentioned him before, did you.'

'D'you think I should have?'

Charlie gulped tea. 'I said this before, or something like it. We could be left holding the baby, if you broke your neck. Suppose your agent wasn't there and they had the place staked out, you all alone doing your *prima donna* bit – '

'If he let us down, we'd make our own recce, that's all. And if they had it staked out I hope I'd be smart enough not to walk into it. But suppose I did: OK, you three'd do the recce, find our man and get him out. You know where we put the boat – and about the offshore R/V with the *gulet* – what the hell else d'you want?'

*   *   *

233

Charles Hislop was woken at a few minutes after 0330 by a messenger from the Special Forces Adviser. Still in a dream-state, or only half out of it, he was off the camp-bed and reaching for his shoes before the petty officer had finished telling him, 'Nimrod's established comms with the Sea-Riders, sir, fifty miles off Cape Greco.'

'Right. Great.' Awake now, more or less; sitting on the camp-bed, looking up at the naval man who, well trained, wasn't going to leave until he was sure the guy he'd shaken wouldn't just fall back again and start snoring. Hislop assured him, 'I'll be along in a minute.'

Thinking, *Thank God for small mercies*. Even more, for big ones. And it *was* a big one: fifty miles off Cape Greco meant they'd come out of Syrian territorial waters. Bacon saved – at least to that extent: and with that primary anxiety lulled, the big question looming was *what about Swale?*

He'd have expected them to have come farther west, actually, by this time. They must have spent longer on shore than Ockley could have intended: and presumably in that gap of time they'd caught up with the Swale party and done the job. Touch wood . . . He had the scene in his mind's eye as he hurried into the JOC, letting the soundproof door thump shut behind him: the sun lifting over that Levantine coast – two hours east of the Greenwich meridian, two light-hours ahead of London – the sea still dark but with the gleam of dawn on it, the Nimrod overhead catching the sun's first rays and with the Sea-Riders as small blips on its searchwater screen, voice communications crackly over the Sarbe link.

He and the admiral, the Duty Operations Director, arrived at the door of the SF cell together, from opposite directions. Each noticing that the other was in need of a shave . . . The admiral, who was wearing a white submarine sweater instead of a collar and tie, told him, 'Our lord and master is ware and waking and yearning for reassurance, Charles.'

'The Minister – he's up?'

'Well, he's awake. And – articulate.' The DOD pushed into the room with Hislop close behind him. 'What's happening, or happened?' Focussing on the SF Adviser: 'Do we know yet?'

'Not – all that clearly, sir.' The Marine major looked

234

troubled. 'Comms so far are somewhat garbled, and — well, Akrotiri's trying to make sense of it, but — '

'What *have* you got, Joe?'

He admitted, grudgingly, 'A first report from the Nimrod that one Sea-Rider's in tow from the other and that there are only four men on board. On board the two of them, that is. Making about fifteen knots, in worsening sea conditions. Then something about one of the outboards having failed.'

'So where on earth — '

The admiral checked himself, choking back what would have been a silly question, since it was obviously in the minds of everyone else in the room. He sat down in the red chair, his eyes moving down the line of computer monitors, their bright faces as bare of relevant information as the teletext at the room's far end. Static hummed from a speaker: a red-headed girl — a WRNS PO — pushed a switch, invited, 'Go ahead, Akrotiri.'

The humming became a high whine which broke off suddenly, replaced by a male voice: 'Nimrod 8 Kilo 6 confirms Sea-Riders have only four crewmen on board. Report from Sergeant Hattry Royal Marines relayed as follows. One outboard failed, major damage not reparable at sea, arrival onshore was thus delayed and enemy group had left the beach. SB team leader decided to remain onshore with intention of reaching target location inland ahead of enemy, to complete task as ordered then withdraw, using boats now located at recent landing-point to make ETA international waters sunrise Friday, Saturday or Sunday. Team leader requests helo lift from boats at time of withdrawal if such helos available. Message ends but further message coming.'

The admiral said in a clear, high tone, 'Jesus Christ Almighty.'

Both his hands were raised: his pipe, ready-loaded with tobacco, was in the left one and a storm-lighter in the other. He seemed to be stuck in that position, like a Tussaud wax-work. The SF Adviser looked from him to Charles Hislop: saying nothing, not needing to, his expression saying it all. Hislop, frowning, wasn't focussing; he was back into his own visual imagination again, seeing a dark beach, an unfamiliar coastline, a distant light's triple flashes above the surfline in

235

the north, a group of dark figures moving inland . . . He was in Ockley's place, then, concentrating in an effort to usurp the younger man's thoughts: and hearing his own words – as Ockley too would have recalled them – *the issue is tremendously important* . . .

The Satcom link from Cyprus burst into electronic life again, and a variety of supplementary information began arriving in staccato bursts, same voice as before. The boats were making for Dhekelia, ETA 0630 Zulu, 0830 local. In the view of Corporal Clark Royal Marines, Clark being a qualified mechanic, either a piston had seized up or the crankshaft had gone. Captain Ockley had said that if he completed the task during the past night his intention would be to lie-up until dark and be offshore (in these other, unspecified boats, Hislop supposed) at sunrise tomorrow Friday. He didn't consider this early completion was likely but requested a Nimrod be airborne at dawn Friday, against that possibility. Alternatively he'd go directly to the target area, and from time of arrival there also through subsequent withdrawal to the beach for embarkation, he'd be ready for overflying aircraft to contact him by Sarbe voice link, if required.

'Expecting we'd send one of those Nimrods *over Syria*?'

A wing commander in blazer, sweater and flannels had murmured this to his neighbour in a tone of incredulity. Hislop glanced at him, but having eight of his own Marines inside Syria already he didn't comment. The Akrotiri Satcom operator was signing off again, and the SF Adviser murmured quietly to Hislop, 'They won't be equipped for an overland penetration, I'd imagine?'

'No.' Not that this was a major consideration . . . 'Look, I'd like to get those four and their boats back to Akrotiri rather smartly. They've a long haul into Dhekelia, you say the first report mentioned sea conditions getting worse, and anyway I want to talk to Sergeant Hattry. What chance of helo lift for them right away?'

The wing commander queried, 'Boats as well?' Hislop nodded. 'Well, I don't know . . .'

'*Saratoga* – ' the SF Adviser chipped in – 'might lend us a Super Stallion?'

'Now *that*'s a thought!'

'They might feel they owed us one.' A glance at the wing commander. 'After that cock-up with the Nimrod being allowed to stay over-time?'

'Try it.' The rear-admiral agreed. 'Washington approved the loan of an E-2, if they could have spared one. In fact it didn't happen, but I've not the least doubt they'll help if they can.'

'Yes.' Hislop nodded. 'That was good thinking, Joe.'

'And meanwhile – ' the admiral was addressing the SF Adviser – 'someone has to tell the Minister that a team of the Special Boat Squadron has entered the Syrian Arab Republic.' He screwed his eyes up for a moment, adding in an even flatter tone, 'With the object of assassinating a former officer of the SAS.' The eyes opened: he looked surprised to be back with them all, as if he'd thought he might have been in a dream . . . 'Major, perhaps *you*'d be so kind?'

The SF Adviser, effectively the DOD's staff and under his command, pushed his chair back and got up. His eyes met Hislop's briefly, ironically, the two of them sharing the thought that *good* news was invariably passed upward through the 'chain of command'. If the Special Boat team had been out and clear, Swale eliminated, the Duty Operations Director would himself have been on the telephone to the Minister by now.

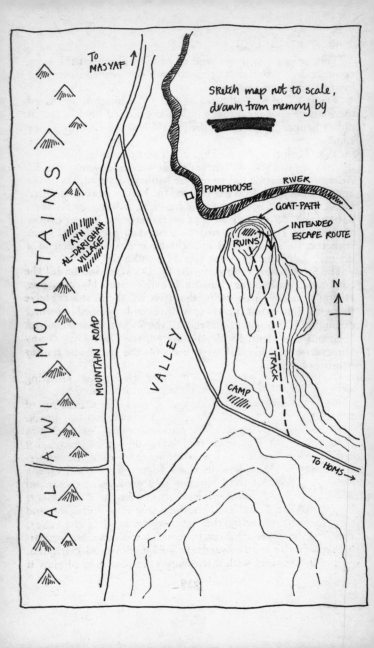

13

Kelso rolled up his strip of map before he switched off the torch. 'First home, let's hope.' Ben, busy with his starscope, muttered, 'Yeah. Let's hope.' But the opposition couldn't have got here ahead of them, he was sure of it. He had about a hundred minutes of pre-dawn darkness left in which to put his team in positions from which to receive them. Or at any rate to see them, see where they elected to lie-up, if they arrived in daylight.

You wouldn't expect them to move by day, but knowing next to nothing about them you couldn't be sure of it.

Darkness was total all around except for a shading of moonlight from behind a slab of mountain to the north. Moon eclipsed by rock . . . He had Laker and Teal with him as well as Kelso. They'd crossed the road – a shelf blasted out of the mountainside – and were crouching among uncomfortably spiky bushes below its outer edge. Above them on the hillside, above this road but also in a position to command the track they'd followed from the west, he'd left Geoff Hosegood and Tony Hall; and he'd sent Ray Wilkinson and Chalky Judge ahead to the right, to the head of the valley, covering the approach from the south but also with a binocular view up this road towards the village of Ayn Al-Dariqhah.

In darkness and with a telescope's narrow field of view it

took a bit of time and concentration to relate mapped features to those on the ground. But he'd got it sorted now, more or less. The moonlight leaking from behind that peak silvered the open northern end of the valley where it widened into the vast spread of the plain, also lit high ground on the valley's eastern side. That spur, the last protruding finger of the Alawis, was about three kilometres long from the head of the valley here on his right to the summit on its tip, a high point commanding the valley's entrance. As it would have done in Crusader days. Right on the end, his starscope picked out shapes like the stumps of broken teeth.

Castle ruin. There'd had to be one about there, and the target would be somewhere near it. On this side: couldn't be beyond it, nothing could, the ridge ended there in a cliff-like drop to the plain.

And from the south, the ridge, access looked almost as sheer.

'See the ruin?'

Sticks grunted. Glasses at his eyes. 'If that's what it is.'

'Map shows the Homs road crossing that ridge at the low part, halfway along. Low this side, anyway. It carries on across the valley slantwise, joins *this* road five or six k's north of here. My guess is where it dips down into the valley – thereabouts – there'll be a village, buildings, *something*.'

'Be dead right for the grid reference.'

'And there was mention of a *qal'at*. Castle. *That* thing. Which is why I'm sure it's not just flat rocks . . . OK, let's – '

He'd been starting to move, but stopped now. Traffic sounds from up there, from the south. Now lights flickered through the tops of the bushes. Diesel, and a lot of crashing and banging. Old banger, literally . . . Geoff and Romeo would have seen it before this but they wouldn't have bothered to break the silence with a warning, knowing that none of their colleagues had cloth ears or carried white sticks . . . Lights accompanied by the sound of churning scrap-iron passed close above, continued northward. The pair on the mountainside would be watching it go, taking advantage of its headlights – if they were strong enough – illuminating some of the village as it got there.

'We'll work round the head of the valley, on to that ridge.

Then recce whatever's down there on the Homs road, and you, Sticks, you with these two guys, suss out the ridge right to its end, including that ruin, then find a place to lie-up facing back to the south. I'll shift the others farther round, this end of it.'

'They'll come this way then, you reckon.'

'Yeah. But you could have one guy watching the reverse slope, couldn't you. In case I'm wrong.' He put the starscope away. 'Right. Back to where we left Geoff and Romeo.'

He felt sure that Swale and company would appear from this direction, no matter which route they might have taken through the mountains. Ten to one they would *not* be coming down from the north, the Masyaf direction, which would have involved a long detour, with no obvious justification for it.

He still didn't know what the target might be. Only a location, and the CO's sketchy outline of the background, something about a hostage who wasn't there. Wasn't *thought* to be there. He'd said, *We're having to guess most of it, but effectively that's it* . . . Swale was supposed to believe that he was coming to extract this hostage, whereas in fact he was being lured in so as to be set up in some way that would incriminate the SBS.

He was mapping the area in his mind as he took the other five to join Wilkinson and Judge, after collecting those two from the mountainside.

'Listen – I'm guessing they'll come by the route we just came on. Probably not before tonight, but – anyway, Geoff, you and Romeo put yourselves somewhere about here. You'll command both approaches. Ray and Chalky'll be five hundred metres to your right, and I expect I'll join them before sunrise. OK?'

'Yeah.' Hosegood had glasses up, studying this view of the peak at the end of the ridge, and the ruins on it. 'Right.'

Wilkinson and Judge, too, would have sections of the southern and western approach routes in view, and also – to their right – they'd look down on the road from Homs. Straight across the valley, they'd see any movements around Ayn Al-Dariqhah.

'I'm going with Sticks to recce along the ridge. Sticks – you,

Ducky and the Doc – the whole bit, up to that summit, scout out the ruins, then find a place on that slope to lie-up with views down this way and across the valley. Main object's to know where they are – if they show up between now and sunset – so we can move in on them after dark. *Soon* after dark – for maximum withdrawal time . . . Remember Swale's a big guy, most likely stand out taller than his chums, and he's the star attraction – if they split up and you had a choice . . .'

Kelso said, 'Water could get to be a problem. Where you're putting me, map shows a river down below us, bottom of that cliff. We three might give you lot what's in our bottles, and I'll send Ducky down to fill ours, when we get there. Down and back up before the sun's up.'

'Your risk – if you can't get down.'

'Human fly, is Ducky.'

Chalky muttered as the water gurgled, emptying three bottles to top up the other five, 'One more duck on a swamp won't notice, will it.'

'Got Puritabs, have we?'

'Course.' Sticks growled, 'Teach your grandmother . . .'

Water was more important than food. Once the sun was high they'd all be reminded of this simple truth. And Puritabs would kill the river water's bugs.

About an hour to go before dawn, Ben thought, when he made the next halt, dropping off Wilkinson and Judge. Then four of them moved on.

The moon wasn't going to show its face from behind that mountain, he realised, wouldn't be either a help or a danger to them in the next hour. Moving downhill, northward towards the Homs road in the dip, Laker was off to his right, the others a short way back on his left. Wanting to get down there reasonably quickly but also exercising caution, the need for which was well ingrained in them, awareness that a twisted ankle or a barking dog could equally bring problems when you were somewhere where you should *not* have been. Dislodging a stone could start an avalanche of other stones, disturb the village dogs: the village, Ayn Al-Dariqhah, was only a couple of thousand metres away by crow-flight across the valley.

242

They'd been picking their way downhill for ten minutes when Laker's voice called softly from the right: 'Ben . . .'

'Coming . . . Sticks?'

'Yeah.'

Moving right, to join the Doc. Who, *last* time he'd called him out of the dark, had found a boat. This time he'd found a road. He loomed over Ben suddenly at a confusing level – about nine feet high, stars behind him . . . 'It's the road, Ben.' He was up on some kind of bank. 'Dry-stone wall this south side. But to my right there's a track branches off, leading north.'

He'd got up there to have a bird's-eye view of it. Ben did the same, and saw that the track led off in the direction of the *qal'at*.

'Your best route, Sticks. You three go on, I'll recce this way solo, maybe pay you a visit after if there's time.'

'Check . . . Luck, Ben.'

The ground still fell away on the road's far side, and the road itself led downhill too, having passed over high ground up on the right, now sloping down into the saddle from which it debouched into the valley. Following the line of it, he was glad of the wall's cover – potential cover – from traffic on the road for instance, if any came. There'd be a certain amount, he supposed, between Homs and Masyaf, it just hadn't started yet.

Light . . .

A pinpoint: high, but bigger and brighter than any star. At the village, some early riser . . . Then a dog began to bark – not here, but from the direction and distance of that light. Early-riser disturbing dog . . . He'd paused – noticing a new amalgam of scents. Well, *smells* – agricultural, biological – and as he moved forward again another hound gave tongue much closer to him: not far ahead, maybe in the road or close to it.

Habitation, then – hamlet, farmstead, whatever? Target location – within maybe fifty metres?

He didn't think *he*'d alarmed the dog. More likely the barking from across the valley had set it going. A chorus now, from that direction, and he was wondering whether this reconnaissance might be counter-productive: however careful

243

or clever you were, there was a danger of being seen or heard, and it was absolutely vital *not* to be.

Creep away, play safe, see it in daylight from a distance?

From across the valley he heard a motor being started. High whine of the starter, repeated spasms of it before the engine fired. The sounds carried very clearly in the quiet night, drowning the dogs' yelps. Then the car's lights showed, seemed to grow out of the darkness and then move away slowly towards the south.

Here, he was close to something – to a village or a farm, a house. It wasn't only the presence of the barking dog, but there were other sounds as well, people or animals stirring, animal smells. Entirely different from the clean, cold air of the mountains. No lights: maybe not surprising at this hour. Except there *was* movement. Might not have electric power but surely they'd have oil . . . He crept forward along the wall, to see what could be seen. Having come this far. The village had to be right on the road, abutting its other side he guessed. If it was a village. He paused again, the headlights passing from right to left and out of his field of vision; at that point they'd have been just below where he'd posted Geoff and Tony Hall.

Light, suddenly, and close . . .

A flare of it. He was crouching against the wall. Hearing what he then realised was the crackling of dry wood, someone lighting a fire. The image that jumped into his mind immediately was that of a camp. Military?

It might make sense. In the context of holding a prisoner – some military unit under canvas. From as much – or rather, little – as one knew of it. Firelight was flickering continuously along the top of the wall now, above his head and for some distance farther along. This would not be a good place to poke one's head up. He turned around – slowly, careful not to let the SA80 clatter against the stones – and began crawling back the way he'd come. Uphill, crawling on until there was no longer any reflection of firelight on the stones.

He was thankful he'd re-touched the cam-cream job on his face. Lifting himself slowly, to see just over the top.

The fire flamed and smoked in the centre of a circle of stones. There was a tripod built over it and a cooking-pot suspended – high, the fire not ready for it yet. Figures crouched or stooped around it. Three of them. Four . . . Behind them – he'd been right with that guess – tents stood in lines. The nearer ones were clear to see in the fire's light, others ranged away into the dark background in straight lines, geometric shapes, the pattern of an officially-organised camp, disciplined. Impossible to count how many: but there were a lot of them.

Those weren't soldiers. He'd caught a sight of grey beard as one moved round to the other side of the fire and squatted to poke at it. Head cowled, Arab-type headdress, an impression of a bony, old man's face. He was back on his haunches now, away from the heat – and light.

Refugees? A refugee would hardly be a surprising thing to find here, but it seemed unlikely in the context of the Swale business. And yet there it was. There had, as everyone knew, been a huge flow of refugees into Syria, driven out of territory now occupied by Israelis, there'd been thousands displaced in various waves at different stages of Israeli settlement and expansion. This might be some more recent, small-scale exodus.

But why would they hold a political hostage in such a camp? Unless it *was* military, those old people just campfollowers?

The dog whined, crouching behind them, firelight like sparks in its eyes. Ben just about holding his breath, not even blinking, not fond of dogs in such circumstances as these. The breeze was the right way, luckily, he could see it in the drift of smoke towards the dog. The barking from across the valley had ceased too, Ayn Al-Dariqhah returning to its slumbers now that its solitary commuter had left. This animal here had its eyes on the cooking-pot, which one old scarecrow had just lowered, letting it down to the heat now that there was less flame, more glow.

His eyes shifted. Back from the fire, somewhere among the tents, a man had hawked and spat.

He saw him – a match flaring in cupped hands. A soldier: the light gleamed along the barrel of a slung rifle before it flickered out. Cigarette, its end glowing red as he drew on it.

Ben smelt it – cigar, not cigarette – and heard the exhalation. He was that close. Lowering himself by about half an inch . . . Military camp, with hangers-on.

The soldier was coming towards the fire, between the lines of tents. Pausing to spit again. He'd die of lung cancer before any bullet got him . . .

No question, anyway. The last thing one wanted was a battle. The requirement was for one man dead, eight withdrawing unseen and unheard-of.

Swaggering way of walking . . . The old people at the fire shifted, making way for him. There wasn't much light from it now the flames had settled, but enough to see that he was wearing shabby green fatigues, baseball-type cap of similar material. He was stretching his hands to the warmth, cigarette wobbling in his dark face, a gruff muttering of Arabic. Ben let himself down behind the wall. From the look of the sky he'd just have time to let Sticks know what he'd found here, then get back to Wilkinson and Chalky.

Thirty hours after he'd had the news that his SB team had vanished into the Syrian mountains, Charles Hislop had to attend a meeting at the Foreign and Commonwealth Office. In the interim – yesterday – he'd been busy enough. First, down to Poole to attend to urgent Squadron business; and while down there he'd actually seen his wife, spent several minutes with her. It had felt like playing truant. Then by early afternoon he'd been back in the JOC for a conversation by Satcom with Sergeant Bert Hattry, who by that time had been at Akrotiri, having been lifted out of the sea with his boats and crews by a US Navy Air Force Super Stallion helicopter sent from the carrier *Saratoga*.

The Cousins had turned up trumps. That Task Group Commander had also said he'd be glad to help again when the team got themselves out of Syria.

When . . .

Hattry had given him the full story of the para drop, the outboard's failure and Ben Ockley's decisions to (a) intercept the target on the beach, (b) continue the pursuit inland. He'd described the boats in which Ockley intended to make his withdrawal, and various other details such as grenade-launchers and a light anti-tank weapon having been cached above the beach in case of later need.

Hislop saw the point, and approved of Ben's forward thinking. The beach was obviously a focal point, and where they'd be at their most vulnerable in the withdrawal stages. But he was also chilled by the prospect of confrontation – on that beach, in the mountains, anywhere on Syrian territory.

It wouldn't happen, he assured himself. With a bit of luck, and reasonably good management . . . The Squadron's very specialist arts included long-range penetration of enemy territory, operating and remaining undetected in that territory, and getting out of it on completion of the task. This was precisely the requirement now; its swift and efficient conclusion was the one and only outcome that would justify the present trauma.

And he was going to have to justify it, or try to. Right after this talk with Hattry he was due to present himself to the Chief of the Defence Staff.

Hattry had detailed again Ben's intention of listening-out over the Sarbe voice link, in case the RAF might consider sending a Nimrod over . . . 'What he said, sir, was if they were stuck you'd want to know was this Swale bloke out of it or wasn't he. Only way he could see to get word out, like.'

'I see. But of course that's not at all likely.'

The way to get word out was for the team to bring it out with them. He wasn't prepared to consider the possibility of their becoming 'stuck'. He'd been thinking on these lines – the only way you could afford to think, in the circumstances – when he'd finished the de-briefing of Bert Hattry and left the JOC just in time to keep his appointment upstairs.

The Commandant General Royal Marines, also Major-General Training and Special Forces Royal Marines, had been present at this interview. They and the Chief of the Defence Staff knew exactly what had happened, in surprising detail, but the CDS had wanted to hear at first hand Hislop's own specialist view of Ockley's actions – and his justification of them or otherwise – and current prospects.

'In terms of the decision he took after he landed on that beach. Up to that point I wouldn't have any criticism; I accept that the task could have been completed before that if it hadn't been for circumstances quite beyond his control.'

Not a bad start. At least Ockley wasn't being condemned out of hand. Hislop glanced at the two Marine generals, guessing that some of this clear-sightedness might have been inspired by them. Then he put himself as it were into Ben Ockley's trainers on that patch of Syrian shingle, and gave the CDS a breakdown from the SB Squadron's angle on the problems/options facing the team leader in that kind of situation.

'Sounds as if you're accepting the responsibility yourself.'

'I think I have to, sir. I'd stressed the importance of stopping Swale, the consequences if we failed. On that beach he'd have known he couldn't be far behind them, still had a good chance, and — '

'And ignored the fact that those people invented an SBS identity for some scurrilous purpose, and he was giving them another eight.'

He kept his mouth shut. When a man was right, and he knew you knew it, there wasn't much point arguing.

'But you'd have done the same?'

'I — believe I would.' He wasn't certain; you'd have had to have been there to be positive about it. But Ockley could have the benefit of the doubt. 'I also think he'll pull it off, sir.'

'Kill Swale and come out intact?' An eyebrow cocked . . . 'Well, let's hope you're right. But my God . . .'

Hislop glanced at the CGRM. Meeting a look of empathy, but also the same appreciation of stark realities: the fact there might be no limits to the size of the upheaval that could follow Ben Ockley's 'local initiative'.

The CDS raised that precise point now. 'You referred to what you call· "local initiative", Hislop. As — well, a doctrine, more or less. Would you say Ockley was under an obligation to exercise such initiative?'

'Definitely, sir. It's the nature of the job.'

'But — ' the Major-General Special Forces interjected — 'local initiative could have been applied the other way — in a decision to withdraw.'

'That's a good point.' The Chief of the Defence Staff nodded. Then looked back at Hislop. 'However. For the time being we've spent enough time on the spilt milk. He's in there

– for better or for worse, and I don't think there's much doubt which . . . Let me hear now what if anything you'd suggest might be done to help him. Any ideas?'

'I'd say it's in his hands, sir. At least until he gets his team off that coast.' An idea was dawning as he spoke; he went on, 'But you very helpfully paved the way for the Americans to send in a Super Stallion, to lift the Sea-Rider team out this morning, and I hear they've offered a repeat performance for sunrise on Friday, Saturday or Sunday. So – *if* so – might they be persuaded to do the job a few miles inside Syrian waters, if that seemed necessary? Ockley's boats won't be exactly speedy, and if the Syrians are even half awake – well . . .' He shrugged. 'The Cousins mightn't want to stick their necks out that far, of course. They've got hostages in Syrian-controlled Lebanon, for instance. But if they would – maybe just turn a blind eye to navigational error?'

The CDS had glanced at the Marine lieutenant-general.

'I really don't know whether they would go that far . . . And on any such question you have to bear in mind that we're looking ahead by one, two, even three days, by which time – well, it's a potentially volatile situation, the fat might be in the fire by then, so what could look like an acceptable risk *now* might by then be something very different.'

'Except –' the major-general offered – 'if Ockley gets Swale and then comes out with his team – which I agree with Hislop he's perfectly capable of doing – plus the fact, as I understand it, that he may be up against not the Syrian establishment but only some group of activists – well, seems to me there's an excellent chance –'

'You may well be right.' A jerk of the head, then, denying it. 'Personally, I'm – less optimistic . . . But don't misunderstand me – I'm with you, in the sense that if we're up the creek so be it, we're up the bloody creek and that's it. All we *can* do, before the hysterics start, is try to limit the political damage by achieving a military success. Then we won't have to look stupid *both* ways, and we'll be less likely to have eight Royal Marines behind bars in Damascus. Right?'

None of them was arguing. The CDS asked Hislop, 'What about this suggestion of sending a Nimrod over to contact him by means of a search-and-rescue beacon?'

'I've just been discussing that, sir, with the sergeant who brought the boats back. Apparently Ockley intended it only as something *we* might want, if we wanted to know what had happened about Swale, particularly.'

A frown . . . 'In those circumstances it would be immaterial whether the Swale threat still existed or did not, surely.'

Hislop nodded. The Syrians wouldn't need to bother with Swale, then. They could throw him away, they'd want to forget him. They'd have no need for subterfuge, they'd have the real thing, undeniable and indefensible.

'On the other hand I'd like to know what he's up to, and whether there's any support we can usefully give him. Such as your suggestion of a coastal pick-up by helicopter. I *like* the idea of establishing communications, if it can be done. One wouldn't lightly contemplate intruding in someone else's airspace, in normal circumstances, but in this instance it might be – might be justified . . . I suppose a Nimrod would be the choice. Fast enough – and it could be lightly loaded, wouldn't want to hang around, would it . . . What about Syrian ground-to-air?'

'At the last count they had twenty-six surface-to-air missile batteries.' The CGRM, or someone on his staff, had evidently been doing some homework. 'Equipped with Guidelines, Goas, Gainfuls and Gaskins. But none deployed in that area as far as we know.'

'Might have that checked out, Mike. Meanwhile I'll have a word with the Minister; and I've a feeling he may want to chew it over with Herself. But I do think the Sarbe proposal's an option we should consider, amongst others. Your boy's landed us right in it, Hislop, but we won't get out of it by contemplating our navels, will we.'

A touch of the 'local initiatives' even at *that* level, Hislop thought. Largely, he guessed, because of the reality and size of the Swale threat. And from that point of view he'd sensed underlying sympathy with young Benjamin.

There was a contrasting absence of it at the Foreign and Commonwealth Office, however, this Thursday morning. The meeting had been called for 10 a.m., and a call to Poole from the office of Major-General Special Forces had caused Hislop to come up for it. He climbed the steps from the courtyard at five minutes to the hour, finding that John Bremner of SIS had beaten him to it.

'Well, Major. You on tranquillisers yet? I'll bet *these* guys are . . .'

The meeting resulted from a research initiative originating in the Ministry of Defence Secretariat and necessarily involving the FCO, but in fact it was a spin-off from that conference yesterday in the office of the Chief of the Defence Staff. Hislop had been on his feet, about to back out from the great man's presence, when MGTSF had come up with a proposal which in fact Hislop had put to him earlier: another para drop, with the Sea-Riders and the same crews, to R/V close inshore with the Special Boat Squadron team at a time and date to be fixed through the Nimrod/Sarbe operation. It had seemed like a good idea – at least to be ready to lay it on at short notice; there was after all no certainty that the Americans would be willing to lift the team out of Syrian territorial waters. Decisions had been made, therefore, (1) to have a replacement outboard motor flown at once to Akrotiri, (2) to take advice from FCO, SIS and other sources as to whether there'd been any unusual activity, either diplomatic or military, inside Syria. Answers to these enquiries might affect decisions on either an air intrusion or the re-use of the Sea-Riders, or both.

It wasn't a big meeting. Hugh Vestey – decidedly on edge, Hislop thought – presided, in a boardroom-like section of his own office suite, and the only others present besides Hislop and Bremner were the MoD's Secretariat Officer – a man named Bennett, who as usual sported a Gunners' tie – and an assistant of Vestey's who took notes.

Not that there was very much to take notes of. Vestey informed his civil service colleague at the outset that 'the Office' had received no reports of any unusual proceedings, diplomatic or otherwise, in Syria, and that in answer to the direct question the ambassador had cabled that with President Assad still away in Moscow very little at all was happening in Damascus.

Vestey looked across the polished mahogany table at Bremner.

'That announcement on the BBC World Service yesterday,

251

John — about an RAF air/sea rescue exercise having ended in a real emergency, a rescue launch breaking down and drifting in Syrian territorial waters, lost all night and finally located by a Nimrod, recovered under tow from a second launch?' His smile was faintly ironic. 'Did I get that right?'

Bremner looked surprised. 'Now you mention it — yes, I read a transcript of it. I gather the statement was put out by the RAF PR department in MoD.'

Hislop had heard of it, too, and thought the seed had most likely been sown by Bremner. Vestey asked, 'D'you think the Syrians will have swallowed it?'

'Don't see why not. *I* would've. Of course, I'm neither a nautical nor aeronautical expert. But I'd have thought it might explain the slow return of the Sea-Riders and all those Nimrod comings and goings.' He shrugged. 'There are people who actually *like* to have their suspicions explained away, you know.'

Bremner then came up with the only 'hard' intelligence there was — and at first sight even this didn't seem all that interesting — namely that Hafiz Al-Jubran had been in touch with his girlfriend, Miss Thornton of the British Embassy in Damascus. Hafiz had telephoned her to say that for a short time he was back at his desk in the Interior Ministry, working like mad to clear it and therefore unable to see her — much as he'd been missing her, longing for a reunion with her, etc. He had to leave town again very shortly, consequently didn't have a minute for anything but work; he'd be back next week, he hoped, and the first thing he'd do would be to call her.

Vestey looked annoyed. 'How did you hear about this?'

Bremner shrugged. 'Gossip. You know . . .'

'And what's its value to us?'

He explained to Bennett, 'I'd say the implication is that he believes the Swale operation's progressing as planned. And it is, of course, from their angle we know it is. The *point* is that it tells us he doesn't know we're on to it.'

'How does it tell us that?'

'The fact he was taking the trouble to keep the girl sweet. Being careful not to appear to have broken the affair off just at this moment, thus confirming any suspicion she might have had that he'd only been screwing her in order to set her up for his planted leak. Thus we're supposed to have accepted the leak at its face value.'

'All right, but – '

'Which I submit indicates that the cat is not among the pigeons. Or wasn't at that stage – yesterday noon. I had the report on my desk last night. But I'm afraid that's the best I can do for you, in terms of what you wanted from this meeting.'

Bennett nodded. 'It's something. In fact – ' a glance at Vestey – 'together with your lack of any stirrings in Damascus, it's probably all we needed.'

Not a difficult man to satisfy, Hislop thought. He and Bremner left together. On the pavement – the SIS man was in need of a taxi, whereas Hislop had only a few yards to walk to MoD – Bremner said, 'You might be interested to hear that our friends at Five have nobbled the lurking mole?'

'*Well* . . . So your scenario was on target.'

'Can't *always* guess wrong. But he was one of my lot. Duty officer that night in the annexe. Due for early retirement shortly, disgruntled, just the guy for it. But he's come clean, and Five know the people who put him up to it – a couple, live in Hampstead, an educational publisher with some funny friends. He was already on the books, they say.'

'So what happens to them all?'

'Whatever Five think best, really. The mole's taken even earlier retirement than he'd expected, but he'll be left alone, keep his reduced pension and so on, as long as he doesn't tip his friends off that they've been rumbled.'

'What if he did tell them?'

Bremner left the question unanswered. 'Funny thing was – or so it seemed at first – he hadn't taken a photostat of the telegram, just had notes on the back of an envelope. When you think about it, it's quite smart. Since he'd have no hard evidence, in all the circumstances it's a fair bet the FCO would've repudiated him and his allegation, denied it totally. Unless of course they'd been less obtuse than I'd give them credit for . . . You see, the row, scandal, would've blown up very quickly, there'd have been no way to avoid a full-scale enquiry, so the telegram would have come to light anyway, the FCO would finally have had the "truth" forced out of them – having prevaricated – and HMG would have been truly over the proverbial barrel.'

'Vote of thanks to your friends, then.'

'Actually it would've been like falling off a log. OK, it's hindsight, but to have recruited such an obvious candidate for moledom was very clumsy. Although, mind you, if we hadn't been on to it as quickly as we were we'd still have been sitting ducks.' He shrugged. 'Really have to watch your back, these days, don't you.'

'Didn't one always?'

'Oh, I think it's more cut-throat now. But there's another line of investigation, quite interesting in its way. That bro-chure, Bluewater Cruises? They've dug out a travel agent who sold four tickets – returns, incidentally, Heathrow to Ercan via Istanbul – where incidentally we were let down very badly – to a woman who looked like a cow and had a strong line of bull, Bluewater Cruises' British agent. Her line was she was setting it up as a pilot scheme, just one boat to start with, she'd share commission, only to get her clients out there and back again. Had an office address that's turned out to have been rented for one month – since vacated, no traces, you'll be surprised to hear. They have the four customers' names, of course – no Swale among them, but Five have lines on two guys with military backgrounds who've deserted their usual haunts, could've been taken on as mercenaries, could be part of it, who knows . . . Charles, I suppose you realise the Hindawi trial verdict's due tomorrow? And did you see that article of Worsthorne's last Sunday, arguing that if it's a "guilty" verdict Mrs T will be bound to kick 'em all out, ambassador first and foremost?'

'Yes, I did.' Last Sunday morning. Lull before the storm . . . 'Suit them well to have us over *that* barrel at this moment, wouldn't it?'

'Let's hope your Captain Ockley knows just *how* well.'

'Major Hislop?'

One of the uniformed security men from inside . . . 'Urgent call for you, sir, Commandant-General Royal Marines.'

'Right – '

'So long.' Bremner raised a hand. 'Don't let him talk you into anything.'

There were about forty tents in the camp. Also, back from the road and on its own, a small stone-built shack with a thatched roof and a guard at its door. It was about the size of a small garage, built with stones like those lying around, the wreckage of whatever had been there before. To the east of it the ground sloped down into a depression with a dried-up watercourse passing through it, and behind it the expanse of rock slope climbed steeply towards the peak where the *qal'at* sprawled.

The guard, with a Kalashnikov on his knees, sat with his back to the wall near the door. Motionless for long periods, probably asleep. He was dressed the same way as the one who'd come to warm himself at the camp-fire in the pre-dawn darkness.

It wasn't a military camp, though. No more than two uniformed men had been sighted at any one time. There'd been very little movement of any kind, in fact, but what signs of life there were had been virtually all civilian, and old folk or infirm, bent, slow-moving. Nobody had visited the camp and nobody had left it, and the door of the stone-built hut hadn't once been opened. This wasn't only Ben's observation, but Chalky Judge, who'd had the last two hours' watch, had confirmed it.

That sentry was still immobile. If there'd been a hostage in there, Ben thought, it would have been easy to have taken him out of it. Even in broad daylight that guard could have had his throat slit before he'd have opened an eye. The hut was a Swale trap, nothing else. There'd been a lot of time in which to study it and think about it, and he was convinced that whatever they wanted Swale for, that was where it was supposed to happen.

Better take a look inside there anyway. If time and other circumstances permitted.

He took a sip from his water-bottle, then re-corked it, making the most of the trickle of lubrication in his throat. It was 2 p.m. now: in London it would be noon. Cool, no doubt, autumnal. Here, the rocks were hot, heat-waves distorted one's view of the valley, over which the pinnacle of rock on which the *qal'at* spread its ruined walls loomed commandingly. The slope leading up to it from the Homs road – Ben had climbed it in the dark, and Sticks was holed up on it now – was not only steep but craggy and deeply fissured. Whoever had picked that site for his castle had known what he was doing.

Wilkinson and Judge were both asleep, in their hides within a few metres of this one. Ben had slept for a couple of hours during the forenoon and he'd rest again before dusk if nothing happened before then. He didn't *think* they'd come in daylight. Probably wouldn't show up all that promptly at dusk, either; because if they'd been close enough to be able to move in here as soon as the light went, they'd surely have made the small extra effort to have made it before dawn. Anyone would have. Also, he was sure they'd have taken about twice as long as his own team had, to make the transit. OK, reduce that difference by about two hours, the time taken up in reconnaissance and settling in this morning, but it still left them several hours' yomp away. The estimate was based on common sense, not conceit; all Royal Marines were commandos and kept themselves fit, but the SBS made a point of being *ultra*-fit. It was hardly likely that some scratch lot of terrorists with a reputedly drink-sodden ex-SAS man in tow would come anywhere near keeping pace with them.

Two Syrians on bicycles were pedalling south on the Homs road. Ben took a look at them through binoculars, then examined the refugee camp again, for about the hundredth time . . .

Helicopter.

The faint beginnings of the sound had been in the back of his consciousness for a couple of seconds before he'd woken up to it. Coming from the southeast, the Homs direction. He looked over to where the others were holed up: checking they *were* in cover, and no weapons or other articles out where they'd reflect sunlight and catch a pilot's eye. He pushed himself well back under the rock. Listening to the hammering beat as the volume of sound increased. Close, now, he guessed it would be about to pass over. Very loud – a biggish helo, he guessed, although he couldn't quite identify it yet. Although he'd heard one of these before . . . The thought triggered recognition about a second before the machine entered his field of view: it was a *Hind*, a Soviet-built Mi-24 gunship.

Big, all right. Fully equipped, it would have a turret-mounted Gatling, rocket pods and most likely bombs as well. The Russians used them in Afghanistan a lot. He couldn't see its nose, from this angle, where the Gatling turret would be, but that gun would blast out something like 4000 rounds a minute and each of the four launcher pods would hold thirty-two 57-mm rockets.

Chalky Judge slid into the hide on Ben's right. 'Looks like it's going to land, Ben.'

It was lowering itself over the village, Ayn Al-Dariqhah. The mountainside above that road looked too steep to land on, but it was a matter of perspective; the village was there, there had to be some level ground.

Ray Wilkinson crawled in. Reaching for his water-bottle, and crowding Chalky on the other side. 'Visitors . . .'

Its noise was bouncing off the mountain: then it was passing out of sight, behind a ridge which also hid part of the village. Abruptly, then, the sound cut out. Wilkinson, who'd picked up some Arabic on a Gulf deployment, said, 'Landed in the *saha*, I dare say.'

'Yeah.' Chalky nodded. 'Never land anyplace else, meself.'

'Village square. Open space among the hovels. Multi-purpose, including stoning adulteresses to death, in some parts.'

The helo's arrival would have some connection with the Swale business, Ben thought, but it didn't have to be performing in the role of gunship. The Mi-24 had started life as a support helicopter, commando-carrier.

'Nutty?' Wilkinson broke a chocolate bar into three parts and handed out two of them.

'Thanks, Ray.'

'I'll scoff all yours later . . . Hey, they're off again.'

The *Hind* had started up. Half a minute later it lifted into view above the village, swept away across the valley and more or less over the top of Kelso's position on that south-facing rock slope, before straightening on course for Homs. But forty minutes later it came back again. Wilkinson reached for his Nikon as soon as they heard it; the camera already had a telescopic lens on it, for taking shots of the refugee camp and the stone cabin earlier on, and he snapped the *Hind* as it flew over towards the village.

'What's that for?'

'I don't really know, Chalky.' Wilkinson shrugged. 'Something to do. Guess I'm a dedicated snapper.' He asked Ben, 'Saw the gun on its snout, did you?'

Shuttle service. Flying troops in, presumably. The obvious guess was they might be staking the place out in advance of Swale's arrival. They watched it clatter down behind that same ridge, and Wilkinson said, putting his camera away, 'Fourteen guys with full equipment, those things take.'

14

Soft whistle from the right, as recognizable as a signature. Ben answered it, and murmured, 'Chalky . . . ' Judge slipped away into the darkness. Having announced his presence, Kelso would be staying put, allowing them to contact him. He and whoever was with him knew roughly where they'd be, and precisely where they *had* been, but also that they weren't nailed down, would very likely have shifted their position after the light had gone.

It had gone now, all right. The night was as black as tar.

Engine-noise, road transport, down on the left. And lights – northbound traffic, the first since dusk. It sounded like heavy trucks – more than one, therefore a convoy, *could* therefore be military: and paranoia was an essential attribute . . . Risking a look straight at it – bad for night vision; he saw headlights on the first, dipped lights on a second, third and fourth. He thought it probably *was* a military convoy.

'Hi, Ben.'

Kelso, and there was one other with him, as well as Chalky. He'd have left either Ducky Teal or Doc Laker up at or near the *qal'at*. Ben said, 'Hang on, Sticks. Need to see if this lot's stopping.' Watching the convoy on the mountain road as it approached the suddenly popular mountain resort of Ayn

Al-Dariqhah. The big Soviet helo was still on the ground there; and a Citroën saloon had come just before sundown from the direction of Homs, joined the mountain road across the valley and turned back into the village. It was still there.

OK, so some villager had a large Citroën saloon . . .

The convoy was *not* about to stop. The leading truck was passing on through the village, grinding on in low gear with its lights licking the wall of rock on its left. The others also coming into sight again: all four, heading for Masyaf or points north. Growl of heavy engines fading, but above it the thinner, high-pitched snarl of a moped; he saw the single light like a bouncing torchbeam southbound on the Homs road.

'All right, Sticks?'

'Ducky filled the bottles again.'

'Good for him.'

'Got sugar-beet too. One here, anyone wants it. Revolting, but edible.'

Doc Laker – squatting, facing out into the night, medical bag strapped on his back, nursing his SA80, had said that. Chalky was covering the other side. It was quiet again, now the moped had snarled away.

'Two points, Sticks.' Addressing Kelso, but it was for the others to hear as well. 'One is I still think they'll come from the west or south, most likely west as we did. And it'd be neat to do the job right there – the junction, where Geoff and Romeo are. Seeing as there must be troops in the village now – we'd be the right side of them, ready to skin out on completion.'

'Unless they've deployed that way themselves.'

'If they have, Geoff'll know it. But point two, we can't count on them coming that way, or on them not sneaking by somehow if they do, but we do know the camp's their target.'

So that was where you'd hit them if you couldn't do it farther west. Specifically not just the camp but the stone cabin which still had a guard sitting outside its door but which no one had even looked into, handed a cup of water or a crust of bread into, let alone entered or exited from, all day.

'They wouldn't be maintaining it for no purpose. Only thing it can be for is to draw Swale. Fits what the CO told us, doesn't it. So look — three guys, adding one to Geoff and Romeo — you'll do, Doc — above that road junction.'

Three would easily handle Swale's group of four, and Geoff could use one as a runner if he needed to contact the rest of them. If those troops did deploy in that direction, for instance.

'Rest of us'll stake out the camp. You and Ducky up on the north end, Sticks. You know your way around that cliff now, don't you. Ray and Chalky this side — here, and right down to the road if needs be, Ray. I'll just move around.'

'What d'you make of the helo?'

'Part of the Swale trap, surely. Once he's wherever they want him, they can deploy fast, can't they.'

'Couldn't've got the buzz *we* were around, you reckon?'

'No, I don't. And OK, it has a Gatling in its nose turret but that doesn't mean it's in the gunship role, it's brought some pongoes to the village, that's all. At least, I *hope* . . .'

Ten metres apart and in single file: Charlie was second in the line, tailing Bob, who'd made a ballsup of the navigation and only come to realise it at dawn this morning when they'd seen the shape of the mountain facing them.

Mountains, plural. Shoulder to shoulder and reaching up three thousand feet, across what they'd expected to be their route eastward, where the gorge they'd been following was supposed to have extended right through and brought them out close to their destination.

If they'd been where they'd reckoned to be, they'd have had only a couple of hours' march after the coming sunset — instead of about eight. The road whose line they'd been following had swung ninety degrees left, short of that mountain barrier, just beyond the point where they'd stopped to lie-up for the day. Bob had tried to disguise his shock, fumbling to get his map out . . . And there it was: two roads roughly parallel, only five kilometres apart but separated by mountains as steep and rugged as those barring the way east. Coming south from where the *gulet* had landed them, Charlie saw — looking over Bob's arm, Tait and Denham crowding in too — Bob must have thought he was on his originally planned route to the interior when in fact he should have continued down to the *next* road. Should have crossed this one, carried on south.

'But we did cross it. Remember that convoy of tankers we had to wait for?'

'Well, in that case – ' Charlie saw the answer, stabbed a finger at the map . . . They'd started inland on the right road, had to leave it to skirt round a settlement on a crossroads, and that was where Bob had led them astray. He'd thought they were rejoining the highway when in fact they'd been slanting off to the northwest.

He'd felt embarrassed for him. SBS, team leader?

'Damn that woman . . .'

Knox meant Leila: he was blaming her for having landed them in the wrong place. Then, intercepting an exchange of expressionless glances between Charlie and Tait, he'd retracted . . . 'I know. My fault, nobody else's . . . But look, all we have to do when we move on tonight is detour to the north a bit – stick to this road, then pass over the hump south of Masyaf – here, right? OK, so we'll lose a couple of hours . . .'

They'd lost at least four, maybe six, Charlie reckoned. They'd got moving again soon after sunset, Bob leading them beside the road at first but then right on it – needing to make up time, so having to leave it to take cover whenever headlights appeared ahead or behind. Once near a bend an Arab on a bicycle had swept by close enough to touch, uttering a loud shriek as he passed, speeding on down.

The road had led them north for about ten kilometres before it began curving right, wavering a bit but generally tending eastward. Finally they'd left it; in the last few kilometres there'd been an uncomfortable amount of traffic on it, and Charlie had reckoned they were getting too close to Masyaf; after another scrutiny of the map Bob had found a track leading off to the right, a steep and winding mountain road, leading to a village which they'd had to by-pass, with some difficulty. Then, when it had begun to seem they were getting nowhere rather slowly, they'd come down at right-angles on to a tarred road cut out of the east flank of the mountains. On its far side was a black void – space, and a steep drop to a plain spreading into unseen distances.

Staring out into the dark, seeing scatterings of lights out there seemingly as distant as constellations in the night sky, Charlie put a map together in his mind. To the southeast would be the town of Homs, while northeast must lie Hama. Sixty k's to one, maybe forty to the other. A motorway linked them, running south to Damascus and north to Halab – better known in bygone days as Aleppo. If you'd taken off from this escarpment in a hang-glider, passing over that road between Homs and Hama and continuing east, you'd have flown over something like four hundred kilometres of desert, camel country, before the sight of the Euphrates warned you that after another fifty you'd be crash-landing in Iraq.

Headlights: a warning flash, car or lorry rounding a bend farther along the mountainside. Charlie led them feet-first over the edge and into undergrowth – thorn, he discovered – which lined the lower edge of the road, rock and earth from the road's excavation having formed a crumbly sort of shelf down there.

Bob, then the other two, had followed his lead. He'd acted instinctively, and the team leader had followed a second or two later. Then the car rushed by, its lights scything through dusty bushes over their heads. Charlie recording another thought: that he'd taken it for granted they *would* follow his lead.

Bob used the cover they'd landed in, getting his torch out to study the map again. You'd have thought he'd have had it in his mind by this time.

'Have to stick to this road now. Only way there is, until we get to this turn here.'

South for a couple of hours, it looked like. To a left fork that would take them down into a valley pushing into the mountains from the open plain. That was the road to Homs, he saw. It led down to cross the valley from northwest to southeast, then passed over more high ground – the eastern enclosure of the valley, a ridge protruding northward. Bob pointed at a *qal'at* on its extremity.

'That's where I should've been at midnight. Come on . . . '

Scrambling back up to the road, Charlie muttered, '*Saab iktir* . . . '

'Right. Lucky there was that ledge to land on.'

263

His comment had been on the steepness of the slope, the sheer drop to the plain hundreds of feet below. But it hadn't been luck, he'd seen those bushes, they'd had to be rooted in *something*.

He wondered why the SBS had been so keen to have a fluent Arabic speaker with them. A second Arabic speaker, at that. Nobody, as yet, was talking to any Arabs.

South now, in single file, ten metres apart and ready to slide down over the edge again when more traffic appeared. Thinking – with the map in mind – that the moon might become a problem, might be risen by the time they got down there and had to cross the valley. Being so late already they'd have to chance it, run the gauntlet . . .

In fact they'd been surprisingly relaxed, he thought, about taking cover. If he'd been leading, he'd have taken a lot more care.

OK, so they'd got away with it. So far . . . But he'd have steered them right, too, not in bloody circles. *And* he'd have got them here in two nights instead of three. He'd have done the job a lot better than Bob Knox had, in fact. A follow-up to this was that right from the start he hadn't given a thought to alcohol. On board the *gulet* he'd been tempted, certainly, there'd been nothing to do for long periods, and the litre of single malt which he'd brought from Heathrow had come into his mind a few times; but he'd put it *out* of mind. And here, liquor might as well not have existed.

He wondered if Anne would have been impressed. Because she was the real reason he was here. That was another thing: he was seeing straight, thinking straight, and one of the things that had become clear was that the drink had been a refuge from his misery over losing her. Not for his wrecked career, but for Anne. Much the same applied to this expedition: he'd instinctively wanted it, but at least half the motivation had been his desire to prove something to *her*. And questioning now whether she'd have been impressed, he couldn't see any answer but a straight *no*, she would not have been. Certainly not enough for it to have made any difference. She'd arrived at her decision, she'd spotted Charlie Swale's feet of clay and that was it, she didn't want him.

That speech she'd made, the last time he'd seen her and

pleaded his case — making a fool of himself, as usual — she'd turned him down with something like *I haven't gone through it just to start again. Might as well face it, Charlie, I don't intend to put my head on the block again . . .*

She'd decided what was safest for Anne, and she was sticking to it. Not what might be streets better because it could turn out to be heaven-on-earth for *Anne and Charlie.* She was concerned only with the risk *Anne* wasn't going to take with herself.

Maybe for her it had never been quite the heaven it had been for him. Although she'd spent a lot of days and nights talking and acting as if it had been.

So there you were — for better or for worse. It had been infinitely better, but also a *hell* of a lot worse, than it felt now.

Getting towards midnight. All in their places, overlooking the approaches and the camp, Ben on the move between them and around generally, and still not a thing happening. The only interruption to the night's peace and quiet came from a transistor at the camp, probably that sentry's.

There'd been no deployment of troops from the village. When he'd visited Geoff and Romeo — leaving Doc Laker with them — Geoff had only just returned from a recce of the area around that road junction, and he'd found the hillsides empty, roads unwatched, unguarded. Whatever troops those were, if they were supposed to be looking out for Swale they weren't making much of a job of it. But it was good that they hadn't deployed, that the withdrawal route to the west was still open; obviously they couldn't have any suspicion that there might be intruders here.

Pitch dark. The moon would be up later but not for a while yet. He thought that when it did rise it would be hidden at first behind the mountains in the north, the west side of the valley at its open end. Then as it slid around it would light the valley, and this north-facing slope, and the lower part of the ridge, but the steep part where Kelso and Teal were holed up would stay dark.

Maybe it would be over by then, anyway. Yomping west, task completed . . .

'Ray?'

'Over here, Ben.'

Wilkinson observed, 'They've let their fire go out.'

'Here. Nutty.' Ben dispensed chocolate, returning earlier generosity. They'd all been chewing slices of sugar-beet, but you could make yourself sick, after a while . . . 'It's not right out. Close up there's still a glow in it.'

Chewing, looking across the valley towards the village, he saw a car come into sight on that high road – coming out of the village. Its headlights jumped up to full beam as it came into view, and its engine sound was a smooth purr, already receding. He hadn't heard it start up.

'Could be the Citroën.'

'You're right, Chalky, it could.' Wilkinson had glasses on it.

'If it turns down on to the Homs road, *I* wouldn't bet against that either.' Because it had come from Homs, or from that direction, a few hours ago. Not that it had to be of any relevance to the Swale operation; it was just that anything that moved invited speculation.

Cold. Not as cold as it had been in the mountains, but it would have been a pleasure to have pulled on a sweater.

Headlights still travelling north. Ray still watching it through binoculars. Ben left him to it, used his starscope to examine the camp, the stone hut, the wall on this side of the road a black streak scored into slightly less dark background.

Ray said, 'Taking the hairpin bend now. It's heading for Homs all right.' There was a distant flash straight into their eyes as the car swung around through a hundred and fifty degrees, its beams then dipping as it nosed into the steep descent to the valley.

Maybe someone had decided Swale wasn't worth waiting for, and was going home. More likely still, it had nothing to do with Swale.

Wilkinson was still following its progress. Ben testing his starscope over longer range, at the valley's wider part where the river looped and irrigation channels cut out a regular pattern of ditches. On that bend of the river, from which Ducky Teal collected water, a concrete pumphouse served the irrigation system. He couldn't see it, couldn't see anything at that distance; in fact a whole regiment of Swales could cross there, scale the goat-path to the *qal'at* ...

The car was down on the flat, its headlights burning towards the ridge. Kelso would be looking down at it from the facing slope; Teal, farther round to the west where he could look down into the valley, would be losing sight of it as it boomed up out of the valley, sweeping up towards the camp. That wall was floodlit, and the nearer tents and the road ahead of it, all uphill to where it passed over the ridge and ran on to Homs. In maybe half an hour's time that driver would be tucked up in a nice warm bed, Ben guessed, very likely in contact with nice warm wife ... The starscope, clinging to the car now, confirmed that it was a fairly large saloon and Citroën-shaped.

Changing gear: having passed the camp, it was slowing, visibly and audibly.

Crawling along now. Then the headlights were swinging to the left: at the junction with the track that led out along the ridge. But swinging out of it again: and stopping, then reversing into that track. The sound of its engine cut off, and the lights went out.

Some Syrian playboy with a lass picked up from the village. If Syrians did that sort of thing, elsewhere than in London.

'Could be the start of something, Ray. See you.' As he moved off to the right Ray Wilkinson was sending Chalky down to the wall at the roadside near the camp, and shifting his own position about a hundred metres closer. Ben was moving east, with the intention of turning down presently to get to the road on the far side of the parked car. Then he'd play Peeping Tom.

He'd covered about fifty metres when he heard a car door shut. Not a slam, but the soft thud was loud enough to hear easily in the surrounding quiet. Then it was repeated, and he guessed that two people had got out. At the same time, distantly, he was hearing an aircraft, without giving it any thought. Sitting, resting his elbows on his knees, he focussed the starscope on that Citroën, and then around it and beyond it.

Two men were plodding up the track, away from the car and towards the high ground and the *qal'at*.

Logic and guesswork said they were going to meet Swale. So the obvious thing to do was to stay with them. But Sticks would have heard those doors, he'd have his scope on them now. He'd stay where he was: as they were going now they'd be closer to him in five or ten minutes' time than they were now. So they weren't likely to become lost to human ken, not for a while anyway, one didn't have to rush after them . . .

Just as well. Focussing on the car again, he was pretty sure there was still someone inside it, behind the wheel.

So he'd leave them to Sticks. To cross the road without being seen by the guy in the car would mean crossing it about two hundred metres higher up, beyond the curve. *Then* catch up on the midnight strollers.

Unless that was only a shadow, in the car . . .

The driver clinched it for him, conveniently in that moment. He must have used a dashboard lighter; no match or gas-flame had flared, but a cigarette tip glowed brightly and then dimmed as it moved downward in a hand that came to rest on the wheel.

The aircraft noise was louder as he detoured eastward. Thinking who else would have seen the car stop and the men get out of it . . . Geoff Hosegood, for instance, wouldn't have seen it but he'd have heard it. He'd know something was happening, and he'd be on his toes – if he hadn't been before this . . . Ben turned down towards the road, still on a slant so as to get out of that driver's field of view. He'd been hearing the airplane ever since it had started as only a hoarse whisper of sound in the southwest: then closer and in the south but still remote, irrelevant to his concerns here. But it was louder still again now, pretty well overhead. It would obviously be Syrian and still didn't have his close interest, although hearing it did remind him of the suggestion he'd made to Hattry about Sarbe communications – if the Crabs would risk it, or *be allowed* to risk it.

Which they would not. Sticks had been right, the idea had been crazy.

He'd crossed the shoulder of the hill: could turn straight down to the road now. Thinking that maybe he should have stopped and switched on his Sarbe. Having told them he'd listen out if aircraft came over, he supposed he should at least have gone through the motions.

Having crossed the road he veered left, over rock and scrub, to get to the track where the going would be easier and faster.

'Foxtrot 2 Bravo, calling Ben . . . D'you hear me, Ben?'

Russell Haig took a breather, holding the mike in front of his mouth but with his thumb off the button for a moment. His co-pilot was doing the driving, and in the middle section of the aircraft Jimmy Drake, the tactical navigator, was watching Syrian airfields – Hama, Al Qusayr, Shayrat.

Haig had brought his Nimrod across the sea at zero feet, crossed the coast near Al Hamidiyah not much higher, over that low terrain where the underground oil-pipes from Iraq reached the coast through the Tall Kalakh pass; he'd climbed steeply up and out of that pass, to nine thousand feet. It was a good height for present purposes for two reasons. One, low-flying would have added to the already considerable risks, encouraging every Syrian for miles around to put two and two together and maybe guess right, which wouldn't have improved Ben Ockley's local standing. Two, nine thousand was an optimum height in the context of the Sarbe's upward reach from the ground, which was in the three-dimensional shape of a cone standing on its apex and extending upwards to a maximum vertical range of ten thousand feet. At nine therefore you were inside the little transmitter's range and had about as much horizontal scope as you could get.

For the umpteenth time: 'Foxtrot 2 Bravo, calling Ben. D'you hear, Ben, d'you hear, Foxtrot 2 Bravo calling Ben!'

'Skipper, they have us illuminated from Hama now.' Drake's voice came tersely over the intercom. 'We're lit up like Oxford Street.'

Radar-illuminated, that meant. They'd had one station fingering them within seconds of that soaring climb out of the pass. What TACNAV would be looking for and hoping not to find was missile-head radar, the kind that locked-on to an intruding aircraft and blew it out of the sky on impact. A Nimrod wasn't designed for dodging missiles.

He'd be watching for Migs too. There had to be a limit to the extent they'd let you twist their noses. And that Hama field was getting closer every moment, on this flight-path.

'Foxtrot 2 Bravo calling Ben. D'you hear me, Ben?'

Seemingly – and sickeningly – not. And not far to go now, not many more seconds over the target area. At any rate the *designated* target area . . . He tried again: same call, same lack of response, and hope of one just about gone, too . . . 'Ben, d'you hear me?'

Turning to port. One last try – talking fast and *willing* him to answer: 'Ben, come *in*, Ben!'

'OK.' He sagged back in his seat, defeated, as the Nimrod turned its tail towards those various dangers. Flying west now, and no more transmissions. Suggestions of trawling across the mountain passes and along the coastal strip had been turned down; if the SBS team weren't in or close to the target area it was to be assumed they were on their way out; there'd be a Nimrod – McPhaill's – over the sea at dawn.

Kelso held his starscope on the two men climbing the track, coming more or less towards him at some moments. At others he lost them, rock spurs intervening where the track wound through them, but always picking them up again as they re-appeared just that much nearer.

Ben would be trailing them, he guessed. Hoped . . . Because when they got to about this level they'd be passing out of sight from here. Unless he shifted his position – which would leave the north side of the camp unwatched. Those two would obviously have come to rendezvous with the Swale party, presumably at the *qal'at* since that was where they were heading, but the target was Swale himself, not a crowd of Syrians before you could get at him.

Ducky Teal was the answer to the immediate problem. Ben might not be all that close behind them, and you couldn't risk losing them altogether. He might be sussing out that car, for instance. So move Teal higher. He was on the west-facing slope, two hundred metres from here, but from higher up he could still keep an eye on the valley while at the same time marking where those Syrians went.

He took another look, confirming that they were keeping to the track, then put the starscope away and moved off towards Teal.   *   *   *

Bloody dark. With the starscope or even binos from a good position you could see over fair distances, especially movements and light colours — like faces, even Syrian faces, that weren't cam-creamed — but on the move you'd be doing well to see a man six feet in front of you.

Ben was on the track now. It was easier going, but it would have been unwise to have yomped it fast, maybe yomped right into them.

One of his trainers had split across the instep, and his toes were out of both of them. Kelso had been right about trainers as footwear for mountaineers.

Stopping to listen, he picked up their sounds immediately. Hard-soled shoes on rock, quite a long way ahead. He moved on again, still not hurrying.

Kelso would have sent Teal up to the top, he guessed. He decided to branch off from the track and confer with him. He'd pick the Syrians up again easily enough; they weren't making any attempt to move quietly. He left the track and began cautiously to traverse the rock slope: it was not only steep at this level, it was a mass of crags, ravines, potential leg-breakers all the way, and only an idiot would try to move fast over it when he didn't have to.

'Sticks . . .'

No answer . . .

He found the place where he'd been, a kind of cockpit among the rocks; and he'd left his back-pack here. Ben squatted, using his ears and getting the starscope out.

Seeing him — within half a minute of putting the scope up — he gave him early warning: 'Sticks, Ben here. Waiting in your hide.'

He'd stopped, but was now coming on again.

'Problems?'

'No . . . Did you send Ducky up to the *qal'at*?'

'Yeah. Didn't know where you'd — '

'Right. Sticks, for your info, there's a guy in that car still. Chain-smoker, doesn't care who sees it.'

'They're noisy too.'

'Yeah. Bless them . . . I'm going on up.'

He went back to the track. Listening from there, hearing

nothing at all, he thought they must have reached the top. The track didn't go all the way to the *qal'at* itself, and if they'd been still climbing, negotiating the last stage which was really a climb, he was sure he'd have heard them.

It took him about three minutes to get to the flat bit where the track ended. It was a plateau large enough to have parked a few cars on, if you could have got them up here. In days of yore the castle's suppliers would maybe have unloaded their carts here; there might have been steps from here on up, or some kind of pulley-hauly arrangement. He crossed the level ground, and climbed that final stage. It was easy enough in daylight, but getting up there quietly in darkness meant taking it very cautiously.

Then he was on the top. Broken sections of wall, crumbling conduits, collapsed arches or doorways, short sections of flights of steps. And – movement – close to his left. *And* – he'd frozen, holding his breath while he concentrated all his senses on identifying it – separating itself from what might have been a chimney, a pillar but rectangular in cross-section – the tall, wide-shouldered figure of Ducky Teal.

'Ducky, where've they – '

The figure jerked round, facing him. Reek of cigarette-smoke, a fag-end burning between his lips. Teal's build but *not* Teal – an astonished Syrian, gleam of white teeth in a dark face as his mouth opened, a gasped syllable of Arabic before Ben hit him twice in quick succession, a spearhand jabbing at his throat to cut out the incipient shout of alarm and then the edge of his hand like an axe where the neck joined that Teal-like spread of shoulder. Ben caught him as he fell: he was crouched, looking for the other one, his eyes probing the darkness as he let the Syrian's body down and then left it, moving to merge into the dark upright of that chimney.

Controlling his own breathing so he could listen: but no sound, no movement.

The co-pilot answered Akrotiri's question: 'Negative. No contact. Over.'

'Roger, Foxtrot 2 Bravo.'

Haig had taken over the driving, and they were over the

sea now, well out. He was depressed by the failure of his mission. He'd been keen to undertake it, but his superiors had been very much against it. The pressure to go ahead had come from London. Now to come out of it empty-handed was galling, and left huge doubts over what might be happening in those mountains.

If he'd been able to establish communications he'd have first asked Ben for a report on the situation there, then told him that the Cousins were offering to lift him and his team out of their boats inside Syrian waters provided a reliable, guaranteed time and position for the rendezvous could be given. They didn't want to mess around, but if it looked like a neat, clearly-defined rescue mission they'd do it.

Would have done it, rather.

Akrotiri was on the air again. Deep in thought, he'd only half-heard that operator telling Foxtrot 2 Bravo to stay clear of the base, maintain present height in a holding-pattern to the south.

He reached for his own mike.

'This is Foxtrot 2 Bravo. May we know what's the hold-up, and how long? Over.'

'Wait, Foxtrot 2 Bravo . . .'

Quite a long wait . . . Then a voice he knew well: 'Russell, we have two Harrier GR3s all the way from the UK and they can't stay up for ever. Give us a break, will you? Out . . .'

'Well.' The co-pilot murmured, 'What d'you know about *that*.'

'Bugger-all . . . Take over, will you?'

It did seem that something must be going on, though. The fact that this unproductive Nimrod intrusion had been ordered from dizzy heights in London, that the Cousins were coming in on the act, plus a rumour that someone of importance to the SB Squadron's operation was on his way out – which was supposed to be why they'd been so insistent on getting a report from Ockley . . . And now RAF Harriers, for Christ's sake . . .

He checked the time: 0128. He'd expected to be Akrotiri's only customer; normally the airfield shut down at 3 p.m.

15

Having used his starscope from a distance he'd thought that the Citroën's driver had taken off, but up close, looking in through a misted window, he saw him sprawled asleep on the back seat. It was better than having him wandering around.

0412 now. He went some way down the road before crossing it and starting up the rocky hillside to Ray Wilkinson's position. The simplest way to get straight to it was to climb up from a recognizable starting point.

The Syrian he'd killed was now in a deep cleft in the rock slope on the west side of the *qal'at*, where Ducky had been climbing up when Ben had mistakenly assumed he'd already have reached the top. The man who'd died as a result of that misunderstanding had evidently been the other one's minder, stationed at the south edge of the ruins maybe to watch out for Swale's approach. About an hour after that event Teal had heard the surviving Syrian call out, evidently summoning the deceased one, then after repeated calls he'd gone to find him, peering into corners as if he'd expected to find him asleep somewhere. The dead one's name had been Yusuf; his boss was quite young, tall and slim, dressed in denims and a leather jacket. Eventually he'd gone back to where he'd been waiting since not long after midnight – a flight of steps with an archway over them. This one smoked too; also – Ducky said

– he talked to himself a lot, in tones of anger and complaint.

Plenty to complain about, too. Swale late, and his back-up absconded. Ducky had expressed sympathy, in a whisper: 'Not his night, is it.'

It wasn't Yusuf's, either.

Ben was shocked at his own blunder. One shout out of that guy, and the whole thing could have been blown. It was sheer luck that he'd been close enough to him to snuff out that shout before it started.

Geoff Hosegood was on the high ground above the mountain road's junction with the track from/to the west. *From* the west if you were thinking about Swale and company arriving – which he was, all the time – and *to* it when you thought beyond that to the withdrawal afterwards. Not too long afterwards either: it was now 0417, which meant the night didn't have much life left in it.

The same applied to Swale's getting here, if he was going to make it before daylight. What was more, it wouldn't be long before the moon put *its* oar in, to complicate the scenario. It was about rising now, would be a little while before it cleared the mountains.

The Swale team did have to be coming, or the Syrian wouldn't be sitting up there. Geoff had had a visit from Chalky Judge, sent by Ray Wilkinson an hour and a half ago to update him on the night's events. Including the gag that Ben had broken a Syrian's neck because he'd thought he was doing it to Ducky Teal.

The moon was up, all right. Looking north with binos there seemed to be a diffuse pallor like mist on the floor of the plain beyond the valley. But it wasn't mist. And – with the naked eye now – there was a lightening of the sky above that shoulder of the Alawis.

'Nutty, Geoff?'

'Yeah, Doc, thanks.'

Marines are natural sharers. They're brought up to be.

'You left the wrapping on, I've fucking swallowed it!'

'All nourishment . . .' Laker caught his breath. 'Hey. *Hey*, what's – Geoff, valley road close to the ridge, two o'clock!'

Hosegood had his glasses up, searching . . .

276

'Yeah. I'm on . . .'

Also 'on' was the moon, which a moment earlier had slid its edge out from behind the peak, catching two ant-like figures – hunched, running now, a rush to get out of that sudden brilliance. Right where the Homs road began its climb up to the ridge. The other side of the road, above it: and Ben had guessed wrong, they *had* come from the north.

They'd escaped the moonlight now, lost themselves in the rockscape that rose from the far side of the refugee camp.

'Doc – get to Ray and tell him, then Ben – or Sticks first if you don't find him easy. And tell 'em I'm shifting down that way – me and Romeo, OK?'

Laker was on his way. Geoff had to collect Hall from his outpost before he could move over towards the action.

As the C130's engines wound down and fell silent Charles Hislop pulled the yellow sorbo-rubber protectors out of his ears and looked around the hold for his gear. One suitcase, packed by his wife in about thirty seconds flat while transport had been waiting outside the house to rush it up to Lyneham, and one duffel-bag from the base containing items which he might need but probably would not: para gear, drysuit, swimfins, ski-march boots, spare items of uniform and the field-stripped components of an SA80 Individual Weapon.

He wasn't expecting to need any of it. He was here to organize and coordinate. But it was a long way to come and not have everything you *might* need with you.

He was the first of the handful of passengers to emerge – emerging into the lights of a staff car out of which a wing commander was climbing. At the same moment a jeep squealed to a halt beside it – Sergeant Bert Hattry at its wheel.

Hattry, Corporal Clark and Marines Kenrick and Deakin sprang out of it as it stopped. Hattry saluting, with a grin on his moustached, well-weathered face. 'Great to have you with us, sir.'

'Nice to see *you* lot. Where did you proff that antique vehicle?'

'Only borrowed it, sir . . . The Nimrod drew blank, sir, not a whisper.'

'Yes, I heard.' They'd told him over the Herc's radio. 'Is the new outboard OK?'

A nod: 'Froggie here's done a routine on it, and we had it in the water, just a quick run, like.'

The wing commander, joining them, looked surprised as he got his first close look at the famed SB Squadron's CO. Under the green beret the expression was so mild, the smile gentle enough for a curate to have worn it at a tea-party.

'Major Hislop?'

The smile turned his way. 'Yup?'

'I'm Jeremy Cox. Group Captain McKenzie's compliments, and there's a meal of sorts waiting, if – '

'Thanks. Very kind of you. And maybe a bit later . . . Look, would you give me just a minute?'

'Of course.'

'Oh, did the Harriers turn up?'

Cox pointed into the dark. 'One's being made ready for takeoff quite soon. 0530?'

Hislop checked his watch: '0330, being still on Zulu . . . Have they painted out the roundels and underwing serials?'

'It was being done, half an hour ago.'

'Great . . . I must see that pilot before he takes off, though . . . Hang on, just a minute?'

He joined his Marines, and continued walking, away from the Hercules, from ears that didn't need to hear.

'Now here's the score. A bit vague, until we get the results of this next recce – if there are any, for which let's keep our fingers crossed. A Harrier's more suitable than a Nimrod – nip in and out a lot faster, and it can go slow when it puts the brakes on, *if* your team leader condescends to switch on his Sarbe. And of course it can look after itself, if it had to. So that's out first move. There'll be a Nimrod up shortly afterwards in any case, in the hope they may appear offshore: and who knows . . . Strictly between ourselves, the broader picture is that it's been decided at the highest level that no effort should be spared to extract them at the earliest possible moment, and in so doing to accept such risks as may be unavoidable. Because whatever the effects might be, they'll be a damn sight worse if we *don't* get them out.' He drew a breath. 'So – we've two options, as of now. One, a Sea-Rider

278

drop, by you four, to collect them and bring them out. This Herc I've just come in will be standing by for it, so we can lay it on at minimal notice once we know they're on the water – or even on or near a beach. The alternative's a pick-up like you blokes had, Super Stallion. The Americans are willing and ready to lift them out of Syrian territorial water as long as we can guarantee an accurate R/V. This is partly what makes it so desirable to establish comms, you see ... But that's it, so far. We'll talk again when the Harrier gets back; if there's no panic by then I'll join you blokes for breakfast – all right?'

He walked back to the RAF car. 'I'm sorry to hold you up.'

'No problem.'

'Can we start in your ops room, or whatever you'd call it? And have that Harrier pilot along?'

'Surely. But Group Captain McKenzie – '

'Maybe he'd like to join us there. I'll look forward to meeting him anyway, but this *is* really rather urgent. I've got recent satellite photos and various things ... This Herc'll be unloaded pretty fast, will it?'

'Like a dose of salts.' The wingco opened the car door, ushered him in. 'And refuelled, and your boats embarked.'

'Oh, God, yes.' He wound the window down. 'Sergeant Hattry!'

They'd have to see to the loading of the Sea-Riders ... Hattry assured him it was all in hand. The boats were on a flatbed truck, had only to be driven over, loaded and secured. Containers were already fitted, with essential gear in them, drysuits, chutes, the lot. 'Gas-tanks full, top line, sir.'

'What about rations? And water? You could be picking up eight very hungry and thirsty guys.'

He sat back, and the car moved off. He hadn't mentioned that if they took the option of a para drop he was thinking of jumping with them. It was a personal inclination, but he was aware that it might not be appropriate to indulge it. For one thing, Hattry shouldn't be allowed to imagine he wasn't regarded as capable of running his own show, and for another he, Hislop, was supposed to be here, running *this* end of it. London was still vivid in his mind: the sense of urgency, based

279

on clear-sighted appreciation of the possible consequences if Ben Ockley and his team didn't make it.

Tait growled, '*Fucking* moon . . .'

Objecting to it because just as they'd been thinking they'd made it across the valley, he and Denham had been caught in that shaft of light. Bob and Charlie, ahead of them, had already been up among the rocks.

They were now in the broken, craggy area half a mile above the camp.

'Somewhere here'll do you.' Bob was winded, getting his breath back before he went on up to meet his Syrian. 'But get into cover; be moonlight *here*, pretty soon.'

The Syrian was going to be spitting blood. Five hours late, almost. He had a ready-made excuse but it still wasn't going to be easy . . . His breathing was now under control; he was squatting, using binoculars to check the topography, make certain of it. Earlier he'd made a fool of himself over the navigation, but he could make up for it now, he hoped. In Moscow they'd had a big scale-model of the area – the ridge, *qal'at*, every detail. The refugee camp was bigger than he'd been given to expect, but in other respects it was like revisiting a place one knew intimately.

'Right then . . .'

'Good luck, Bob.'

He'd planned on following the track that led up the east side of this ridge, but it would take time to get over there, over all the rough stuff, and time was what he didn't have. This would be harder going, but so much shorter that it had to be quicker too.

The most significant effect of arriving this late, apart from personal annoyance to the Syrian, was that the action would have to be delayed. They'd have to lie-up for the daylight hours, and make the move after dark this evening. There'd be no moon then, either: and in a way he was glad to have a day's respite – time to get himself straight, get his nerves in hand. It was going to demand quite a lot of nerve: he'd seen this coming, and feared it, ever since that first briefing in Moscow by Gudyenko and Vetrov. He remembered clearly how he'd felt – Gudyenko had been describing the operation, the fake atrocity, and Leo had been startled almost into panic, visualizing the problems not only of setting it up realistically enough to con Swale into believing that SBS personnel were indulging in mass murder, but also somehow to coerce the pseudo-SBS into actually *doing* it, opening fire on a crowd of refugees. But the general had said off-handedly at an earlier stage of that briefing, 'This is detail, you'll get it all later': so he hadn't cared to question *that* 'detail' either, he'd had to assume it *would* be explained later. Then when he hadn't been able to restrain himself from interrupting – on that same, insuperable obstacle, as he'd seen it then, asking Gudyenko, 'They've got to be hoodwinked, but also join in the pretence?' – Gudyenko had answered flatly – flatteningly – with the one word, 'Exactly . . .'

At that time, he'd discovered shortly afterwards, they had not had any answers to those problems. Hadn't even seen that the problems existed. He, Leo Serebryakov, and the planners, Gudyenko's backroom brains, had been expected to provide solutions so that the overall plan, the general's own brilliant concept, could be implemented. Leo had wondered how often such plans might have been dropped as a result of the impossibility of building any structure that could support them: and whether it wasn't about to happen in this present case . . . But they'd licked it, extraordinarily enough, and really quite simply. A staff officer named Pavluchenkov, whom Leo had disliked for his tendency to sneer, had come up with this *Doppelganger* plan. Pavluchenkov was a German specialist and linguist, and he'd supplied the label as well as the solution itself.

Geoff Hosegood left Hall with Wilkinson and Judge, the three of them spaced at intervals along the drystone wall facing the camp. This became in effect the base-line. It was as close to the target as guns could be placed, and there was deep shadow this side of the wall so that they had good cover and a well-lit area in front of them – road, tents, the stone hut.

'Ray.' Geoff pointed: 'I'll cut over – like *there*, see?'

Meaning he'd cross the slope from right to left well above the camp, aiming to end up somewhere close to where the Swale team might be. Sticks was above them, and so was

Ducky and most likely Ben, and by this time the Doc would be up there too. With these three closing off this end of the covert, Geoff would be the dog that went in to flush out the game. Or maybe just to point at it.

'Be at the top, maybe, where the Syrian guy went.'

'Yeah.' Geoff nodded. 'And what goes up must come down. See you, lads.'

Sticks had his starscope on the climber. He was in moonlight a lot of the time – the climber was, not Sticks – and hadn't any clues about moving quietly or using cover. Another thing obvious was that this was not Swale. He was no more than average height, if that; and no ex-SAS man of Swale's experience, even if he was drunk, could be so clumsy.

'Sticks . . .'

He'd heard, but he kept the starscope on his target. 'Yeah.' Turning very slowly to the right, following the guy up. 'See Ben, did you?'

Laker grunted an affirmative. 'Gone up to warn Ducky, told me to join you.'

'This wally'll be out of sight in a minute. Hear him, can you?'

'Yeah . . .' Doc got the climber in his binoculars. 'Ben and Ducky'll be hearing him too . . . Not tall, is he.'

'Right. The big fellow'll be down *there*, someplace.' Indicating the rockscape below them. There was a lot of it, and it was very broken up, a jumble to the eye that made a kind of camouflage pattern of its own, but with the moon getting to it now it wasn't quite the needle-in-haystack game it might have been.

Laker emitted a grunt of satisfaction. 'There. Five o'clock, four hundred metres, guy going creepy-crawly left to right.'

'Be one of our blokes.' Sticks left the climber to get on with it, turned with his scope held ready. Laker muttered, 'I'm on him now. He's approaching the line your chum's taking . . . Dare say you're right, though.'

Sticks grunted then, as *he* found the new target. Still hearing the other – behind them, up to the right . . . He murmured after a moment, 'Geoff, that is. Moves like a fucking mantis – see?'

'Maybe *I* should – '

'Hang about.' Watching Hosegood, and still hearing the unidentified climber's scramblings receding, and thinking over that suggestion ... 'Yeah. Get down there. Halfway, say.'

'Right. Below Geoff, or – '

'Piss off, Doc.'

The climber was almost at the top. Ben tapped Teal's arm, pointed to the right, saw him squirm away into the moon-streaked dark. Moon and shadow ... He flattened himself close to the lower courses of an ancient wall; the entire area was covered with the relics of the centuries-old fortification, all of it throwing long shadows for the benefit of those who knew how to use them. Picnickers' leavings too: behind him in an angle of this metre-thick wall was a heap of broken glass and bottles, some intact and some smashed, as if some-one clearing up the site had tossed them into that corner. Crawling, you had to look out for the glass.

The Syrian was exactly where he'd been for most of the last five hours – on crumbling steps, framed in an archway that was still intact and now in silhouette against the moon. He'd made another search for his missing back-up, Ducky had reported, searching around the ruins and calling, stopping on the brink above the drop to the plateau and staring in the direction of the car. Then he'd given up again, returning to his steps, grumbling to himself and lighting what must have been about his fiftieth cigarette of the night.

If this climber went directly to him, he'd be passing between Ben and Ducky. Ducky would then withdraw, fade away to take up a position down on the track, the east side of the ridge; it was a good bet they'd move down that way, and you'd want to stick to this fellow then, in the expectation he'd lead you to Swale.

The visitor rose into sight, moonlight. Twenty feet away. And the Syrian had heard him, had been watching and now saw him. He jumped up, started forward – peering, not sure whether this would be the guy he'd spent the night waiting for or the missing Yusuf. This one meanwhile doubled, hands on knees, panting like a dog. The Syrian advanced towards him, peering aggressively through the darkness: 'Leo?'

It had sounded like 'Lay-oh' . . .

Now a stream of fast, hissing Arabic, incomprehensible except for its tone — that of a man barely keeping his fury under control. The other one, upright now, raised his arms as if in surrender to the torrent of invective: 'Hafiz, Hafiz . . .'

They'd got over the first stages of recriminations, and now they were at loggerheads again. Leo insisting, 'Out of the question. Don't you see he'd never go along with it? *Nobody*'d believe we'd pick a time like this!'

'The fact remains, it has to be completed right away. Now, or not at all, we call it off. It was not *I* who came so late, you know!'

'Listen. Hafiz . . . If I went down to them now and said we're breaking him out right now, before dawn, they'd refuse. Swale knows we'd need darkness to get away in, there's no *chance* he'd be persuaded.'

'So it's cancelled.' Hafiz flung down his cigarette and stamped on it. 'It's *finished*!'

'But you've only to wait — what, twelve hours — '

'My people will never trust Moscow again. I'm sorry for you — Moscow won't love *you*, you realise?'

'Why not wait for sunset, Hafiz?'

'Because the people I have here can't be kept indefinitely. They're not here officially, it's only the unit commander who happens to be one of us. The army commander knows nothing, battalion commander knows nothing. These men will happen to be on hand, by chance, because they're here on exercises on the unit commander's own initiative. As it was planned, he'd achieve a coup, get nothing but praise, but — ' Hafiz spread his arms, let them flop against his sides. 'Leo, you persuade us to risk our lives and futures, and — '

'*I* persuaded nobody to do anything. And I was late because that woman — *your* woman — lost her nerve and landed us in the wrong place . . . But all right: yes, all `right — '

'Uh?'

'I've got the answer. I can handle it.' The solution had come to him just at that moment, and it was so simple he wished he'd thought of it before, avoided the argument and the threats, the appearance of surrender to threats now. All he had to tell them was that the hostage was about to be moved – today . . . 'So listen, now.' Putting his mind to the nuts and bolts of it. 'I go down there. They're five hundred metres above the camp – that side, I left them there because I was trying to cut corners and save time . . . Now, we'll move over, I'll put Swale where he has to be, tell him he's there to cover us while we get the prisoner out and withdraw – because we'll be withdrawing *that* way, I'll explain, across the road and up into the high ground on the other side.'

'What you tell him is your own affair.'

'It has to make sense to him, so it has to make sense to you and me, I'm checking it out as I would've done during the day – *all right*?'

'Don't shout at me, Leo.'

'Is your side of it ready?'

'Well, of *course* – '

'The *Doppelgangers*?'

'All set up.' He put a hand on Leo's arm. 'Come, let's get down there . . . But yes, they're at the camp. Dressed – ' he glanced down at Leo's fatigues, and nodded – 'as you are. I've had them play-acting, keeping guard on that cabin.'

'What for?'

'For your men to see. You could've been lying-up here all yesterday, it had to look right to them, didn't it? I sent those four down here two days ago, *I* couldn't sit here with them for days on end!'

'But Leila must have telephoned, saying this past midnight?'

'For us to meet, yes. But a cautious man would have been here with a good margin of time, I'd have thought.'

Leo bit back a caustic answer: there'd have been no mileage in it. Hafiz said, 'I'll alert them now. They know exactly what to do.'

Leo had given Smotrenko, in London, a note of Tait's and Denham's heights and weights. This information would have been passed to Vetrov in Moscow, and from there it would have gone to Vorontsev, the GRU Resident in Damascus. Vorontsev in turn would have informed Hafiz Al-Jubran, who'd have arranged for the two *Doppelgangers* plus two others (heights and weights immaterial) to be hired from one of Fatah-Abu Mussa's training camps. The requirement had been for two trained men of roughly the same height and build as the two mercenaries. At a distance, dressed similarly and most likely in bad light, Swale would see them as Pete and Smiley.

He'd *know* that was who they were.

'So — you'll have them hidden near the stone building. I bring my two along — quietly, of course, we'll be creeping up. When we're out of Swale's sight, your gunmen kill them from ambush. No warning, close range, in the back, no chance of mishap. Swale will hear the shots, and then I'll be waving and calling to him to join me. As he comes rushing, he'll see the *Doppelgangers* — and me too — shooting into the tents and killing the refugees who run out. Shooting, killing, tent after tent . . . He'll be like a madman, won't believe what he's seeing — and before he reaches us, those same two get *him*. From behind, with a stun grenade before they shoot him — in the legs, a whole clip if they want but *only* in the legs, that's vital — huh?'

'I said — they know exactly what to do. He'll get worse than that, in fact, he's got to be unconscious for a while, has he not.'

They were climbing down to the plateau, then, to get to the track. Leo still running the scenario through his mind. Swale would have no doubt that his attackers were Stillgoe's guards. Nor could he doubt that he'd witnessed a mass-murder of old people by Bob Knox, Smiley Tait and Pete Denham, all of the Special Boat Squadron of the Royal Marines. That would be the horror-picture in his mind when he regained consciousness — strapped to a stretcher, badly wounded and no doubt in a lot of pain, and either in or about to be loaded into the Mi-24 helicopter which he'd believe had rushed Syrian troops in just too late to prevent the atrocity.

The helicopter would transfer him to a prison hospital in Damascus. Denham's and Tait's bodies would be amongst those of slaughtered refugees, but they'd have been stripped of their green fatigues before the incoming troops saw them. And the four militiamen would be on their way to remote camps in Libya within hours.

'All right.' Hafiz reappeared, brushing dirt off his leather jacket. Moonlight didn't touch this plateau, which was shaded by the peak above it. 'Thought Yusuf might have been down here. He's got some troubles coming his way, believe me.'

'I believe you . . . ' Leo asked him, 'D'you have to go to the camp now to warn them?'

'No. A signal. My car's on the hill, they'll have been watching for two flashes on the headlights. Then when it's all finished – and when I'm ready for them – three flashes will bring the helicopter down. Simple, eh?'

Mention of the helicopter prompted another question . . . 'When it's finished – I can't afford to be seen by Swale. If he's conscious. So I can't go in the helicopter, can I. But I have to be on the first available flight out of Damascus. So – *how*?'

'Well.' Hafiz had stumbled . . . 'Well, that's simple, too. I'll drive you, in my car.'

Like stating the obvious: but somehow as if the thought hadn't occurred to him until Leo had raised the question.

Ducky Teal saw them separate, one turning off westward and the other continuing down the track. It was the one who'd be returning to the Swale party who mattered. He let him get a head start, and then followed.

It wasn't difficult. The guy was hurrying, and about as agile as a camel. But he was covering the ground quite fast. Within a few minutes he was crawling up that central spine; on its other side he'd be not only in the moonlight but also in Sticks Kelso's field of view.

Sticks would then start moving down, Ducky thought. Another guess was that by this time there'd be others in that chaos of moonlight and shadow, crags and fissures.

He watched him clamber over the spine: moonlight full on him for a moment, then he'd gone over, out of sight. Ducky could move fast then, on fingertips and the torn remains of trainers . . .

Over the ridge: over very smartly, horizontal and rolling over, avoiding that guy's compulsion for self-exposure . . . He picked him up again – acoustically, *then* visually – within two minutes of having lost him. Real clown: but clearly in a hurry . . . A low shelf of rock, throwing about as much shadow as a snake might need, came in useful now, enabling

287

him to cross what was otherwise an open, brightly moonlit area and bringing him slightly downslope of the man he was following. He could afford to pause here: the guy had changed *his* direction, also downward.

Waiting, watching. It would surely come to a head soon now. There *would* be others in the vicinity, and they might even have the Swale party pinpointed by this time. Ducky used the time to drag up his right trouser-leg and push its cuff under the haft of his diver's knife, which was holstered on that leg, so he could get at it quickly when he needed to. It had a wooden haft shaped to his palm, and a nine-inch carbon-steel blade a quarter of an inch thick with both edges serrated, sharp as a Gurkha's *kukri*.

Fifty metres on Ducky's left, Doc Laker wormed forward another metre and then stopped again, having achieved the object of being able to raise his head while still having it in shadow. He thought the Swale group couldn't be very far in front of him. But the guy he'd been watching – up to the right, slanting down now, hurrying and thus making himself easy to see and hear – would no doubt locate them shortly, thus saving further efforts and the attendant risk of alerting them. He was all right here, but ahead of him the ground was less well endowed with cover, as well as moonlit.

Patience was therefore called for. Despite frustration: and knowing Kelso was up there with his starscope and caustic comments as applied recently to Geoff Hosegood. Who would no doubt be somewhere ahead there, maybe *beyond* the Swale group . . . Laker moved cautiously, adjusting first the position of his SA80 and then the bag containing his medical equipment, making these adjustments so that he'd have unimpeded right-hand access to his knife.

Geoff Hosegood heard the wally coming. Couldn't see him, and it wasn't safe to raise his head. He – Geoff – was within forty or fifty feet of them, he reckoned; and one of 'them' had surely to be Swale. For whom one had come about two thousand miles and through various exertions and privations.

If he'd been licensed to use his SA80 Individual Weapon he could have cleaned them up in approximately ten seconds, he thought — if his guess was right and that was where they were holed up — but Ben didn't want any advertising of the SBS presence. Dead right, too: with troops and a helo in the village, and a long yomp over mountains between here and the next square meal. The SBS motto was *By Stealth, By Guile*, not 'fix bayonets and charge' . . . Meanwhile it was a step forward to have them even roughly located: he'd heard low voices — not recently, they'd gone silent since, and he'd only heard it for a second, just long enough to freeze and cock his ears. But whoever'd been that close was *still* that close.

Maybe. You couldn't ever be completely certain. Sound-effects could be deceptive, and some guys were incredibly adept at the silent movement bit. Swale might be one of them . . .

Over to Geoff's right, the Citroën started up. Brief *whirr* of the starter, then the engine fired and revved before it settled to a smooth purr. Lights then — sidelights and a red glow astern, and movement: out into the road and turning right, downhill. Then it had stopped again. Headlights up: dipped. Then the same again. A double flash, could have been a signal.

To the village?

Sixty yards upslope, Sticks Kelso heard and saw that performance too. But after flashing its lights the Citroën reversed into the track again, then came out swinging left — and away, towards Homs.

He whispered, 'Ali Baba's pissing off.'

The man who'd met 'Ali Baba' at the *qal'at* was clambering straight down the fall-line now. Homing in on his chums, no doubt, on Swale . . .

Ben had gone down the west slope from the *qal'at* fast enough to have joined Kelso and for both of them to have been watching for that one when he'd come over the rock spine with the moon on him like stage lighting. Obviously thinking he had the place to himself: which made for a promising situation. Ben knew (from Sticks) that both Hose-good and Laker must by now be somewhere close to Swale; and Teal would have tailed this one over from the track so he'd be somewhere at hand too. Then there were three at the wall, and himself and Sticks moving down now to close the box – with a swathe of moonlight, unfortunately, streaming across the slope in front and below them.

The temptation to use the SA80s had clearly to be resisted. Because of that helo up at the village. He was half expecting movement from up there now, anyway, reaction to the light-signals from that bloody car. If there *was* any such move, OK, you'd use the guns, and *fast* . . .

Leo stopped, crouching. 'Charlie?'

'To your left, Bob.'

He was on top of them before he saw them: they were in a cleft of rock, extraordinarily well hidden. Leo slid in, crowding them: Charlie whispered, 'Car just drove off?'

'The guy I met. Listen, we're going to do it now, right away, so—'

'With an hour to sunrise?'

'No option. Simple reason the guy won't be here tonight, they're moving him – *today*.'

'Fucking hell, Bob – '

'Hold it, Smiley . . . Tell us, Bob.'

Leo pointed. 'Start-point's east of the camp, hundred metres above the road. Straight there, *now*. You stay there, Charlie, watch our backs while we move in quietly and get him. Then you withdraw with us but covering us in case there's any reaction – we don't know what shape he'll be in, we may have our hands full. Over the road, up into the high ground up there, lie-up all day then split off west, whole night for travel . . . All right?'

'Yeah . . . Yeah, I'd – '

'Right, let's *go* . . .'

Ben saw them moving – and the thought in his mind was that the Syrian had signalled to *them*, not to the village. From right to left, a huddle of men covering the ground quite fast – the going was probably not too bad down there, less rugged than it was up here. In patchy moonlight the group was indistinct and bunched up, they were running crouched, no individual separable from the others. Tense with frustration at that moment, he realised soon afterwards that anyway there'd been nothing he could have done about it; even if it had been possible to identify Swale and even if the range had been three hundred metres or less he wouldn't have used his SA80. Several of the others *would* have been in range, but one shot and you'd have had those troops deploying from the village. He'd warned them about it, collectively and individually, stressing that there'd be no dividend in killing Swale and then having the whole team trapped here. He was on his feet – so was Kelso, off to his left – getting down the hill as fast as the broken ground could be covered. Not knowing exactly where Doc Laker or Geoff might be: they *could* be right in those people's path, in which case they might have a chance.

Laker saw Charlie Swale clearly for about two seconds. The moon had been on him – one tall guy in a group of four, the other three like peas in a pod. The difference was obvious even when they were bounding away stooped like apes: just as you'd notice a *big* baboon loping along in a family of standard-sized ones.

Cursing, mentally, at seeing them go, after that long stalk . . . But even if his reactions had been unbelievably fast – faster than anyone's could have been, in the circumstances – he couldn't have used his gun. It was slightly mollifying to remember this now; his first reaction when the chance had seemed to have come and then gone had been to ask himself *Christ, what's the* matter *with you?*

Geoff saw them go: he'd heard a snatch of voices before that, just as the guy who'd joined them had stopped: and like the Doc he'd been close enough – initially – to have noted Swale's height in comparison with the others, close enough to have cut him down – cut *all* of them down – but in that space of about one second he could have picked off Swale with a snap-shot in the back.

He was thinking now that maybe he should have, should have turned a deaf ear to Ben's orders. One squeeze of the trigger and it would have been over, Swale dead, withdrawal the only remaining problem.

A major problem, maybe, if one *had* stirred up the locals. Starting across the slope, more or less on those people's tracks, he accepted this point, and that he could not possibly have been justified in disobeying that clear and very necessary instruction. Although soon – *very* soon – he'd find himself wishing to God that he *had* snapped off that single round and finished it.

'This'll do. All right, Charlie?'

'Sure. Go ahead.'

Settling himself between two rocks and checking on the terrain around him, fields of fire, line of sight to the camp and the way they'd come out of it – where he'd converge with them, covering their withdrawal.

He hadn't argued about Bob's decision to put him here while the three of them went in to get Stillgoe. He didn't much care what job they gave him, and if they, the SBS, wanted to spring the guy on their own – OK, let them.

He focussed his glasses on them. They were keeping low, advancing cautiously and slowly towards the camp. So Bob was capable of moving quietly. You wouldn't have known it, earlier.

They'd need to move fast, though, when they'd got this guy: there was a hint of dawn in the sky already. He was looking up that way, guessing at how long they might have before sunrise, when he saw the car coming back, over the rise from the Homs direction.

It stopped, just this side of the crest, and its sidelights went out. Bob's pal would be getting a grandstand view.

Except there shouldn't be anything for him to see. Barring accidents, and if they did the job the way it ought to be done. Charlie unslung his Uzi, checked that it was ready to fire and put it down beside him. Then lifted his binos again, focussing them on the stone hut this side of the camp.

16

Leo blew it, by looking back. Smiley Tait saw him do it, and was warned; Smiley was doomed in any case, but he took the PLO killer with him, and the carefully planned drill was ruptured from that moment on.

There was a depression in the rock slope on that side of the camp, and it was in this dead ground, out of sight from Charlie's position, that Smiley and Pete Denham were to be killed. The two gunmen – not the *Doppelgangers*, whose start-line was to be the stone hut, but the other pair – were hiding among the rocks, and were to shoot Smiley and Pete from behind and at close range as they passed. Leo had almost passed through the dip, was climbing the far slope, looked back to see it happen. Smiley saw his turn, maybe saw something more than that in his posture, and with the instant reactions of a highly trained commando he was diving sideways as those two stood up and opened fire. Tait's Uzi blasted out one short, accurate burst even before he'd hit the ground; Denham had gone down on his face, killed by a single shot in the back of the head, bullets were screaming off the rocks where Tait had been a second earlier, and Tait's second *blip* of three or four rounds killed Denham's murderer. The other was on his knees, solidly hit but groping for his dropped gun, and Smiley finished him with calm precision before he was

293

killed himself, by Leo. Leo's gun-barrel had been an inch from Smiley's head when he'd squeezed the trigger.

Still clear-headed at this stage, he saw no reason why the plan shouldn't go ahead. He'd have to attend to the crippling of Charlie Swale himself, that was all. Charlie could still be treated to the sight of the *Doppelgangers*, shades of the two slaughtered Brits, massacring the old people. He wouldn't see Bob Knox taking part, but that was all he'd miss. Leo yelled towards the stone hut in Arabic, 'Start the killing, start killing them *now*!' Then, down in the dead ground with the bodies, knowing he had only seconds in which to get ready for Charlie – who'd surely be on his way, having heard those shots he wouldn't just be sitting there – and that the first essential was a stun grenade. Crouching over a PLO corpse, patting at it to find the bulge of a grenade . . . Getting desperate: hearing shots from the direction of the tents at last, relieved that Charlie would be seeing it, but then it also sounded like shots coming from the hillside. Imagination: echoes off rock, an acoustic illusion . . . Confusion brought stirrings of panic all the same: scrabbling at that body, then realising this one didn't have the grenade, the *other* one . . . Expecting Charlie to come charging at any moment, having of course no way of knowing that Charlie *had* been coming, sprinting, had just been hit by a burst from Ducky Teal who'd dropped on to one knee for a long shot at the fast-moving target and continued skidding down the slope in that telemark-like position which must also have been agonising, but sighting and aiming-off skilfully enough to score, hitting the tall, sprinting figure which he'd realised had to be Swale. Charlie went into a spin; he'd dropped his Uzi – he'd been hit in that arm and shoulder and the arm was hanging, useless – and the other arm was stuck out in a kind of involuntary balancing act as he revolved, the impetus of that motion having been his sharp turn, just before Teal got him, towards three sources of automatic fire, three unknowns pounding down the mountainside. He'd tripped then, and fallen, bouncing and rolling down the incline. Leo was then rising from the PLO body – he'd found no grenades, was utterly confused by the volume of gunfire seemingly from all directions – with his Uzi up, waiting for Charlie. Geoff Hosegood appeared on his left – above him, looming tall with the moon behind him — and Leo fired, although in the same moment his attention was diverted — Charlie arriving in an avalanche of loose stones down the slope on his right: Geoff was hit, but aiming at the Uzi's flash in the shadowed depression he squeezed off a burst and hit Leo harder than he'd been hit himself.

Which meant, *hard*. Geoff was down, his legs having folded under him.

From the direction of the tents meanwhile there'd been more shooting and a bedlam of shouting, wailing, screaming. A Syrian in green fatigues had begun firing bursts at random into the tents, and Chalky Judge had come over the wall and blasted him with a stream of 4.85-millimetre. Romeo Hall had cut down the other *Doppelgangers*, who'd been about to kill an old woman. She'd been on her knees, in front of him, pleading, terrified. The gunman had just pushed a new magazine into his AKM and had been about to shoot her when he'd seen Chalky kill his friend, and he'd decided to fix him first, swung his weapon that way. Chalky hadn't seen this, but Romeo Hall had, and he'd used a whole clip, virtually gutting him.

Ben was there now. And Sticks. They'd been the farthest away when it had started. Hall pointed at the *Doppelgangers*' bodies: 'Bloody murdering 'em. Jesus, I mean, they — '

'Would've had me too. Thanks, Rome.'

Doc Laker arrived, limping heavily. He'd fallen and sprained something. And Teal shouted, near the stone cabin, 'Geoff's been hit, he's — '

A blast of SA80 from the road interrupted him. Two hundred metres uphill the Citroën's headlights and wind-screen shattered. The car had been free-wheeling down this way with no lights on, Ray Wilkinson told them afterwards, he'd seen it coming and decided to discourage it. It was reversing away up the hill now, its engine screaming in the high gear.

'Where *is* Geoff, what's — '

'Doc's gone to him, Ben.'

'I'll be there in a moment.' He was looking up at the village: seeing no movement yet, but knowing he'd better get the team out of here double quick . . . 'Ducky, did you kill Swale?'

'*Someone* bloody near did.' Shambling towards them, one arm dangling straight down and a mask of blood over that side of his face and the shoulder. He'd come to a halt: peering round at their faces as SA80s homed in on him. Wilkinson said, climbing over the wall and joining them, 'Thought this guy *was* dead. I was on him myself, saw him go down. Swale, is it?' Charlie stared at him – one-eyed, the other was full of blood – then lurched round, shifting the glare to Kelso, someone his own size . . . 'Mind telling me who – ' he'd swayed, that eye half closing, and the colour sergeant put out a hand to steady him – 'who the *fuck* . . .'

Flight Lieutenant Malcolm Worrall in his Harrier GR3 smashed inland over the coast, over the Lebanese border, at a height of fifty feet and with his throttles wide open, flying therefore at 1180 k.p.h., crossing the coastline just less than fifteen minutes after taking off from Akrotiri.

Over the sea, dawn had been a soft tinting of the eastern sky; this much closer to the inland mountains you wouldn't have known it. Hugging the ground, contour-hopping, although in a moment he'd have to bring her up a bit – his first overland leg was on 080 degrees through the Tall Kalakh valley and out of it on a direct course for Homs. It was fifty-two kilometres from the coast to the turn, less than three minutes, under all and any radar, virtually scraping the ground except that *now* – roughly halfway – to be doubly safe in relation to pylons and power-lines in this area he was coming up to a hundred and fifty feet. For twenty seconds: he stretched it to twenty-five, by which time he was getting to the end of the leg. Like – *now* . . .

Banking, a left-handed turn through 97 degrees on to a course of 343. There were – *had been* – pylons on his right and smokestacks beyond them as he'd gone into the turn, and a mass of masts and other obstructions on the periphery of the town of Homs about five k's – twenty seconds' flying – dead ahead if he'd held on.

He had the eastern escarpment of the Alawis close to his left wingtip, shutting out his view of the sky on that side, and a run of twenty kilometres into the designated target area.

Entering it – *now* . . .

Throttling back from 1180 k.p.h. to 120 — like slamming on brakes in a very, *very* fast car — he adjusted his altitude upward again, to two hundred feet. There'd have been some advantage in going higher, to broaden the scope of the Sarbe transmissions, but the dominating factor was Syrian radar, the need to stay below the lower curve of its reach. He put a gloved hand down to switch on the radio, which was pre-set to the Sarbe voice frequency.

'Victor 4 Tango calling Ben Ockley. I say again, Victor 4 Tango calling Ben Ockley.'

If he got any answer he could put himself right over the guy and go into hover. Not for long, because hovering Harriers guzzled fuel at a colossal rate, but long enough . . . In fact he wasn't expecting to make contact. That crazy bastard in his Nimrod hadn't scored, and there was no reason to expect anything to be different just because six hours had passed.

He began again, 'Victor 4 Tango, calling Ben Ockley . . .'

'Christ's sake, what can you lose?'

Time, that was what. Kelso nagging like an old woman. Turned on by some low-flying, slow-flying, ultra-loud air-plane's racket to the east of them. Ben didn't *have* time for it: partly because he didn't like it, he was expecting his problems here to escalate and he was well aware that Hama, spitting-distance in that direction, had an airbase with a swarm of Migs on it.

The SBS team was withdrawing. Not westward, but up the ridge to the *qal'at*. With Geoff Hosegood a stretcher case — he'd been shot in the legs — and twelve hours of daylight imminent, and that gunship at the village, there could be no question of starting the long haul through the mountains.

God only knew why the *Hind* hadn't moved yet, after all the shooting. But you could bet it damn soon would.

'Ben, do us a favour, just *see*?'

He pulled his Sarbe out of the rucksack. Thinking that maybe they were waiting for daylight. He told Romeo Hall — who'd been doing some useful foraging, collecting ration-packs that wouldn't be wanted by dead men — 'Go with the stretcher when they're ready. Hurry them up, will you.'

For a stretcher they were going to use the door off the stone hut; Chalky and Teal were getting it off its hinges.

He pushed the selector to 'voice', and switched the Sarbe on. Immediately, like turning a tap and getting water out, a voice crackled out of it, a West Country accent demanding, 'D'you hear me, Ben Ockley?'

Astonished: Kelso laughing in the darkness above him, and Laker's voice telling Hosegood, 'You'll be OK, Geoff. Fix you up a lot better when we're up there, OK?' Ben said into the Sarbe, 'Ockley here. Hearing you two's, threes – you've passed to the east of me. Who are you?'

'Victor 4 Tango, Harrier GR3. Delighted to hear you even twos, Ben Ockley. Turning back to you now. On the ridge, are you?'

'Right. Where the road crosses over, nearer the west side than east. Did you say Harrier?'

'Out from UK yesterday, two of us. Listen, Ben – report wanted, by your CO. What's new?'

'I've got Swale. Alive, wounded, no threat now. Otherwise – less good. We've had a firefight, details obscure but I've a sergeant wounded, stretcher case, it'll slow us down. You getting this?'

The noise was increasing as the Harrier returned – west of them, low over the valley. Deafeningly loud but not visible, the moon gone, slipped behind the *qal'at* peak, this whole area in shadow again. Ben squatting, hunched over the Sarbe, concentrating on hearing this and trying to shut out the thunder up there in the darkness. The Harrier pilot had told him affirmative, getting it on the recorder, go ahead.

'Well – we have to sit out the daylight hours so I'm withdrawing to the ruin on the tip of this ridge, and we'll sneak out westward after dark. Can't hang about – ammo's short, ditto rations, and there are Syrian troops, two Mi-24 loads so maybe thirty, also the Mi-24 that brought them, at Ayn Al-Dariqhah village. No idea why they haven't deployed yet, could be waiting for daylight. But we'll hold out up there until sunset, I'd guess . . . Got that, Victor Tango?'

'Roger. Message from your CO now. Starts: American Super Stallion will lift you out of boats inside Syrian waters if you can give them an R/V they can count on. Alternatively

298

Sea-Riders will para-drop and take you from boats or from any beach – repeat, from any beach. Message ends. OK, Ben, in your situation you obviously can't give any R/V forecast. Expect me or my oppo back later, maybe after sunset. Anything else for your CO? He's at Akrotiri, by the way.'

'*Is* he . . .' That was good news. But he couldn't think of anything else: and time was short . . . 'No. Nothing more. I'm moving now.'

He switched off, and as if that touch on the switch had done it the Harrier's ear-splitting din changed its pitch; he was looking straight up, and saw it, a black shadow moving slowly at first against lightening sky but then *gone*, catapulting away southeastward, ripping away in a trail of deafening then swiftly falling sound. Ben was on his feet: the dawn was *here* now, every minute counted; he admitted, to the gleam of Kelso's eyes, 'You were right.'

Those two were coming with the door.

'Chalky, what's the casualty situation look like there?'

'One old guy killed, shot through the throat. That's all, except most of 'em's having heart attacks.'

You couldn't blame them. But they'd been lucky . . . He swung round: 'Yeah, Ray?'

'Swale.' Wilkinson had his arms full of weapons and spare magazines. No less than six Uzis, and two Rumanian-made 7.62-mm AKM assault rifles. 'He wants to bring along this joker who conned him into believing he was a Bootneck.'

'Says he's Russian, now.' Swale loomed behind Wilkinson. The improving light did nothing for his appearance. Not that any of them were exactly beauties by this time, but Charlie was a walking ghoul. 'He's prepared to tell everything he knows, and I want to hear it.'

'Didn't Doc say he was dying?'

Looking past Swale, seeing Geoff being loaded on to the door . . . Thinking about several things at once: ammunition, water, rations, weaponry, that helo . . . Swale said, 'He's not dead yet, anyway, and he could be useful. Syrian intentions and so on?'

'How would you get him up there?'

Meaning, up to the *qal'at*; but staring up at the village

299

again and wishing he'd brought the grenade-launcher and the LAWs . . .

'Carry him.' Swale glanced at Kelso. 'If you'd put him over this shoulder for me.'

The left one. The other wasn't usable. A stream of 4.85-mm slugs from Teal's SA80 had scored the side of Charlie's head like a tiger's claws, ripped that ear, smashed the collar-bone and upper arm. This had been Doc Laker's instant assessment; he'd been more concerned with Geoff Hosegood, which was natural enough.

Leo Serebryakov felt himself being grabbed and picked up, and a spasm of agony shot from the region of his elbow through all the nerves of his body, shrivelling his brain. He'd let out a shout, and a voice said gruffly, 'Better give him a shot. Got it to spare?'

'Haven't, really.' Laker said, 'Early in the day, and Geoff's going to need some. This guy too.'

Charlie said, 'Don't worry about me, *I'm* not feeling any —'

'You will, though.' That was the other voice again. 'Give us a hand, Doc . . . Stoop a bit, er — Charlie?'

The pain was fading. It had been as if that elbow, which he guessed might have a bullet in its joint, had snagged against itself. He couldn't feel his left leg at all; earlier, making an attempt to stand, he'd found it simply didn't work.

'OK?'

A grunt . . . 'Yeah, just — just get him balanced . . . Hang on a mo', might —'

'Sure.' Kelso asked quietly, 'Where's he hit?'

'Which?'

'*This* one.'

'Left arm — elbow — and two clean through the chest. Those I know about, but you saw how the leg dragged, too . . . Sticks, I'm going ahead now with Geoff, OK?'

Gudyenko, Leo thought, wouldn't want to set eyes on him again. Safer maybe if he didn't, at that . . . Facing this now — because he was locked into it, nowhere else to go — facing what had been a recurring nightmare to be dismissed in daylight hours as paranoia, the suspicion that he mightn't have been intended to survive in any case. The way Hafiz had answered his question about transport to Damascus had stirred it up again, the doubt which he'd been suppressing but which had surfaced from time to time in periods of sleeplessness: over and over, rehearing Gudyenko telling him about the leak that was being set up, some traitor in London they'd been manipulating; Gudyenko of *all* people to be dishing out highly sensitive information to someone who didn't need it, couldn't use it, wouldn't do his job any better as a result of possessing it.

Because by the time it blew up he wouldn't have been around to talk about it?

In fact he wouldn't have boasted of his knowledge. But there were plenty who might have, and it was the kind of unnecessary risk that Gudyenko not only didn't take, actually prided himself on *never* taking.

'OK, there?'

Charlie's voice. Plodding more slowly, slow rhythmic lurchings, left arm up to hold the burden on his shoulder. Hunched forward, eyes on the ground a few feet ahead of each footfall, probably unconscious of dawn's light growing to light the sky and the rocks, the peak up there where they were going burning in the first direct rays of the rising sun.

'Can you speed it up, Charlie?'

Kelso, behind him, closing up behind to urge them all on faster, increasing daylight adding to the sense of urgency and also enabling one to see enough to push it along a bit . . .

'Here, I'll take him, Charlie. Stop a minute, let me have the bastard . . .'

'What they'll have been waiting for, I bet. Signalled on his lights before, didn't he.'

A hundred metres downslope from Charlie and Sticks, Ben and Ray Wilkinson had their glasses up to watch the Citroën race across the valley. They'd known it by its shattered windscreen when it had appeared over the rise from the Homs direction a few minutes ago. When it got to the mountain road it would hairpin left: then it would be in the village, and his bet was that a deployment would ensue.

'Ray — go on up, tell Sticks what's happening, get 'em all up there and into cover, quick . . . Except Teal plus one —

down the other side for water. And beets while they're at it. Tell him Christ's sake watch out for the helo.'

'Right – '

'That was a smart move you made, Ray.'

Shooting the car's lights and screen out, he meant. Otherwise it would have been at the village a quarter of an hour ago, or signalled anyway, and with Geoff immobilized they'd have been caught with their pants down.

The wing commander – Cox – leant across his boss's desk to switch off the tape. Group Captain McKenzie sat rock-still, frowning slightly, pale eyes resting on Charles Hislop. They'd been listening to the tape of Victor 4 Tango's exchanges with Ben Ockley; it was a relief to have made contact, but it hadn't been happy listening.

McKenzie said, 'I suppose if he *can* sneak out tonight, being slowed by this stretcher case he'd still make it in about three nights, wouldn't he?'

Hislop was thinking that if there'd been thirty Syrian soldiers and one *Hind* gunship there before this firefight, there'd damn soon be a hell of a lot more. And sneaking in through the mountains had been one thing, sneaking away again after stirring up the hornets' nest would be quite another.

Three nights' yomping, say. Or four. OK, more bimbling than yomping. And allowing for hold-ups, the fact they'd be hunted now and might have to detour or lie-up for longer periods, and so on . . . Further Harrier visits would be necessary, to maintain contact and arrange the pick-up. He looked round at the Harrier pilot: still in his flying gear, helmet dangling from one hand.

'*Certain* you had no radar on you at any time?'

'Positive. Not a flicker.'

'You wouldn't be worried about doing it again, then. Could you drop food to them?'

'Easy.' Worrall glanced at his seniors. 'Containers of some kind, one each side under the wing pylons.'

Where in different circumstances you'd have a 1000-lb bomb each side. The wing commander nodded. 'Something could be improvised.'

302

Rations and ammunition, Ben had mentioned. Battalion headquarters at Dhekelia might have some 4.85-mm, he supposed. The SA80 family of weapons was still new, by no means all Army units would have switched over to it yet.

'Comes down to this.' Holding McKenzie's calm, analytical stare, and thinking aloud. 'In normal circumstances, Ockley'd have no problem bringing his guys out. But when the Syrians know (a) where he is now, (b) more or less where he's got to get to – and there aren't so many routes to choose from – *and* he's got wounded men to carry with him . . . Well, the odds change, rather.'

'Quite.'

Cold fish, Hislop thought. Cold eyes, detached manner. Doing his best to help, but . . . Anyway he was only bouncing thoughts off him, trawling for inspiration.

'If they were trapped there, we're back to square one, it might've been better if we hadn't reacted to the threat in the first place. *But* – well, as some very senior generals decided yesterday, this is spilt milk, they *are* in there, and we've got to accept whatever risks may be entailed in getting them out.'

McKenzie frowned. 'I wish I knew what to suggest.'

'I've one suggestion. Logic says that if he can't get to the coast, he's got to be extracted from where he is now. And the only helicopter that could do it, in terms of capacity and range, is the Super Stallion. The Cousins have offered to lift them out of Syrian waters – that was a big step forward, now I'd say we might try to persuade them to take another, pull them out of Syria.'

'Your logic's sound enough, and I'm sure they'd want to help us out. After all, it's common cause, basically. But I'm sorry to have to tell you – I really *am*, the last thing I *want* to do is pour cold water – that you don't stand a hope in hell. In plain physical terms, they couldn't do it.'

'If I call London – by Satcom, right away – I'd like to, if I may – do I do it from your Communications Centre?'

'More conveniently from *this*.' He nodded towards a green telephone. 'But of course if you'd prefer – '

'From here would be marvellous. Thank you . . . The point is, I've reason to believe that the Chief of the Defence Staff himself – '

'Oh, yes.' A nod . . . 'The CDS would talk persuasively to the chairman of the Joint Chiefs, you were going to say.' The group captain's hands separated, joined again as if they'd decided there was nowhere better to go: a small gesture of helplessness, from a man not given to gestures . . . 'I know. He might not even risk *impasse* at that level, the Minister might persuade Mrs Thatcher to speak to the President. I'd guess she wouldn't need much persuading, and I'm certain the President and the National Command Center would react favourably, 6th Fleet would be told to cooperate to the maximum extent, etc. But that's where you'd hit the brick wall, Hislop. I don't want to bore you with avionics, but – frankly, I was astonished to hear they'd agreed to send a CH-53E into Syrian waters. It's the US Navy Air Force version of the machine first used in Vietnam, popularly known as the "Jolly Green Giant". They still use that nickname for the CH-53C – C as distinct from E – which is the US Air Force, not *Navy* Air Force, combat search and rescue helicopter. Operated by US Air Force Aerospace Rescue and Recovery Squadrons. *Those* could and would be used in the kind of mission we're talking about. The Super Stallions on board the *Saratoga*, however, the aircraft that picked your boats out of the sea, are CH-53Es, used exclusively in the role the Yanks call VOD – "vertical onboard delivery", meaning transporting supplies to the carrier battle groups. They're unsuited to combat missions – that's to say any task in which they might come under attack.' McKenzie paused, shook his head. 'Sorry to be such a wet blanket. But nobody in his right mind would dream of sending one of those into hostile territory.'

Hislop glanced round; but the Harrier pilot had left, after a murmured exchange with Cox, the wingco. He looked back at McKenzie. 'What if we – you – gave it an escort of two Harriers? To sneak in and straight out again, in the dark?'

'Not a chance. No matter what Downing Street and the White House might say to each other . . . Just as you don't want to leave your Marines there, they'd be averse to losing a Super Stallion and its crew. Remember what happened to some helicopters in the Iranian hostage rescue mission?'

'I take the point . . .'

304

The bottom line being that the only guy who could do anything about this situation was still Ben Ockley.

The helicopter had landed in the road beside the refugee camp, disgorged soldiers in DPMs, then flown back to the village and brought down another load. This time it had put itself down above the camp, close to the stone cabin. Ray Wilkinson had counted twenty-six uniformed men in the two shuttles.

Teal and Hall had taken half a dozen empty water-bottles down to the river. Wilkinson was holed up on the lower side of the plateau, and Chalky was on the plateau itself, simultaneously keeping an eye on the approaches and acting as communications link with Ray. Kelso was prowling the *qal'at*'s perimeter.

Doc Laker was cleaning and disinfecting the hole in Geoff's left hip. Leo had been swivelling as he'd fired that burst, and the shots had slanted across the middle part of Geoff's body, hitting him in that hip then missing more vital parts but smashing the right leg above the knee. He was in pain, but without morphine it would have been a hell of a lot worse.

Ben squatted beside the Russian. Charlie Swale was beyond him, unconscious, propped against the wall. He'd passed out on arrival, after the exertion of the last steep climb, and Laker had attended to him first, having fixed Geoff up in a preliminary way down at the camp. Charlie had lost too much blood, he'd said; he and Geoff both needed specialist attention in a hospital as soon as possible.

That was *all* . . .

They were in the shelter of the section of crumbling wall where at some time or other a load of bottles and other rubbish had been dumped.

'He didn't say what kind of troops he'd borrowed? Trainees, commandos, or what?'

'Only that they were supposed to be here on exercises. Their unit commander was in on it, but not the higher command.'

'Rank of the unit commander?'

'I don't know.'

Those troops hadn't deployed until Hafiz had got to the village. They would have, presumably, if he'd given them the signal on his headlights; Leo had remembered that much. But the civilian, Hafiz, was effectively in command, it seemed.

'*Jesus!*'

'Sorry, Geoff . . .'

The military unit had just sat there, waiting to be told what to do, and this suggested that its officer/s and/or NCOs weren't briefed on the Swale plot. Otherwise surely they'd have moved on their own initiative when things began going wrong. According to this Russian with his Scots-flavoured standard English, refugees were to have been massacred, Swale was to have been left alive to go on trial and swear that the murderers had been Royal Marines. The scheme had been hatched in Moscow and launched in collaboration with an anti-Assad Syrian faction in which Hafiz figured prominently. But the troops had been provided only to witness the atrocity and arrest Swale: so they might be trainees, cooks, drivers, clerks, any rag-bag collection from the local barracks.

'You and Hafiz had no idea we might be around?'

'None at all. I still don't see how – '

'You don't have to see. Just answer my questions.'

Hafiz had been on the hill in his car when the action had started. Keeping his own skin safe, of course. Maybe he'd have seen Ducky and Geoff charging down the rock slope: having heard shooting from that side. But he'd have been expecting to hear shooting, mightn't have seen so much. The flash-hiders on the SA80s were effective, certainly . . . The point being that Hafiz, the guy who was still running this, most likely didn't have much idea even now about what had gone wrong, who'd caused it to go wrong or who was up here now. The shootists plunging down the mountainside could have been the two mercenaries who'd come with Swale, if he *had* seen them. Those two could have started the rot. He'd probably realize there'd been some "outside" element involved: he had the mercenaries' bodies down there, and those of the four PLO. The only bodies he did not have were Swale's and the Russian's, and he'd hardly believe *they*'d combined to rat on him.

Except that having such tendencies himself, he might . . .

306

And one of them could have shot up his Citroën. Unlikely, but he couldn't *know*, he'd be guessing.

'The odds are, Geoff, the sod who's running this may still not have a bloody clue about us being here.'

Hosegood's head turned. Bearded, streaked with dirt and cam-cream, hollow-eyed . . . 'Seen us on our way up here, won't he?'

'I'm not sure he could have, between the time Ray put the fear of God in him and when he got up enough nerve to come back.'

'Wouldn't 've known it was clear for him to come back, otherwise. He'd 've parked his motor up there, come back on his feet. *Must* know we're here.'

'All right. Let's accept he knows someone's here. And he's lost Swale and this sod, so he knows they're part of it. But what else he knows – well, roughly fuck-all, I'd guess.'

Laker was resecuring Geoff Hosegood's trousers, having done his best on the hip-wound and plastered it. Ben looked back at Leo.

'You. What's-your-name.'

Leo's eyes opened. Bloodshot, otherwise ice-blue.

'Your Syrian pal will be trying to cover it all up, won't he? Now it's gone off the rails?'

'I suppose – yes . . .'

'So he'll want us dead, but he won't be shouting for help. Right?'

'You mean – '

'For more troops, helicopters, mortars, whatever.'

'No. No, he won't.'

'The troops he has here now, you said he can't keep them here for long. That was what *he* said, you told me. Did he indicate *how* long?'

'No, he didn't. And it could have been only to force me to agree to acting at once instead of waiting for tonight. I don't know.'

Laker had finished with Geoff; he brought his bag over, dumped it beside Leo. Glancing at Charlie: then stooping to check his pulse and breathing . . . He told Leo as he came back to him, 'I'll have a go at you now . . . All right, Ben?'

He nodded. 'Do your worst.'

Hosegood murmured, 'Hear, hear.'

'How is it, Geoff, bloody awful?'

'Dare say I'll live.'

'You'll be in hospital soon enough. We'll be out of here tonight, don't worry.'

'With me and Charlie there deadweights . . . Taking the shithead, are we?'

Ben shrugged. He wasn't sure of the answer; there could be advantages in taking the Russian back, but it might not be physically practicable or on balance worth the effort. The guy could be dead by then, anyway . . . But he wouldn't have wanted him to hear an answer at this stage, even if he'd had one: he changed the subject, stooping to pick up a wine bottle that had lost its neck but was otherwise intact. 'Yeah. I wonder . . .' He tapped the broken end against the wall until it was down to about jam-jar size, then showed it to Geoff: 'Just about right. Look . . .' Squatting beside him, he reached into his DPMs for a grenade. He was almost sure it would fit . . . 'Well, it'll slip in neatly enough when the pin's out. See?'

'*Right.* Then you'd shoot, and – '

'You're still on the ball, Geoff.' Needing another twenty-three bottles, he began collecting them and knocking them down to size. Laker glanced up at him while he was lining the finished products up on the wall. He muttered, 'The nerve's severed in this leg. Couldn't find a hole at first, but the bullet went in up here and came out there, back of the knee.'

Sticks called, 'Ben – looks like they're deploying.'

Hislop recognised the voice of Joe Lance, former SBS major now in the Ministry of Defence . . . 'Glad it's you has the duty, Joe, my good luck . . . You'll have seen the transcript of the Harrier tape?'

He was using the green telephone in McKenzie's office. Wing Commander Cox had set up the Satcom connection for him, while his boss had gone off to get breakfast.

Lance said yes, he had it in front of him at that moment, had just been discussing it with the Duty Operations Director. 'Not too promising.'

308

'Well, it doesn't seem we can do anything useful from here except lay on a ration drop by Harrier tonight. Otherwise it's up to Ockley to get his team to the coast, and I'll take the Sea-Riders in and grab him off some beach. But I agree the outlook's not good, and an alternative which you might be able to promote – please – could be to persuade the Cousins to go right in there tonight with a Super Stallion.'

'We could – promote it, sure, but – '

'Hang on. Technical advice received here is that the carrier-borne Super Stallion – ' he was checking his notes – 'the CH-53E, that is, is unsuitable for the task and they'd be highly unlikely to agree spontaneously. Unarmed, or only lightly armed, I don't know, may be a question of armour. But this would be the stumbling block, I'm told, so any instruction for its use would have to stipulate that the risk *is* to be accepted. Otherwise it won't wash. You with me?'

'Makes it twice as unlikely, of course. But we'll try. It'll have to go through channels – but with strong backing, *maybe* – '

'Make it quick, Joe?'

Ben had Sticks, Ray and Chalky with him among the ruins at the edge, above the plateau, watching the Syrians' rather half-hearted deployment. Ray and Chalky had slipped down among the rocks, crept around placing the grenade traps – eight on a radius of 300 metres, another eight at 250 and the rest at 200. He'd been right that with the pin out the anti-personnel grenades fitted neatly into the bottles, with the handles held in place. When a bullet from an SA80 smashed the glass, there'd be a pause of four seconds before the blast. It should be a useful deterrent, he hoped.

The *Hind* was still sitting there, its motionless rotor glinting in the sunlight. Two men with binoculars – one of them Hafiz, the other uniformed – were watching their men spreading out and upwards, while about half their number still lounged around the helicopter.

'My guess is that thing can't be armed. They're waiting for these goons to be in position to take pot shots at us, then it'll try to land up here with the rest of them.' He pointed. 'There, wouldn't you expect?'

On the plateau. Apart from the *qal'at* site, which was cluttered with obstacles, it was the only level ground.

'Why d'you say it's not armed?'

'If you had one with clout, wouldn't you've sent it straight here to mallet us, by this time?'

'Yeah. Maybe . . .'

'Fits the picture. What *he* told us.' He jerked his head towards the wounded, where Doc Laker was still working on Leo's wounds. 'Borrowed troops, borrowed helo, all rear-echelon stuff. That's Fred Karno's army down there.'

'You reckon . . . Here's our water.'

Hall and Teal . . . Teal said, 'Quick work, eh? We got beets, an' all. Get up and down that track blindfold, now.'

'You may have to, Ducky.' It was one of the things he'd been thinking about. 'May well be our best way out, tonight.'

Back exit: and across the valley before moonrise for a withdrawal northward. If he hadn't had the wounded he'd have banked on getting away south and west, sneaking through despite the presence of those Syrians.

He told Teal and Hall about the grenade traps. Some were visible from here even without binoculars or the sights on the SA80s; they'd placed them where they could be seen from this side but not by Syrians climbing up towards them, and at points where the route looked invitingly easy or where they might group in cover.

Charlie muttered, summarizing what Leo had told him, 'So I was to be put on trial. Yeah, I get it . . . Had me sewn up, didn't you, you bastard.'

'It wasn't my idea, Charlie, and it wasn't – personal . . . I was told what the plan was, and tasked with carrying it out. Swale was just a name, I didn't know you, did I.'

'Reluctant, were you, after we'd established our beautiful relationship?'

No answer . . . Charlie was racked with the shame of having been so easily and thoroughly suckered.

'How'd you get to pass yourself off as a Brit? Born in the UK or something?'

'I was born in the USSR. Georgia. I am – have been, I should say – what's called a *nyeznakonnii*. "Illegal." I was given an identity — passport, family background, everything — well, it's a long training, very long and intensive.'

'And you expect these guys to keep you alive now, do you?'

'I'll tell them all I know. That's a lot, believe me, I've a great deal to offer, I'm sure that from your security services' point of view — '

'I'll tell you one thing. Even when you had me conned into believing you were Bob Knox, Royal Marines, I thought you were a prize shit.'

About an hour after they'd placed the bottled grenades, they were watching two Syrian soldiers getting close to one of them. Sticks murmuring, 'Come on, lads, come on . . .'

He was sighting on the bottle, on the sun's gleam on it, with his SA80's sights at maximum elevation. He was getting the privilege of this first shot because he happened to be one of the Squadron's best marksmen, and at three hundred metres half a bottle wasn't all that big a target. He was standing, using the remains of an ancient buttress as a rest for his left arm and shoulder, and waiting for the Syrians to come within a foot or two of the grenade. At close quarters the L2A1 A/P grenade had what the manual called 'a high degree of lethality', but outside a radius of ten metres its 1200 fragments would barely scratch a man's skin.

'You're getting warm, boys . . .'

Wilkinson and Ben both had glasses focussed on the climbers, who were coming to the trap as surely as if someone had been leading them by their noses. As long as they kept coming . . . They might well have stopped before this, tried the range with their Kalashnikovs, if they'd had any target visible to shoot at. Ben was pretty sure his guess was right, that their tactic would be to put themselves where they could make the defenders keep their heads down while the helo put a sizeable attacking force on that plateau.

Sticks fired. Sunlight glittered on flying glass. Both men had whipped round: then the grenade exploded. The nearer of the two fell backwards, his arms jerking upwards like a puppet's and the rifle flying, clattering away downhill: the other stood for a moment with his hands clasped to his face, then folded down into a heap that didn't move.

All the other visible Syrians had stopped climbing. It would take them some time to work out what those two had walked into. Kelso said, lowering his gun, 'Shame, really. Might've put a stun in, just warned 'em, first time round.'

He was right to the extent that there was no satisfaction in killing those people. But there was even less in having them kill *you*, and they weren't being sent up here for any other purpose. The grenade traps might be frightening enough to keep them away until the light went this evening, but they wouldn't be much of a deterrent if they left them with nothing more than headaches. In any case that hadn't been a practical suggestion; Kelso had only been reacting to the shock of his own effectiveness.

Or 'lethality'.

The sun was high now, and hot, and there was a need to conserve water in order to have enough to take with them tonight. To keep the heat off the wounded the stretcher-door was set up across piles of masonry.

'May as well go into two watches, Sticks. If you want to get your head down, I'll shake you in a couple of hours.'

But there was a ration distribution to be made — Israeli rations, and slices of sugar-beet — and other chores to see to. Like field-stripping the SA80s and cleaning them, sorting the Uzis and AKMs and ammunition. The AKMs could as well be used now, in fact, and left behind this evening, as one wouldn't want to be burdened with their extra weight.

By midday one more Syrian had died, shot at long range by Romeo Hall, and for a while afterwards the rest kept their distance. Hafiz would be getting impatient down there, Ben guessed; in fact he might have been getting desperate. But in fact the Syrian's troubles — and his own, for that matter — were yet to come.

There'd been a certain amount of traffic on the road, and two or three times cars or lorries had stopped, no doubt to enquire what was going on. One of these transients might well have precipitated the crisis: maybe one of the southbound drivers, dissatisfied with whatever yarn they'd fed him, had pressed the panic button when he got into town. It started, anyway, at about one thirty with a Gazelle helicopter arriving from the Hama direction and landing beside the *Hind*. There

312

was a lot of running to and fro, and the reluctant skirmishers were called down from the mountainside. Half an hour later a column of military vehicles appeared from the south, bringing in troops who looked a lot more business-like than the crowd Hafiz had had on loan; they put a roadblock on the rise behind them, the Homs side, and one vehicle drove on across the valley to do the same at the junction with the mountain road. Another, which had halted with the rest of them at the camp, re-embarked its troops and moved off in that direction, but then swung off the road on to the dirt floor of the valley, bounced northward over the flat, hard ground for about two kilometres to offload its passengers close to the bottom end of Ducky Teal's route to water.

Sticks came back from observing that part of the swift, unpleasantly efficient deployment.

'Ben, you know that pumphouse on the river?'

Ben was kicking himself for having been so complacent in recent hours, having taken so much for granted. He glanced round at Sticks: 'What about it?'

'Machine-gun section, on its roof. That was going to be our way out, right?'

17

Charles Hislop, in a borrowed goon-suit, peered down from the Wessex HU-5 helicopter at the wrinkled blue Mediterranean so close under it that the downdraught was making it look as if a school of whitebait was trailing them at high speed. Not that a Wessex was all that speedy, despite this sea-level transit for optimum economy and time-saving. Hislop was sharing the rear compartment with the helo's observer, a flight lieutenant, both of them linked to the pilots only by throat mikes and earphones. They were an hour out of Akrotiri and flying west – *away* from the SB team's predicament, a fact of which he was uncomfortably aware.

The invitation had reached him at midday, after the US Task Group Commander in the aircraft carrier *Saratoga* had spoken personally to the Air Vice Marshal who was GOC of the sovereign bases in Cyprus. Admiral Fermenger had suggested that Major Hislop might care to visit with him on board the carrier, to discuss ways in which American assistance might be given to his team in Syria. The Air Marshal had passed this message on via Group Captain McKenzie, who'd offered the Wessex as a taxi to and from the *Saratoga*, then about 450 nautical miles away, north of the Gulf of Bomba and steering for the Antikithira Channel while her aircraft maintained surveillance of that Soviet squadron.

He'd accepted because he'd been achieving nothing in Akrotiri. There was nothing to do at the moment except wait, maintain communications with the JOC in London and pray that Ben Ockley would be able to pull his own chestnuts out of the fire. Meanwhile the Sea-Riders had been unloaded from the Hercules; there couldn't be any para drop for at least two days, and he'd been assured that another C130 would be provided when the time did come. All one could do meanwhile was be ready for it . . . He had a briefcase full of maps and recent satellite pictures, and one of the Harriers would be going in again this evening to get Ben's update on the situation and to drop ration-packs and ammunition. SA80 ammo had been available at Dhekelia, and was being sent down by road.

But this visit wasn't likely to yield any great dividend. A Satcom call from London in mid-forenoon had confirmed that the carrier-borne version of the Super Stallion would never be used in a combat situation. Joe Lance, the SF Adviser, had spoken to a US Navy airdale commander on the staff of CINCUSNAVEUR in North Audley Street, and he'd given him chapter and verse on the subject. This was perhaps what the American admiral would also be explaining. But it was conceivable that something might emerge that could help later: for instance, instead of the para drop, the offer of a pick-up out of boats inside Syrian waters. If the team could get themselves off the coast, to take advantage of this offer, getting the wounded men to hospital that much more quickly might save a life or two.

In fact, a Super Stallion might lift them out of the Sea-Riders. Para drop to pick them off the beach, then an R/V at sea. Maybe.

The Wessex soared suddenly, climbing steeply, and the pilot's voice in Hislop's headset told him, 'We made it, Major . . . See them?'

The observer tapped his arm, pointed out to starboard. Frigates, or destroyers: four of them in line astern. A beautiful sight: white wakes brilliant on the sea's blue gloss. Beyond them, with another small warship in attendance close astern, was the *Saratoga*. Sixty thousand tons of flat-top; the 'island' amidships, smothered with antennae, from this angle looked like a small pimple on that expanse of flight-deck.

Beyond her, another four destroyers ploughed a single vivid furrow. You could see the movement on those smaller ships as they dipped across the swell, but the carrier looked static, immovable in her dignity . . . Those would be Tomcat F-14s, he guessed – about eight of them parked near the 'island', which was looming higher and bigger as the Wessex clattered down and touched gently, flight-deck crew running out from the superstructure to secure it.

'Did you get any lunch yet, Major?'

'I did, sir, thank you.'

'So you'll take coffee, right?'

Tom Dubyak said sure, he'd like some too. A tall, ginger-headed Navy captain, he was the Task Group's Operations Officer; he'd met Hislop down below, led him up here through a maze of passages and ladderways and introduced him to Admiral Fermenger – a small, square-built man with a balding head, glasses, and a wide, infectious smile.

'Sit down, make yourself at home, Major.' He said into a telephone, 'Coffee in here for three of us, and bring us some of those sandwiches, will you?' He put the phone down, and came over to dump himself into an armchair facing Hislop; the stateroom was spacious, as well furnished as any town-house reception room. 'I've heard a lot about you and your Special Boat Squadron, Major, and I'm glad of the chance to welcome you on board.'

'I'm grateful for the invitation, sir. Also for your offer to lift my team out of Syrian territorial waters, if things go that way.'

'Well, we'll get to that.' From the glance he exchanged with the Operations Officer, Hislop guessed that they'd changed their minds. So – para drop, and Sea-Riders, back to square one . . . He didn't let his disappointment show. The admiral was saying, 'We're well cognizant of your problem, Major. You have my sympathy, and 6th Fleet Commander's, and also – now – the personal concern of the President of the United States. Did you know your Prime Minister spoke with him this morning?'

'No. I guessed it could be a possibility, but – '

'Yeah, I guess you would have.' The smile was dry. 'Anyway, I don't have to tell you, I'd like to help in any way that's possible, so would every man in this Task Group. You can take that as fact.'

He looked round as the door opened: two stewards, bringing coffee and open sandwiches, a mixture that looked like chicken and mayonnaise. Hislop realised he *was* hungry, after that flight. Tom Dubyak enquired during this interruption, 'Did you have a good flight out from Cyprus, Major?'

He looked as if he was really interested in the answer. Hislop studied him with interest, knowing he couldn't surely give a damn what kind of flight he'd had . . . Then a second question: 'And you're based in London, that right?'

'Well, no – '

'Here, come on now, help yourselves.' The admiral showed them how . . . 'I was saying – we want to help. I have to tell you, though, right after I'd said to your people OK, we'll snatch those guys out of Syrian waters, my staff here gave me a hard time. Fact being, and I believe you've caught on to this yourself, Major, that our Super Stallions, the 53Es, are not suitable for missions that could involve confrontation with enemy forces. This is for technical reasons which if you like Tom here will show you, down in the hangar, before you leave us.'

'No – I mean, thanks, but it was explained to me this morning, sir.'

'Well, I mention it because, in that transatlantic telephone call which I referred to just a moment ago, there was a suggestion that this could be just some kind of lame excuse we'd offer. It happens to be no such damn thing, and I want you to know this, Màjor.'

'I – believe I do know it, sir.'

'Don't you take sugar in coffee?'

'I had some.'

'Oh. Well, *I* didn't . . . OK. That was the point I had to make.'

'Somebody must have confused the issue, after I spoke to our Ministry of Defence in London early this morning. That was after the recce flight by the Harrier, the bad news. I'd just been told about this technical snag, by a senior Royal Air Force officer. I mentioned it to the guy I was talking to, explaining that he'd better know about it because any instruction sent from Washington would need to state clearly that such a risk was to be accepted. My point was that unless they could give that specific directive, a blanket instruction wouldn't be worth having, however much goodwill existed, because there'd be no way you could act on it.'

'That makes sense.' A grin, at Dubyak. 'Of a kind . . . I guess someone higher up the tree got something or other in a twist.'

Dubyak nodded. 'Would seem so, sir.'

The admiral peered at Hislop over the top of his glasses, and said in a somewhat fruity tone, 'Didn't want any damned excuses, were we going to help or were we *not*?'

Hislop blinked. 'My God.'

'Yeah . . . But OK, that's disposed of, Major. Now we can move on to the nitty-gritty, as they say. I told you – I got bawled out for saying we'd do that. And they were right. So, I scratched my head, sent out a few enquiries – and I was fortunate in having the support of my boss down the road here – and – well, bottom line is that in about thirty minutes –'

A glance at Dubyak. 'Thirty, Tom?'

The Operations Officer checked the time. 'Twenty, sir.'

'Twenty minutes, you'll see one US Air Force HH-53C touch down out there. Flew from south Germany to Sicily last night. I knew I should not have made that promise, see, but I didn't like to go back on my word. And this led to a successful exercise in what we call joint service coordination.'

Hislop was staring at him, hardly daring to believe it.

'HH-53C . . . Combat search and rescue . . . Might it be able to fly into Syria tonight, sir?'

The admiral spread his hands. 'I don't know what the hell else they'd be here for.'

Mid-afternoon, baking hot, and they had the place surrounded. The mountain slopes were infested with Syrians, there was a large detachment of them around parked transport at the camp, and they'd reinforced the group who'd set up a GP machine-gun on the flat roof of the pumphouse. More trucks and men had arrived in the last hour, and a few had left, taking away the old folk from the camp. Transport in various shapes and sizes had been spaced around the area in a way that made the intention easy to read: after dark, all the approaches – and exits – could be floodlit. One scout-car had driven as far up the track as they could get it, and they'd parked it aslant and on the incline so its lights would blaze clear across the hillside.

Now it was all static and quiet. Dispositions made, the *qal'at* surrounded and isolated. Siesta time.

Ben, Kelso and Ray Wilkinson were flat among the ancient stonework and rubble on the *qal'at*'s south edge. Hall was keeping lookout on the other side, above the goat-path; the others were resting, maybe even getting some sleep, in patches of shade among the ruins.

Ben put his binoculars down for a moment, massaged his eyes. 'They want us alive. Any other way they'd be blasting us off this rock with mortars. Or a gunship or two. Incidentally, that one's *not* armed, can't be.'

'Plan on moving in on us after dark, won't they.'

'Yeah . . . Mind you, they can't know how many we are – or who, or what . . . All they know of for sure is Swale, and their ally who may have ratted on them. But anyway he's not *those* guys' ally, is he, he was tied up with Hafiz, who's a dissident, very likely has electrodes clamped to his balls by now . . . But whoever they may think we are, they'll want us alive – for that kind of purpose.'

Sticks said, 'Something to look forward to, then.'

It was the pattern of things, though, the hostage and show-trial syndrome. A mountain summit with a scattering of foreign bodies on it might make for some kind of propaganda picture, but corpses couldn't have confessions screwed out of them.

'They'll do what I thought the others might try. Send that helo up while they pin us down from all around.' He glanced sideways at Kelso. 'And we could handle *that*, all right. Mind you, I wish I hadn't been so fucking clever with those grenades, could've used some up here now . . . But a *Hind*'s capacity is fourteen, fifteen guys, with weapons. Suppose they crammed in twenty – short hop like this they might – five of us could take them, huh?'

'Five?'

'One mobile, one on the goat-track.'

'So what then? Ammo won't last long. OK, so we take out your lot of twenty, but they're coming over the slope too, aren't they.'

Sticks was right. Ammunition would *not* last very long. As the Syrians would be well aware. *They*'d have no problems, they could sit it out as long as it took, exert a certain amount of pressure so that ammunition got used up, hang on until there wasn't any more.

'You're right, Sticks. Dead right.' He had his glasses up again, watching various small movements around the camp. He did have an answer to the problem now, although he'd been through a bad time, mentally sweating over it, a touch of panic stirring deep down, seeing *no* way out . . . Back there on the beach a couple of days ago it had looked easy, straightforward: and it had been entirely his own decision, local initiative by Ben Ockley, rightly famed for his nerves of steel and head of bone . . .

Then, recollection of that snide comment had jerked him out of the negative thinking. 'Bull at a gate' was another phrase he'd heard applied to himself: but he told himself now that bulls who charged gates had been known to smash through them – and at least had to know what a gate looked like when they saw it.

It was up there on the Homs road, on the rise.

'Hinges on timing, Sticks. Initially, that is. I want to start the move out of here as soon as it's really good and dark, but – '

'Move – ' Kelso took his glasses from his eyes – '*out*?'

The main clue was that the east and west faces of this peak were sheer, unclimbable, therefore didn't have to be guarded up here or staked out by the Syrians down below. But the east side wasn't all that sheer right up near this summit, it fell away gradually for a while before the vertical drop to the plain. You couldn't get up or down on that face, but just below the edge of the *qal'at* you might get *around*, in cover of darkness. It would bring you to the far side of the track, well east of where the track curved in behind the central spine and up to the plateau. That was very rough, craggy terrain, with the sheer drop on your left as you'd be coming down. Geoff would have to be carried. Charlie could make it on his feet – with some help, maybe – but the Russian would have to be left here.

It was simply *an* answer – the only one he could see – to an otherwise hopeless situation.

'Sticks, that flat piece below us is the only spot they could put their helo down, right?'

'I'd say so.'

'I wouldn't think there was enough unobstructed space anywhere up here, I mean.'

Kelso agreed: 'That's where they'd land it.'

'So we could prepare it for them with Romeo's PE, right?'

With plastic explosive charges linked by the explosive Cordtex and with several igniters. When they touched down on it, they'd wish they hadn't. And that would be the moment to break out, while the besiegers were preoccupied. Down the east side and around. No stretcher: Sticks would have to take Geoff on his back. Around the side of the peak and then south, diverging from the track, and if that area was staked out too the Syrians would have to be dealt with quietly, one at a time, in ways in which all members of this Squadron were proficient. Actually he didn't think there would be Syrians in that stretch of broken rock; they were concentrated in front here, doubtless in the belief that between the track and the west edge of the ridge they'd have all the southbound routes covered.

For the same reason, that strip wouldn't be floodlit either. None of the trucks pointed that way. If there was any significant leak of radiance from the one halfway up the track you'd have to shoot its lights out before you started: one guy down that way ahead of the main force, then cutting across to join up lower down.

When you got to the road, the roadblock, that of course would be something else. But again, one had the skills: as long as one could also bank on a reasonable share of luck.

The Wessex lifted from the *Saratoga*'s deck, swung up and away, feeling to Hislop as if it was standing on edge as it turned and he took a last look down, seeing a foreshortened

322

bird's-eye image of Tom Dubyak walking back to the screen-door in the superstructure. The pilot asked him — that soft Devon burr in his headphones — 'Good visit, was it?' and he told him — remembering the throat microphone and speaking quietly — 'Absolutely fantastic.'

Ten minutes earlier, when he'd returned to the admiral's quarters to say goodbye after an hour with staff and flying personnel in the carrier's War Room, he'd wrung the Task Group Commander's hand and told him truthfully, 'I don't know how I'd even begin to thank you, Admiral.'

Harry Fermenger's broad grin: 'Well, I'll tell you. Just give me a good reference to a certain female person, huh?'

Then on the flight-deck Tom Dubyak's farewell had been, 'What are cousins for, for God's sake?'

He was checking through his notes now, of things to be attended to as soon as he landed at Akrotiri. Like cancelling the rations drop. The Harrier was still to go in, just ahead of the Super Stallion, but not to drop food. Food — sandwiches would be easiest for them — plus gallons of hot tea — was to be prepared at Akrotiri for loading into the giant helicopter when it landed to top up with fuel. Sergeant Hattry could organize that supply of provender: he and Corporal Clark and Marines Deakin and Kenrick were to be ready to embark with it, in fighting order, and Hislop would be with them. The RAF was to be asked to provide at least one doctor and maybe two medical orderlies, with all necessary equipment including stretchers, and the base hospital was to have beds and an operating theatre ready, surgeons standing by for when they got the wounded back. Refuelling was to be laid on in both directions not only for the Super Stallion but also for one Grumman Hawkeye E-2C early-warning aircraft, the kind they'd wanted earlier in the week, and two Grumman F-14 Tomcat fighters.

When they went in for something, these Cousins, they really did go in for it.

It wouldn't be long before the sun dipped behind the Alawis.

'Let's hear it, Ben.'

He nodded. 'It's a good plan, Geoff.' Then the time-worn joke: 'If it works.'

'Change your name to Houdini, if you get us out of this one.'

'Am I going with you?'

The Russian . . . Ben said, without looking at him, 'Not because any of us want you. Only because they'll want to interrogate you in England.'

Charlie had asked him, half an hour ago, 'Those *gulet* people, Leila and co – obviously they're not Israelis, but – '

'Palestinian originally. It's her own team. They worked for Abu Nidal once or twice. There was a killing in the yacht harbour in Larnaca a while ago – remember?'

'That was a Brit – a Brit and some – '

'You always need backup, Charlie.'

Leo asked now, 'You'll carry *three* of us, to the coast?'

'No, two. Charlie's legs are OK . . . Charlie?'

'Walked up here, didn't I.'

He was still in shock, at the extent to which he'd been fooled. And the horror they'd had in store for him. Underlying that now, Leo's cool confession: as if it was a game without any rules at all until suddenly you felt like stopping, or were stopped: then he reckoned to just cash in his chips and walk away. Be *carried* away, for Christ's sake . . .

'And one arm's strong, you could tote a Uzi one-handed . . . And you've got both arms, Geoff. If we propped you up – a wall behind you? I'm talking about the next hour or two.'

Hosegood nodded. 'Sure.'

'Doc, get him on that door again, then some of you car him over this side.'

Leo offered, '*I've* one good arm – '

'So fuck yourself with it.' Ben walked away, explaining to Sticks, 'I only want Geoff where I can talk to him, away from that prick . . . Suggest to Charlie he tries his legs out, will you?'

Ten minutes later he had them all together, near the southern edge. Charlie had made it, after an uncertain start Ben had a feeling they'd end up carrying him as well; and Laker had said he'd lost too much blood through that smashed shoulder, which it had been virtually impossible to staunch.

'OK, here's the masterplan . . . First thing is Romeo'll se up a booby-trap for that helo. Can't be much doubt they'l

324

ry to land it up here when the light goes, or later. We'll have them peppering us from all round, then it'll fly in an assault eam and put itself down on Romeo's PE. And we'll start out vhen it blows. If I'm wrong and this doesn't happen we'll nove anyway as soon as it's good and dark . . . Oh, incidenally, I'm *not* taking that shit. No point telling him before he eeds to know – we'll just leave him here, the Syrians can ave him. OK, Charlie?'

'They'd have made a meal of him in London.'

He nodded. 'I know. Might have cleared our yardarm for s, too. But that can't be helped . . . Geoff, Sticks has kindly ffered to transport you on his back. Got morphine left, Doc?'

'Not a lot.'

'Give Geoff a shot before we pull out. Carrying him that vay'll hurt, won't it. You'll stay with him, Doc – with Sticks as minder. I'll lead with Ray and –' glancing round – 'you, Chalky. Behind us, maintaining contact with Sticks and letting ie know if they're stopped or in trouble – you two.' Ducky eal and Romeo Hall. 'Two halfbacks and three strikers, you night say.'

He explained the route, and that the withdrawal was to be ilent.

'So we get to the Homs road.' Sticks rubbed his bearded aw. 'Roadblock above us, half a battalion below.'

Neither his tone nor his expression were as cynical as the vords might have implied. Ben nodded. 'Yeah. I'd thought f crossing the road and sneaking up to where some of us vere yesterday. But we can't hang around, food and water as : is, and these two . . . So – Sticks, you hang back with Geoff nd Charlie, put Geoff down, sit tight in cover while the rest f us push on and take out the roadblock. Looks like half a ozen guys there, and no support nearby. Softly-softly aproach therefore, and knives, whatever.'

Nods. So far, no insuperable problems.

'Then we jump in that truck. Me driving. It's pointing ownhill so we run down to the junction – unless there's eason not to, in which case I'll turn it up there on the ill. While I'm doing it, Sticks, you lot join us and willing ands'll haul you in. They may be shooting at us by then, nay not be. With real luck their attention will still be on this

place, and if they're not bothered there's no reason we shoul
be. Either way we'll take off towards Homs, then north
Nobody'll see the turn northward – please God – but I'v
worked it on the map and I'm sure they'd expect us to hea
south – and then west, that's the obvious way to go. But we'
circle right up near Masyaf – thataway. If we have to we'
dump the truck in one of those ravines, but if we're luck
we just *might* make it to the beach before dawn. Barrin
roadblocks, helos, or an empty gas-tank, etc. So that's abou
it. We'll be getting that Harrier over us before long, s
Akrotiri'll have warning and be looking out for us.' H
paused. 'How d'you like it?' Picking on Kelso, the heavy
weight: 'All right, Sticks?'

'Yeah.' The colour sergeant's sombre gaze met Ben's. 'Yeal
it's a chance. *Good* chance.'

The snags were obvious; Ben could see them registering i
Kelso's by no means unshrewd mind. The terrain they'd hav
to get over swiftly and quietly despite the complication o
moving with the wounded, the fact that Charlie for all his gu
might *not* hack it, and the chance of running into opposition a
such a range that it couldn't instantly be silenced. Then gettin
the truck and turning it on that narrow road: there could b
Syrians on the road by then, *other* trucks . . . But he wa
accepting it – they all were – because none of them was stupic
they could all see it was a chancy scheme but also that it wa
the only chance they had.

Hislop, coming from the Communications Centre where he'
been talking over the Satcom link to Joe Lance in Londo
joined Wing Commander Cox at a window in the contr
tower, to watch the arrival of the Cousins.

Earlier in the day at the Old Bailey, Lance had told him,
verdict of 'guilty' had ended the trial of Nezar Hindawi, th
Jordanian terrorist on the Syrian payroll, who'd tricked h
Irish girlfriend into carrying a bomb that would have blow
an Israeli jet-liner to pieces in mid-air. And about now in th
House of Commons, the SF Adviser had confided, the Foreig
Secretary would be telling crowded benches of MPs that th
Syrian . ambassador and his staff, deeply implicated, wer
being thrown out of Britain. Syrian signals traffic, Lance ha

reported, had increased sharply during the day; the trial and the rupture of diplomatic relations might be enough to explain this, but there might also be other contributory causes – such as an intruding force holed up in the mountains. Until now the consensus of opinion had been that the Swale conspiracy was probably only a factional operation not involving the High Command or political establishment; minds were now open to the possibility of that situation having changed.

He watched the Super Stallion in its US Air Force warpaint lower itself ponderously to the apron. Almost as it touched the noise began to wind down, the 72-foot-diameter, seven-bladed rotor gradually becoming visible as it slowed. Personnel and vehicles were already closing in around it, a welcoming party which included Group Captain McKenzie heading for its front end, starboard side, where the crew entry door was situated. Then as that sound ceased, from the west you could hear the next one coming.

Cox said, shielding his eyes against the westering sun, 'Here's your E-2.' He glanced round, saw Worrall, the Harrier pilot – he'd come looking for Hislop – and turned back to watch the Hawkeye lining itself up to land. Telling Hislop, 'Turbo-prop, not all that quick, but it's a very efficient early-warner. Little brother to the AWACS.'

He'd asked Joe Lance whether the Americans were aware of the flurry of signals traffic in and out of Syria, and of that possible implication. Joe's answer had been affirmative: National Command Center was watching the situation closely.

He checked the time. Aware that the Pentagon *might* still pull the plug on this, if it began to look like going public . . . The E-2 was settling down towards the runway. High-winged, with a large, saucer-shaped radar rotodome on top. Touching down – now . . . Then it was racing up the tarmac, with a full attendance up at this end preparing to receive it, and through the open window the sound of more aircraft coming.

Worrall caught Hislop's attention, while he had the chance. 'Anything new or changed, sir, for my transmission to Ben Ockley?'

'You're telling him to be ready for a quick pick-up by the

327

Super Stallion twenty minutes after your own departure. Right?' Worrall nodded. 'And that's all . . . Well, if you have the time, you could add that I'll be on board with four Marines, the Sea-Rider crews. We'll disembark and hold off the opposition while he gets his wounded and the rest of 'em on board, so he doesn't have to think of anything but that embarkation. And we want it *quick* . . . I thought the other Harrier'd be making this run?'

'Well, as I know the way . . .'

Cox said, 'Here come the Tomcats.'

Two F-14 two-seater fighters, their variable-geometry wings adjusting themselves to the reduced speed as they came in to land. They'd be patrolling high off the coast, controlled from the E-2, which would pick up and track any threat that might develop. The expectation was that their presence in the area, with their speed of Mach 2.4 and armament including Sidewinder, Sparrow and Phoenix missiles, might be enough to ensure that no threat *did* develop. In any case, for most of its time in Syrian airspace the Super Stallion would – like the Harrier – be well below the reach of radar.

The Tomcats came screaming down. Like darts that changed shape, feathers opening up as they slowed, thundering down out of the sky . . .

Refuelling this force was going to take about fifty minutes, and by then it would be getting towards takeoff time for the Harrier. The helicopter, with a top speed that was only half the Harrier's, would take off at the same time, so as to be hammering in over the Syrian coast a few minutes after the Harrier emerged seaward; emerging, Worrall was going to divert northward before turning towards Akrotiri, so the Super Stallion's pilot didn't have to worry about head-on collisions. The Hawkeye would be over the sea and high by that time, while the F-14s could sit on the runway for another forty-five minutes and still be out on the job in time.

The light was going. It wasn't truly sunset yet, there was still luminosity reflecting downward from overhead, but the sun was behind the peaks and effectively this was dusk.

The troops who'd scattered themselves across the rockscape were moving up. Not hurrying, but there was an observable upward drift that would soon bring the front-runners to the outer radius of grenade traps.

'Pick your bottles . . .'

While there was light enough. There wouldn't be for long.

It wasn't a happy situation. His own move depended on the enemy moving first, and the enemy might not oblige. And he wanted the Harrier before that anyway. It was a lot to ask for: for a man who'd bitten off more than he could chew to ask for. A biblical proverb recalled from childhood made him wince: *As ye sow, so shall ye reap*.

Hall was with Wilkinson on the other side, the goat-track approach. Laker was roaming loose, all-round surveillance as well as being available as necessary to the wounded. Geoff Hosegood was sitting upright with his back against a section of wall, clasping an AKM, and Charlie was on Ben's left with an Uzi in his good left hand; he'd found he could use it well enough by raising that knee to rest it on.

Ducky Teal called, 'Customers . . .'

'How many?'

'Three of the sods.'

Ben had swung his glasses that way just as Teal fired. The same crash of splintering glass, and a pause before the burst. One man down, a second crawling – a loud, high cry – then collapsing; and the third – he was down too, there were two bodies in that sprawl. Numerous Syrian rifles fired, bullets screaming off the centuries-old fortifications; but they could have had no targets in sight. Lucky them, with enough ammunition to afford to waste it . . . Chalky called, 'Got a single here, Ben, just plug him or shall I use the bottle?'

'Use it. If you miss it, *then* plug him.'

Chalky didn't miss. One of Charles Hislop's stock remarks in appropriate situations, Ben recalled, was, 'We don't train our guys to miss.' That Syrian screamed as he staggered back, vanished into the dark jumble of rocks. And another SA80 barked out a single shot from the right; Kelso told himself complacently, 'Nice one, John.'

The light was in its last moments of extra time, sky darkening overhead. Ben let his glasses drop on their strap and raised his SA80, sighting on a dark splodge which he happened to know was one of the few remaining bottles on that 300-metre radius. Two DPM-clad figures were clambering up towards it: about five metres apart, unfortunately. But maybe they'd close up, in that gap. The bottles had been well placed, exactly where climbers would naturally choose to pass . . . Sighting, letting the first guy pass it: a shot cracked out on his right, glass shattered, the grenade exploded and Ducky Teal recorded, 'Two, that was.'

It would be about the last, Ben guessed, at the rate the light was going now. You'd be shooting at shadows or rifle-flashes from now on. At anything that moved. The bastards *had* to be held off, kept back for as long as possible and far enough back not to know the withdrawal was starting when it did start. But they hadn't been sitting on that hillside all afternoon for nothing, they'd surely be turning on the pressure soon.

Shots from the goat-track side. He called, 'Sticks, see if they need help.' He pushed his selector switch from single shot to automatic, cradled the weapon in one arm while he swept the dark rockscape with his glasses. Teal fired again, drawing several shots in reply. They'd sounded closer than he wanted them. He had movement in his binoculars, brought the gun up for a snap shot while keeping his eyes on that spot, snapped off a short burst and heard a shout, then the thud of a body falling, hitting rock.

It couldn't last. Ammunition wouldn't last more than half an hour at this rate. Nobody'd come here equipped for trench warfare. Sticks told him, returning, 'They're OK. Goon was climbing the track, Ray did him.'

He needed that *Hind* to come. For the blast, sheet of flame, helo burning and bodies scattered, Syrian confusion. As it was going now you couldn't think of pulling out; the pressure wasn't overwhelming but it was constant, despite the fact Syrians were getting killed; if you tried to withdraw and the shooting stopped they'd know it, be on to it in seconds.

'Charlie?'

Glancing round: Charlie was a dark oblong against pale-coloured stone. 'Hear me, Charlie?' A burst of firing from the right, an SA80 in action . . . Charlie moved: 'Want me there, Ben?'

'No, stay there.' He went to him, crouched close to him, to be heard . . . 'I'm going to have to shoot your Russian.

Because —' his words were lost as Teal fired a short burst and shifted target for another — 'tricky enough anyway, without leaving him to tell 'em which way we went . . . D'you agree?'

Charlie let it sink in. Understanding Ben's reason for asking. Killing men in combat was one thing, killing a prisoner was another. But it was necessary: and *his* job. Leo had brought him here, and *he* was the reason these guys were here; Geoff Hosegood was going to be crippled for life — that was old Charlie Swale's doing too . . . 'Yeah. You're right.' He added — back to those other thoughts and talking to himself as he began to struggle up, 'And we're not out of the bloody wood *yet*, old son . . .' An SA80 blared ten feet away: in an ensuing silence Kelso told Ben, 'That was a grenade then. Closer by fifty metres, sod 'em.'

'Ben, hang on —'

He'd cursed, swung back to him: 'Where you going, Charlie?'

'Kill the Russian. *My* Russian — right?'

'Yeah. All right.' Ben turned away: listening into the dark, into the pauses between outbreaks of gunfire. It was already louder, clearly *not* just wishful thinking . . . He shouted, 'Sticks, all yours now!'

'Harrier?'

They're going to wear us down, he thought. Wait for us to use up all the ammo. *Then* they'll send the *Hind* up. In the circumstances, and assuming they'd want prisoners on the hoof, it was the obvious way to play it. They'd know that whoever was up here couldn't have any great reserves of ammunition. In fact they'd know they had it made, didn't have to rush it or waste their own men's lives.

So we have to move out. Now.

He crouched on the steps where Hafiz had spent most of the previous night, and switched on his Sarbe. Ray Wilkinson's — he'd swapped, since the other one's battery might have been running low.

The Crab was there — on tap, on cue . . .

'Victor 4 Tango calling Ben —'

'Hearing you — threes . . . Listen, we're in a jam here, in action, have to make this quick — you hearing me?'

'Closing you. Hear you fours. Ben, *you* listen, this is *urgent*!'

'We're under fire, surrounded, I'm pulling out in about one minute, stealing transport if I can, *might* hit the beach by sunrise. Got that?'

Close now, hovering, the noise filling the night, clogging the ears and brain with sound. Crouching over the Sarbe, cupping both hands at his ears right above it: the Harrier pilot's voice again: 'Twenty minutes after I leave you, you'll have a Super Stallion here. Be ready for immediate fast embarkation. Your CO with four Sea-Rider crew will disembark to cover your withdrawal, leave defence to them. Twenty minutes from *now*, OK?'

Surprise so stunning it was like a punch between the eyes: a sense of the unreal, you had to struggle through it, out of it . . . 'Where – *Christ*, where'll it land?'

'Right there, where you—'

'Flat part below is mined. Flat rock down there – *explosive*. And up here obstructions – ruins – all over. Tell 'em they'll have to –'

'Leaving you, Ben, sorry, timing's tight on this one. Good luck . . .'

Charlie sat, close to Leo Serebryakov. He'd prepared the Uzi before he'd come over, gripping the little boxy weapon between his knees and using his only working hand to jerk the magazine's top round into the breech. The Uzi's small-looking spout was an inch or two from the right side of Leo's head, Charlie's forefinger curled around its trigger, that hand and the gun's weight resting against stones that had been piled on each other six or seven hundred years ago.

Leo shouted, 'When it leaves, we moving?'

'Well.' Charlie hesitated. The head turned, he had to pull the gun back to avoid contact. Leo asked, suddenly suspicious, 'They *are* going to take me, are they?'

Straight question: straight answer. He took a deep breath, and it hurt that shoulder. 'Since you ask – no, they aren't.'

Shouting through the noise, into each other's faces . . . 'Charlie – *Christ*, Ben *promised* –'

'Keep *your* word, do you? Soul of honour – Bob?'

'Charlie, listen, we can deal, you know the value of the info I can—'

332

'Goodnight.' He let him feel the gun against his head, felt and heard the convulsive reaction, shock and terror. He tightened his finger on the trigger.

Jammed . . .

He'd tried to fire and couldn't. Couldn't do anything about it quickly one-handed either. Leo swung his right arm, back-swiping at him, Charlie turning to protect his smashed side, in a spasm of pain that made his head swim.

'*You there, Charlie?*'

Voice from Outer Space, thin, far away through the aircraft's thunder. He'd got his knees up to jam the gun between them so he could work at it. No joy in it for Bob meanwhile, extending his period of blue funk. Although in Damascus under sentence of death after giving evidence against one's own people the final hours mightn't have been all that rosy. Leo still convulsing and the Harrier departing – like ripping a hole in the sky to let the sound out. Ben's voice suddenly clear then, clear and close: 'If you haven't killed him, Charlie, *don't!*'

The Sikorsky pilot, Major Gregg Swensson, glanced round from his armoured seat and raised a gloved thumb to Charles Hislop. 'Your guy's on his way out, just turned that corner. It's running like clockwork, Major!' Hislop nodded to him and to the co-pilot, put down the borrowed earphones and went aft. The flight engineer, a heavyweight sergeant by name of Wayne – Pete, not John – grinned at him as he passed. Same kind of slow grin: could well have been a grandson . . .

Swensson had been referring to the Harrier in that statement, and would have had his information from the Hawkeye, now at twenty-five thousand feet and running this, controlling also Tomcats 105 and 107 who were on their way out from Akrotiri, climbing to their offshore patrol positions.

In the big helo's cabin, extremely spacious and unbelievably noisy – well, believably, if you knew you had two turbines right over the top of your head – Hislop joined Bert Hattry, Froggie Clark, Wee Willie Deakin the Judo expert and Frank Kenrick the grim-faced young Aberdonian. All in DPMs and trainers, armed with SA80s and grenades, faces cam-creamed, even Kenrick's expression showing his pleasure at finally getting into the action. These four had exactly the same commando and specialist qualifications as the others, just happened to have drawn the Sea-Rider crewing jobs on this deployment.

Hislop sat behind them, in the array of nylon-webbing seats. Across from him were the two doctors – one RAF, one Army from the battalion at Dhekelia – and two medical orderlies, one RAF and male, the other a Royal Navy girl, QUARNS, on exchange posting at the base hospital. They had four steel-framed cots rigged and ready with drip-feed stands and other gear beside them.

The only other occupant of this compartment was the hoist operator, Airman Dave Latta. He was at the after end, near his gear, chewing gum and reading a paperback. The Tannoy broadcast hummed, and Gregg Swensson's voice boomed at them: 'We're now over Syria. Hummer 602 reports no activity on Syrian airfields. Looking good, this far.'

The Hawkeye was cruising at twenty-five thousand feet, riding the night sky at a modest 140 knots thirty miles clear of the Syrian coast, with two pilots up front but mission command back where the CICO – Combat Information Center Officer – was controlling the 'big picture', liaising with the ground at Akrotiri and with the *Saratoga*, and overseeing the functions of his ACO – Air Control Officer – who controlled the fighters, and Radar Operator who was in communication with the Super Stallion. The RO was also the trouble-shooter on the Hawkeye's equipment, and that was certainly no sinecure; the computer-controlled radar assembly could detect, automatically track and analyse anything that moved in something like three million cubic miles of airspace; it could pick up a target as small as a cruise missile at up to about three hundred kilometres, and handle marine surveillance while simultaneously tracking six hundred airborne targets and directing up to forty intercepts.

It could handle a lot more than it was likely to be required to do tonight, in fact.

The ACO, Matt Zimmermann, was murmuring into a microphone, 'Roger, Tom One Zero Five. No chores for you at present, Harry.' He nodded to Digby O'Donnell, the CICO. 'That's the both of 'em.'

Both on patrol at fifteen thousand feet. And the Super Stallion was on the point of turning on to the inland leg of its approach to the target, altering to a course that would take it up the east side of the Alawis. The moment when that outsize US helo *might* become illuminated by Syrian ground radar was when Swensson climbed to get to his LZ on the high end of the ridge; and that was when the Tomcats might get some work to do.

O'Donnell leant forward, pushed some keys. Intent on his computer monitor. He reached again, tapped in a coded question.

'Matt, check this one?'

Wanting it double-checked although he was already 99 per cent sure what it was. The computer profile was detailed and precise, and the computer never forgot a face. This one was on the sea, roughly the latitude of Tripoli, twenty-three miles offshore.

The ACO concurred: 'No doubt of it, none whatsoever.'

'Small world, huh.' The CICO began to call the *Saratoga*, for a directive as to whether that *gulet* they'd been told to look out for and destroy on sight was still on the 'wanted' list.

'That was good, Max.'

Max was at the wheel, perched up on the high stool; he'd taken over from Joseph, who'd gone forward. Glancing round – scrawny, lizard-like, a lizard's eye half-closing in a surreptitious wink as he peered round at her. She'd only commented on the food in order to encourage the two passengers to offer some similar plaudit: because Max needed that kind of thing, had a tendency to depression. But they didn't even glance up from their meat balls in rice. They were from Islamic Jehad, and men of influence, VIPs recently in Teheran; they'd joined the *gulet* in Al Lathqiyah and were to be landed in Tripoli. A pleasure trip, breath of sea air. The *gulet* was required in Tripoli in any case. Leila hadn't been told precisely what the next job was, but Joseph had heard something about a shipment of weaponry northward.

From Asala, the Armenian group based in the Bekaa Valley, maybe, an arms smuggling run to their brothers in Turkey. The *gulet* was perfect for that job, of course.

Leila edged out from behind the table. 'I'll leave you to finish on your own.' One of them glanced her way, sauce running down his chin as he eyed the bulge of her thighs, but he didn't speak and the other one had eyes only for the food.

She went up the side to the foredeck. Joseph was lounging there, smoking a cheroot and watching the stars. He asked her, 'Are they happy?'

'They're pigs.'

He laughed. 'Prefer your last passengers, eh?'

'They'll be dead by now.'

She got up on the cabin-top. The *gulet* was pitching rhythmically, seas swishing brilliant white from the heavy timber bow as it lunged through them. The plastic-covered mattress on the cabin-top was running wet; but so was the woodwork, and she didn't care. It was a fine night and there wouldn't be many left to come now, you'd soon have strong winds and rough seas on this coast.

She drew her legs up, hugged her knees, began to croon in her low-pitched, husky voice – and thinking of that last lot they'd carried, since Joseph had mentioned them – '*Ma hala, ma hala, gatl en Nasara . . .*'

How sweet, oh how sweet, to be killing Christians . . . Joseph put the cheroot between his lips, gently clapped his hands, encouraging her to continue. Tomcat 105 would have been about twelve miles distant at that moment.

The pilot of Tom 105 was Lieutenant-Commander Harry Biro, and his RIO, Radar Intercept Officer, was Lieutenant Josh Hughes. Hummer 602 had obtained confirmation from USS *Saratoga* that the *gulet* was a terrorist conveyance currently engaged in terrorist operations, to be treated as hostile and in appropriate circumstances destroyed on sight, and the Hawkeye's ACO had then guided Tom 105 down towards the target until Hughes had acquired it on the fighter's own radar. The F-14s' radar was pretty good, but limited in azimuth.

Biro said, 'Two Sparrows. Firing from two miles.' Hughes

locked the Sparrow radar to the target. The Tomcat was by this time travelling faster than any bullet: Hummer 602 had told him, 'Make this fast, Harry, might need you back here where the *real* work's liable to be,' so he'd gone on to his after-burners and smashed through Mach 1, putting his fighter into a ten-degree dive from ten thousand feet. He'd selected Sparrow because it was the most suitable missile for the task. Phoenix was air-to-air, Sidewinder heat-seeking; Sparrow being radar-guided seemed a surer bet, since he doubted whether that slow-moving timber vessel would be emitting all that much heat.

Hughes' voice now: 'Five to go, starting *now*. Four – three – two – one – '

'Birds away!'

Birds twelve feet long, high-explosive warheads, flying at Mach 3.5 . . . The double flash was like a giant match rasped into ignition on the black surface, golden nucleus expanding into a fireball as the *gulet*'s hull burst open, timbers scattering over acres of glaringly bright seascape. Biro dragged his stick back, threw Tom 105 round to port, to get back to where the *real* work might be.

'Want help?'

Romeo Hall's head turned, and Ben heard the shouted answer, 'Better on me own' before a multiple outbreak of automatic fire and some single shots from up here in the ruins ended a brief respite in the action. The attacking Syrians' fire seemed to be coming from every square metre of the mountainside – and from much too close now. In that pause, he realised, they must have been moving up.

There'd been another attempt at forcing the back door, the goat-track entrance, but it was easy to defend and Ray Wilkinson was handling that side on his own. Ben, Sticks, Laker, Teal and Judge were spread over this south-facing curve of the ruins, replying mostly with single shots to the stammering flashes of Kalashnikovs, while Hall was on his way down to the lower level to defuse his helo trap by removing the igniters and disconnecting the Cordtex.

Igniters were spring-loaded triggers, would be activated by the helo landing on them, maybe even by its downdraught when it was close enough, to fire a .22 cap and detonate the Cordtex — instantaneous explosive fuse, lengths of it criss-crossing the rock down there, the ends knotted as detonators embedded in the PE.

Dead right that Romeo'd do it better solo. Knowing exactly where he'd laid the charges and placed the igniters, and having to wriggle around on his belly in the dark . . . Teal meanwhile blasting with his SA80 on auto: shifting to a new magazine, surely his last, shouting, 'Bugger was right up on the side there!' *That* close: Ben knew their chances of getting away would have been very slim by this time: but in fact he wouldn't have hung around this long, if the helo hadn't been coming he'd have had them moving out right after the Harrier's visit.

Bullets smacked into ancient masonry close to his head: and he heard Chalky yell, 'Romeo's *hit*!'

Laker got there first, to where Hall had been — on the edge, about to slide over. Laker's anger in a scream: 'Oh Jesus, *damn* it!' In the next moment Ben's fingers were in the mess at the back of Romeo's head where the Kalashnikov round had smashed its way out.

Simultaneously, first sound of the Sikorski giant helo, its deep hammering distant but unmistakable, coming from the south.

Had to do *something*: and quick . . .

'Put him over!'

In the hope that the body might hit an igniter, do the job it had been about to do when it had been Romeo Hall. With the bonus that any Syrians on that lower edge — where Teal had just shot at one — would be wiped off . . . Ben and the Doc crouching — trying to stay low, but doing this you couldn't — hefting the body and launching it into the dark. A bullet grazed the back of Ben's neck as he dropped flat: he and Laker on their faces, waiting for the explosion . . .

There wasn't one. Romeo's body misused to no effect. Saluted by Kalashnikovs in chorus, SA80s more and more economical in their replies, signalling clearly that the defence would shortly fold through lack of ammunition.

The Syrians would also be hearing the Super Stallion now. Anyone's bet whether they might think it was one of their own or guess at the truth, but either way it might encourage them to try a rush.

It was also anyone's bet whether the Harrier pilot had taken in the message which he hadn't acknowledged, about that lower level being mined.

'Sticks — ' bawling at close range — 'try shooting at the PE!'

Back among the rubble, then, crouching over his Sarbe . . . 'Stallion pilot, Ben Ockley calling, d'you hear me, Super Stallion?'

Should have given him *that* message too — to listen out on Sarbe frequency. His hope was they might have thought of it anyway. 'Stallion pilot . . .'

Kelso had no SA80 shells left. He'd switched to an Uzi: one magazine in it and one spare. Ears filled by the helo's noise . . . He sprayed the far side of the rock plateau — for insurance — as he moved forward, crouching, to try his chances of hitting Cordtex or an igniter or some of the plastic itself. With no idea of where or how Romeo had set it out . . . A figure loomed close, lurched against him: 'You, Ben?'

Charlie Swale. Bloody great target, upright though favouring the wounded side, in full view of the snipers . . . Sticks screamed at him to get out of it, get back into cover. Then pushed on, closer to the edge.

Ben, knowing this was hopeless, tried the Sarbe link again, one last time . . . 'Ockley calling Super Stallion, come in, Super Stallion . . .'

Waste of time — time he didn't have, the whole night pulsing with the giant helo's racket. He heard Charlie's shout: 'Ben? That you, Ben?' Charlie was brandishing an Uzi: and that would do — to join Sticks, double the long-odds chances . . . 'Charlie, give me that!'

'No ammo — sorry — '

Apologies, for Christ's sake . . . Anyway he'd remembered where they'd left the spares. Although it would be worse than fairground odds, shooting blind into the dark with millions-to-one-against chances of hitting something the thickness of a pencil. The Super Stallion's deafening noise was to the left and lifting, and the gunfire, Kalashnikovs' flashes, from the front had thinned. Syrians maybe thinking this was the helo assault they'd been told to expect? He grabbed an

Uzi, one of two he'd dumped for emergency use in close-range fighting if it came to that stage of desperation, and ran back. The Super Stallion was now overhead, still high but its downdraught already kicking up a cloud of dirt and rock particles. Its searchlight then: stabbing down into this murk, lighting the whole scene around the central core of brilliance. The helo was moving, the beam moving with it, sliding away and over the lip to plumb that lower level. Coming *down* . . . Ben was close to the edge, not far from where Hall had his brains shot out; crawling forward, glancing to his right at stabbing flashes of automatic fire which had seemed to be aimed at him but evidently were not. Then a vision of Chalky kneeling, crazily exposed, blasting with an AKM at some attacker; but in the next second he was upstaged by Charlie Swale — an apparition loping forward in the floodlight's glare — tall, lop-sided with his smashed right side and strapped-up arm. *Really* lop-sided, though, some burden in the crook of the other arm — a stone, cube of antique rubble for a missile to hurl down at the explosive charge: it would bounce on rock, bounce around a bit, wasn't a bad idea — and he nearly made it, shambling towards the edge, gunfire out there immediately thickening: and he'd checked, twisted round, staggering, dropping his block of antiquity close to the edge, he'd so *nearly* made it. He was staring up into the glare that was descending fast towards him, the light's focus narrowing as it came down and the noise expanded, downdraught a gale of grit and muck, Charlie's face upturned to it and his good arm lifted either to shield his eyes or in futile warning. Then he'd been hit again: or Ben thought he had, seeing the tall figure stoop suddenly, lunging forward and outward in a sprawling dive. The helo was coming down, straight down still, its point-five machine-guns spitting fire, and Charlie had gone head-first over the brink. His body might have bounced once on that steep drop, in the rising cloud of debris, or his dive might have taken him clear of the slope; whichever, when he hit the rock floor he blew the charges.

Hislop had thought it was curtains. As if a missile or shell had burst right under the Stallion's belly. The enormous helicopter was buffeted upward, flame was vivid outside all its plexiglass windows as if the fuselage was ablaze. Passengers had gone flying in all directions, gear flying too, smashing. Medical gear especially, a lot of glass smashed. Then the external flames snuffed out or fell back and the Stallion was under control, Swensson getting his ship up out of it, clear of whatever had come so close to finishing them – *would* have, if it had gone off a few seconds later when they'd have been right down on top of it. Hislop and the other Marines had been ready to disembark, having unstrapped themselves from their seats a minute earlier; they'd been flung in heaps, and he was disentangling himself somewhat bloodily from a smashed drip-feed stand when Swensson's smooth tones came over the broadcast system: 'May be OK on that rock now, but my feeling is once shat on twice shy, d'you agree with me, Charles?'

Latta, the winchman, was helping the pretty nurse to salvage and re-stow equipment. All of them at it, but it looked like he was helping *her*. Hislop crabbed forward: the flight engineer told him, 'No sweat, Major, you'd be amazed what this baby can take.' He looked proud. Hislop said, 'I'm amazed already.' In the cockpit, then: 'I agree.' He yelled, 'Too many Redskins that side anyway.'

'So you wanna break your neck. OK, on your marks . . . '

Ben had thought they were finished, too, he'd thought the Sikorsky was on fire and crashing. He'd been dazed by the blast, and singed – on the edge, emptying a magazine down at the PE to no effect, he'd been more or less *in* it. Now he saw the massive helo go into hover above the west side of the qal'at, saw the cargo door open under the after end of the fuselage, abseil ropes snake down and the first pair – Hislop and Hattry – on them, rushing down . . . Ben seeing to it that Kelso and Chalky were staying put until those others got here – they were being profligate with their Uzi ammo now, and Ray Wilkinson was busy on the other side, Laker and Teal getting Geoff on to the makeshift timber stretcher and rushing him into the helo's thunderous downdraught. Then one of them back with the board to put the Russian on it. The CO had been taking over by this time: Ben met him in sudden close-up as they raced in opposite directions, Hislop sprinting with Frank Kenrick at his heels, SA80 in his left hand, a grenade in the other and pulling the pin out with his teeth as he ran. They'd brought a lot of grenades, were distributing them like confetti. There'd been a ladder dangling now, abseil ropes were being pulled up out of the way, Laker had got Geoff strapped into one stretcher – the medics had thrown some down – and Geoff was on his way up on the hoist, Laker and Teal back again with the Russian and on their knees fastening a stretcher around him. Each of them had two SA80s: Geoff's and Romeo's, which Ben had left with them: and they were to go up on the ladder themselves once the Russian was off the ground. Chalky was running for the ladder now, sent back by the CO; he had an AKM slung on his back as well as the SA80. Then Kelso, carrying his own gun and two Uzis, but Ben intercepted him, took the Uzis and threw them into the dark in opposite directions. It wasn't possible or necessary to explain. He was on the southern edge again after that, between the CO and Bert Hattry who were lobbing grenades clear over the plateau to explode as they rolled down the slope beyond it. Deakin and Kenrick were then also on their way: it was about ten minutes since the explosion, maybe five since the helo had dropped the first ropes.

Ben pulled the trigger on an empty magazine, his last. Hislop sent him away: he'd already sent Hattry. Ray Wilkinson and Froggie Clark had come from the goat-track side and were climbing like monkeys, and Ben waved Sticks on to the ladder ahead of him. He himself was about halfway up when the CO passed him –.one foot in the strop of the winch-wire, getting a free ride, but both of them going up fast then because Gregg Swensson wasn't hanging around unnecessarily, his winchman had been counting heads and he had his Stallion rearing up into the night. The searchlight had been switched off, Ben was climbing the twirling, swaying ladder through a hurricane of downdraught up towards the oblong of light awaiting him.

Mugs of tea, beef sandwiches, and a reek of disinfectant . . .

Bearded, blackened faces, eyes all with the same deep-sunk, cautious look about them. Not the eyes their wives or mothers knew. The caution might have been an unreadiness to trust in this apparent safety, in being alive while there were some who weren't.

Geoff was on a cot, with an Army doctor and the girl attending to him. Leo Serebryakov on another had a drip-feed into his undamaged arm, a hypodermic needle sliding at this moment into a vein in the other one. Ben asked the Crab doctor, having to scream to be heard over the noise, 'This guy going to live?'

Laker hadn't been at all sure he would. The doctor didn't look up: he shouted, 'No reason I've seen yet why he shouldn't.'

Not much reason he should, either, Ben thought, moving to a seat behind the CO's. Especially when Romeo Hall and Charlie Swale were dead.

The Russian would provide good insurance, though, alive. He leant over to shout to Hislop, who cupped an ear as he turned his head.

'They'll get plenty out of that guy. Seems to *want* to tell it all. He was briefed in Moscow – GRU. False identity, Brit passport, recruited Swale so as to frame him for some show-trial, he was working with some dissident faction in Syria . . . And he murdered one of the mercenaries he brought here with Swale – a Brit – in cold blood, *admits* it.'

Hislop nodded, shouted, 'Not bad for starters.'

'Not even Assad could say we weren't justified.'

Hislop's eyebrows rose. '*Couldn't* he . . .' He paused, then turned again: 'Anyway, should do you and me a lot of good.'

'We going to need it?'

A shrug . . . The round, bland eyes were non-committal. And the shouting made conversation too difficult. They'd be on the ground at Akrotiri in about an hour, there'd be time enough then for the questions and answers.

And to call Mary.

But questions like how come the Cousins had got into it this deep. And whether he'd have made it his way – the backdoor exit, grabbing that truck for a high-speed dash to the coast. Hall might have been alive now: others *might* have died. You'd never know . . . But something he did know – and he'd have it in and out of his mind as long as he lived –

343

was what John Kelso had shouted in his ear a couple of minutes ago: 'That guy – Charlie – he bloody *dived*!'

Charlie Swale had a wife – or had had. See her, tell her?

Or maybe the CO would . . . And meanwhile a point that needed to be made right away, in case London might want to use it, was that he'd left Israeli ration-packs and Israeli weapons on that hilltop.

Someone had pushed a sandwich into his hand. He was leaning forward – elbows on knees, tea-steam in his face, cocooned in noise. The noise was a blessing in its way, a refuge.

ROUGH CUT

GORDON McGILL

The perfect script for blackmail and revenge . . .

John Brodie's agent just loves his new filmscript. His bank manager loves
the six-figure fee. Film star Henry Harper loves his new leading role.
Brodie's beginning to hate the whole thing . . .

There's his mysterious backer – Vietnamese millionaire Han Lo Phu.
There's Han's new screen goddess, Marie – the 'successful model' no-one's
ever seen. And then there's the question of Harper's past, and the secret
that haunted his old Vietnam buddy.

Caught up in a web of blackmail and violence, Brodie finds himself acting
out a plot that's crazier than anything he's ever written. Crazier – and
deadlier . . .

0 7221 5880 7   ADVENTURE THRILLER   £2.99

SPECIAL DYNAMIC

Alexander Fullerton

ON THE RUN FROM THE SOVIETS
IN A DEADLY ARCTIC WILDERNESS . . .

Former SBS Captain Ollie Lyle is assigned to a
civilian expedition into Norwegian Lapland.
A nationalist movement has sprung up among the
Lapps, and their actions have seemingly escalated
into terrorism and murder.

As Lyle and his expedition penetrate further into
the icy interior, they discover the terrible truth
behind the killings: a vicious Russian undercover
operation serving as a prelude to a full-scale
invasion of Lapland.

What began as a peaceful, fact-finding mission is
now a deadly struggle against two implacable
enemies: the brutal, highly-trained Soviet guerilla
force, and the pitiless Arctic winter. Hampered by
his inexperienced companions, Lyle must use all his
combat and survival skills to stand any chance of
coming out alive . . .

0 7474 0087 3   WAR/FICTION   £3.50

RICHARD HUGO

FAREWELL TO ★ RUSSIA

Running desperately. Shouting breathlessly. His voice screaming itself to soundlessness for want of air: 'Get away from here! Get away from the water!'

The unthinkable has happened at the Soviet nuclear plant at Sokolskoye. An accident of such catastrophic ecological and political consequence that a curtain of silence is drawn ominously over the incident. Major Pyotr Kirov of the KGB is appointed to extract the truth from the treacherous minefield of misinformation and intrigue and to obtain from the West the technology essential to prevent further damage. But the vital equipment is under strict trade embargo . . .

And in London, George Twist, head of a company which manufactures the technology, is on the verge of bankruptcy and desperate to win the illegal contract. Can he deliver on time? Will he survive a frantic smuggling operation across the frozen wastes of Finland? Can he wrongfoot the authorities . . . and his own conscience?

'Immensely well-researched . . . growls with suspense . . . even without the recent memories of Chernobyl the novel has an authentic ring'
Independent

'Diverse loyalties are suspensefully stretched and nerve ends twanged'
Guardian

0 7474 0061 X　　　THRILLER　　　£3.50

JUNIPER

James Murphy

'Knowing your enemy is not the primary consideration. You have to know what you are defending first of all. Then the enemy will show itself.'

Oliver Maitland joined MI5 to defend his country. To defend freedom and democracy. He's served his time in the hell of Northern Ireland, battling for a peaceful solution. Now he's transferred to counter-subversion, fighting, not the IRA but ordinary men and women.

Phone tapping, mail interception, burglary – it's a dirty war. And when Maitland finds out the truth behind the Mountbatten murder he begins to wonder who the enemy really is.

Operation JUNIPER, brainchild of Maitland's sadistic boss, 'The Butcher', is the deadliest campaign yet. It's going to smash the peace movement and sabotage disarmament talks. Maitland knows the butcher doesn't care how many British agents have to die to fulfil his plans. What he doesn't know is that he's top of the hit-list . . .

Also by James Murphy in Sphere Books:

CEDAR

0 7474 0059 8   ADVENTURE THRILLER   £3.50

THE PALACE
PAUL ERDMAN

The flash of a wheel, the twinkling spin of a ball, the fat slap of a heavy wallet as glazed eyes ignite and bejewelled fingers tremble, urging that faithless harlot, Lady Luck, to stretch out and offer her all. Gambling – compelling, glamorous, sleazy and addictive – is wickedly exposed in Paul Erdman's masterly novel of financial skulduggery on the Big Game circuits. From the vast money-making centres of Las Vegas and Atlantic City to the shadowy, underground gambling dives of London and Beirut, he spins a spellbinding tale of wealth and treachery, intrigue and mob conspiracy. Proud, aristocratic international bankers, sharp-eyed card tricksters, corrupt politicians, professional criminals are all in on the game in this devastatingly suspenseful, cracking-paced thriller that will have you hooked from first page to last . . .

'Mind-blowing financial scams . . . lively narrative spanning two decades in which fortunes are won and lost . . . very funny and very sharp'
LITERARY REVIEW

Also by Paul Erdman in Sphere Books:
THE LAST DAYS OF AMERICA
THE CRASH OF '79
THE PANIC OF '89

0 7474 0259 0   THRILLER   £3.50

A selection of bestsellers from SPHERE

FICTION

STARK	Ben Elton	£3.99 □
LORDS OF THE AIR	Graham Masterton	£3.99 □
THE PALACE	Paul Erdman	£3.50 □
KALEIDOSCOPE	Danielle Steel	£3.50 □
AMTRAK WARS VOL. 4	Patrick Tilley	£3.50 □

FILM AND TV TIE-IN

WILLOW	Wayland Drew	£2.99 □
BUSTER	Colin Shindler	£2.99 □
COMING TOGETHER	Alexandra Hine	£2.99 □
RUN FOR YOUR LIFE	Stuart Collins	£2.99 □
BLACK FOREST CLINIC	Peter Heim	£2.99 □

NON-FICTION

IN FOR A PENNY	Jonathan Mantle	£3.50 □
DETOUR	Cheryl Crane	£3.99 □
MARLON BRANDO	David Shipman	£3.50 □
MONTY: THE MAN BEHIND THE LEGEND	Nigel Hamilton	£3.99 □
BURTON: MY BROTHER	Graham Jenkins	£3.50 □
BARE-FACED MESSIAH	Russell Miller	£3.99 □

All Sphere books are available at your local bookshop or newsagent, or can be ordered direct from the publisher. Just tick the titles you want and fill in the form below.

Name _____

Address _____

_____

Write to Sphere Books, Cash Sales Department, P.O. Box 11, Falmouth, Cornwall TR10 9EN

Please enclose a cheque or postal order to the value of the cover price plus:

UK: 60p for the first book, 25p for the second book and 15p for each additional book ordered to a maximum charge of £1.90.

OVERSEAS & EIRE: £1.25 for the first book, 75p for the second book and 28p for each subsequent title ordered.

BFPO: 60p for the first book, 25p for the second book plus 15p per copy for the next 7 books, thereafter 9p per book.

Sphere Books reserve the right to show new retail prices on covers which may differ from those previously advertised in the text elsewhere, and to increase postal rates in accordance with the P.O.